CURSE
OF THE
ELIXIR

First Edition

Copyright © 2023 by D.G. Mooney

The moral right of the author has been asserted.

This is a work of fiction. Names, characters, places, and incidents either are the product of the authors imagination or are used fictitiously. Any resemblance to actual persons, living or dead, events, or locales is entirely coincidental.

Developmental Edit by Adam Wilson
Copy Edit by Tim Major
Beta Read by Nicola Hodgson
Cover Art by Felix Ortiz
Book Design by Nat Mack

ISBN (Paperback): 978-1-7392270-0-5
ISBN (eBook): 978-1-7392270-1-2

For those who feel lost, lonely or redundant.
Never give up.

CHAPTER 1
THE CATHEDRAL OF FAILURE

Jonathan Burton tried to crack a smile towards his jolly neighbour, but the corners of his mouth refused to curve. His mood was always the same when he set off on this particular journey.

"Cheer up, it might never happen," his neighbour joked.

"That's what I'm worried about."

"Where are you headed?"

"Nowhere."

Burton's black-and-white scarf started flailing around as soon as he left the front gate. He tucked the soft material inside of his long grey peacoat to form an extra layer against his chest. The wind was wild even for late November, and every step he took was met with force. He leant into each icy blast as it tried to push him back home. *I guess this is the start of Storm Jessica.*

Before long, he passed an extensive field covered in big white tents. The area had been closed off to the public for months. Glancing through the silver metal bars, he could see that the temporary structures were sturdy and unyielding to the elements. The people visible through the fence appeared excited by their work despite the conditions. Some carried clipboards whilst others had brushes, rope and chisels. They were hugging and shaking hands with one another whilst gazing into a man-made chasm in the ground. *It must be nice to find your calling.*

Initially, details surrounding the tarpaulin jungle had been vague. Burton had hoped it might be a big Hollywood movie production, but North East News had recently announced that it was an archaeological dig.

It's crazy to think that enormous lizard creatures once roamed the Earth. People almost seem to pass it off as fiction these days. Dinosaurs could have fought to survive on this very ground. Real teeth, real blood, and no CGI. Nobody would believe a word of it if they hadn't found the bones.

Wallsend High Street was itself a land that time had forgotten. Local businesses had battled through a recession caused by two global pandemics. Burton glanced at Oriental Buffet, a Chinese restaurant missing the 'I, E, N and T' from its flickering red sign; it looked like something else entirely. Any working-class area will struggle when there is little work to go around, throw a national energy crisis on top and it becomes almost dystopian. Sometimes, Burton wished the locals were still required to wear protective masks so he couldn't see their beaten down expressions. *Such a waste of life. They're miserable zombies. They're nobodies, and I'm one of them.*

A middle-aged woman walked towards him with a can of cheap lager in her hand. She aimed a vicious squint at Burton. Her beady eyes were buried in wrinkly skin that looked like ancient tree bark. *Does she think I'm the guy who locked her in the Stand 'n' Tan?*

Burton tried not to make eye contact and hurried toward an underpass as dead-eyed children threw stones from the metro station steps above.

"Oi, ginger pubes!" a feral teen shouted, referring to Burton's rust-coloured mullet that protruded from his maroon beanie hat.

A fist-sized rock hurtled down and crashed off the path. A piece of shrapnel sprung against Burton's cheek, just missing his eye. One teen hung over the side of the railings above and spat. Burton stopped and attempted the same threatening glare he had received from the 'tree-bark' woman, but the feral teens just laughed.

They should be at school. The high street is so damn creepy these days. I hope this is only going to take ten minutes. Please, God, no longer. Burton shook his head in disbelief.

And there it was, his emasculating cathedral of failure: the Wallsend dole office. He pushed the heavy door and entered.

"Hi, Jonny," a familiar woman greeted him. She was short, fat, and wore a flowery blouse that didn't match the dreary tone of the room.

"Hi, Jean," Burton replied in a low voice. He always thought the greeting sounded like a demand for cleanliness and feared it might insight an altercation with the scruffier attendees.

"Here to sign on again, laddy?"

"Yeah."

"If you take a seat, someone will say your name shortly. You've been coming a while, haven't you, laddy?" Jean sounded concerned.

"Almost a year now." Burton looked down at the floor. "But I'm waiting on news from an interview."

"Good for you. Good luck, laddy!" Jean shook her fist as if to suggest an upcoming triumph. She started to stare just below Burton's eye line. "Here, you're bleeding. Bet it was those kids outside again." She handed him a tissue to wipe the stinging cut on his cheek.

In the open-plan office, work-search coaches lined the walls and were hunched behind computer screens. The tapping of keyboards accompanied mundane questions and basic answers. One coach was suggesting to a blank-faced teenage girl that she should apply for a role stringing tennis rackets. Another was offering an old man a course in IT. A heavy-set security guard trundled back and forward, and the repetitive thudding of his boots added an ominous rhythm to the room.

Burton took a seat opposite a young mother jerking a pram back and forward, her movements making her big fringe, earrings and on-display cleavage wobble in unison.

"Stop doing that, you little fucking idiot," she ordered her older child as he climbed on the furniture. His sausage roll was flaking pastry all over the seat and the floor. A third boy came over, trying to read a piece of paper he'd taken from the bulletin board.

"Mam, what's an… anal… an analyst?"

"How am I supposed to know? Shut the fuck up and sit down."

A pale man close to Burton's age sat next to him. A poorly executed flame tattoo climbed up his neck from under a tatty blue sports coat. His hair was shaved around the sides but long on the top.

Get me out of here. Please. I'll give anything. Please, for the love of God. How did I end up here? He pictured himself on his knees with his face becoming a skull, aging through an eternity of nothingness.

"JONATHAN BURTON!" a work-search coach shouted at the top of his voice.

Burton hurried over before his name was called again. He sat down opposite a youngish man with gelled-back hair, stubble and an intense expression. The smell of his cheap aftershave burned Burton's nostrils.

"So, Mr Burton, you've been coming here almost a year. I need you to reconfirm some details. Could you tell me your marital status?"

CURSE OF THE ELIXIR

"Still single."

"Address?"

"Still living with my parents."

"Any large savings?"

"Still no, unfortunately."

"Any change to your health?"

"I ran a half marathon for charity a couple of months ago, and it was a real slog."

This garnered no reaction.

"And under the type of work you're looking for, you've put 'Artist' or 'Designer'?"

"Yes, that's right."

"Can I see your work search diary, please?"

"Certainly."

"Okay, it says here you haven't actually applied for any jobs this week. You know you must apply for at least two."

"I didn't apply because I was concentrating on an interview. I had to prepare a presentation."

"But you haven't applied for two jobs."

"I had an important interview," Burton snapped.

"You should know the rules by now. I'll need to put a black mark on your record, and you may not get your jobseeker's allowance if this happens again."

"That's ridiculous. Surely a big interview supersedes anything else?"

"I've added the black mark as a warning, Mr Burton. Please ensure you follow the correct procedure, or your benefits will be stopped. I suggest you consider widening your job search, as the arts are hardly a realistic line of work to aim for. Next time we can discuss something more appropriate, like an admin or analyst role. That will be all." He gave a superior smirk.

Burton charged for the door. *I'm never coming back. I could do his job standing on my head. What a shithole.* He pulled on his maroon beanie and smashed through the door. It didn't seem so heavy now that he was enraged.

"Nicely done, Frosty!" a female voice said sarcastically. The swinging door had almost hit her foot and splashed droplets of water across her face.

Burton slowed and took a deep breath as she wiped the drips away with her cuff and stared right at him. Her gaze didn't break as she sat on the wall, kicking her heels off the bricks. Ultraviolet hair hung from the hood of her furry blue parka, and the opening offered just a glimpse of symmetrical features and judging, cat-like eyes. The girl stood out like an influencer who had just recorded a video about 'cool stuff' and posted it for her 200,000 subscribers online. Transfixed, Burton forgot to look where he was going, and walked into a bollard, which gave him a dead right leg. He panicked and limped away without even saying sorry.

"Watch out for the metal thing. That's Eliza's tip of the day!" the girl shouted from behind him.

Sleet and negativity followed him all the way to the front door of number 7. *Oh my God, I'm so dumb. Why do I always make such an idiot of myself? And that stupid prick saying I should apply for a job in admin. He doesn't know my talent. He hasn't seen my paintings.*

Burton's dad opened the front door of their modest semi-detached home. He was an old man but looked strikingly like his son, despite standing a few inches shorter. The mirror image always acted as a reminder of how much he was letting his parents down.

"Hi, son. How was it?" he asked and glanced at the nail varnish on Burton's right hand. The fourth fingernail was black and the little fingernail was white, it had been a recent image experiment. His dad let out a deep breath.

"Okay, I guess."

"Hi, son." Burton's mam came into the sitting room from the kitchen and hugged him as though he'd been away in the army. "What would you like for tea? You can have pasta, bangers and mash, fajitas. What do you fancy?"

"Pasta... please," Burton replied. The words seemed to fall from his mouth.

"No problem. Now get changed out of those wet clothes," she said in her usual caring yet commanding way. "Wait, what's that on your cheek?"

"Nothing. I just scratched it on a door."

"It doesn't look like nothing. It's nasty. Give it a good wash."

Burton carried himself up the stairs. His bones, blood, water and muscle were a single heavy mass. He entered his box room and sat on the end of his single bed. His old artwork hung on the walls. The paintings were a mix of abstract expressionism, impressionism and futurism, styles at which he had excelled during his art degree all those years ago. He looked at a piece above his bed. He had titled it 'A Maze Of My Own Making', but now he could only see his mistakes and poor technique. Many sheets of crumpled-up paper lay below a blank easel in the corner of the room.

We've got pointillism already. Maybe I can call my style 'point-less-ism'. Nobody's going to see it, nobody's going to like it, nobody's going to buy it.

His mobile phone rang. He recognised the displayed number. It was the agency where he'd had his interview. His hand started shaking as he accepted the call. This was it.

"Hi, is that Jonathan? It's Tom from White Robot. Are you well?"

"Yes, good thank—"

"It was fantastic meeting you last week. You've got an outstanding personality. My colleagues all loved you, and you'd fit in great here at White Robot."

Burton's palm was sweating so much that the phone was slippery in his hand. A smile started cracking on his face into the forgotten territory of his cheekbones. He visualised running downstairs and telling his parents he'd got the job.

"Unfortunately, on this occasion, you've been unsuccessful in your application."

"What! Why?" Burton asked, unable to hide his desperation.

"We've given the role to someone with more experience using our in-house programs," Tom replied.

"But I would be an incredible designer. You said yourself that my portfolio is stunning. I just need someone to give me a shot. I'd learn how to use your system in a week."

"Well, we gave a promotion to someone in-house. They've been using the system for a long time already."

"So I was a tick box? You never intended to give it to anyone else, did you? You've just wasted my time. That presentation took me all week to prepare."

"Everyone had an equal opportunity, and we'll keep your details on file."

Burton hung up. All sensation left his face. He touched his right cheek. Nothing. It was numb. His lips, numb. His eye sockets and forehead, numb. *If what goes around comes around, I should be due for years. When will this ever end?*

He looked at his bare wrists and the thick blue pulsing line underneath the flesh. There was a scalpel he'd used to sharpen his colouring pencils on a chest of drawers in front of him...

...

...

...

"Have you seen this, Jonathan?" his dad shouted up the stairs.

"What?" Burton shouted back.

"Come and have a look at this on the TV."

"Okay, okay, I'm coming." He replaced the scalpel.

"They've found something at the site. They've found the remains of a temple."

Before he headed downstairs, Burton stopped in the bathroom to wash his face and erase any trace of his crippling sadness.

CHAPTER 2
PROJECT PANACEA

Burton could hear his mam putting out plates and cutlery in the kitchen. The gas hissed under pans, and tea was nearly ready. His dad sat in his favourite chair under a picture that his second son had painted of St Mary's Lighthouse. Family photos filled every surface in the room, and there were cushions everywhere; Burton took one off a chair in order to make space to sit down.

His dad turned the TV channel over by accident and looked in dismay at the remote "What have I done?" he asked.

"You've turned it over."

"I just wanted to turn it up. Here, quickly."

He hurled the controller underarm, and Burton caught it in two hands like a wicketkeeper. When he put the news back, it showed a scientist with thin weaselly features and round, black-framed glasses; the caption identified him as Dr Frederick Wortham.

"This is quite incredible. We've uncovered one of the most unspoilt sites I've ever seen. This part of the world has a lot of Roman and Viking heritage, but we have yet to identify which era

this temple belongs to. There are even elements of the architecture that may link it to Ancient Greece. I'm sorry, I have to go."

"Thank you, Dr. Wortham," the interviewer replied as the scientist headed back into a tent. *"Now, over to Keith with the sport."*

"Quick, change the channel," his dad said, pointing to the remote vigorously. Burton switched to a random evening quiz show.

"What was that in aid of?" Burton asked.

"Do you honestly want to see a replay of that goal against us again?"

"Tea's ready," Burton's mam announced from the kitchen.

Burton's dad loved food almost as much as football. He yanked himself up from his chair and let out an involuntary shout induced by old age, before limping towards the grub. Burton moped behind him into the kitchen. The island in the middle was small, but his mother ensured the food upon it was always plentiful and delicious. They collected their plates and sat down at the table.

Minutes passed before anyone spoke. Burton pushed pieces of chicken and penne pasta around aimlessly. A meal that he would normally have devoured remained untouched.

"What's wrong, son?" his mother asked.

"The advertising agency called me. I didn't get the job… again. I'm sorry. I don't know what I'm supposed to do." Burton lowered his head and looked at his lap.

"Don't apologise. It's understandable you're disappointed but keep trying. Just put it behind you." His mother stood up and hugged him as if to shield him from the cruelty of the world. "You just need a bit of luck. I've got a feeling it's coming for you soon."

Burton heard the letterbox tap.

"What d'you think that is?" she asked.

"It's not the milkman. He got his money on Tuesday."

"I'll get it."

As he looked through the small window in the front door to see if anyone was there, Burton could've sworn he saw ultraviolet hair bouncing away. At his feet was a note addressed to him, written in purple pen:

Jonathan Burton
Meet me on top of the Pit Heap at 8 o'clock TONIGHT.
Love Eliza X

What? How does she know my name and where I live? Did she follow me up the road? Why does she want to meet me? Does she fancy me? Why the Pit Heap? Eliza is such a cool name.

"What is it?" his dad asked from the kitchen. In his days filled with predictability, anything different was a delight.

"A flyer for a new Indian takeaway," Burton replied. He folded the note and put it in his jeans pocket.

"Excellent," his dad replied. Burton pictured him licking his lips and rubbing his belly as per usual.

"You've just finished your tea, fatty buster," his mam joked from the kitchen.

Burton headed up the stairs two at a time. Various scenarios ran through his mind. The Pit Heap had a small wooden bench at the top. Maybe she'd kiss him, maybe she'd rob him, or maybe she'd kill him.

Walking through a country park at night doesn't seem like the safest thing to do. Maybe not taking chances has been my problem, though. Maybe that's why I'm stuck in limbo. I just want to feel something. Anything. Fuck it.

"I'm going to meet Adam for a drink tonight," Burton shouted down to his parents.

"That's great, but wrap up, it's getting colder," his mam shouted back.

Although the Pit Heap was close to home, it wasn't a place you could say you were headed to at night without raising questions. It pained Burton to lie to his parents, but it would spare them worry.

He lay back on his bed and listened to music. He was a walking encyclopaedia of his favourite band, indie four-piece The Lull. At 7.30pm, as their rousing rock anthem, 'God Loves a Trier' played, he pulled on his coat, scarf and beanie as the lyrics that he knew so well lifted him:

They say that God loves a trier
They say that God loves a trier
Well, I can't try any harder

~

The silhouette of his mam waved from the lit doorway as Burton walked up the street. He pulled his black-and-white-striped scarf up over his mouth and marched through residential streets towards the country park. *Let's see what the hell is going on.*

He could smell smoke as he got closer to the gate of the park. It sounded like unruly kids were using up the last of their discount fireworks, but grey sheets of cloud obscured any colours. *On behalf of all dogs, fuck off.*

Radgies lingered by the entrance. One circled on his bike as the others passed around a two-litre bottle of cider. *Great. Don't make eye contact.*

Cold was under his coat, but he didn't know if it was the temperature or his nerves making him shake. These kids were liable to do anything. He continued towards them, his right hand forming a fist in his pocket, his house keys between his fingers. One kid stepped in Burton's way and barged into his left shoulder. Another sprayed deodorant into a lit lighter, and Burton felt a quick blast of heat against his right side.

"He's shitting his pants," the junior arsonist proclaimed.

Burton kept walking.

The radgie on the bike rode up next to him. "What's your problem, you lanky prick? You're so ugly." He seemed desperate to get a reaction, but Burton kept walking, clutching his keys in his pocket. The kid on the bike pedalled back to his mates for another swig of cider before issuing another incoherent threat.

Burton let out a deep breath that floated visibly in the winter air. His size and silence had deterred the radgies. They didn't want to mess with some guy walking alone in the dark. *They probably thought I was unhinged. Maybe they're right.*

The trees had a gothic appearance without their leaves and their skeletal branches were stretching high on either side of the path. No streetlamps guided the way and not even the moon could break through the cloud. Burton walked off the track into an uneven field and looked up.

The Pit Heap was a grass-covered mound formed from coal mining centuries ago. Dr Wortham wasn't the first to try and find riches underground in Wallsend. Burton's calves stretched as he ascended towards the wooden bench at the summit. It wasn't colossal, but it was high enough to see across the entire town from the top. The archaeological dig in the distance illuminated its surroundings and looked like a UFO crash site from a sci-fi movie. It was the first time Burton had seen Wallsend from a height at this time of night, and he experienced a sense of ownership. As he sat down on the wooden bench, snowflakes started falling onto the arms of his coat. A few landed on his nose and melted before he wiped them with his scarf. There was magic in the air, and he couldn't wait for Eliza to turn up.

At 8pm exactly, he heard someone call from down the hillside, behind him.

"I like a man that's on time," a male voice shouted.

As Burton turned, he saw Eliza walking upward toward him alongside an older man. He was wearing a Stetson and a long business coat, with a red cashmere scarf tied around his neck. The long, grey ringlets poking from underneath the hat made him look like an eccentric antiques dealer. He held a large black umbrella that covered both him and Eliza.

"Hello there, Jonathan," the mystery man said as he finished his ascent. Now Burton could make out his features. There were prominent crow's feet around his eyes and deep wrinkles that resembled thin rivers on a dusty map all over his face. Despite his age, he appeared unchallenged by the steepness of the hill.

"Hiya, Frosty," Eliza said, and smiled as she reached the top. Burton tried to work out if the man was her dad, boss, brother, or uncle.

"Hi, Eliza. Nice to meet you. Sorry about earlier."

"Don't worry about it," she replied. "How's your leg?"

"Bit bruised. Who is this? Is he your da—"

"David O'Fagan. A pleasure to make your acquaintance," the man interrupted.

O'Fagan had an air of class that couldn't be confused with bravado. He offered Burton his hand to shake, but Burton took a couple of steps back. For once, it wasn't because of social distancing.

"Can I ask what's going on here?" he said. "If you two are kinky doggers, then I'm afraid that's not my thing."

He'd heard stories of a dogging area further into the country park, near the nature pond. At school, they used to call it 'Pervy pond' and joked about the flabby porn the ducks must have endured.

"Don't worry, son. There will be nothing taken out and waved about. I wouldn't want to lose my little sausage to frost-bite." O'Fagan let out a booming laugh that seemed almost too loud for his frame. Burton noticed that Eliza laughed and smiled at every gesture he made. "What I have for you is a business proposition. I hear you are looking for work? We are just waiting for one more attendee, then I'll tell you all about it."

"Do you not have an office?" Burton asked.

"You have no idea," O'Fagan replied with a wide grin.

Suddenly, a firework whistled past, missing Burton by a metre. The makeshift missile burst into greens and violets alongside the Pit Heap. The radgies from the gate had deployed halfway down the hill.

"He's shitting himself! Fire another one," the alpha ordered to his feral minions. He looked almost threatening in his newly applied SAS balaclava.

Burton wasn't sure what to do. He didn't want to run, but the kids were too young for him to retaliate. Not that he knew how to fight anyway, bar a few things his brother had shown him. *Would I go to prison for hitting a sixteen-year-old?*

A figure emerged from the snow that was now falling heavily. "Come on then, you little fuckers," he threatened in a rough northern accent.

O'Fagan leant over to Eliza and asked, "That'll be our guy?" and Eliza nodded.

Two of the radgie boys backed off as their leader confronted the figure, only to be punched on his concealed nose.

"Hey, he's just a kid!" Burton shouted as the man kicked the minor in the stomach.

"If I ever see you again, I'll rip your head off!" the figure shouted.

The defeated teenager clambered to his feet and ran.

"You Eliza?" the man shouted up at them.

"Come here and we'll introduce ourselves," O'Fagan shouted, and pointed to the wooden bench.

This is wild. Burton's heart pumped in triple time.

The radgie-basher approached, trying to light a cigarette in the wind. The only permanent flame around, however, was climbing up his neck – it was the man from the job centre. His tatty blue sports coat was soaking, but if he was cold he wasn't letting on.

"That was a pay-per-view punch! Here comes the new heavyweight champion of the world," O'Fagan boomed like a ring announcer, his arms stretched into the air. He was certainly charismatic. "I'm David O'Fagan. Pleased to meet you, champ. Where did you learn to hit like that?"

"Dunno," the man replied.

He'd probably been fighting all his life. By the looks of him, he would've thrown stones from metro station steps and launched fireworks when he was sixteen.

He didn't introduce himself, but Eliza skipped over to him. "This is Dan," she said, stroking the newcomer's arm. Her head was only up to his shoulder; he must have been six foot five.

"Well then, Danger Dan, let me explain what I can offer all of you," O'Fagan said. "Please sit down."

Burton, Eliza and Dan sat on the bench and O'Fagan looked at each of them in turn like a football manager about to give a vital team talk.

"I am a businessman, a philanthropist, a philosopher and, sometimes, a philanderer," O'Fagan began with a glint in his eye.

"You should change your name to Phil," Eliza joked, and giggled. Her thigh was pressed up against Burton's. It was the closest physical contact he'd had with the opposite sex in a long time. These days, he counted himself lucky if he got to see a random bra on a washing line.

O'Fagan scowled at the interruption. "Let us be serious now, Eliza," he said in the stern tone of a headteacher.

"Sorry."

"I know hardworking folk when I see them. Jonathan, Dan – I want you to work for me and I will reward you generously."

"How much?" Dan asked.

"I can offer you one thousand pounds each just for coming on board. I bet you could have a good Christmas with that."

"I'm in." Dan stood up and shook O'Fagan's hand.

"Hang on there, Dan, we aren't done yet." Eliza grabbed the tattooed man around the waist and sat him back down. "What about you, Jonathan?" she asked.

"I don't even know what the job is. What are we talking about here?"

The snow continued to fall around them. The grassy Pit Heap was slowly changing to resemble a fresh white canvas.

"The right question," O'Fagan said. "As you can see, I'm getting older, and I don't quite have the energy I used to." He gave a sigh and shake of the head that was surprising, given his quick ascent up the hill. "Basically, I want you to be my hands and do the things I no longer can. This is not a boring desk job where someone will make you put numbers into tiny boxes. You will deal with people and have to think on your feet, but you will be rewarded for it. Think of all the new toys you could buy for your nephew."

"I'm not selling drugs," Burton said. "Hang on, how do you know I have a—"

"No, no, no! You won't be selling drugs. I told you all to be serious. Am I wearing a bum bag full of pills? I think not. I don't want you to sell drugs, but I need you to do something tonight. Are you in?" O'Fagan asked impatiently. "Or would you rather go back to the job centre?"

"C'mon, Frosty," Eliza said. "We need your help. It'll be

fun." Her voice was muffled due to her tightened parka hood. Her hand patted Burton's knee.

Fun. I can't even remember what that feels like. Burton paused, thinking about Christmas and how embarrassed he'd be if he couldn't buy his nephew anything. He thought about the dark and irreversible idea that had crossed his mind after the White Robot call.

Everyone was looking at him. He glanced into Eliza's big, hopeful eyes through the gap in her hood, before opening his mouth.

"I'm in. But what are we doing on the Pit Heap in the middle of winter? What's so important that it needs to be done tonight?"

"Well, my new colleagues, I need you to collect an item and bring it to my office in the morning," O'Fagan explained. "Eliza knows where it is."

"Where from?" Burton asked. He stood and started bouncing on the spot to keep warm.

"That should be obvious by now." O'Fagan folded his umbrella and pointed it at the big white tents at the dig site.

Burton's eyes widened. "You want us to steal something from the site?"

Dan shook his head. He'd been doing so whenever Burton asked a question.

"No, no, no!" O'Fagan said. "You are just collecting two bags from my associate. She'll be doing the heavy lifting for now. Go to the north-eastern corner of the perimeter fence and wait."

"Do you need all three of us? Is there any design work I could do for you instead? A logo, perhaps?" Burton asked. He had cold feet in every sense of the word.

Everyone ignored him.

"*How* you bring it to me is up to you. *Why* can wait for another time. I'm a chilly old man. There will be two thousand pounds waiting for each of you when I get the package."

"You said a grand before," Dan piped up.

"Oh, did I? Is two okay for you?"

"Quality. That'll buy a few cans, aye," Dan replied with a grin.

"I guess," Burton replied.

O'Fagan reopened his umbrella and started walking down the hill. He raised his voice to call out, "Okay, then. I'll see you all tomorrow. Welcome to Project Panacea. Good luck."

CHAPTER 3
THE BIG WHITE DIG

"Gang, here's what we need to do. This isn't my first rodeo." Eliza pulled her hood back and pointed at them. "Be casual, okay? To everyone crazy enough to be out in this blizzard, we're just three mates out for a stroll in the snow, yeah?"

"You've done this before?" Burton asked.

"Yeah, twice now," Eliza replied, "but I think we might get what we're after this time."

"What's in the bags?" Burton asked.

"Something that will help a lot of people."

"Who cares?" Dan added. "We've got two grand coming our way in the morning."

"Exactly," Eliza said. She didn't appear to want to over-complicate things.

The three began walking down the Pit Heap and onto the streets. Burton felt good to be moving again, and the motion warmed up his joints. He filled the awkward silence with more questions.

"Is there anything else you can tell me about Project Panacea? What 'panacea' even means would be a start."

"A panacea is a cure for all life's difficulties. It's a Greek word. The project is something David started up, and it's cash in hand. Don't expect to find a website. He'll tell you more tomorrow. As bosses go, he's okay. I've had a lot worse, believe me."

Although Eliza smiled, she had a look behind her eyes that made it seem superficial. She was struggling with something but Burton didn't pry. The nicer he had been to his last girlfriend, the less she'd seemed to respect him. In the modern day, people often misconstrued kindness as weakness. *Exploiting her pain is not a noble way to win her over. Maybe she'll tell me one day.*

Moisture invaded Burton's trainers as they made their way along a quiet Kings Road.

"So how long have you worked with Mr O'Fagan? And what else do you do?" Burton's questions kept coming. Dan sighed.

"It's been a bit like a computer game so far, if I'm honest," Eliza replied.

"In what way? I like a game now and then."

"For kids, them things," Dan chipped in, underlining himself as hard and manly.

"I've been doing fetch quests. Go here, talk to this crazy person, pick up a thing, take it to someone else, get the reward and build up experience. D'you know what I mean?" Eliza asked.

"Yes – like an RPG."

"What's an RPG?" Dan asked.

"A role-playing game," Burton explained. "You play as a hero and complete tasks to unlock better equipment, in order to beat bigger and stronger enemies."

"Fucking nerds."

"Are you not cold, Dan?" Eliza said. "Maybe when you level up, you can unlock a better coat." Her zinger made Burton burst out laughing.

"No, I don't feel the cold because I'm not a puff," Dan

responded. He was as rough as they came, and also, it would appear, a massive homophobe.

"What do you usually do for work?" Burton asked.

"I was a bricky, but one day I chinned the chargehand. Not found any graft since."

"Bloody hell, I'm not surprised," Burton said. He was quite envious as there were a few ex-bosses he wished he'd done the same to.

"Okay, quiet, you two," Eliza instructed them. "We're getting close. Put your hood up, Dan."

"I haven't got a hood," Dan replied.

Eliza shook her head. "Okay, well, pull your cap down a bit."

"If this is a computer game, then I hope we're on easy mode," Burton said to Eliza, detecting the nervousness in his own voice.

"Shhh. Follow me, I know a shortcut."

Eliza wriggled between the perimeter fence and the garden wall of a large, detached house.

"I think this is too narrow. You're a lot smaller than me," Burton whispered as he squeezed through. The brick of the wall was grazing his ear.

Eliza ignored him until they were all on the other side at the north-eastern corner of the dig.

"A bag will be passed over to each of you soon," she explained. "Take it home and meet me at two o'clock tomorrow afternoon by the monument in Newcastle city centre. Once David has the bags, you'll get your money."

"Aye, whatever," Dan replied.

"And one last thing. Do *not* open the bags." In a single movement, Eliza pointed her index finger at Burton and then at Dan.

The perimeter fence was metal-barred, seven feet high, and spiked at the top. It was hardly Fort Knox, but it wasn't inviting either. Burton looked around for escape routes; they weren't far from his house, and he knew the area well.

"What now?" Burton asked as Eliza texted someone on her phone, one hand cupped over the screen to shield it from the elements.

"We wait," she whispered.

A blur came towards them on the other side of the fence. The figure was dressed all in white and the face covered, like a ninja. They moved almost silently. A rumble came from the front entrance of the dig that sounded like a truck. As the mysterious figure got closer, Burton made out military-style clothing with clips and belts all over their arms and legs, plus studded leather straps hanging from their waist like a Roman soldier. Without stopping, they threw two black satchels over the fence.

"Catch them!" Eliza whispered frantically.

Burton grabbed one, and Dan the other. One had a green tag on the handle; the other was red.

"Switch bags, quickly," Eliza ordered.

"Why?" Burton asked.

"Just do it." Eliza pushed the green bag into his hands.

"They are here. You must go. Now," the figure whispered. Burton could see focused emerald eyes above their white mask. They had broad shoulders but sounded female. Burton's pulse raced as he looked at Dan and Eliza.

"Go. For a better world," they ordered before pulling something from a holster and running back from where they came.

Burton stepped backwards. *That looked like a gun.*

His stare was interrupted as Eliza yanked his arm and pulled him around to look at her.

"Remember the plan. Go home. Now."

"I can't be arsed running; think I'll walk," Dan announced.

"Do what you want, but don't say I didn't warn you. The people who just arrived in that truck don't mess around."

Burton started sprinting. His trainers could barely grip the ground, he slipped and scrambled on the snow-covered path. The dig behind him was oddly silent, he'd expected to hear fighting.

Burton reached his front door breathless and shaking. Adrenaline was pumping through his body. It was almost 10pm, but it seemed like mere minutes since he had left his home to meet Eliza. His parents had already gone to bed. Thankfully, his mother hadn't fallen asleep in her chair waiting for him, as she often did.

Burton sat on the settee, staring at the bag between his feet.

Should I look inside? I'd better not; they said not to open it. I don't want to know. I shouldn't have brought it here. Who was that ninja lady? I wonder if Eliza liked me? Will I even get the money? Should I call the police?

With his mind racing, Burton carried the bag upstairs, removed his wet clothes and lay on his bed. For every second that the clock ticked, his heart must have pounded five times. He was awake until the sun came up.

The eternal night had ended. Burton's body stepped up out of the bed and carried him to the bathroom and shower. It was like his head and consciousness were still outside in the storm. The hot water cascaded over his body as he recalled all of his actions from the day before. *I should ask O'Fagan for a contract; I need to get some assurances. Should I tell Mam, Dad and Paddy that I've got a job? Does this even count? I need to get the bag out of the house. What if it puts everyone in danger?*

"You've been in there for twenty-five minutes," Burton's

mother shouted up the stairs. "Have you forgotten about your doctor's appointment?"

His parents might have gone to bed early, but they were always up before Burton. They seemed to be on a quest to see as much daylight as possible in their remaining years.

The doctors! I completely forgot. I need to go. This nonsense will be over after today. It's more important that I find out what's wrong with me. I'll have time to meet Eliza afterwards. It's just another side quest.

The moment the shampoo rinsed away, Burton dived out of the shower cubicle. He dried and then pulled on his jeans, threw on a plain white T-shirt and his black cable-knit jumper.

"Do you want a bacon sandwich?" his mother asked as he entered the kitchen. The smell filled the whole downstairs. "I've made one for your dad."

"Yes, please, but I'll have to be quick. I'm going to have to get there fast." He glanced at the clock on the wall. "Actually, no, I don't have time."

"Here, son, you have this one. I'll get the next batch." His dad handed him a toasted butty with tomato sauce. "Did you have a good night?"

"It was okay. I was back early." There was no way Burton could explain what had happened. Not yet, anyway.

"That's good. I've put your scarf on the radiator to warm it up. I thought you might struggle to get back home last night?" his mother said.

"It's the reason I came back early – it would've been difficult to get a bus or taxi in that weather." Burton was rubbish at lying, and he tried to keep his fibs as simple as possible.

"Okay, eat that quick and get yourself away or you'll be late," his mother ordered with love once again.

Burton had a hunger. He wolfed the butty down, grabbed his black and white scarf, and picked up the black bag.

"Where's that from?" his mam asked. She missed nothing.

"Adam left it in the pub last night. I'll probably meet him in town this afternoon and give him it back."

"You're going to be late, you'll have to run," his dad said with a usual forecast of doom. It made Burton remember how close the medical practice was to the dig.

Shit, I better leave the bag here. I need to be more switched on. I can't wear the same clothes either; people might be looking for me.

He placed the black satchel next to the front door and took off his dry coat, warm scarf, and hat.

"Don't be daft, it's freezing. Your coat isn't even that damp." His mam placed the back of her hand against the material.

"There's only one way I'll be able to keep warm, then. See you later."

Burton opened the door and started running. If he took any route other than straight past the dig, he'd miss his appointment. The deep snow crunched under his feet. His hamstrings were strained from the night before and it made finding his stride difficult. The icy air penetrated his lungs and phlegm filled his nose and throat. His half-marathon fitness had left him despite all of his training earlier in the year. *Why can't I just store my progress? It's so frustrating to keep going back to square one.*

A police car was parked by the entrance of the dig, and multiple areas were cordoned off by yellow and black tape. A siren started screeching behind him.

Oh God, this is it. Burton stopped, but the police car kept bombing down the road. It wasn't out of the ordinary; he saw them every day, but never as a potential suspect. A weasel-faced man crossed the road and approached Burton. It was Frederick Wortham, the scientist from the news. He had a video camera in his left hand, which was pointing directly at him.

"Excuse me, there has been a break-in at the site. Did you see or hear anything in this area between eight and ten o'clock last night?"

"No, I didn't." Burton started walking.

"What were you doing at that time?"

"I don't think that's any of your business."

"Hey, stop that!" A police officer ran over the road. "What have we told you? Leave the investigating to us. We'll find out who did this."

"They desecrated my work! While you and your cronies drink coffee, the thieves roam free," Wortham said.

"Sorry to bother you, sir," the officer said, addressing Burton. "I can assure you that Dr Wortham will destroy the tape and adhere to GDPR guidelines."

"I don't know what GDPR is and I'm late for an appointment, so I can't help, sorry." Burton sped away.

Shit, I'm a criminal. I'll go to prison. Shit, shit, shit, fuck.

Burton sat in the doctor's waiting room, watching for his name on a red LED display above the reception. OAPs sat coughing and spluttering all around him. This was probably the only human interaction these people had each week, hence their determination to brave the weather. They were catching up by listing their ailments in graphic detail. As disgusting as their illnesses sounded, at least they weren't talking about anything caused by a new pandemic. Just as one virus was controlled by vaccinations, another seemed to take its place. It had been hard on his parents, who had been advised to shield for the duration. Even though the general public were gaining confidence again, it felt inevitable that something nasty would be brewing.

A loud beep filled the room and *Jonathan Burton to Room 6 —Dr Wright* appeared on the display. Burton loved having a doctor called Dr Wright; it suggested his diagnosis could always be trusted. He walked along the short corridor and knocked on the familiar orange door.

"Come in," the doctor said from inside.

"Hello, doctor."

"Please take a seat," Dr Wright replied in a calm and inviting tone. He was in his late forties, bald, and wore a smart white shirt with a thin green check. An expensive-looking pen protruded from his top pocket, but no salary was high enough for him, in Burton's opinion.

"How have you been since the last time we spoke?" Dr Wright asked.

"I've still been feeling exhausted. Most days I don't even want to get up, washed or dressed. I'll speak to family and as soon as I'm in a different room, I just start crying. My fingers and feet are kind of tingly, my head is killing me, and my shoulders feel almost locked, like they need oil."

Burton's leg twitched as he spoke, and he could hardly look up. He always felt so guilty using the doctor's time when everyone else's problems were bound to be worse and more worthy of attention.

"You're sweating and out of breath. How do you feel this morning?"

"I ran here because I was late. I've had more exercise in the last two days than I've had in the last few months."

"Okay, well, that's one of the best things you can be doing. The good news is your bloods have come back and they're clear, so we can rule out any nasty viruses. You're right as rain in that respect."

"Thank God," Burton said under his breath. "So why do I feel like this? I don't understand."

"What you're experiencing is depression mixed with hyper stress and anxiety. You have a lot of tension, which will explain the feelings in your hands, feet and shoulders. It's your body's natural fight-or-flight response, and you've been fighting for a long time. It's all built up in you, Jonathan."

All of what Dr Wright was saying made sense. Burton always felt like a knight in the mud, holding up a broken sword against repeated blows.

"Now, other doctors might be quick to prescribe medication. I'm sure you've heard of anti-depressants? These can help, depending on the person, but I'm sure you can come through your situation without them. You have a wonderful family and you're in good health, apart from this blip. Seriously, people would kill for your blood pressure." Dr Wright offered a warm and reassuring smile. "Talk to your parents, continue to exercise in the fresh air, be creative, take this time away from work to try things you've always wanted to do. In time, these symptoms will settle and you'll start to feel back to normal. Honestly, you're only 34 and you've got a lot going for you. Of course, if you feel you would benefit from speaking to a counsellor, that's something we could look into as well. I know it's not a quick fix, but does that sound like a plan? Remember, you can come back and see me at any time. If things seem like they're getting worse instead of better, just make another appointment."

"Yes, doctor. Thank you for your time and thank you for your help. You've been fantastic," Burton replied. He held the National Health Service in very high regard and looked upon doctors and nurses as real-life superheroes.

He left and walked back up the Kings Road to his house, monitoring everything going on at the dig as he passed. People continued to rush around the site, and their frantic footsteps had already flattened and compressed the new snow. As he approached his house he saw his brother's car parked outside, a black people carrier that he used to taxi the family around when he wasn't working. *Paddy must have a rare day off.*

Burton stepped through the front door and into the sitting room, where his brother Patrick was talking to his dad. Although he was fifteen years older, Patrick was stockier, much better-looking and had a trendy dark beard with no grey hairs. He was wearing a tweed business suit that exuded a higher class than where he'd been raised.

"Alright, Jonny? How was everything down there?" Patrick asked.

"I'm… okay," Burton replied. "My blood test was clear. It's just going to take a bit of time – I've been very stressed."

"You should come to ours this weekend. Matthias would love it, and you haven't seen the dog for a while either, have you?"

His brother was always positive, refusing to acknowledge anything morose or negative. He always focused on what he could do. Patrick had become the CEO of a huge pharmaceutical company called Biovax, which was based in the North East. He would have given Burton a job if he could, but said the board members had expressed concerns that nepotism would cause unrest.

"Are you having a day off?" Burton asked.

"No, I've had a meeting near here and I've got another one in town soon. I just called in for a cuppa."

"Did you watch the match at the weekend?" Burton asked.

Now his favourite subject had been mentioned, their dad took over the conversation and interrupted. "How did the keeper let that one in?" he asked passionately. "He's useless. If we don't get relegated, I'll eat my hat."

"I'm going to jump on the bus and meet Adam," Burton said. He ignored his dad.

"Okay, here, take some jam tarts before you go," Burton's mother said, emerging from the kitchen. She'd been busy again; her apron was covered in flour.

"Thanks, Mam. See you later." Burton grabbed a few jam tarts, shoved them in his mouth and picked up the bag.

"Where are you going? Do you want a lift?" Patrick asked.

"Town." Burton replied so quickly that he spat wet crumbs all over his brother by accident.

Patrick glanced at his watch, which had a raggedy, worn leather strap and a cheap-looking metal face. Burton never understood why he kept it, even though everything else he wore or used was top of the line.

"Right, let's go or I'll be late. You know me, though – family first. And thanks for that." His brother wiped the splatter of jam tart off his expensive suit and led the way out.

CHAPTER 4
CACTUS GIRL &
BALLOON BOY

The brothers headed for Newcastle city centre in Patrick's luxury vehicle. Burton experienced a strange sensation on his arse and put his hands underneath it to check.

"Don't worry, you haven't pissed yourself. It's a heated seat." Patrick laughed and pressed a button on the dashboard to start his Christmas music playlist.

"Phew, I thought I might've done."

The bag rattled at Burton's feet. It sounded like a soldier's canteen bouncing around inside a metal tin.

"What's in there?" Patrick asked, taking his eyes off the road to glance down.

"It's my mate's bag. I was out with him last night. Do you remember Adam? He left it in the pub. I'm dropping it off."

"Don't remember him. Is he the one that moved to Scotland? No, the one who works in America? No, was it the London one? Christ, all your mates moved away, didn't they?"

"Yeah, he's the only one still here. He's got three kids, so I hardly ever see him."

"Did you have a good night?"

"Snowed off. I was back in the house at ten o'clock," Burton replied.

"You're joking! There would've been loads of lush lasses desperate for someone warm to snuggle up to. You absolute plonker." Patrick shook his head in disbelief.

"They wouldn't snuggle up to me if I was the last man on Earth with a hot water bottle," Burton replied, half joking and half embarrassed.

"Stop being such a wet blanket. If you don't shoot, you don't score – simple as that." His brother turned up the music. "I'll drop you here, if that's alright? I need to go to that meeting."

"Yeah, great. Thanks," Burton replied. They were near the top of Northumberland Street, which was a central hub for shopping.

During the journey Burton had almost forgotten about everything going on. Patrick had a sunny disposition that made everyone around him feel good. *If only he could bottle that.*

Burton weaved through the Christmas shoppers as a busker played acoustic guitar and stamped on his tambourine. The crowd got busier the closer Burton came to Grey's Monument, a 135-foot stone column with a statue of some old prime minister at the top. Burton's dad had once told him how lightning had struck it during World War Two and blown the head clean off. With all the bombs dropping at the time, it seemed strange that nature was the thing to leave a mark. Apparently, a carpet salesman put the head in his shop window and said even the prime minister had come to see his low prices.

The Christmas market was in full swing around the base of the monument, and the scent of strong mulled wine from a nearby stall filled the air. Other stalls sold baubles, carved reindeers, tinsel, wrapping paper and dancing Santas that boogied on the shelves. Despite the festive atmosphere,

Burton expected to be swarmed by police. He couldn't see Dan or Eliza. Sweat flooded his armpits. He scanned from side to side and used every inch of his six-foot-one height to look over the crowd. A little elf tried to usher him along the one-way system before an arm linked his from behind.

"FIVE GOLD RINGS!" Eliza sang with gusto along to 'The Twelve Days of Christmas' playing in the background. "That's the only bit I know."

She pulled herself in close to Burton as they walked.

"You've got green hair now? Are we not trying to blend in?" Burton asked.

"Think of it as Christmas camouflage."

"Where's Dan? Shouldn't we wait for him?"

"Dan's... not going to make it. Come on, we're nearly there."

"But he had a—"

"Chill, okay? No more questions until we meet David," Eliza said.

She stopped in front of a large, modern, glass building. Looking up, Burton noticed that someone had painted all the windows on the top floor black. He'd passed this office a thousand times on his route to watch Newcastle United play and never given it a second thought. A panel beside the revolving doors read *Maslow Fairchild Solicitors* in a strong, classy font. Eliza led the way inside to the reception desk.

"Hi, we have an appointment with Mr O'Fagan at one o'clock," Eliza said to the receptionist, who had perfect flowing dark hair, straight white teeth and flawless, tanned skin. As she checked the details on her computer, Burton caught himself staring down her burgundy blouse. *Wow. If only.* He was practically drooling.

"Please take the lift to the eighth floor and have a seat in the waiting area by the boardroom." The receptionist's words seemed to form without any change in her smile. As she finished her instruction, a tall man placed a cup of coffee next to her with a smarmy grin. His black hair was gelled back, and he was wearing a pinstriped suit. *Is she not supposed to get coffee for the lawyers?*

"Thanks," Eliza replied, and pulled Burton in the direction of the lift. They waited in silence before stepping inside.

"I think somebody might like someone, aye?" Eliza teased.

"Me? Who? No?" Burton spluttered, failing to stay cool.

"Maybe I should talk to her on the way out. Have you got a girlfriend?"

"No, don't, I just—"

"Why d'you get so embarrassed all the time, Frosty? She's gorgeous. Those bouncing betties were something else. Am I right? I don't think she's your type, though."

"Why's that?"

"She's a cactus girl."

"What does that mean?"

"She's always surrounded by pricks, and she likes it that way."

"What does that make me, then?" Burton asked.

"You're a balloon boy." Eliza laughed. She prodded him on the shoulder and shouted "POP!"

"I better watch out." Burton took a couple of exaggerated steps away from Eliza. She was right. He'd floated too close to many a girl and ended up popped or deflated.

"Press the button for the eighth floor, dummy. And quick, before that pervy grease monkey tries to give me a cup of slime as well."

He was enjoying the back and forth so much that he had neglected to press the button. He obeyed. The doors closed, and they ascended.

"Things might get weird up here," Eliza said, "but I want you to stay with me, okay? It's not as bad as it looks."

Burton didn't reply. He just wanted his cash and, if possible, a few answers.

The lift doors opened on the eighth and uppermost floor

to reveal a luxurious space containing water coolers, plants and expensive-looking leather couches. Flat-screen TVs on each load-bearing column played the news.

"...*a local man was found murdered in Wallsend this morning,*" Burton overheard the newsreader say as they passed through the lobby. "*It is reported that the 31-year-old male had both of his hands removed and his throat cut...*"

Removed? What the fuck? Was it Dan?

"Come in." O'Fagan beckoned from the boardroom and used a remote to switch off the televisions. A strong-jawed bald man walked out of the room and approached Eliza and Burton. He reached out to shake Burton's hand firmly.

"Maslow Fairchild – pleased to meet you. I'm a friend of your brother's. He's a good man."

"Patrick? I've just seen him. Pleased to meet you too," Burton replied, in awe of Maslow's stature.

"Nice suit," Eliza added, gesturing to Maslow's grey three-piece suit, beneath which he wore a black shirt and tie.

"Thank you. Stay safe," Maslow replied, and walked into the lift. He maintained a knowing smirk as the doors closed. Burton rubbed at his right hand, following the powerful handshake.

The order and cleanliness of the surroundings seemed to be abandoned as they entered the boardroom. There were books everywhere; literary towers standing nine feet high. Papers, maps, protractors and pencils littered the enormous table in the middle of the room. O'Fagan appeared in the midst of his work, whatever that was. Burton's eye was drawn to a short sword displayed behind him, lying horizontally on a stand.

"Give it to me," O'Fagan demanded.

Burton handed over the bag immediately. "Listen, I'll just take my money and be on my way. I don't want to disturb you," he said.

O'Fagan gazed at the bag as if he was about to devour it, like a toddler with a Mr Whippy ice cream.

"Nonsense," he said. "You're part of the gang now. You've done well. Don't you want to know what this is all about?"

"Is it the real deal?" Eliza asked.

"Let's find out, my dear."

O'Fagan opened the bag and pulled out a red metal tin. He opened this in turn to reveal two pyramid-shaped vials. They were each about six inches tall. Their surfaces were misty glass that had been partially covered by a decaying leather casing. O'Fagan dusted the casing off one vial with his fingertips and held it to his eye. He then swished it in his hand like a goblet before smashing it to the ground. Burton jumped as the glass shattered and dust covered the board-room floor. O'Fagan grunted. He picked up the next vial and dusted away the casing once again. Burton glimpsed green liquid inside.

O'Fagan's eyes widened. "Yes, it's the real deal, my dear."

Eliza clapped and cheered.

O'Fagan picked up a small statue from a shelf at the rear of the room and placed it on the table. It depicted a white muscular man holding a staff with a snake wrapped around it. A dog lay at his feet. "Tell me, Jonathan, have you ever heard of the Cult of Asklepios?"

"Erm, no," Burton replied.

"Asklepios was a healer, a god of medicine in Greek mythology. His worshippers represent one of the longest-lasting organisations in antiquity. They originated in Epidaurus in ancient Greece and spread to Italy, the Eastern Mediterranean, North Africa and beyond. His followers shared their wisdom by transporting a sacred serpent to different sites at which they performed incredible feats of restoration on the sick and the lame. It is said that on one occasion Asklepios even raised the dead, only to be punished by Zeus." O'Fagan no longer spoke with charm or a glint in his eye; he was deadly serious. "How are you with snakes?" he asked Burton.

Burton shuddered. *Demonic predators with unpredictable movements and changes in speed.* The collar of his jumper felt tight. He ran his finger around the top to free up some space to breathe.

"Hear him out, okay?" Eliza whispered.

"Follow me." O'Fagan marched over the broken glass of the shattered vial and into another meeting room. It appeared that any solicitors were based on the floors below.

This is getting weird. The windows of the next room were all painted black. In the centre was a large glass case filled with foliage and a big, jagged rock. O'Fagan walked toward it.

"Wars are breaking out everywhere. *White this* and *Black that* are hurled as both insults and unifiers. 'Your god is the wrong god', 'I was offended by something you said', et cetera. Isn't it embarrassing? We are a limited race bickering into extinction." O'Fagan was now so close to the case that his nose touched the glass. A thick black shape slithered amongst the plants. O'Fagan handed Eliza the vial before rolling up his shirtsleeve, revealing a tattoo on the underside of his left forearm: a snake wrapped around a staff. Eliza passed the vial back to him with the utmost of care, using both hands.

"We class the Aesculapian snake as non-venomous and native to Europe." O'Fagan said. "The male can grow to around six feet six inches. That's bigger than you, Jonathan." He grinned.

Burton was panicking, and his armpits were miniature versions of Niagara Falls.

"You should never judge a person by the colour of their skin, or indeed a reptile by its scales," O'Fagan said. He reached inside the tank with his tattooed arm and yanked out a huge black snake speckled with white dots. He held it at a point just below the head and the snake's jaws opened.

O'Fagan looked straight into the fanged abyss and poured some of the pyramid's green contents into it. The serpent stopped writhing and became subdued. O'Fagan placed it back into the tank, then sealed the top.

"Keep your money," Burton yelped, his voice breaking. He took two big strides back and spun around to run for the lift.

Within seconds, a muscular woman stepped from behind one of the columns and pushed him to the floor. She appeared solid, wearing a white vest, dark cargo pants and laced-up black boots that could kick him to the other side of the room. Two short boxer braids arched tight against her scalp. Burton peered into the same focused emerald eyes he had seen last night. It had to be the mysterious figure that had thrown them the bags.

"Stay. No danger yet," she said in broken English. She offered her hand to help him up, but Burton slapped it away. He crawled sideways like a crab, clocking that she had the same snake tattoo as O'Fagan on the underside of her forearm. He got to his feet, but stumbled backwards over a brown leather settee and banged his elbows off the thinly carpeted floor.

"I won't let you feed me to the snake," Burton said. He grabbed a long bronze lamp and swung wildly at the woman. She looked at O'Fagan who raised his eyebrows and smiled, as if Burton's efforts were comical.

Eliza tried to calm the situation. "You've got the wrong end of the stick… or, in this case… lamp. I know it looks mad, but—"

"Nefertari, stop this," O'Fagan said. His patience seemed to have come to an end. "He'll disturb the workers downstairs."

~

Burton opened his eyes to see O'Fagan and his muscular, boxer-braided bodyguard in front of him. His head was on Eliza's lap, and he was lying on one of the leather settees. She was mopping his forehead with a cold, damp flannel to soothe the pain from the blow he hadn't seen coming. He wasn't sure how long he'd been unconscious.

"Jonathan. Just let me say my piece before you go," O'Fagan said, still chuckling. He threw the same black bag Burton had used to deliver the pyramid vials against the settee. It thudded as it hit the floor and seemed to be full again. "Two thousand big ones for your troubles."

The snake-wrestling businessman didn't have prominent crow's feet around his eyes anymore. It must have been a trick of the light, or maybe the effects of concussion, but he could've sworn O'Fagan's irises were now piercing green circles.

"I sorry, too much noise," the bodyguard said to Burton with genuine remorse.

"This is Nefertari," O'Fagan explained. "She is one of the most incredible women you will ever meet, and also the toughest. Daughter of an Egyptian poet and a Japanese yakuza. Not too keen on working in a team, but she's getting better. I would tell you more, but I don't want a crack over the head myself."

Two blood-red marks were visible on O'Fagan's arm. *A snakebite?*

Burton sat up, bewildered and groggy, looking at Eliza as if it were all her fault. She remained silent and bit her lip.

"Wh-what is this?" he said. "Why have you involved me in this?"

"The Greeks regarded snakes as sacred creatures and used them in rituals to honour Asklepios," O'Fagan replied. "They believed venom to be a remedy, and skin shedding a sign of new life. You can even see the Asklepion symbol in the medical profession today; it is no secret." He pointed at his tattoo. "Of course, venom can be deadly, but it has also been used to produce medicine to combat cancer, blood pressure, strokes, Alzheimer's, Parkinson's and many other terrible things that you pray that your loved ones will never have to face. This is a good thing, is it not?"

"Of course, medical workers are superheroes," Burton said with conviction. "The work they do is unrivalled, and I hold no profession in higher regard."

"If I'm not mistaken, that was your exact social media update that piqued my interest in you, young man. When I looked closer, I could see that you raised money for charity and were a damn good runner as well, which helps in this profession. The Great North Run in one hour and fifty minutes – remarkable."

"And what exactly is this profession? Are you a lawyer?" Burton asked.

"I find the justice system intriguing, but it was never my calling. I rent the space from Maslow, the man you met on the way in. He can always find a solution to your problem, if the price is right."

"As in, he paid him a shit-ton of wonga," Eliza whispered.

"But why me?" Burton asked. "If this is so important, why not hire a professional?"

"We needed to find someone quickly who knew the area, and you fit the bill," Eliza said. "You seemed like a guy with a good heart as well."

"We have plans for you, Jonathan. I hope you will consider working with us further. I have no doubt, despite your little outburst, that you will prove very useful indeed," O'Fagan said with a sterner tone.

"Did you kill Dan? Why isn't he here? Did you spy on him as well?" Burton retorted.

"The Caballion tried to take the vials for themselves."

"Caballi-what?" Burton asked.

"Caballion. Foot soldiers of those with a different point of view," O'Fagan replied.

"Proficient warriors, trained in the ways of Sparta," Nefertari added.

"And… hunters," Eliza said, her words hushed. It was the first time she'd sounded less than one hundred percent confident. She rubbed the top of her right arm as if the memory of an old wound had returned.

"One attacked Nefertari, while the other tracked Dan to his home in the town centre. Thankfully, you and Eliza disappeared into the blizzard. Equally thankfully, Eliza thought to give Dan the decoy bag," O'Fagan said.

"He was a moron," Eliza said. "Dan was always going to get caught. We just needed to confuse them with extra numbers."

"Caught? They were talking about Dan on the news when we walked in. How stupid do you think I am? They chopped his fucking hands off before killing him," Burton replied.

"Removal of hands is punishment for stealing what they think theirs," Nefertari explained.

"What if I was tracked? What about my parents?"

"Impossible. Once I deal with weakest hunter, I watch you home. Only two." Nefertari spoke with a certainty that she had completed her mission.

"Listen, I don't care what you think. I'm going home and I want nothing more to do with you, the snake, these 'Caballi-maniacs', or anything else. I'll say nothing to the police if you promise not to come near me ever again."

"Please, you earned the money – take it," O'Fagan said, pointing to the bag.

Burton picked it up and held it to his chest. He edged towards the lift, all the time bracing himself to be knocked down again. Nefertari looked to O'Fagan, who shook his head. Burton moved backwards, knocking a vase off a plinth that shattered on the floor. Before the lift doors fully closed, he saw Eliza watching him with an anxious frown.

Burton jogged through reception and saw three men vying for attention in front of the receptionist. *POP!* Burton thought as he hurried back home.

CHAPTER 5
THE HMS BACON SAVER

Burton burst into his sitting room. *Thank God.* His dad was watching Leicester City vs. Crystal Palace, while his mother was sitting in her armchair, doing a crossword. All was normal. He hugged his mother before she had even had the chance to rise from her seat.

"I'll get your tea straight away," she said. "Pie and mash sound good?"

"Two-one!" his dad shouted as the Leicester striker fired a shot in off the post.

In the week and a half that followed, Burton stayed indoors and played online video games with friends based all over the world. Topics over voice chat included football, social-media models, and parties from a bygone era. When the others were all too busy changing nappies to play, Burton listened to 'The Ether' by The Lull:

It's only right
That I should feel like
A shadow sometimes
Waiting in the Ether

He was trying to rid his mind of those nightmarish two days by escaping into make-believe worlds. The thought of the grotesque snake wrapping around O'Fagan and biting into him was emblazoned in his mind. The fever dream of Eliza seemed an unfulfilled addiction and she inspired him to pick up an HB pencil for the first time in a while. At first, he tried sketching the oval outline of her face, then her button nose and her judging, feline eyes. *It's not good enough.* He couldn't capture her essence, maybe because he didn't yet know who she was. What motivated her? What was she scared of? What made her laugh? What did she love?

One night, after ordering his nephew's Christmas present online, he heard the faint tap of the letterbox again. He darted from his room to see a note lying on the mat at the bottom of the stairs. *Eliza?*

He opened the front door and ran barefoot to the gate, but she was nowhere to be seen.

"What are you doing? Shut the door, you'll freeze the house out!" his mother barked from the sitting room.

Burton snatched the note and retreated to his room. Excitement rose in him again: he had a fix.

Balloon Boy
Meet me at Tynemouth Priory, 8pm tomorrow.
I need to see you.
I need your help.
Please.
Eliza x

Should I go? Surely I'm putting my family in danger if I do. Why does she need my help? What if something happens to her and I could've done something? What will O'Fagan do if I don't go? What if the caballi-people are looking for me?

Burton's thoughts spiralled with question after question, worry after worry. At 7.05pm the next day he lay on his single bed, looking at the walls of his safe little box room. They seemed to be getting closer together with every year that passed.

He stood up. *I'm damned if I do, but I'm especially fucked if I don't.*

"I'm heading to the coast to meet Adam!" he shouted down to his parents, who were watching a quiz show on TV.

"Okay, son. Enjoy. Have a good night," his parents replied together to the point that Burton wasn't sure who had said what.

"It's Denmark," his dad said to the TV.

"You were too quick for me there," his mam said. "I'm sure I've got some Viking blood in me. It's supposed to be the happiest place on Earth, you know? Can we all go before we're too old? It might be our last chance."

Burton stepped outside for the first time in almost two weeks. He took a moment to readjust to the fresh air; it made him lightheaded for a few seconds. His destination was Tynemouth, a little coastal town that was only a short bus ride away.

Burton stepped onto the 306 double-decker bus, paid his fare, and scanned the seats downstairs. A plump middle-aged couple sat holding hands, their mix of perfume and cologne blending into a pungent aroma that said, 'We still love a night out'. The headphones of a twenty-something produced a tinny drumming noise that had the potential to drive Burton crazy. Upstairs was the only option.

A mean-looking dark-skinned man was sitting near the back. He had a short back and sides and wore a black leather jacket. Burton collapsed on a seat about halfway along the bus and wiped the condensation from the window. Would everyone be a potential threat now? Should he expect to be strangled every time he left the house? *Maybe it would put me out of my misery.*

The bus stopped to pick up more passengers. Burton heard bustling and sarcastic laughter coming up the stairs. *For fuck's sake, more radgies?*

The two gangly teens that emerged had baseball caps balanced on the tops of their heads. They sounded as thick as wet clay. Their limbs were so long and thin that their bodies appeared sharp.

"Can you fuckin' believe Donna let me finger-blast her last night?" one of them shouted at his accomplice, making sure the whole bus could hear.

Well, there's someone else with a better love life than me. How could anyone let a moron like that anywhere ne—

Burton's thought process was broken as the finger-blaster snatched the beanie from his head and marched to the back of the bus. Burton turned to see the teenager spinning the hat around his finger as he sat down.

"This is mine now, unless you want to come and get it back, freak," the finger-blaster shouted down the bus. His smaller accomplice was sniggering and revelling in the anarchy.

"Give it back," Burton said.

"What are you gonna do about it, ginger pubes?" The idiot's honking laugh underlined how dense he was. Burton heard that insult a lot; it was as though all these kids were connected by a brain-dead hive mind.

Once again, they didn't look intimidated, and they were

bigger than the lads on the Pit Heap. Burton was about to stand and approach them, but the man in the leather coat snatched the hat with one hand, then glared at the finger-blaster.

"Woah, we were only messing, mister. We were going to give him it back. We're just kids – I'll get my dad and uncle onto you if you hit us."

The man walked down the aisle and handed the hat to Burton. Close up, his nose was flat and looked as though it had been broken more than once. His jaw moved as though he were chewing on a wasp and enjoying it.

"Thanks," Burton said, dipping his chin and speaking in a lower register to try and sound tough. He put the beanie on his head before thinking. *Ugh, I hope the finger-blaster has washed his hands since last night.*

The man in the black coat hadn't made a sound, but he was one hundred times manlier than anyone else on the top deck. He sat down again, unperturbed. There was utter silence until Burton got off at his stop, Tynemouth Front Street.

Front Street had cool bars, art boutiques, and several respectable cafes, not to mention a great fish and chip shop called Must Do Batter, which was owned by one of Burton's former teachers. In the summer, colourful bunting joined the two sides of the street to welcome all visitors. The community had stood by each other and ensured their standards never wavered through hard times. The street led towards St Eddie's Bay, a stunning sunken beach overlooked by the colossal priory on the cliff. Quintessential English culture mixed with salty sea air and the sound of waves; it was idyllic.

Burton knew little about the history of the priory, only that the former kings of Northumbria had been buried there. This was why Tynemouth's coat of arms featured three crowns. What he did know, however, was just how stunning the broken ruins overlooking the ocean appeared. In the sunshine, the yellow stones radiated warmth, yet now they were gothic and grey. Every time he visited, Burton filled his social media with images of the structure. Forgotten power emanated from the broken walls that clung desperately to their foundations.

He looked towards the gatehouse. A woman with platinum blonde hair flowing from her blue parka hood leaned her back and raised foot against the closed portcullis, snow falling around her. The scene looked like the most perfect vinyl album cover. Eliza was always on time.

"Balloon Boy!" Eliza shouted and waved with a delighted look on her face.

Burton felt a smile forming but tried to hide it as he approached. Eliza went to hug him, but he stepped out of her reach.

"You don't look as worried as your note made out," he said.

"I didn't think you'd come."

"You said that last time."

"I thought you'd be spooked."

"I am."

"But you came."

Every time she used the word 'come', Burton tried to ignore primal urges rumbling inside him. Her parka made her look like a big present, ready to be unwrapped. His fantasy kept igniting, and Eliza didn't even need to try. *Stop it, I mustn't think like this. I'm turning into a seedy old man. She needs my help.*

"You must spend a lot of time at the hairdressers. Your hair has been a different colour every time I've seen you. Looks nice, though."

"Thanks. I do it myself with Samurai Dye."

"Samurai Dye?"

"Yeah, you know. 'Use Samurai Dye or pagoda hell!'" Eliza quoted in a deep voice.

Burton couldn't hide his smile any longer. "C'mon, then – what's going on with everything, apart from your rainbow hair?" he asked.

"Let's walk along the promenade and chat. If you see any dog walkers, just make sure you change the subject, yeah? Here, hold my hand so it looks like we're out for a stroll."

They were a metre apart. Eliza grabbed Burton's hand before he could even think about moving it away, not that he wanted to. *This is the most romantic thing I've ever done, and it's all pretend.*

They started walking along the long stretch of seafront. The waves lapped on their right, in and out, in and out.

"The archaeologist, Wortham, has reported the theft to the police and the Caballion are in the area. They're looking for whoever took the Elixir," Eliza said in a hushed voice. "The police are pretty useless, but the Caballion… they don't mess around."

"Took the what?" Burton asked.

"Elixir. It's what we call the green stuff in the vial."

"What do you intend to do, and how does the Caballion play into this?"

A woman approached, holding onto two leads that restrained bounding Labradors, one black and one golden.

"And then he shouted, 'My fajitas!' It was so funny!" Eliza blurted out.

The punchline was for the dog walker to hear, although Burton recognised it from one of his favourite sitcoms. Eliza squeezed his hand and leaned into him until the dog walker was forty feet away. Burton heard the Labs barking in the distance.

"Okay, so Nefertari told me that the Caballion are foot

soldiers who represent the Cult of Asklepios," Eliza said. "They're sent out to fetch the Elixir from sites around the globe as temples are discovered."

"Asklepios? As in the Greek guy O'Fagan mentioned?" Burton asked.

"Yep. He would've explained it better back at the Maslow building if you hadn't freaked out. David is one of the Four Columns, a boss. Here's the problem: he wanted to make the Elixir public during the last pandemic and see if it could be mass-produced. The global suffering really got to him. Two of the leaders opposed him and wanted to continue distribution in small quantities. They've always carefully vetted recipients to prevent this stuff from being corrupted and abused."

"I wonder why. Wouldn't Asklepios have healed the whole world if he could?" Burton asked.

"You'd think – but in their eyes he was a god and capable of anything. They want to follow tradition to the letter. It's like how some morons hate gay people because of references to them being stoned in the Bible. Backwards, right? They're prepared to allow pain and tragedy in order to honour an archaic medical practice. The Elixir is becoming almost impossible to find, and it's making the cult violent and unpredictable." Eliza was becoming more animated, her voice rising.

"The last pandemic was a horrible time for so many," Burton said, still processing the information. "They should've helped."

"The Elixir is a cure for ev-ery-thing. Whether it came from Asklepios, aliens, God, a fucking snake, I don't care. All I know is that my mam is sick, and I want her to get well. Jon, I just want her to be better." Eliza stopped. She looked at the ground and bit on her lip. Her eyes welled up. "David says I'm first in the queue. I just need to help with Project Panacea."

Burton was about to comfort her when he saw two figures

in the distance, advancing towards them. They were hooded and draped in crimson tabards that fluttered in the wind. Their bowed heads and clasped hands suggested that they were monks enacting a penance in the icy temperature.

Eliza looked back over her shoulder and snapped out of her vulnerable and fragile state. "Run. Now. It's the Caballion."

They both broke into a sprint, Burton's blue trainers in parallel with Eliza's purple feet smashing against the ground as the waves crashed against the priory rock behind them.

"What will we do?" Burton asked.

"Keep running."

"Where to?"

"I don't know, I don't know."

"What about the lighthouse?"

"How far is it?"

"Must be four miles. Can you run that far?"

"Yes, go. Quickly."

Burton had been worried that Eliza would struggle to keep up, but if anything it was the other way around; she was like a bullet. He dared not look back and pushed himself until his heart was almost beating out of his chest. They were close to St Mary's Lighthouse, which grew larger and prouder with every passing minute.

Eventually they stopped, gasping for breath, both bending forward with their hands on their thighs. Eliza pressed the bottom of her right knee and grimaced, it must've been sore from the sudden burst across the concrete.

"Pace yourself," a smug runner said as he passed them.

"Fuck off, Spandex," Eliza snapped back.

The runner's lime fluorescent headband and bumbag bobbed into the distance. Beyond him, two dots that resembled droplets of blood in a sugar bowl confirmed the hunters hadn't run after them at all.

Eliza looked over the railings at the lighthouse. "We didn't think this through, did we?"

Panting, Burton looked up to see that it was a high tide. The concrete causeway was submerged and there was no way across to the decommissioned lighthouse.

"Damn," Eliza said.

"What do we do?"

"We need to hide."

"They'll see our footprints."

"With this much snow? They'll be gone in minutes… I think."

"But what will we—"

Eliza cut him off. "Don't fucking ask me that again." She fell silent, thinking. "There!" She pointed at two old rowing boats overturned on the grass. In summer, they were used as the frame for a Nordic-themed flower display, but for now they offered refuge. "This one's got stuff underneath. Lift the other one slightly and if it's empty, I'll get in. Try not to knock the snow off the top."

Burton fumbled around the frayed blue angler's net draped over the rowing boat, searching for a good grip.

"Okay, you ready?" he asked.

Eliza pencil-rolled under the boat and held it up from inside, just long enough for Burton to slide in. They lay face to face on the grass.

"Don't make a sound. Don't even breathe," Eliza mouthed.

They lay still, but Burton heard no hurried footsteps, no baiting calls, nothing.

After ten minutes, the hunters drew near. The crunch of compacting ice beneath their feet was slow and considered. Through a centimetre gap between the ground and the rowing boat, Burton could see the black soles of rubber boots.

Burton shut his eyes. When he opened them again, Eliza was still staring right back.

There was a crash of wood. The boat next to theirs had been overturned. It probably contained lobster cages that had been used for the display. *I hope I'm not catch of the day.*

The black-soled boots sauntered away. *Christ, they must've just thought this one was full of junk as well. Unless they were just trying to scare us?*

Burton and Eliza lay face to face for another twenty minutes until she broke the silence. "This is your captain speaking. Thank you for travelling on the HMS Bacon Saver."

They both tried to stifle their laughter, but hilarity ensued in their cramped proximity.

"I'm freezing," Burton said. He was cooling down after the prolonged sprint. Eliza pushed herself closer to him until their breath mixed visibly in the cold air.

"I'm wet," she whispered.

A thousand carnal thoughts battled Burton's inner Morality Knight, a warrior so noble that he had cost Burton many pleasures. Within seconds, the moment had passed.

"You're one of the nice ones, aren't you?" Eliza said. "Will you help me?"

"Tell me what you need." Burton felt strange, as if he'd passed her test but lost her interest at the same time.

Eliza spoke softly as they lay like lovers on pillows. "We need a meeting with your brother. We've tried to reach out to him before, but he's always turned us down."

"Paddy knows you?"

"David has tried to speak to him, but he won't respond. I mean, I'll admit the snake stuff is super creepy, but you can't ignore how David looked after it bit him."

"His eyes were bright green circles."

"Exactly – this is not normal stuff. He says the Elixir has the power to cure anyone, we just need to figure out how to mass-produce it. That's where your brother comes in. He has an army of scientists and equipment at his disposal."

Burton was struggling to understand. "Why is this not

already being researched by scientists at Oxford and Cambridge?"

"David's worried about it getting into the wrong hands and wants to keep an element of control. He trusts your brother will do the right thing, and so do I."

"You're using me?" Burton often received online friend requests from people wanting to be one connection closer to his brother. He was used to it, but never this intimately.

"I'm sorry, but we had to involve you. You're the key to getting him to listen. Don't you want to save the world?" There was hope in her voice.

Burton paused for thought, "Let's go see my bro. I'll ring a taxi."

"Fantastic. Let's get out of here. Are you ready?"

Burton nodded, and they squeezed out from under the boat together. There was no sign of their trackers.

"I think it'll be best if he sees you alone," Eliza added as Burton slid his hand into the pocket of his soaking jeans to retrieve his phone.

"Are you sure?"

"Meet me back at O'Fagan's office tomorrow at three o'clock. I'll give you my number but send nothing about all of this – you never know who's watching or listening." Eliza took Burton's phone from him and typed in her number.

"Don't worry, I won't send any dick pics either," Burton joked, then wondered if he might have crossed a line.

Eliza was looking down at the screen, the light illuminating her features. "Hey, nobody said you couldn't send those." She gave a wicked little grin without looking up, before handing the phone back.

"David asked me to give this to you as well. Tell Patrick to give it a closer look." Eliza pulled down the zip of her coat and lifted a bronze necklace from around her neck. There was a marble-sized locket attached. "Here is one drop of Elixir for the Super Burton Brothers." She performed two little punching jumps after the locket was handed over.

You've been a lucky little necklace, tucked in there. Burton put it over his own head. *Stop it – you're doing it again.*

"Okay. I'll go to Paddy's house and talk to him. We'll sort this out and make a plan tonight. I'll ask for two taxis and you can get home. Where to?"

"I'll tell them when they get here. Promise me you'll convince him?"

"I'll do my best."

"Good lad."

The two new friends stood at the top of the steps that led down to the ocean-covered walkway. The old lighthouse, tall and proud, had guided its first travellers to safety in many years.

CHAPTER 6
THE PRISONER'S WATCH

The taxi pulled up outside Patrick's beautiful five-bedroom detached house on the corner of Jesmond Dene. The Dene was a wooded valley in the centre of Newcastle, a wildlife corridor where families walked when the weather was fine. Patrick owned the biggest house on the street and a mega-rich Newcastle United footballer lived next door. Patrick had talked of moving somewhere even bigger once he'd been in his CEO role a little longer.

I'd never want to move. As Burton approached the front door, Tino the cockapoo barked; he must've sensed that his best mate was nearby. Before he had even knocked, Dominique opened the door and Tino sprinted out with a greeting that only a canine could offer: the pristine mutt started rolling on his back in the snow.

"Hi Dominique, I'm s-sorry to b-bother you so late. Is P-Paddy there?" Burton imagined he might have icicles hanging from his nose and earlobes.

"Oh dear, is everything okay? What's happened? You're soaked right through. Come in, come in. I'll get you a towel and some hot cocoa."

Dominique seemed ready for bed. She stood barefoot in

red silk pyjamas, and her shining dark hair looked as though it had been brushed a thousand times. Her hazel eyes were warm and welcoming despite the time.

"Ho-way then, come in, ya bugger," she joked, adopting a deep voice and mimicking Burton's accent. "Tino. In. Now." Tino ran back into the house and sat by the door waiting for his paws to be dried. He was the most obedient pup ever. "It's too late for dog angels, you silly thing."

Paddy came down the stairs wearing chequered lounge pants and a grey T-shirt stretched across his barrel chest. He handed Burton a warm towel and an identical set of spare loungewear. *He must've heard me come in.*

"What's up, Jonny? Everything okay? Are Mam and Dad okay? How are you this soaking? Have you been swimming in the Tyne? Get changed and we'll have a sit down. I've just finished a call, so it's good timing."

Dominique took Burton's heavy coat and handed it to her husband. Burton stood dripping onto the ornate black-and-white mosaic tiled floor of the hallway. Dominique shot a glance toward Patrick as he went to throw the wet coat over the banister. He walked down the hall to place it in the utility room instead.

Dominique was on top of Burton's late arrival with the efficiency of a military leader. "I'll get this menace sorted and bring you a drink. Why don't you stay over, and you can see Matthias in the morning? Get changed in the utility room."

"Yes, thanks. I'll message my mam and let her know," Burton replied through the towel as he mopped his hair and face. After jumping into the utility room, he got changed quicker than a superhero's alter ego. He noticed an A4 drawing by his nephew stuck to the spare freezer. Little Matthias had drawn a crowned stick man running and had written *uncy jony* at the top. *I won't be his hero for much longer; he's nearly old enough to work out what a loser I am.*

The brothers sat down in identical clothes, although

Burton didn't fill out his T-shirt in the slightest. Patrick's sitting room was immaculate, like the cover of *House Wonderful* magazine. The 70-inch TV didn't even seem too big on the wall. Bound books and family photographs lined the sunken shelves on either side of the screen. The open-plan area boasted dark brown leather settees, a small bar, and even a pool table with grey cloth to match the décor. Tino sat in the perfect spot at Burton's feet to get a good head scratch.

The brothers watched the sports news, mitigating any emotion they might display. The volume had been turned down low.

"Right, what's wrong?" Patrick asked, as if he'd be able to solve any issue without a thought. He didn't wait for an answer. "You know, Jonny, things change. Your work situation has been unlucky. The second pandemic battered the economy. There are loads of people in your position. Just keep trying, keep swinging, and never give up. I'm doing my best to use my contacts and get you in somewhere. It's just a shame I'm working all the time. You know you never have to worry about your money situation either, right? You've never asked for anything, but if you needed it—"

"I do, thanks. I'm trying. It's not that, though, it's—"

"Girls? You need to get out and about. Go to the clubs in town, get a few drinks into you and relax. Don't be so serious all the time. Be confident. You're quirky and funny when you relax – it's an excellent combination."

"Actually, I think I might have met someone. I think we might've hit it off. That isn't why I'm here. I need to ask you about—"

"What? Who? Stop the press. Dom, get in here! Jonny's got a girlfriend. Will I get the champagne out? I'm ringing the North East News."

Dominique emerged from the kitchen carrying two large mugs of hot chocolate. She stood perfectly balanced, an almost celestial homemaker, with the silk dressing gown flowing behind her. She was laughing at her husband.

"Stop it, Patrick, he's blushing. What's her name, Jonny?"

"Eliza."

"That's such a pretty name. You can tell me about her tomorrow. I must go to bed. I'm exhausted. I gave a speech at the Sage today about climate change."

"That's great. Did it go well?"

"Yes, thanks. The weather put some people off, but it'll be uploaded online tomorrow."

"I'll watch it, I promise."

"Did you know, if there were no insects or worms we would cease to exist within ten years? If humans didn't exist, the planet would thrive."

"We don't treat our planet with any respect. It can't go on indefinitely," Burton replied.

"Exactly. I often wonder if all these pandemics are just Mother Earth fighting back. Don't you stay up drinking all night, Patrick, do you hear me?" Dom chuckled to herself and headed off to bed.

"Goodnight," the brothers said in unison like little school-boys as they sipped their cocoa in their matching pyjamas.

Patrick made his next comment as soon as his wife was out of earshot. "Come on then, tell me about Eliza. Is she lush?"

"Yes. I mean no. I mean… That's not why I'm here." Burton sensed the conversation getting away from him.

Patrick's eyes grew with delight, like a cartoon wolf observing his prey. "Does she have big—"

"What do you know about the Cult of Asklepios?" Burton asked.

The mood changed. Patrick changed. His laughter stopped. He stood up and walked to the pool table, lifted a cue from the holder, placed the white ball down with a scowl and smashed it into the other balls with ferocity.

"Who told you about them?"

"They need your help. You should get back to them."

"I can't believe they've spoken to you. Is this how you met Eliza? If so, they're using you."

"The world has been on its knees. You could save so many people."

"You've got to be fucking kidding me," Patrick muttered to himself. He smashed the pool balls again, producing a loud rattle.

"Let me tell you a story." He chucked his cue down and spun the black ball on the spot before leaning against the table. "There was a boy who had lazy teachers at school. They'd hand out textbooks and ask the children to read quietly while they sat at their desks and dreamed of being poets and rock stars. If a child complained, they were made to stand outside. The boy taught himself the best he could and scraped through his exams."

"I can see where this is going," Burton said.

"Can you, though?" Patrick asked. "The boy used his charm to get a job at a local pharmacy. He answered phones and managed orders. He also delivered prescriptions. Often, at a certain door, a timid woman would answer with a black eye and bruises. Sometimes her scruffy little husband answered. Greasy hair, chinos, vest, little moustache, you know the type. Scum.

"Then, on a drunken night out in Newcastle, the boy saw the bastard, and a scuffle ensued. The boy beat the man, hitting him with a bottle and kicking him while he lay on the ground. He was aggressive and asserted his dominance. The woman just watched with a smile as he kicked her husband from pillar to post.

"Guess what. They charged the boy with assault and battery. The judge dismissed the evidence of domestic abuse as rough sex. If the wife's testimony was to be believed, she enjoyed being manhandled. The boy went to prison for six months and it was hell."

"Eh? You've never been to prison." Patrick had been the subject of Burton's own childhood paintings. The notion that he was a criminal sounded preposterous.

"I did. Remember when you were a kid and mam said I was in America studying at Harvard? Nope, I was in a cell in Durham. I wasn't complaining, though. I was absorbing any reading material I could find in the prison library. My six months would've been tougher without my cellmate, Sergio."

"He doesn't sound like a Geordie," Burton stated.

"He was from Merida in Spain, near Madrid. Have you heard of it?"

"I don't think they've got a good football team, so no." Burton had hoped to lighten the mood, but it didn't work.

"One day, we'd experienced an unpleasant exchange with some thugs in the canteen. I was shaken when we got back to the cell, and Sergio started talking about Merida and how he'd ended up in prison, or 'prision' as he pronounced it. He blamed something he called the Cult of Asklepios.

"Sergio opened up to calm me down. Merida had been a Roman colony and acted as a retreat for veteran soldiers to retire and heal their scars. His brother was a server and his sister sold flowers to tourists. He couldn't find a job or offer any support to his family, and it crucified him. One day however, an Englishman with ringlet hair approached him with a proposition."

"O'Fagan?" Burton asked eagerly.

"Yes. There was an excavation around something the locals called the 'Aqueduct of Miracles'. O'Fagan asked him to steal an ancient vial before the archaeologists could find it."

"The Elixir! This is exactly what happened to me. I took a bag from the site on King's Road." Burton was elated to find that Patrick knew so much already. "How did Sergio end up in England?" Patrick shook his head and muttered something including multiple expletives under his breath before continuing.

"After his initial success, he said that they inducted him into the cult and sent him to England. Sergio held a vial for ransom, and that's when his luck ran out. It was his way of trying to secure the future of his family. The Caballion cut off his hand, killed his parents, brother, sister, and framed him for the murder. Animals."

"O'Fagan is a philanthropist. He doesn't seem the type. He's a good guy."

"A violent mistake is one thing…" Patrick tapped his chest to present himself as proof, "but murdering an innocent flower girl… come on." Patrick looked at his brother sternly as though ready to condemn any defence about to be made.

"Look, it's horrific, but Sergio stole from them," Burton said.

"Are you having a laugh? It didn't belong to them, or anyone else. Sergio and I became good friends in prison. Before I left, he asked the guards to give me his watch, the only thing he owned in the world. He told me that whenever I checked the time I should remember to work harder for my family. He showed me his stump and joked that he didn't have a wrist to wear it on anyway.

"With his words ringing in my ears, I climbed the career ladder and became the CEO of Biovax. Can you imagine how hard that was with a criminal record? You've brought danger to my door, Jonny. Why the fuck should I involve myself with these lunatics and risk everything I've built?"

Burton took off the necklace and held it outstretched in his fist. The bronze chain dangled from his fingers. "This is why."

"What's this?"

"One drop of Elixir. Proof. Take a closer look at your lab tomorrow. You owe it to the world."

"Did you just listen to a word I said?"

"O'Fagan hasn't turned his back on Asklepios, but he

believes their ways need to be modernised. He chose us because we're an honest family."

"He chose us? Like he did with Sergio?"

"The cult has four leaders – it might not have been O'Fagan who gave the order to murder his family. Just check it. If you don't want to help after that, I'll tell him we're out."

"I was never in."

"Come on. Imagine if you used it to discover a cure for cancer. Wouldn't that be worth the risk? Wouldn't that be worth anything?"

Patrick glared at Burton and the two stood facing each other. Patrick held out his hand and Burton released the locket.

As Burton lay on the double bed in his brother's luxurious spare room, a picture message came through on his phone. It was Eliza, pulling a goofy cross-eyed face with her hair wet and bedraggled. The caption read, *Thought I looked cute, might delete later*, and was followed by a laughing emoji.

Lol, see you tomorrow. PB is going to take a look, Burton replied.

Good boy xxx, came back instantly, with a kissing emoji at the end.

As Burton drifted to sleep, he thought about a positive future for the first time in years.

CHAPTER 7
LAB ATTACK

The Burton brothers stood in the immunology lab at Biovax HQ. Everything was white: the walls, the floor, the desks, the microscopes, the shelves, even the test mice in their transparent cases. It made for a sterile environment.

"Is there anything I can help with?" Burton asked.

"No, just take a seat and don't touch anything. I'll have to call in my lab assistant – there's too much to get through on my own," Patrick replied through his white disposable facemask.

"Should we not keep our circle small?"

"It's not an option. I need his skills. Anyway, he hasn't got the balls to say anything." Patrick pressed a button on a desk phone. It buzzed straight through; he didn't need to lift the receiver.

"Yes, boss?"

"Egan, get to the immunology lab, please."

"Right away."

Patrick was wearing a long white lab coat with his security pass tucked into the top pocket to prevent it from dangling. He stared into a microscope.

Egan came into the room with a sense of purpose. His face was so pale it almost matched the walls, and his chequered shirt was faded as though he'd washed it a thousand times. One of his ears was pointy, like a little goblin. *Wow, he looks like he's never watched sport in his life, never mind played it.*

"Hi, I'm Jonny."

"I have a PhD," Egan replied.

Burton didn't know how to respond. This oddball might have been smart, but he didn't know how to socialise.

Patrick took over. "Egan, we have a special project. I need you to help me run some tests and we need to start right away. I must ask for your discretion regarding whatever we find."

"Oka boss, anything."

The scientists began investigating how the droplet reacted to certain stimuli in a petri dish. Patrick muttered to himself as he switched between his microscope, computer and notepad. He handed apparatus to Egan along with communicative gestures and looks. They were in the zone and operated as one unit.

After some time, Patrick seemed to realise Burton was sat there doing nothing and tried to involve him with an explanation. "I'm testing the intracellular membrane traffic, cell-to-cell interactions and also the distribution of antigens and their co-localisation with intracellular markers."

The way his brother jumped from cheeky northerner to absolute boffin dumbfounded Burton.

"In English, please?" he said.

"Immunocytochemistry is the best method for visualising the behaviour of intracellular proteins. Permeability is all about puncturing cell membranes and detecting intracellular antigens. I've introduced this after preparing the fixative agent to initiate protein cross linking."

"Nope, didn't understand a word of that either." Burton

wouldn't have even been able to repeat it. Egan looked up and tutted.

"What? No. Don't you dare!" Patrick shouted at his petri dish. "Jonny, I've never seen anything like this. I need more to test. This could be world-changing. This could win me a Nobel prize."

Egan's head popped up again. Patrick was becoming keener with every hour of investigation.

"When Biovax couldn't manufacture a vaccination during the last pandemic, I received a lot of criticism," Patrick said. "My credentials were mocked, and my position questioned. All you get at the top is backstabbing from people who want to replace you. This will blow them away. I'll meet O'Fagan. I must have more Elixir. Tell him to come here now. And if he tries anything, he'll get this." Patrick slammed his fist into his palm, making a crack. He'd never been afraid of anyone or anything.

"What makes you think you can do something with the Elixir if you couldn't help produce a vaccine during the pandemic?" Burton asked.

"Reverse engineering," Egan butted in arrogantly.

"Exactly, Egan. It's like taking the hardest test in the world, but with every formula and solution written right in front of you," Patrick explained.

Burton texted Eliza. *P wants to meet D at the BV building. Bring more.*

A response came through instantly: *30 mins.* They were on their way.

"Okay, done. They'll be here in half an hour," he said, putting his phone back in his pocket.

Patrick looked off to the right side. "It's going to be strange to look this old man in the eye. I don't trust him."

He wheeled his plastic chair to one area of his chemical playground after another. He continued to work, scribble and pour things into tubes until the voice of a receptionist came through the speakerphone. "There is a Mr O'Fagan, a Miss Contra, and someone who won't tell me her surname here to see you."

"Thanks," Patrick said. "I'm expecting them. Give us five minutes and send them to meeting room G, please."

Contra? Is that Eliza's surname?

"Follow me." Patrick's long white lab coat flapped behind him like a cape as he made his way to the meeting room.

Meeting room G wasn't as lavish as the Maslow Fairchild boardroom. It had a small white plastic table in the middle, surrounded by white plastic chairs on wheels. Three walls were used as a single large whiteboard; they had equations written all over them. A board rubber and coloured markers sat in a pot. Behind Patrick was a large window.

"Wow, bro, I don't think I've ever appreciated how smart you actually are," Burton said, looking at the mathematical gibberish surrounding him. "You've always seemed so... normal."

"I didn't do these – that was Egan. He's got a brain the size of a house. It helps to surround yourself with smart people in my line of work." The assistant sighed through a smile, which hinted at a deep-rooted frustration.

"Patrick," he said, "can I continue working elsewhere while your meeting takes place?"

"Of course. Use the time well."

As Egan moved toward the door, Patrick leant over to Burton and said, "He can write this shit all over the walls, but he can't talk to people face to face. He spends his nights on his laptop ruining the ends of films and books for people. He even has the username Spoiler." Patrick's whisper was slightly too loud, and Egan's pointy ear picked it up. It was almost as though Patrick wanted him to hear.

Someone knocked on the door just after it closed.

"Come in," Patrick said in a commanding tone.

Eliza entered first and did a little nervous curtsy while grinning at Burton. She was wearing one of the spare lab coats. "Hi, I'm Burton's friend Eliza."

"Hi, Eliza, nice to meet you." Patrick stamped on his brother's foot twice under the table in approval, before standing to greet the other visitors. Nefertari didn't come in or even speak, she wedged the door open and stood guard.

"And I'm David O'Fagan. What a pleasure it is to finally meet the self-made pharmaceutical giant, Patrick Burton."

O'Fagan removed his Stetson hat and placed it on the white table, along with his red scarf. He stood upright in a pinstriped suit. The wrinkles weren't as prominent as Burton remembered, but the glint in his vivid green eyes remained. *How old is this guy?*

O'Fagan reached out for a handshake, but Patrick didn't acknowledge it. Despite his brothers smile, he was glaring at his guest.

"I'm sorry," O'Fagan said. "I always forget we aren't advised to do that anymore. It's so sad to see an age-old tradition die. If only the big companies could have done more to help during the last pandemic, we wouldn't all still be so worried about infection."

"We did all we could," Patrick replied. "And speaking of tradition, I heard you've turned your back on yours. Is that correct?"

Burton and Eliza sat quietly as the tycoons locked horns.

"You are right to a degree, but what I hold dear remains," O'Fagan said. "To be a healer, you must make sacrifices. I hope we can find some common ground today."

"You call yourself a healer, but I've heard something very different. To heal is to save lives, not to take them."

"Sacrifice, young Patrick. I once cured a group of boys in Cape Town whose eyes were burned by captors. They believed the boys would make more money begging blind, you see? We introduced the captors to our Caballion, and they never stole another son. We healed an entire village with our actions that day. Naturally, tyranny rose again, but we did the best we could. Sometimes violence is the only way."

"You're quite the Samaritan."

"I try."

"And these Caballion butchers just follow your lead on who to murder?"

"Our ways have been archaic. You are quite right to question them. I come to you today, cap in hand and begging for your help. The past is the past but the future… the future is full of endless possibility, if only you try."

Patrick's eyes narrowed. It was so hard to read what either of them was truly thinking.

"Tell me more about the substance you shared with us," Patrick asked.

"In Ancient Greece, Asklepion temples acted as rehab sanctuaries. Villagers would travel there and take part in a purifying ritual. They would then enter an Abaton, an incubation chamber where they received a healing dream under the influence of an Elixir. Sometimes these dreams are said to have included a visitation from the divine physician himself. Over time, these shrines spread across the globe with the Roman Empire. The Caballion investigate forgotten shrines around the world, acquiring the Elixir before it falls into the wrong hands."

"So, you hallucinate while this agent works through the body; interesting." It was clear that Patrick wasn't wanting a history lesson, only anything that could aid his upcoming research.

"Yes, but don't get carried away. You may be rejuvenated and free of illness, but you won't be punching through walls, shooting rays from your eyes, or flying through the clouds after consuming it. Without training, you'll merely be able to withstand a heavier beating and prolong your agony. I know how much Jonathan likes his superhero movies."

Patrick shrugged, as though his brother's childish hobbies were none of his concern. "Any nasty side effects?"

"Just a constant guilt that you're not doing enough with your gift. There have been some that became addicted to their hallucinations, finding the real world difficult to return to after consumption. It's important to stay motivated on a goal to avoid this."

"Interesting." Patrick seemed to be calculating every word. His index finger was pressed against his bottom lip, as if he were trying to solve a crossword puzzle.

"The Caballion return the vials to the Four Columns when they are found, which is becoming less and less frequent. Nefertari was the best of them, and she stands outside this door protecting us right now. Count yourself lucky she defected with me."

"I think they chased us through Tynemouth. We hid," Burton said.

Without leaving her post by the open door, Nefertari spoke, "If they did not engage, they still in tracking phase, ensuring target is correct. Once they sure, no hiding."

Nefertari's robotic delivery and broken English only made the threat more chilling. Burton fidgeted in his seat. His leg was shaking up and down under the table. He felt Eliza's feet stretch out to try to keep him still.

"Why are they coming after you?" Patrick asked. "Are you guys not on the same team?"

"Do you know what the last words of Socrates were?" O'Fagan asked.

"The philosopher? Something about dust in the wind or sand in an hourglass?" Patrick replied. It seemed like an educated guess.

"It's time to be serious, Patrick. They were 'Crito, we owe

a cock to Asklepios. Pay it and do not neglect it.' They sentenced the greatest mortal mind ever to walk the Earth to death. They said he corrupted Athenian youth and failed to acknowledge the gods of the state. Although urged to flee by those close to him, he continued to speak our truth. He hoped his martyrdom could help heal a city torn apart by war and corruption.

"The cult was driven underground, and we adapted. That is how anything survives after all, is it not? We operated in much smaller numbers, serving the people in secret and passing on the knowledge of our godly substance through generations. I believe it is time to resurface and share the Elixir with the world. The others do not. They are prepared to kill for their cure."

"How many are in the cult?" Patrick asked.

"Initially we were many, but power is a terrifying thing in the wrong hands. We have altered our methods since 399 BC, finding that four groups of three may achieve as much as an army.

"Twelve? That's it?" Burton asked.

"What is easier to see on a beach, a grain of sand or a boulder? Those whose lives we impact are sworn to secrecy. Next time you see someone with vivid green eyes, check for the mark of Asklepios on their arm." O'Fagan showed Patrick his tattoo. "They will be your ally should you need them. It is a symbol showing that they were once saved."

Patrick leant forward in his chair. "Okay, can we end the history lesson before I fall asleep? Can we reproduce the Elixir? It seemed to evaporate after a short amount of time outside of the casing. We need more to test."

"This is why the cult travelled with a sacred snake. Inside a living host, the Elixir is more durable and long-lasting. The fangs acted as needles, a prehistoric means to administer their futuristic cure," O'Fagan explained.

"I need more to test," Patrick repeated more directly.

O'Fagan reached into his middle pocket of his suit jacket and placed the vial on the table. "This should be enough to know if it can be replicated."

As the vial touched the table, a small metal object crashed through the window and began spewing black smoke that took the place of space and light. The fire alarm and sprinklers kicked in within seconds. Burton now struggled to see his brother across the desk and everyone's words became muffled by the noise.

"Caballion here – move now." Nefertari beckoned everyone towards the emergency staircase as the sprinklers soaked her white apparel.

Burton heard another thud and looked towards the shattered window to see a crimson figure ziplining towards them from the roof of an adjacent building.

"Nef!" Eliza shouted as the fire alarm screeched like a hundred police cars.

O'Fagan snatched the vial as the hunter flew into the room. The group scurried and moved behind Nefertari as the aggressor extended a pointed metal baton. The figure wore a red tunic covered in tight crimson body armour. A red face-mask and dark hood concealed most of their features. The hanging leather straps from their belt made them look like a gladiator from a modern-day coliseum.

The figure swung the baton and took a chunk out of the wooden doorframe. They drew a gun and fired two black-feathered darts into Nefertari's abdomen. She didn't go down but staggered into the wall, smudging the writing and knocking the pot of pens onto the floor.

Tranquillisers?

Nefertari took a deep breath. She picked up a chair, used it to deflect the next baton strike, and then threw the shattered parts at her opponent. As they held up their arms to block the incoming debris, she moved in. Her biceps flexed as she picked them up by the throat and slammed them down through the weak fibreboard table in the middle of the room. The attacker tried to get up, but she stamped down on the outside of the calf that was holding their weight. It made a horrific sound, like a thick, jam-covered cracker biscuit being snapped in half. Nefertari had broken their leg.

"We need to go!" Eliza yelled.

Burton banged on the door of the neighbouring meeting room and alerted Egan as the others ran towards the stairs.

"Unless he fly, he in trouble," Nefertari announced as she re-joined the group. She pulled the darts from her abdomen. *Did she throw the masked guy back out of the window? He'll be dead!*

As they hurried to the ground floor, another dark cloud was waiting. Darts fired out from it and into the gathering in the stairwell, hitting O'Fagan and then Patrick. The two business moguls fell unconscious and dropped down the last few steps and onto the floor.

"Stop!" Nefertari shouted, launching herself down the stairs, ahead of Burton and Eliza. A second hunter exited the smoke and threw her to the ground, dropping their gun in the process.

Burton stopped and tried to wake his brother on the steps by shaking his shoulders. He heard shoes slapping on the wet vinyl floor as if someone were running away down a nearby corridor.

The second hunter was on top of Nefertari, hands around her throat and pressing a knee into her stomach. Burton caught her eyes through the smoke and water, they were cold and calm.

Eliza stopped tending to O'Fagan, picked up the gun, and aimed it at the crimson warrior's backside.

"No help," Nefertari forced out.

She jolted their wrists to loosen the grip around her throat. Then she snaked herself to the left to force the opponent's weight onto her right hip rather than her stomach. The next move in her grappling master class was to lock up their ankle behind her own bent leg and rock her attacker backward. They lost their balance and cracked the back of their head off the wet floor. Nefertari stood and pulled a bronze bar from her back. With the press of a button, it extended into a spear with a lethal tip. As the gladiator struggled to their feet, Nefertari skewered them to the wall. She unleashed a flurry of lightening quick strikes until her opponent hung like a tattered old coat on a peg. Burton lay on the steps in awe.

"You're going to have to help – get him out," Eliza ordered.

Burton dragged Patrick outside by the underarms before going back and doing the same to O'Fagan.

As Burton knelt beside his unconscious brother, he performed a headcount. "Where's Egan?"

Eliza was crouched, trying to wake O'Fagan. Nefertari had carried the hunter out of the building and was watching over them without blinking.

Two fire engines, an ambulance and a police car were parked a hundred metres away at the front of the Biovax building. Hundreds of staff formed orderly queues behind the emergency services, no doubt as they had practised in drills.

"The alarm triggers automatic emergency calls," panted Nefertari.

Where is the one with the broken leg? Did they get away?

Two paramedics ran over to Patrick and O'Fagan.

"They've breathed in a lot of smoke," Burton said, standing over them.

The paramedics checked their circulation, airways, and breathing. O'Fagan woke just as a paramedic was about to perform CPR.

"You'll need to buy me a drink first," he said. Even in a daze, he was quick. The male paramedic, who had been seconds from locking lips, backed away. The second paramedic handed a packet to Nefertari. It contained a silver sheet to keep her warm.

"Thank you." Nefertari bowed to the female paramedic and smiled. Her face had been grazed and bloodied only moments earlier, but now she appeared untouched. "I fine. You very nice. Thank you." She bowed again. Then, as two police officers began to handcuff the downed gladiator at her feet, she added, "Careful, very dangerous."

Patrick came to after medical assistance and sat up amid flashing blue lights and gawping colleagues. As if afraid of his employees seeing their CEO weak and vulnerable, he rose to his feet, using the bonnet of a blue hatchback for stability.

"Is everyone okay?" he shouted, deflecting the weakness back onto his workers. "There has been no fire, so don't worry, your work will be intact. This was an attack on our building by animal rights protesters, possibly the Three Blind Mice activists again. Don't worry – there will be a group email offering support and information before the close of business tomorrow. Everyone take the rest of the day off. Collect your things and go home."

The workers chatted amongst themselves as they began to disperse.

Another white-haired police officer approached Burton and his brother. "The black smoke has all but cleared. We've bagged this – some kind of canister. A fire-fighter spotted it when conducting a sweep."

"It looks pretty hardcore, like something you'd find in the military," Patrick said. He tapped his head and looked at blood on his palm. "They must've bought it on the dark web."

"These guys were well kitted out for activists. We've apprehended one and will take him to the station for questioning."

"Thank you, Officer—"

"Detective Glover."

"Thank you again. We'll look into upping our security."

Burton could see that Patrick was already plotting as he gazed up at the evacuated building.

O'Fagan was patting his jacket and looking on the ground and under the cars.

Glover noticed. "Have you lost something, sir?"

"Just my glasses, officer. They were expensive."

"We'll find anything once the smoke fully clears. I'll be in touch, Mr Burton." Glover walked over to his colleague by the squad car.

The group made their way back inside to reconvene and get warm.

"Who has it?" O'Fagan was restless, searching his pockets and scanning the floor. "Tell me one of you has it."

"I don't." Patrick looked to Burton.

"Me neither." Burton looked at Eliza.

"I don't." Eliza pulled out the pockets of her soggy lab coat and let them hang.

"It was mayhem in there. Could one of the Caballion have taken it? The one you threw out of the window perhaps?" O'Fagan asked.

"No. They didn't get close to you. I make sure. I search the other when he hanging from my spear," Nefertari replied.

"Hey, where's Egan?" Burton asked.

"Looks like the little pointy-eared boffin stole our vial," Patrick announced.

The group sat in the furthest corner of the Biovax canteen as staff exited through the main reception. A young barista brought over coffees with snowman art swirled into the top, and the aroma replaced any remaining smoke in Burton's nostrils.

"I hope you're okay, Mr Burton," the barista said to

Patrick. Her hands were shaking as she placed the cups down on the table.

"Thanks, Jolene, I really appreciate this. Get your stuff together and go home with the rest."

"Thank you, Mr Burton."

"Please, as I've said before, call me Patrick."

As soon as the barista was out of earshot, Patrick's focus switched back to Egan. "That ungrateful little freak. The time and knowledge I've shared with him over the years, and he does this. He sniffed it. He sniffed the fucking glory. I knew he was ambitious, but I didn't expect this."

"Where would he go?" Eliza asked.

Trying to think logically, Burton said, "The first thing he said to me was that he had a PhD. Might he go to his university?"

"Yes, Jonathan, I like your thinking." O'Fagan scowled like a mob boss who had been disrespected.

"He might go to Northumbria University, or he might have a makeshift lab setup at home. The boy never stops working." Patrick was marching up and down the canteen while the others sat. His natural stamina was unbelievable.

"He sell?" Nefertari asked.

"Not a chance. If there is industry respect to be won, he'll want it for himself. I'm going to kill him."

"What about other pharmaceutical companies?" Eliza added.

"Going elsewhere would only mean working with others and sharing the glory. He'll want this for himself. Trust me."

"Give address, I'll go to house." Clearly, Nefertari didn't want to waste time.

"Jonathan, you and Eliza go to the university in the morning," O'Fagan said assertively. "I doubt there will be many people around with it being almost Christmas. Patrick, can you progress your studies at all?"

"Potentially."

"Okay, we have a plan," O'Fagan said. "The hunt is on."

"Cult will be back. We must find fast," Nefertari said.

"Jonathan, stay at my house again tonight," Patrick said.

"Okay. What do I tell Mam and Dad?" The others looked at him in surprise – a thirty-four-year-old still tied to his mother's apron strings. He regretted saying it immediately.

"Just say you're enjoying the change and it's like a holiday," his brother replied. "It's easy."

"Eliza, you stay with me again, just in case," O'Fagan said.

"Sure." Eliza looked pleased. Burton lowered his head as Patrick glanced over at him. His brother seemed to read his mind.

"Why don't you stay with us, in the spare room?" Patrick suggested to Eliza. "You'll be able to go to the university together in the morning,"

"No, it's okay. I'll see you tomorrow, Frosty. Eight o'clock sharp."

Patrick handed Nefertari a piece of paper with Egan's address, and she left without another word.

O'Fagan guided Eliza towards the door with one hand and applied his Stetson hat with the other. "I'll return here tomorrow, and we will continue. Don't stay up too late. We have a rat to catch."

Burton returned to Jesmond. Matthias wanted to play their version of hide and seek – or, as he called it, the 'action roll game'. It warmed Burton's heart to see the joy on his nephew's face every time they played, but it was too late to be commando crawling into hidey places. They played computer games instead, but no high score could take Burton's mind off Eliza. All his paranoia now centred on her safety instead of his own. *O'Fagan's an old man. Surely he wouldn't take advantage of her? Do they have a relationship beyond what they've shared?*

After Burton retired to get ready for bed, Patrick remained sat downstairs, drinking red wine with Dominique. He could hear them laughing and joking as he brushed his teeth. *Paddy and Dom are so comfortable together and they know each other inside out. Must be nice to be part of a team like that.*

CHAPTER 8
Z-GIRLS

Burton and Eliza walked across the grounds of Northumbria University. Raised grass areas bordered the pavement, creating a walkway that would usually herd hungover students to their lectures during term time. A long ramp on the left led up to the library.

"I used to watch the performing arts students pirouetting through that window over there," Burton said.

"Bet their debt was the only thing that was truly spiralling," Eliza retorted. "What job were they expecting to get with a performing arts degree? Seriously?"

"About anything they wanted if they worked hard enough. Dancer? Actor? Singer? I suppose it's difficult to break into the industry when your parents aren't famous or rich already. Remember when the government suggested all artists should retrain? What do they think everyone was doing during their enforced lockdowns? Listening to music, watching films and reading books. I can't believe how they treat creativity with such contempt. Arseholes," Burton cursed under his breath.

"What were you doing looking in the windows anyway? You big perve," Eliza teased.

"Put it this way: at least they got to entertain one person in their career. Looks like they've installed heavier blinds since then." Eliza grinned and slapped his upper left arm playfully. "You're not wrong, though. I studied Art here a long time ago, and it led absolutely nowhere."

"You're standing next to me, so it's not all bad. I think you'd be an excellent actor. You have a unique face. You could play a troll."

Eliza's words cut him pretty deep. He looked away from her to hide his features and their laughter was cut short. Burton changed the subject. "Follow me. The science classes are held here. The striker from my uni football team dated someone on the Biology course. We used to spend ages waiting for her to come out and meet us at reception."

"Early is on time, and on time is late, as my mam always says. Why was she taking so long?"

"She was shagging another member of our team in the library basement each week. My mate was such a likeable lad, and she humiliated him. At least she got kicked off the course."

"Sounds like an own goal to me," Eliza commented.

"He was depressed and didn't end up finishing his degree. We came second in the league without him. I hate her nearly as much as he does."

Eliza bit her lip and looked away. To fill the awkward silence that followed, Burton asked, "Did you go to university?"

"You know the drill. I do the talking," Eliza said, ignoring his question. She came to life again as they approached the reception. The words *We're here to help* were displayed on a blue wall behind a crescent-shaped desk. Miniature models of knights and goblins lined the entire curve.

Burton began, "D'you not think it would be best, as an alumnus, if I—"

"Hi," Eliza said to the teenage porter and stepped forward. As he looked up, he jumped and dropped a small plastic knight he was in the middle of painting. He wore thick-rimmed jam-jar glasses that magnified his eyes comically. Long, mousy brown curtains flopped down, partially obscuring his spotty face.

"Busy?" Burton asked. Jam-jars scowled.

"We think our classmate is here borrowing some equipment, and we need to give him a message about coursework before he goes home," Eliza said, making up a cover story on the spot.

"What's he called?"

"Egan," Burton replied. He stepped forward, but Eliza slapped his chest to make him go back.

Jam-jars scowled again. "You're old for students. I haven't seen you here before, and I don't forget a face."

"This is a help desk. Do I look like a girl who needs a lot of help?"

"And I'm a mature student," Burton said. "You should never stop learning," he added.

"What's his second name?" Jam-jars asked, his magnified bug eyes narrowing.

"Erm, we don't know," Eliza said. "He's little, with a pointy ear, and looks a bit like a gremlin."

"You don't know your fellow student's full name?"

"We just use his online nickname," Burton intervened.

"Which is?"

"Spoiler."

"Filth." Jam-jars stood up from his seat. "I once asked a university message board about the running time for *Knightsblood 3,* and the Spoiler replied. He said Princess Felicia was a Syrenite."

Burton was familiar with the series and tried to use it to their advantage. "That was the big twist of the movie!"

"I'd waited five years for it to come out and he ruined it. I've never forgotten the username." Jam-jars was incensed, but clearly happy to find a fellow fan at the same time.

"Did he ruin the Battle of the Siamese Gate as well?" Eliza asked.

His face lit up. "When Magnus brought the portcullis down on the bogtroll? Incredible – no words can do it justice."

"Anyway, d'you think he's been through here?" Burton asked.

"No, nobody has. Practically everyone is home for Christmas. I've been painting my Knightsblood models for the last hour. Would you like to look at them?"

Eliza tossed her head back and grunted at the ceiling. "Fucking hell, why didn't you just say so straight away?"

"Just fancied a chat. Do you collect the cards? I'll trade some."

Eliza picked up a figurine, walked through the automatic door, and threw it off a tree trunk.

"No! My Felicia!" Jam-jars ran outside to save his plastic princess, wading into the slush and mud, desperately cupping snow and searching under the tall tree.

"That was harsh," Burton said, passing Eliza to help him look.

Jam-jars was looking upward. "That's funny, the window isn't normally like that."

"Which window?" Eliza asked.

He pointed. "Look at the Biology building."

"I can't see anything." Burton said. The campus courtyard was surrounded by windows. "How strong are those glasses?"

"They give me the vision of a Hawkranger."

"*Knightsblood 2: Fable of the Fall*?" Eliza said immediately. Burton couldn't have been more impressed.

"Exactly!" Jam-jars scurried over to the window. It was a few centimetres open but remained on the latch. The wood was scraped, as if someone had tried to prise it open in a hurry and failed. "I need to tell my superior. That damn Spoiler will get no help off me. I'd rather be fed to a bogtroll."

"Sorry about your model. If I get any cards to trade, I'll know where to come." Eliza seemed to want to make things right after losing her temper.

"It's okay, and please do. My name's Jimmy. Here, you can have this." Jimmy Jam-jars handed the small wet model of a princess holding a spear to Eliza, and she placed the dismal trinket in her coat pocket.

The trail had gone cold, but Eliza started analysing their small discovery. "Egan was too weak to get in. I'm surprised he even tried."

"He's a scientist, not a burglar. He obviously needed something, though. Let's get back to Biovax."

As they travelled back to Biovax, they talked about *Knightsblood* all the way. Burton loved discussing his favourite characters, music and storylines from the three classic action movies. Before long, they were back in the building that had been attacked twenty-four hours earlier.

As they entered the immunology lab, Patrick started his questioning immediately, "Find anything?"

"Egan's been there alright, but we missed him. He'd tried to get in through a window but couldn't," Burton explained.

"What a pansy," Patrick muttered.

"Would it be such a bad thing if he cracked the code? Isn't that what we're trying to do? Regardless of who gets credit?" Eliza asked.

"It's dangerous. Trying to manipulate something like this

without help, proper equipment or a way to test your findings is impossible to do safely," Patrick explained.

"But you got so much done yesterday," Burton commented.

Patrick pointed. "You see that microscope?"

"Yeah."

"It costs nearly six thousand pounds, and it's not even the best one. That's a single item in the lab. D'you think he can afford anything near this setup?"

"I doubt it very much," Eliza replied.

"So what? He's just the equivalent of a guy recording a raw song in his bedroom instead of a recording studio. That's how a lot of hit records are made these days," Burton summarised, trying to elevate his answer with metaphor.

"I like raw-sounding songs better. They've got more soul." Eliza had to be a punk, in the best possible sense. Raw music, coloured hair, snarly attitude, it all added up.

"But you don't inject a number one record into your bloodstream. People will be hurt if Egan continues alone," O'Fagan said. He was looking out of the window with his back to the group.

Nefertari entered the lab. For someone returning from an all-night stakeout, she looked fresh. "No sign. He lives in a small dorm room in the student hall of residents. He not stay last night, only small number of foreign students. What about parents?" Nefertari asked. She was ready to go again.

"They live down south somewhere," Patrick replied.

Her questioning continued. "Friends?"

"He doesn't talk to anyone apart from his computer," Patrick said, dismissing Egan's entire lifestyle once again.

"Eliza, didn't a teaser trailer for Z-*Girls* come out today?" Burton asked.

She took a couple of seconds to catch on. "I remember hearing something about it."

This was a Eureka moment for Burton. "Why don't we ask a question online, like Jimmy Jam-jars did?"

"What are you two talking about?" O'Fagan asked.

"*Z-Girls*. It's a movie about two royal sisters who were born into a brutal regime. They've got blasters and neon leggings. They rock," Eliza explained.

"What has this got to do with our problem?" O'Fagan asked.

"I think I like where you're going, Jonny," Patrick said. "Keep up, David. Egan likes geeky movies – or rather, he likes to tell people the endings before they get to see them."

"How pathetic," O'Fagan replied, and shook his head.

"Yep. Maybe we can fish him out?" Burton said, unsure how his suggestion would be received.

O'Fagan seemed to be struggling to follow their references. "How?"

"We'll mention the movie online and see if he spoils it. There are always set photos, leaked scripts and actors accidentally slipping information prior to release. If he does, we can try to strike up a conversation. The cinemas may have all closed down, but streaming services still have a big audience."

"Well, I suppose a gull can tap its feet to mimic rain. Let's see if the worm rises," O'Fagan said, adding a touch of class to the planning process.

"He'll have downtime whenever one of his crude tests is concluding," Patrick said. "You never know, he might look. I often check if the wife wants anything in between my own tests. Eliza, try it. Use my tablet."

Patrick passed over a silver tablet and Eliza got to work. She headed straight for a popular streaming site and created an account named FeliciaSyren92. After a quick search for the *Z-Girls* trailer, it played. A female voice with a Scandinavian accent spoke over pulsing synth music.

"*Since birth they taught us only cruelty, in a land where the rich rule and the poor obey. The time has come to denounce our lineage and return to the dirt. We are rebellion. We are... Z-Girls."*

"This looks so good," Eliza said, lost in the trailer.

Patrick had far less time for fiction. "Get on with it, you two – it sounds crap. Has he left anyone a message yet?"

"I've searched for his username, but there's nothing yet. If he responds to my comment, I'll get a notification on my account." Eliza started typing.

FeliciaSyren92: Z-Girls looks awesome. I've been looking forward to this all year. Those costumes are sexy!

"Do you have a picture on your account? Pick something or it won't stand out." Burton said, taking charge.

Eliza looked up and smiled, obviously having noticed his upturn in confidence. Burton puffed out his chest.

"Erm, here." Eliza reached in her pocket and took out the plastic model Jimmy Jam-jars had given her. She took a picture and added it to her profile. "What do we do now?"

"We wait," Burton confirmed in a tone of authority.

"No, we don't." O'Fagan looked at him, and Burton deflated instantly. "There's a chance this pest won't answer at all. We need a Plan B."

O'Fagan pinned a map to the wall. "If we don't retrieve the Elixir from our pointy-eared friend, we'll need a replacement vial. My investigations suggest two potential locations." He pointed to Albania on the map. *This must've been why he had all those maps at the Maslow building.*

"Why there?" Patrick asked.

"Butrint is home to Byzantine and Greek ruins. The Roman influence is unquestionable. There is an aqueduct set for excavation that could contain an Asklepion shrine. The area is a picture of tranquillity and a retreat from the Mediterranean sun. It perfectly aligns with other Elixirs that have been found in the past."

Patrick wasn't impressed. "Nothing closer to home?"

"There is somewhere a lot closer. The Bowl Hole. In 2007,

ninety-nine skeletons were excavated in the sand dunes beneath Bamburgh Castle. Archaeological research has been taking place ever since. At first they were suspected Viking raiders, then Anglo-Saxon settlers, but recent reports are referring to them as 'elite individuals'. Research has suggested they were unusually tall and robust and showed little evidence of disease. Isotope analysis states that only ten percent came from the immediate area and the rest were from other parts of Britain, continental Europe and even further afield. Although no Greek influence has been mentioned, I suspect this could've been a rare gathering of the cult, a meeting that turned sour. An opening has been discovered in the dolerite rock next to the dunes. It's listed only as a site of special scientific interest."

"Bamburgh? Why did you not say that first?" Patrick asked.

"It's likely to be a lot more dangerous. The cult is already here in the North East."

Patrick countered, "Speaking of which, what will become of the incarcerated hunter? Could we get to them and extract any information?"

"Pointless. Caballion no speak." Nefertari stated without a trace of doubt.

"How did the one you threw out the window survive?" Burton asked. "It was pretty high."

"Elixir grants strength and stamina that can be honed under training. They likely broke many bones but rebuilt upon impact. Caballion learn to disconnect pain from their bodies, a skill that comes after experiencing such breaks repeatedly." O'Fagan said.

"Not invincible but tough to kill." Nefertari said. She seemed to speak from experience.

"Why don't you know where their leader is?" Patrick asked O'Fagan.

"The Four Columns remain elusive, even from each other.

We used to communicate by encrypted letters bearing wax seals. Now, we use... email. It took some getting used to. Our words used to be filled with compromises and philosophy, but now I only experience demands and threats. The other three Columns go by the names of Nicoli, Mukhtar and Gorgone. Make no mistake, they're coming."

"So, we should act quickly. Surely it's better to head for Bamburgh right away?" Burton suggested.

"The shortest path is not always the best route to take," O'Fagan said with a lowered brow.

"I go where you decide. We are, how you say... democracy," Nefertari added. Her English was improving every day.

"Jonny's right, it'll be much quicker," Patrick said. "Eliza, you have the final vote. Just know, if it's not what I want to hear we may scrap this system going forward. I'm not keen."

"Bamburgh it is," Eliza decided. "Get in and out of there fast, Nef."

"As much as I disagree, it is a system that Socrates would be proud of. Nefertari, prepare for Bamburgh. It may be difficult to navigate," O'Fagan ordered. "Investigate the skeletons first before heading into the dolerite cave. I'd like to know more about them."

"I will leave tonight, and I will go alone. It could be dangerous," Nefertari confirmed.

She is such a badass. How is she not afraid? How does she not tire or show any apprehension?

Burton rubbed the top of his shoulder as the muscles tightened and cramped into the centre of his back. It was a twinge compared to the aches he usually had at home while doing nothing. He ignored it and continued to speak. "What happens if the Caballion come back when Nefertari isn't here?"

"They are regrouping. If they come, run to a crowded place," Nefertari replied, then exited the lab. As soon as she left, the group seemed exposed.

For the next three days they congregated at Biovax. Burton passed the time by imagining the celebration they'd have if Patrick could pull this off. The eureka moment hadn't come yet, but he kept faith. There was no response from Egan; he must've been busy with his own work. On the third night, Patrick and Burton sat watching the news after Dominique and Matthias had gone to bed.

"Today's top story: Two brutal murders were committed in different parts of Newcastle last night. Julia Jay is reporting from cRave nightclub in the city centre."

The Burton brothers looked at each other and shifted to the edge of their seats.

"Thanks, Kim. According to reports, a 22-year-old man exited cRave at approximately 1.45am. He screamed, 'I am the Last Dance Destroyer' and stabbed a young couple."

"Did the perpetrator know the couple?"

"Apparently not. Eyewitnesses saw him observing many young couples throughout the night, but at this point we aren't sure of any relationship with his victims. He has also been described as having 'wild violet eyes'."

"And there have been similar reports elsewhere in the city?"

"Yes. A man aged 29 was arrested last night after murdering three former line managers on a redundancy rampage. Witnesses report that the man's irises were also glowing violet, much like the case at cRave nightclub. The police have suggested that a powerful new drug may be circulating, although they refuse to make an official statement."

"Thank you, Julia." Kim looked directly into the camera. *"We will bring you more on this story as it develops."*

"It wasn't you, was it?" Patrick joked. He knew his brother had hated his last few bosses.

"That's not funny. It has to be Egan supplying the drug though, right?"

"He must be testing his formula on the public."

"Why would they be murdering people?"

"Medicine is a balancing act. Cocaine, for example, stimulates the nervous system and can lead to a sense of euphoria. You experience a sensation of strength that replaces fatigue and fear. Imagine that but amplified – you'd do whatever you wanted. People are on the edge after the events of recent years.

"How could they be getting this stuff?"

"He's live testing in limited quantities. It's the only way he'd be able to gather any reasonable data. We need to find out how he's distributing this new concoction."

Burton's phone vibrated silently on the arm of the leather chair.

"Hang on," he said, "I've got a text from Eliza. It just says, 'He's replied'."

CHAPTER 9
HOT CROSS BUNS

The Aesculapian snake had been transported to Biovax overnight. The reptile's glass chamber now stood at the rear of the immunology lab. Burton couldn't bring himself to get within ten feet of the creature. Patrick had designated the whole area off limits to staff, claiming it was still being investigated by the police.

"Did you see the news, Patrick?" O'Fagan asked.

"Yes – looks like Egan is testing a compound," Patrick responded.

"There's been another murder this morning. Brutal stuff. A dentist recognised a new patient who had ignored her messages on a dating app. She removed more than his wisdom tooth."

"Ouch." Eliza covered her own teeth with her lips to make it look like she didn't have any.

"I know a few people who should have their wisdom teeth put back in," Patrick quipped.

"These people are acting without restraint. I took the liberty of pinning them on the map," O'Fagan said. He had stuck a map of Newcastle onto a whiteboard and added three red pins to mark the locations of the murders. None of the pins were far apart, and red string lines connected them to make a triangle.

"You can't beat a good old-fashioned manhunt," O'Fagan said.

"Just an old-fashioned man," Patrick replied. He was playing the alpha game and took a dig at O'Fagan as he led the conversation. "The centre of the triangle is Ouseburn valley."

"Indeed. He must be near," O'Fagan replied.

"He doesn't have a network or any runners or dealers. I can't see him distributing it himself. Maybe this is a dark web thing?" Patrick said, thinking out loud.

"What did Egan's message say, Eliza?" Burton asked.

"It said 'The Z-Girl sisters end up battling each other in their mother's throne room. Alanah wins.' He responded to loads of people in the comments. Look at this." Eliza was sitting cross-legged with the tablet resting against her knee. "They're going crazy. He's ruined it for hundreds."

"What are they saying in response?" Burton stepped closer. His head was right on Eliza's shoulder, and he thanked the lord he'd just brushed his teeth.

"One comment says, 'I'm going to find out where you live and put a swarm of wasps through your letterbox.' That kind of thing. Tame, really."

"You can almost hear the nerd-tears hitting the keyboard," Patrick said with a smirk.

Eliza shook her head and didn't hold back. "Just because you don't like something, it doesn't mean it's wrong or weak. You sound so narrow-minded."

"Has anyone ever responded positively to him?" O'Fagan asked, ignoring the squabbling.

Burton was confused. "What d'you mean? Why would they?"

"It's like he loves to see their rage and said tears hitting the keyboard. What if Eliza responded with a spoiler of her own? Give the loner some kinship?"

"There must be a leaked script online. Let's see if we can spark the wimp's curiosity," Patrick said.

After a quick search, Eliza had it. "Oh wow, apparently there is a Draug skeleton in the movie that connects it to the *Knightsblood* saga. Oh my god."

"*Z-Girls* takes place in the future of the *Knightsblood* universe?" Burton and Eliza shouted at each other in excitement.

"What the hell are you two talking about?" Patrick asked, baffled.

Eliza started typing.

FeliciaSyren92: Oh yeah!? Well there is a Draug in the throne room, which connects it to the Knightsblood universe. Mic drop!

"Perfect," Burton said. He loved the 'mic drop' addition.

"We need to be proactive while we wait" Patrick said whilst rubbing his dark beard, "I actually know a guy who could help."

"Is there anything special about this one?" O'Fagan asked.

"I went to school with him."

"Oh, well, that will solve all of our problems. Another genius?" O'Fagan asked with more than a hint of sarcasm.

"Actually, he's well acquainted with a certain type. He's the kind of guy you keep at arm's length, but you're happy he's on your side."

"When you say 'certain type', does that mean someone like you?" O'Fagan asked.

"Worse, and he seems to know everyone in the North East."

"What is he called?" O'Fagan asked.

"Cal. We always called him Kinky Cal at school because he talked about sex so much. His exercise books were filled with pencil-shaded cocks and biro fannies."

"Don't all boys go on like that anyway, even when they're sixty?" Eliza asked.

"Not quite this bad. I haven't seen him for a good few years, thankfully. There was a time, however, when he was a regular fixture in my life." Patrick leant against a bench and looked off to one side, as if wondering if this was the right play.

"Why?" Burton asked.

"I was going through a rough patch at the time and needed a distraction."

"You? You needed a pickup?" Burton was surprised. His brother was always so energetic, positive, and in control.

"Yes. I'd meet up with Cal and he'd provide me with certain 'performance-enhancing' substances. This went on for a few months. He called us the Alumni High. Then I met Dominique and he'd pass comment about her constantly. I hated the fact he even knew her name."

"He might've been jealous?" Eliza suggested.

"Well, who could blame him? I still get emails inviting me to his 'parties', but they're not the type of thing you go to if you have a family."

"Why is that?" O'Fagan enquired with a grin. It was a safe assumption to say he knew all too well.

"He was bad enough during the Alumni High days, but I've heard some dodgy things about these parties. He sounds worse now."

"So how can this pervert help, exactly?" O'Fagan asked, his tone suggesting that he had run out of patience.

"Cal is connected. If he hears people are buying Egan's stuff, he'll want in. I wouldn't be surprised if the drug was circulating at his next party, which is actually tonight."

"What type of people will attend? Are they druggies?" Burton asked.

"Not who you'd expect. The attendees are often success-ful. He always offers me free entry with a plus one for

Dominique, but he charges anything between one and five thousand pounds per head, depending on how good-looking you are. Strange, considering the parties also require you to wear a silver cherub mask and a black robe."

"Simple, then – you can ask him," O'Fagan said with finality.

"No way I'm going. I'd be risking my marriage and everything I've built."

"Well, your brother would be welcome, I'm sure." O'Fagan grinned at Burton.

"I'm not sure he'd be able to handle it. Literally." Patrick looked upward and scratched his beard again, as if he were calculating all eventualities.

Burton thought for a moment, then took a deep breath. "I'll go."

"And I'll be your plus one." Eliza stood in front of Burton, looking up at him.

"Watch yourself around him, Jonny," Patrick warned. "He won't kill you, but he knows people who will. Mind your Ps and Qs."

"We'll keep our masks on and heads down," Burton replied, addressing Patrick with the respect of a private in the army.

Eliza saluted Patrick and shouted, "Sir, yes, sir!"

"Oh, something tells me you won't want to miss a thing." O'Fagan said, looking at Eliza. "Oh, to be young again."

"How will we know which one is Cal?" Eliza asked.

"Once you're there, you'll realise how ridiculous that question is," Patrick replied. "This is the address. It's at seven o'clock tonight and the password is 'horse'."

Eliza peeked as the address appeared in a text on Burton's phone. "Darras Hall? That's an expensive area," she said.

"He's the reason we haven't moved there," Patrick replied.

"How does such a reprobate afford a property like that?" O'Fagan asked.

"Cryptocurrency. Cal created a token system for pornographic websites called 'Titcoin'."

"I don't want to know," O'Fagan replied.

"Now, if you'll excuse me, I've got some experiments to run," Patrick said, pressing his silver tablet, presumably to review data. "Don't be late for the party and don't forget your mask and robe."

"Here. Take this." O'Fagan counted out £500 into Eliza's hand, as casually as if it were loose change. Burton noticed some of the wrinkles had returned around his eyes. *Is it wearing off?*

O'Fagan rolled up his sleeves and Patrick examined the bite marks on his arms. No stone was being left unturned in the quest to learn the secrets of the Elixir. Eliza and Burton put on their coats and headed out.

"Okay, where to?" Burton asked.

"Joke shop. I know just the place. I was there a couple of Halloweens ago before I met David."

"What did you do for work before all of this?"

"I worked with my mam in her pub for a while, but I wanted some independence. I ended up at a company that made digital thermometers, basically wrapping up parcels every day. It was so boring."

"I bet that toned your arms up, though?" Burton asked.

"When I was furious, I'd go through to the warehouse and the guys would let me smash up storage crates with a hammer. I think they just liked to watch me get sweaty to be honest, but plywood's not that strong and it felt good."

"What was the final nail in the coffin? Why did you leave?"

"My boss liked to vape. He'd leave enormous clouds of stinking smoke around me all the time. I'd asked him politely to stop on numerous occasions, but he kept doing it. One day, I slapped the vape out of his mouth and pushed him into a big pile of cardboard boxes. Not had another job since."

"Oh wow, that's amazing. That was the same problem Dan had – he mentioned it on the way to the dig in Wallsend. It was one of the last things he said."

There was silence as Burton recalled the seriousness of their situation. People were losing their lives.

"It's a shame there's no way to rate bosses online. They'd think twice about messing people around if it was added to their permanent record," Eliza said.

Has she forgotten about Dan already? Does she even care that he's dead?

"I wish I'd battered a few in my time," Burton replied.

"I think that's where you and me are different – you seem very restrained."

"I'm not sure how good it is. The frustration builds up and I end up beside myself."

"Hey, that's not a bad place to be, Frosty." Eliza timed a bump on Burton's shoulder to make him walk into a bush covered in snow.

"I'll get you back for that," Burton said with a chuckle as he wiped the wet off his shoulders.

"Good luck, Frosty."

The two chatted and bantered all the way to a fancy-dress shop called Clown College. Each letter of the shop sign was a different colour, and masks of characters from popular franchises sat lifeless in the front window. An overpowering smell of dusty old rubber hit Burton as they entered the shop. Eliza picked up a plastic scythe and started swinging it around her head, then began looking at the female costumes on the wall.

"Why do all the costumes for girls need the word 'sexy' attached?" She asked. "Sexy Nurse, Sexy Nun, Sexy Police Officer, Sexy Shark, Sexy Hot Dog, Sexy Witch, Sexy Skeleton."

"How can a shark be sexy?" Burton asked.

"Maybe I should put it on and find out?" Eliza hummed an ominous tune from a famous shark movie and put her hand above her head like a fin.

The shop assistant cleared his throat. He was gaunt, old and balding on top. His remaining scraggly grey hair had traces of crusty green paint. His nose was rough and red, with indentations on either side. He was a clown that had given up.

"Welcome to Clown College. How can I help you find your fun today?" His voice was high-pitched, like a ventriloquist's dummy, which didn't match his bored tone.

"We're looking for two cherub masks and two robes," Burton replied.

"Ordinarily, they're £150 each."

Burton looked behind him. Eliza was wearing joke glasses with orange frames, and the plastic eyeballs dropped down to her knees on springs in perfect comic timing.

"What? £150?" Burton asked in disbelief.

"They always get popular around this time of the month, and I'm limited to how many I can order. We keep selling out, so it's supply and demand. We're coming out of another recession and Flowerpecker needs his squeezy money." He gave a wide grin, and a little drool escaped his bottom lip. *I don't want to know what 'squeezy money' even means.*

"You said 'ordinarily'," Burton said.

"We're sold out of the masks. The last two went this morning. There are plenty of alternatives." Flowerpecker waved a hand at the shelves of terrifying rubber caricatures.

"What will we do?" Burton asked as he turned again to look at Eliza.

She grabbed two random masks from a shelf and put them on the counter, along with two black robes.

"£100, please," the old clown said.

"This is still robbery," Burton said.

"I can't be bothered arguing about the price." Eliza slammed the money on the counter, then pushed over a hat stand as she walked out, sending oversized comedy apparel everywhere. "Kiss my ass, chuckles," she said without looking back.

Burton followed her, worried and impressed by her temper in equal measure. Outside, they stood looking at the masks they'd bought.

"A werewolf and a giant fluffy yellow bird?" Burton said doubtfully. "Are you sure they'll let us in wearing these? Patrick said they needed to be cherub masks."

"We'll be fine." Eliza scrunched her face and shrugged, then laughed, as if to acknowledge they'd be anything but.

"This is going to be completely demented," Burton said.

"Sure sounds like it."

"What will we do until the party?"

"Pizza? I'm starving."

"Hell yeah. I could do with a bit of normality."

The pair walked to a pizza restaurant called Lend Some Dough, which gave a percentage of its proceeds to the homeless shelters and food kitchens in the area.

"What you gonna get?" Eliza asked.

"Just a plain cheese."

"Come on, are you joking? We've still got four hundred big ones here." Eliza patted her jeans pocket three times to remind him of the remaining cash.

"I don't feel great. I'm just thinking about later. We could invest it all in Titcoin instead?" His suggestion was a joke, but somehow sounded sensible compared to what they were involved in.

"I know what will make us feel better." Eliza waved to the server. "Hi, can we have two ice-cold brewskies, please? Also, I'll have a twelve-inch meat feast and my friend will have—"

Burton hesitated, trying to process what Eliza had

requested. She kicked him under the table, and it prompted his order, "A twelve-inch pepperoni, please."

"Coming right up." The server disappeared and arrived back within a minute, holding two frothing beers.

"I needed something meaty. And this might calm our nerves." Eliza held up her glass. "Cheers."

"Cheers.".

From the moment they clinked, the time disappeared. They drank, ate pizza, chatted and laughed. Eliza wasn't Burton's girlfriend, but in that moment he allowed himself to pretend that she was. He wondered if this was what his friends felt when they were with their wives and partners. It was wonderful to experience such camaraderie. As the alcohol loosened his tongue, he pried a little.

"So, have you got a boyfriend?" he asked.

Eliza rolled her eyes. "I had a fiancé. Then one Sunday morning he just left and didn't come back. Can you believe it?"

"No, I can't. Why?" He watched her as she stared at her plate and snapped bits of leftover crust. *How could any man let this woman go? He must have been the biggest moron in the history of the universe.*

"I don't know if I am who you think I am. I'm not actually that nice, y'know." Eliza hiccupped.

"Well, I'm an excellent judge of character. It's my superpower."

"How come you haven't used it to find anyone, then?"

"I don't know. The stars just never aligned."

Eliza made a 'ppft' sound. "Love stinks. If you want my advice, just forget about all that crap. I've ditched the idea of a long-term relationship. I'm just having one with myself. If you don't let anyone in, they can't mess you up."

Burton frowned. It wasn't what he'd wanted to hear.

Eliza hiccupped again. "Oh my god, I think I'm pissed.

Are you pissed?" She staggered as she tried to stand up and let out a loud cackle.

"Shit, I think I am a little bit," he said. The pizza restaurant blurred around him as he stood. "What time is it?"

Eliza looked at her wrist, but she wasn't wearing a watch. "Hair past a freckle."

"Seriously, it's 6.40 – we need to hurry. I'll ring a taxi." Burton was only slightly more in control than her; both of them were slurring every word.

"I'll get the bill. Garcon!" Eliza shouted across the restaurant.

The pair put on their masks as the taxi entered Darras Hall, the most expensive and exclusive estate in the North East. Burton wore a werewolf mask with a long snout and grey fur. Eliza was an Easter chick with a bright yellow quiff and a little orange beak. As they stepped out of the car, they slipped into their long robes, which were black satin with white drawstrings at the neck.

Eliza shouted "Thank you!" at the taxi driver and clambered against a plant pot that made her fall over. Burton slipped as he tried to help her up and fell forward. An enormous man on the front door, the bouncer, was looking over at them.

"What a gentleman! Thank you for coming to my aid." Eliza stood and linked Burton's arm.

"You're not coming in. This isn't your kind of night," the bouncer said. His broad shoulders blocked any light from the open doorway behind him, and his deep timbre was frightening. The bouncer unfolded his arms and put the knuckle of his left index finger against his chin. His hands were broad like shovels.

"You don't get to decide what my kind of night is. I am

woman, hear me tweet," Eliza slurred, pushing a finger into the bouncer's chest. The angry Easter chick looked ridiculous trying to threaten such a colossus.

"Miss, remove yourself from my personal space immediately."

"Or what?"

"Hang on, is that you?" Burton lifted his mask slightly to look at the bouncer. "Kolo? Kolo Holloway?"

"Jonny Burton. You've hardly changed."

"You know this bozo?" Eliza asked.

"We were at school together. I was there when he enacted revenge on all the bullies. To this day, it's one of the best things I've ever seen. The teachers just turned a blind eye. The bastard bullies didn't bank on you sprouting to six foot six, did they? He half killed the lot of them."

"Almost everyone in that school was a bully. You were one of the only lads that was kind to me. Listen, you can come in, but you'll still have me to deal with if you cause trouble," Kolo threatened. "I need this job."

"Cheers." Eliza made a move to walk inside, but Kolo's solid left arm smashed against the doorframe to block her path.

"What's the code?" he asked.

"Erm, 'please'?" Eliza had forgotten already.

"She's joking, she's joking." Burton said, then blurted, "It's… 'horses'. I mean, I mean, 'horse'." He looked behind him to see if anyone had heard. Nobody else was arriving; they were going to be last.

Kolo nodded and Eliza limboed under his arm, shouting, "How low can you go!"

～

They entered a narrow hallway. The interior was pleasant and tasteful, with purple painted walls and a white dado rail across the middle. The wooden flooring had a dark and light brown chequered trim The only thing that seemed out of place was the devilish art on the walls, which clashed with the calming pastel décor. Burton recognised a print of Henry Fuseli's painting *The Nightmare*, which depicted a woman dressed all in white lying in deep sleep. An ugly old demon was perched on her chest.

"This place isn't quite what I had in mind," Burton said.

"Don't speak too soon."

A door opened at the end of the hallway and a long-legged woman walked elegantly towards them as though she were part of a fashion show. She was dressed only in black high heels and suspenders, and her blonde hair cascaded over her breasts.

"Can you see my eyes popping out?" Burton whispered.

"It wouldn't be my eyes popping out that I'd be worried about if I were you." Eliza gave Burton a playful tap on the backside as if they were jocks in a locker room.

"Strip. Everything but your underwear," the blonde demanded in a Scandinavian accent as she stopped in front of them. "Your outfits are not regulation, but I've been told to make allowances. Robes, masks and underwear only beyond this point. You have just made it. Come on, chop chop."

Eliza was quicker to remove items of clothing than Burton. She had tattoos on both of her arms and legs, but she moved too quickly for Burton to make out exactly what they were.

"It's okay – nobody will see who you are," Eliza encouraged him as she stumbled back onto the stairs while taking off her ripped jeans. A vase wobbled on a table next to her and Kolo glared at them as he closed the front door. Burton slipped off his trainers, and the rest followed under the fixed gaze of the Swedish supermodel.

"These will be looked after. Come, follow."

This is horrible. I don't want people to see me naked. Each time Burton's robe flapped open, he pulled it shut.

The wolf and chick were led through the door and into a sitting room. Gangbang pornography was being projected onto a blank wall as they walked through. Burton's mask was filling with condensation by the second.

"The huge Ruby Room extension has been built especially for us. Mind your robe on the red paint, it may still be a little… moist. If you need anything, hold up your hand and an au pair will grant your wish." The term was odd, an au pair was generally hired for housework or to take care of children, it was so creepy in this context. She opened a set of red double doors, and they stepped through.

The Ruby Room contained at least a hundred cherubs, each of whom must have either been invited or paid a fortune to attend. Burton and Eliza's different costumes attracted some unwanted attention, but the majority were having too much fun to care. In the nearest corner, Burton could see a blindfolded au pair holding two trays on the palms of her hands. Cherubs were taking turns to add weights. As she buckled under the strain, they all cheered and the 'winner' was permitted to spank her bare arse. In another area, a blindfolded, muscular man stood statuesque as cherubs queued up to rub baby oil into his arms and chest. The cherubs swooned and laughed as they brushed against his covered manhood, pretending each time it was by accident. Nearby, a naked body was laid across a table with all manner of fruit resting on it. Cherubs plucked at grapes and bananas and sipped their drinks through straws. If anyone needed a refill, they would raise their hand and an au pair would bounce over and take their order. All of this was just in Burton's immediate eyeline; God only knew what else was going on. There were different levels of depravity: it appeared that an au pair dressed in black was a sex worker, he overheard haggling and watched them being fondled. Au pair's in white were bar staff and off limits, the punters left them alone. There were rules here.

The most attractive au pairs, both male and female, wore purple.

"Wow." Eliza was watching a moaning brunette with her head and arms in stocks. A buzzing came from behind her, speeding up and slowing down. It looked as though cherubs were taking turns to control it.

Burton was speechless. The carnal sights were sobering.

"What shall we have a go on first?" Eliza asked, as if they had entered a depraved theme park.

"I hope you're joking."

Suddenly, there was a loud whistle and the cherubs obediently separated and went to the edges of the room. Some got red paint on their robes without noticing. Everyone fell quiet. The only sound was the buzzing machine; the au pair tried to contain her moans by biting her bottom lip.

"Somebody switch that bitch off!" a camp voice shouted from the hallway.

An au pair ran over and halted the buzzing before returning quickly to her post. Burton heard a tacky sound like a dog walking on wood, but soon realised that it wasn't paws he could hear but hands.

A leather covered gimp on a leash crawled along the floor, followed by a man that Burton presumed was Cal. He wore a pink glittery robe that flapped open to reveal various crude tattoos on his thighs. He was short and skinny, but completely owned the Ruby Room as he paraded through. His gimp sniffed Eliza's bare feet in passing.

"Hey, that tickles," Eliza said, acting as though it was actually a dog.

At the far end of the Ruby Room was a throne modelled as a giant pair of lips. As Cal sat, he gave his first command.

"Newcomers step forward." Cal gave dramatic arm movements and spoke with an effeminate tone. Burton and Eliza stepped forward. There were around fifteen or sixteen newcomers, by Burton's count.

"There is one rule you must follow here tonight, which is—"

"I am a slave to the Ruby Room," the experienced cherubs chanted in unison.

"Yes, you must give yourself to it and let go of your inhibitions. Inhibitions are just no fun, and when things are no fun, I don't want to come. Remove your robes. Let's get a good look at you before the first game. If there are any friends among you, don't worry – I always take care of my friends. Isn't that right, Rudi? Yes, it is." Cal patted his gimp on the head and scratched his leather-covered chin.

Game? How will this help us? This is a nightmare.

Burton looked at Eliza. She had already removed her robe and stood with her hands on her hips in nothing but a chicken mask and underwear. Seeing Eliza remove her clothes should've been a 'thank you God' moment, but the situation was too twisted to amass any enjoyment from it. Burton couldn't bring himself to take anything off at all.

"So you're a grower, not a shower. Don't worry, plenty of guys are like that. Just take it off." Eliza pulled the string around Burton's neck and pushed the robe back over his shoulders. She had a quick look down. "You see, nothing to worry about."

Burton looked along the line of newcomers to see a variety of sizes, body types, and ages.

Cal looked them all up and down whilst licking his lips. "Scrumptious! Look at all those fresh new buns, Rudi. Okay, time to get super serious. A game of Hot Cross Buns." Cal stood up and raised his arms in the air like a game-show host.

"What's Hot Cross Buns?" Eliza whispered.

"I think… I think it's a kids' game?" Burton whispered back.

"We've got a couple of chatterboxes over here." Cal leapt out of his seat to stand in front of Burton and Eliza. The gimp also bounded over on all fours. "A wolf and a chick, what a bizarre combination." He thought for a moment. "I love it. Why copy everyone else, right? Rules are for fools! Everyone could learn from these two." Then he whispered in Burton's ear, "Don't worry, you'll be glad you came, Jonny."

How does he know it's me? Has he watched us since we entered?

Cal clicked his fingers. An au pair ran over with a chef's hat and placed it on his head like a crown. He sat back down on his throne of lips.

"Everyone, the rules are as follows. Some of you are single, some of you are married, some of you have partners. Pish. None of these things matter in the Ruby Room Bakery. You're all my hot cross buns, and I'm a massive master baker." Cal chuckled. "We'll sing and you'll wait for the shoppers to come and pick you. If you like, you can indulge each other with your bulges. If not, leave and never come back, because you're no fun. Now, together everyone…"

The cherubs chanted the old nursery rhyme as the first two male 'shoppers' walked along the line and examined each female.

Hot cross buns
Hot cross buns
One a penny
Two a penny
Hot cross buns

The first two 'shoppers' were clearly gym regulars, with six-packs and muscular arms. At first, they stopped and took an interest in Eliza, but moved on when she hiccupped. They picked a similarly athletic-looking lady with an hourglass figure and breasts that heaved in her nervousness. She nodded at each man, and they led her away.

"Happy shoppers, happy shoppers. Again, again." Cal clapped like a giddy schoolgirl as the crowd chanted again.

Hot cross buns
Hot cross buns
One a penny
Two a penny
Hot cross buns

Next, there were three shoppers, one tall and tanned, one short and fat, and another wrinkly all over. Burton could just make out green flakes encrusted in his thinning hair. *Flowerpecker the clown.*

Burton noticed that all the shoppers so far wore purple wristbands, as if they had been granted access all areas. *This place is so grimy. What happens if Flowerpecker chooses me?* Burton's worry lasted only for a second, as they headed straight for Eliza.

"Just shake your head," Burton whispered.

"Go with the flow," Eliza replied and nodded to them.

What? What's she doing? Flowerpecker and his gang spun her around and started pulling her hair back and putting their hands on her before leading her away.

"Happy shoppers!" Cal exclaimed. "Now, this next one is very exciting. A special lady has visited the bakery."

They took her somewhere. What if they do something to her? They were touching her, and she didn't even flinch. Burton stood on his tiptoes to look over the line and see where she'd been taken.

He was no longer listening to Cal and had started hyperventilating. As he continued to look along the line, he could hear his rapid breaths hitting the inside of the rubber. Sweat was dripping down from his brow and into his eyes.

A hand pressed softly against his chest. He looked forward again. *Wait, I recognise her. That's a pornstar – Christina GG?*

"Yes, ladies and gentlemen, American porn starlet Christina GG is here tonight for your pleasure," Cal boasted.

"The gravity-defying temptress of the internet oozes sexuality. Just look at her. How does she even stand up? The Ruby Room spares no expense for its cherubs."

"Let's see how big and bad you really are," Christina GG whispered into Burton's wolf ear.

"The shoppers look happy – are you? Everyone, is this a sheep in wolf's clothing? He's so mesmerised he can barely nod."

Christina GG gave a slow nod to encourage him to accept. Burton was so bewildered and shell-shocked that he copied the movement, and before he knew it he was being led away by her linked arm. Her high heels clip-clopped on the wooden floor.

"Where are you taking me?" Burton asked Christina.

"To heaven and back, sweetie. I'm gonna blow your house down."

They went up some stairs and entered a side room. It looked like a library, but upon closer inspection the books were just a pattern on wallpaper. Thick dark curtains hung either side a window. The fact that they weren't drawn gave an impression the world was watching, even though nobody could possibly see inside. A lamp straddled in thin red drapes bathed a wooden four-poster bed in dim, seedy light.

"Where is my friend?" Burton asked.

"There's at least one part of you that doesn't need to care," the pornstar commented. "I wanna hear you howl, wolfy."

This was the ultimate fantasy of many, but it seemed so wrong. She was prostituting herself. The connection he had experienced with Eliza in the pizza shop was the only thing Burton cared about; anything else would be a betrayal of what he wanted.

"We came together. I just need to see if she's okay," Burton explained.

"Well, maybe you can finish together." Christina GG

stormed toward a second door and swung it open. Burton moved toward it.

Eliza's reflection in a mirror on the wall revealed she was bent over with her mask off. Thankfully, another step inside the room revealed she was looking for clues in a chest of drawers by the bed. The gang stood in an orderly queue waiting for her. *Are they following her orders like she's their dominatrix or something?*

Christina stood by Burton and briefly rubbed his crotch. He stepped away and held out a hand to signal 'stay back'.

One of the men approached Eliza. His fingers rested on her bare shoulder as he spoke, "C'mon darling, I'm sick of waiting."

"I said no touching." Eliza stood, grabbed his index finger, bent it back and hoofed the man in the nether regions with her right foot. He keeled over, winded.

"Hey Cal, I put on my form that I wasn't into that kind of thing," the man gasped. It was peculiar, as Cal was not currently present in the room.

"Keep your grubby hands off her," Burton demanded.

"Have you two taken a Violator or something?" Christina GG asked. Burton assumed this was the first time she'd been rejected in her personal or professional life.

"Violator?" Burton asked. "What do you mean? What's a Violator?"

"I've heard a couple of stories about girls barely escaping their clients this week. The punters eyes were glowing bright violet, apparently, like they were possessed or something."

Flowerpecker stood in a wrinkly state of arousal. "Get back here, girl. I paid big squeezy money for this. I wouldn't mind a kick."

"Stop, Flowerpecker," Cal shouted as he came up the stairs. He sounded disappointed. Burton could also hear the slapping of Rudi the man-dog, who then ran past the door, chasing a rubber ball. Cal had either been watching or listening the whole time.

"Why are my shoppers not happy?" Cal asked.

"I'm sick of these games. We need to talk. Now," Burton said. He was furious.

"Are you not both entertained? Did you not like my special game? I could've got boys if you preferred. Maybe *this* boy." Cal ran his finger slowly down his own chest and shuffled closer to Burton, pouting his lips for a kiss.

Burton pushed him away. Rudi growled.

"Quiet, Rudi." Cal turned back to Burton, "I expected your girl here to be the star of the show. We were all looking forward to watching her."

"Watching?" Eliza asked hesitantly.

"Yes, we all watch the initiations on the big screen in the Ruby Room. It's funny – people wear a mask and forget their inhibitions. Something tells me you don't have many."

Eliza charged forward and slapped Cal, who halted Rudi as he went to defend his master. Rudi growled louder.

"You're so feisty. I love it. Are you looking for work?"

Burton lost it. "We're looking for the guy who's selling Violators, you fucking creep," he snarled.

Cal's beady eyes locked on him. "Christina, Cherubs, leave us. Cut the link to the Ruby Room." Cal sat on the end of the bed. "Let's talk."

"Let's," Eliza said sternly as the perverts were ushered away.

"I want a refund," Flowerpecker sulked as he stomped away. "This isn't good enough, Cal. You hear me?"

"That was very disappointing, chick," Cal said. "And Jonny, your bro said in his email that you needed some TLC. The crowd was cheering, and you let them all down. You let *me* down, your friend." Cal had no shame, and Burton knew he was pushing buttons to see a reaction.

"I'm not your friend. You're twisted. These poor women don't deserve this," Burton said.

"Poor? Christina is anything but. I paid her a fortune, and the other au pairs live well, bar a few sordid hours a month. There's never a recession when you've got big tits and a pretty face. What's the alternative? Swiping tins of baked beans on a checkout for pennies? Who are you to shit on their chosen profession? They're swimming in Titcoin, thanks to this place."

"What do you know about Violators?" Eliza asked, changing the subject.

"You mean this?" Cal reached inside his pink robe and retrieved something that looked like a washing machine pod, the type that kids died from eating in a bizarre online trend years ago. It was bright violet.

"Where did you get that?" Burton asked.

"A funny little creature called Spoiler hooked me up, in exchange for an evening with an au pair. Apparently, it's rather potent. Haven't tried it yet. He was too nervous to even get it up. The poor little gremlin. Ironically, I guess he's impotent."

"It's turning people into murderers."

"Oh, wow, that sounds fun."

"Fun?"

"It must be some trip, to harness your demons like that."

Eliza was edging toward the door and seemed keen to get out. "Where did he hand it over? Can we have it?"

"Why are you asking? Are you like that wizard and his do-gooder mates in those films?"

"We're trying to stop people from getting hurt. We need to find Spoiler. *Patrick* needs to find Spoiler."

"He's probably sitting on the dark web now with his nonce mates. He had created a message board called Purple Reign. That's how I got in touch. 'KinkyCal' – I couldn't believe that username wasn't taken, can you? He advertised a new drug that gives you the greatest high of your life and makes you look younger. Beats another visit to my surgeon. Me and Rudi met him in an underpass near the Lumber Yard Bar in the Ouseburn. We should all go!" Cal shrieked in excitement. "Why don't we meet him in our little gang? I can be the funny and unpredictable one, the crazy one. When things are fun, I wanna come. Oh, and apparently there's also a massive chance it could turn me into a crazed killer? Cool."

Kinky Cal put the pod in his mouth and chewed. Liquid spilled down his chin as the pod popped like a fresh berry. He dropped to his knees and looked up. His irises glowed bright violet, but the whites of his eyes turned bloodshot; there was hardly any white left.

"Oh… this… feels… fabulous!" he screamed, first clutching his head and then the tops of his arms.

"Are you okay, Cal?" Rudi the man-dog asked, speaking for the first time.

Cal picked up the high-backed chair and smashed the whole thing over Rudi before anyone could stop him. He threw a broken wooden chair leg at the window and the glass broke. Cold air penetrated the room.

"Never break character, ever." Cal leapt towards Burton, trying to kiss him again. "You're mine, boy. Then I'm going to put that nosey drunk slag of yours in the stocks."

Burton turned his face away from Cal's tongue. He closed his eyes and kicked and pushed without any idea of how to stop the assault. Kolo stormed into the room, he must've been alerted by the broken window.

"He's trying to fucking rape him," Eliza shouted. "Get him off!"

"Remember who pays the bills," Cal shouted over his shoulder.

But Kolo was having none of it. He dragged Cal off Burton and cracked him three times across the jaw. Each punch was delayed a few seconds, suggesting he didn't expect it to take three.

The crazed host lay dazed on top of the broken chair parts. Burton noticed another pod fall out of the pocket in Cal's robe as he attempted to get up again.

"Huh? What has he taken?" Kolo asked.

"A Violator," Eliza replied.

"Shit. Get out of here – I'll deal with him. Just don't call the police."

"We don't have time for the police," Burton replied.

"Good. Get your clothes from the hall and don't come back. I'll tell the cherubs Cal's sick and that they need to leave."

"He's sick alright," Burton said.

"Pays good, though," Kolo said, still trying to justify his job even as he beat Cal down again and cuffed him to the bedpost.

"Kinky," Cal said groggily.

Burton and Eliza made their way to the door. Eliza picked up the pod as she passed Cal's barely conscious body and concealed it in a loosely closed fist.

Burton and Eliza didn't speak as they left the seedy house in Darras Hall. Cal had played with them like a child checking the anatomy of a new doll. They stood in silence on the slippery pavement. Burton looked at the ground and felt it shifting beneath his feet. Those people were everything he was not. It had been a sobering experience and the opposite of how he had felt at Lend Some Dough.

The minutes seemed like hours before Eliza spoke. "Don't tell anyone about what happened in there," she said.

"Of course I won't. You didn't do anything anyway, did you?"

"I'm not a slag."

"I know. Cal said that, not me."

"Blokes do whatever they want, and it's celebrated. The more notches on your bedpost, the more of a man you are, huh?"

"I didn't even touch the girl. That's not what I want."

"I'm under all the stress in the world. Maybe I should've picked out a handsome guy. That's why you like me, anyway, right? All about the outside, like the rest of them?"

"What? No. We weren't there for that. I didn't want it to be like that, and you know it." This was the first time Burton had spoken to Eliza sternly. "I didn't even consider doing anything with that prostitute. If there's no connection, there's no point."

"You act all 'nicey, nicey', but I've seen the pervy looks you give me. I'm a person."

"I meant nothing by it. I thought you found it fun—"

The front door opened, and cherubs started exiting after their evening of debauchery. Kolo must have broken the news to them after he'd broken Cal's jaw.

"We better get a refund – it took ages to find a babysitter," a woman muttered in a posh accent to her partner as they passed.

"Can we try that thing the au pair did when we get home, honey?" another man asked as he reapplied a wedding ring.

"We need to go," Burton said nervously. He couldn't predict the response he'd get from the volatile Eliza.

Eliza was looking at her phone. "Egan messaged me again while we were in there." She read it out. "'Touché, but I knew that already. You can't spoil the Spoiler.' But he's followed me, which means I can direct message him."

FeliciaSyren92: Hey, I'm from Newcastle and I'm a friend of KinkyCal. I want to try some of your stuff. He showed me the Purple Reign message board. I've got the money.

This time, the response was instant.

Spoiler: Can you meet me at the underpass next to the Lumber Yard tomorrow night at 8?

FeliciaSyren92: Yeah, definitely.

Spoiler: I'll wear a beige jacket.

FeliciaSyren92: Cool.

Spoiler: Come alone. The price is £250 per pod.

Eliza put her phone back in her pocket. "Yuk."

Burton spotted a hole in the plan. "He knows what you look like, though – he saw you at Biovax."

"I'm not going to meet him. We know where he's going to be, so you can follow him."

"Aren't you coming?" Burton asked.

"Do you always need someone to hold your hand?" she replied abruptly. "Just do it and text me. I'll update David."

She turned and walked down the street without saying goodbye.

Burton stood alone.

CHAPTER 10
THE SOUND OF SIRENS

Burton crouched on a grass verge, dressed from head to toe in black sportswear. He'd borrowed a sweatshirt from Patrick and bought the rest from a discount shop. He was waiting to get a sight of Egan. From his high position, he had an unobstructed view of the graffiti covered underpass. The Lumber Yard pub to the right looked empty bar one mortal-drunk smoker in the beer garden. Burton exhaled through his gritted teeth and felt the breath push past his incisors.

I just don't understand Eliza's outburst. I didn't even say anything bad.

Burton sat waiting for around forty minutes, pondering his relationship with Eliza, anguishing over every word that they'd traded up to this point. Another person might have focused on what they'd seen in the Ruby Room, but he was deep in a different obsession. *She's literally driving me wild. I feel like an animal up here in the long grass.*

Finally, the little oddity appeared in the underpass wearing a quilted beige jacket and navy-blue scarf. Egan shuffled from side to side and kept patting the contents of his coat pocket. He took out his phone. *I bet he's messaging Eliza.*

After waiting for around ten minutes, edginess consumed Egan. He spun and scurried back in the direction from which he had come, splashing in puddles. Burton stayed high on the wet grass and moved swiftly to catch up with him. *He's on his phone again.*

The roads were busy, and headlights whizzed past Burton at the top of the bank. The sounds of spinning wheels and engines masked his footsteps. Egan looked back a few times but hadn't twigged, despite Burton slipping. *Where is he headed?*

The pursuit continued. Burton was running out of bush to hide in; he'd soon need to move onto the pavement. He crouched within the last few feet of foliage and surveyed the area. The Ouseburn was a poorly funded area that had been adopted by creative types. Having a hobby was expensive, and Burton admired anyone that kept trying to share their talent in these testing times. Nearby was a building that held art displays, a recording studio for local musicians, a block of flats popular with hipsters, the White Robot advertising agency and a small building called the Warerooms that rented out storage space. There was also a Chinese takeaway called Triple Dragon. Egan stopped and called in for something to eat.

He must be hiding out in the Warerooms; it's the only place he'd have any space and privacy around here. The flats would be way too expensive for him. He'll not be long if he's ordered ahead of time. Shit, what do I do? Keep following him? He'll see me and run. More people will get hurt if I don't do anything. Burton took out his phone and dialled 999.

"Hello, please state the nature of your emergency?"

"Hello, I've seen someone looking suspicious. I think he's just sold drugs in the underpass next to the Lumber Yard pub in Newcastle. He's wearing a beige coat and a blue scarf. He's just walked into the Triple Dragon Chinese. I think it might've been the drug that's turning people into killers."

"May I please take your name?" the operator asked.

"Erm, no." Burton hung up.

He pocketed his phone, then looked up to see a drunk man with long grey hair exit the takeaway. He was wearing Egan's coat and admiring the material.

The bastard's swapped coats. The sound of sirens was getting louder already, nearby units must have dropped everything.

Egan exited the takeaway in a stained grey sweatshirt. Now with a carrier bag of food, he scurried up the street as police swarmed around the drunk in the beige coat. A patrol car performed an unnecessary handbrake turn to come to a stop. Detective Glover stepped out of the driving seat and another officer exited on the other side.

"Get down on the ground and interlock your fingers behind your head!" the officer shouted.

The drunk threw up all over the coat and sank to his knees in a single motion. A police officer searched for a weapon on his person, then took a Violator pod from the jacket pocket and showed it to Glover. The officer's blue plastic gloves were dripping with vomit when the search ended.

"Care to explain this, sir?" Glover asked the man, but he only hiccupped and looked at him vacantly. He was on a different planet. "Had a few today, have we?"

Glover turned away and spoke to his colleague. "I told you, didn't I? The locations of the murders pointed to this area. It's a good job we were nearby. We'll talk to him when he's sobered up. I want to check CCTV from the area and any security footage the Triple Dragon has set up. He turned his attention back to the drunk.

Burton pulled up his black hood and walked along the other side of the street and around the corner. As he approached the double doors of the Warerooms, he could no longer hear the officers. *It won't be long before they track Egan back here, assuming the Triple Dragon has security cameras.* He entered.

A fat guy was slouched behind a desk. He looked like a dropout, with an unkempt beard that contained crumbs. The man looked up from the movie playing on his phone, grunted, and took his headphones out.

"Which room are you here to use?" the man asked. "Or do you want to rent a space? There are a couple of rooms free. We're discreet, if you know what I mean?"

"I'm just here to see a friend. Is it okay if I surprise him? It's his… birthday."

"Sure, whatever, head on through," the man replied. Clearly, he didn't give a shit.

Burton walked into a thin corridor with multiple sets of dark blue double doors on either side. Rumbling bass guitars, inconsistent drumming and singers struggling to hit high notes screeched from behind the walls. A door opened and Burton braced himself. A tall guy with long messy hair, a tight black T-shirt and ripped jeans walked towards him.

"Hey, d'you like rock and roll? Check us out at the Lumber Yard in a few weeks. We're called The Antibodies. We play hard and fast. Add us online. We're nearly done, but you can stand and listen if you like?" The rock-star wannabe strutted off and into the toilet next to them. Burton heard the guy's piss hitting the pot; he hadn't shut the door behind him. The sound overwhelmed even his buddies making the racket.

Burton walked along the corridor. *Which door are you behind, Egan?*

There were four double doors on each side. A few rooms were being used by bands and another was open and full of storage crates. Burton walked to another door. His nose picked up the potent smell of takeaway curry, the type his dad would treat him to if his mam wasn't around to cook.

Gotcha. He pulled the handle and entered.

The place was an absolute mess. Looking around, Burton saw the takeaway bag on a bench with a sleeping bag laid out underneath. A crude chemistry set bubbled away on a waist-high shelf on the back wall. The flasks and Bunsen burners cooked up violet liquid in a makeshift assembly line. An old computer with a massive external hard drive displayed information on a beefy monitor; a progress bar showed that something was 70 percent complete. Egan had also written equations on the faded yellow walls in black marker, just as he had done in the offices of his former employer.

"Christ, did you win all this from an online clearance auction?" Burton said. "Give back what you stole. People are dying."

"I've made your brother rich over the last three years." Egan's voice came from a large crate in the far-left corner of the space. He sounded calmer than Burton had expected. "He got the promotion to CEO because of me. My hard work, my theories, my brain. Because he's good-looking, he gets the big pay packet and the trophy wife."

"Hand over the Elixir. You can't keep using the people of this city as your lab rats." Burton walked towards the crate confidently, knowing the pointy-eared wimp presented no physical threat. He pulled open one side of the plywood crate that was on hinges. He was expecting to see Egan cowering and crying, but instead he discovered an old PA speaker inside, a python was wrapped around it.

Huh.

"Say hi to Si." Egan's voice came from both the speaker and from behind Burton. A large metal object hit into the back of Burton's Achilles tendon and knocked him forward inside the wooden crate. He yelled. The door slammed shut behind him, then latches clicked and locked from the outside. He was trapped.

The body of the snake slithered against his hip in the dark. *It's wrapping around my leg. I can barely see now the box is sealed.* The paralysis of complete panic started to tense through every muscle.

He wanted to scream, but he was terrified the snake

would react and bite. *This is going to be the worst way to go.* He heard Egan disassembling his equipment on the other side of the wood.

Hang on, didn't Eliza say that the plywood on these storage crates isn't that strong?

Burton grabbed the PA, tilted it against the panel and pushed all his weight steadily. He heard the wood of the crate splinter, and the snake hissed. *There isn't enough room to use it as a ram. What do I do?* Burton backed up as the snake wrapped further around his leg and squeezed.

He kicked full force against the front of the crate with his other foot and the wood splintered again. A sharp pain stabbed in his Achilles tendon where he'd been struck. The snake hissed louder as if threatened, then clamped its fangs onto his arm.

"Jesus Christ! Help!" Burton screamed.

With a crouched shoulder charge, Burton smashed out of the wooden panel headfirst. The sharp splinters ripped and stuck into his face and arms. The snake's jaws loosened slightly as it was dragged out with him.

"Everything alright in here?" The loud pisser's head appeared from behind the door, a guitar now strapped around his shoulder. "No way, dude."

"Get it off!" Burton shouted, as the snake began to crush his entire torso. He couldn't breathe.

The Antibodies punk raised his Telecaster and smashed it over the head of the python, splattering it flat.

"Mate." A skinny longhaired man carrying a bass guitar stood behind his frontman. "Rock and fucking roll."

"I'm a snake killer and a lady thriller! Write that down before we forget it." The musicians looked at each other as if the coolest thing ever had happened.

Burton couldn't care less about the snake; it had been him or the limbless demon. The Antibodies had just saved his life.

"Give me two minutes." Burton hobbled as quickly as he

could after Egan and into the car park. There was no time for emotional thought, he had to act now. Egan was just about to get into a rusty blue van, but Burton slammed into him from behind and knocked him onto the tarmac. Burton put his knee on Egan's stomach, just as the Caballion warrior had done to Nefertari. He punched him again and again, and only relented when the pain in his wrist became too much. The thieving scientist spat blood all over the pavement.

"Stop. Please. My inside pocket," the feeble Spoiler coughed and spluttered.

Burton reached inside and grabbed the vial of Elixir.

"You've used nearly all of it." Burton couldn't believe it. As he pulled back his shaking fist again, Egan lay still, unable to defend himself. He heard sirens, which were getting louder by the second. *The police will deal with you now.*

Burton stood up and stepped away from the beaten boffin. He turned away from the spoiler and hobbled back inside to The Antibodies.

"I can't thank you enough," he said. "I'll make sure I'm at one of your next shows and I'll buy you a new guitar as well. Just leave it with me. Here's my number. Apologies – I have to go."

The Antibodies all high-fived. "Awesome! Our first fan."

Burton was experiencing all manner of pain across his body that stung, stabbed and ached. Despite the challenges his new injuries presented, he took out his phone and captured quick photos of all the mathematical equations scribbled across the walls. The band kept photo bombing like it was their first ever photo-shoot. "Hey, can you send them to us? They're album cover material."

Burton took a picture of the band before charging for the exit, "I will later. Thanks again."

He staggered and stumbled into the night, hiding behind cover whenever he could. His eyes were wide and alert, and his breaths were quick. He was a wounded animal in survival mode. Kicking the crate and being whacked from behind had given him a severe limp. Splinters were buried in his hands and face. His senses seemed heightened and amplified. He jumped at any car that drove past and trembled each time someone walked towards him on the street. It wasn't unlike how he had felt during his bouts of acute anxiety. Every nerve was on fire. *But it's worth it. I've accomplished something.*

He didn't know what would happen to Egan, but at least he wouldn't be spoiling anything for a while. Maybe he'd get jailed for life. He stopped and looked back at the Warerooms. The police had caught up, and the building was bathed in blue light. Burton moved forward again.

Suddenly, an enormous explosion came from behind him and Burton turned to see Egan's Pound shop lab and the Warerooms on fire. Although it was in the distance, he could hear the crackling of the flames. *Has he destroyed the evidence?*

There was no time to worry. Burton's homing beacon had kicked in. It was just like the end of a night out drinking when he felt disorientated and dumb. The comfort of number 7 was calling, but he couldn't return to his parents and put them in danger. He thought about phoning Patrick and asking to be picked up, but he didn't want to risk his brother being stopped and questioned so close to his former employee.

A fire engine sped past towards the explosion. On Burton's side of the road, a Q2 Quaylink bus was approaching. He widened his limping strides towards the stop. The driver must have seen him in his mirror; he slowed to a halt. *He's actually waiting.* Burton struggled to step up onto the bus because of his injuries.

"Where to?" the driver asked.

"Where are you going?" Burton replied.

"Quayside, Haymarket, St Mary's Place. All the major stops in the city centre."

"Quayside, please."

Burton grimaced as he put his hand in his pocket. His

right wrist was sprained and swollen. He rummaged within the pockets of his wet and muddied tracksuit bottoms before realising he'd lost his wallet; he didn't even have a couple of pound coins.

"I can give you it tomorrow, I swear," he begged. "I'm sorry. I'll give you twenty pounds tomorrow."

"Just sit down, lad – don't worry about it. You look like you've had a bad night. There are people who can help and places that offer shelter, I mean, if you needed it, mate... Maybe look in the morning. Food banks, counsellors, that kind of thing. Just try not to bleed on the seats."

He thinks I'm homeless...

"Thank you so much. I will." Burton collapsed into the nearest seat. Although he didn't feel like he was crying, water just fell from his eyes. The kindness of the driver moved him despite his incorrect assumptions. *Every now and again, you'll meet a person who restores your faith in humanity. Most drivers wouldn't even have stopped.*

Burton rode to the quayside without taking out his phone, as he didn't want to destroy the illusion of the driver's good deed. Instead, he thought about real homeless people and wondered how they survived. He had struggled with his own mental health so much this year, despite an incredible support system. What kind of person was he for sinking so low in such comfortable circumstances? He felt gigantic waves of guilt. However, his low mood swings were happening less since he'd been introduced to the Cult of Asklepios. *Has all this danger been good for me? Is it forcing me to grow?*

Burton rained praise on the driver as he stepped off the bus at Newcastle Quayside. "Thank you so much, mate. The world needs more people like you."

"No worries, buddy. Look after yourself," the driver said with a smile before pulling away.

Burton rested against a waist-high metal fence by the River Tyne and slowed his breath. The water looked black, and the depth was unfathomable. He gazed across to the Baltic Centre for Contemporary Art, a converted flour mill where he'd enjoyed exhibitions with his best mate before he moved away. Next to it was the Sage, a huge, silver music venue. He thought about the time he met his high-school crush there for a perceived date, only for her to ask, "Where's everybody else?" Her embarrassment still got to him ten years later. Similarly, Burton lamented his last kiss in a nearby pub. The next day, the girl was offered a job in Manchester and left his life forever. It seemed like every time he grew close to someone, an invisible current pulled them away.

To his right: well, there it was, the arching Tyne Bridge overlooking everything and everyone. It was a fantastic feat of architecture and the symbol of Newcastle. Whenever you left the city and returned, it was the sight that let you know you were home. It looked so romantic all lit up at night, with green highlights accentuating its curves in the dark. On the flipside, it was a popular spot for suicide, and the walkway across it was lined with notices for helplines. A red heart-shaped balloon was tied to the fence near Burton, maybe it was to commemorate a poor soul who had taken the plunge recently.

Burton took out his phone and called Patrick.

"I've got it."

"Jonny, I've never been happier to hear your voice. Where are you? I'll come to get you."

"Quayside, opposite the Baltic."

"I'll be twenty minutes. You absolute legend."

Burton used the time to message his mother.

> *Having a great time at Patrick's with Tino and Matty. Feeling better. Patrick says I can stay as long as I like. Don't worry.*

The reply was swift, as if she'd been watching her phone and waiting for a message to come through.

> *That's fantastic, son. It'll be good to get away from us oldies for a while. I miss you though and can't wait for you to be back. You*

just need to find some inner strength. I'm sure you'll feel even better
soon. Not long until Christmas xxxxxxxx

After fifteen minutes, Burton heard Patrick speeding from a mile off. The people carrier screeched to a halt in front of him and Burton dragged his weary body inside.

CHAPTER 11
THE PRISM

Burton looked at his brother from the passenger seat. Patrick seemed to be calculating his next move.

"We should head straight to the lab," Patrick thought out loud. Burton knew he wasn't asking; he never did. It was surprising they'd had a group vote when he was involved, although looking back it was perhaps to mask that it was on a matter he knew little about. They would do whatever he decided, as Patrick was indisputably the smartest.

"I can't. I'm done. I need to rest."

"What am I going to tell Dominique? That you were fighting? Matty can't see his uncle like this, can he?"

"No, I don't want him to."

"We're going to Biovax. Message Eliza."

"But—"

"We're going. I don't want that stuff near the family. You understand? Man up."

"Don't say that. I hate it when you say that."

"Man up? Why? That's what you're supposed to do."

"It's such a dangerous concept that men can't be vulnerable. Do you know depression kills more young men than cancer?" Burton asked.

"Of course I do. But you're not depressed, Jonny. Snap out of it and text Eliza."

"I… I…"

Burton looked down at the vial in his hands, wondering where it would lead him next. His fragile emotional state was cracking under the pressure, and he could feel it starting to take hold. Depression was like standing within a fog that debilitated and slowed him as the world continued at full speed. He never knew how long it would last, and at times it felt like he might be trapped in it forever. His grazed knuckles stung as they brushed the inside of the pocket, and his hand was still shaking as he pulled out his phone. *I need to do this for her.*

> *Eliza, we've got it. Heading to Biovax now. Can you and O'Fagan come tonight?*

She sent back a 'thumbs up' emoji. It wasn't the usual enthusiasm or quirkiness that Burton had come to expect. *She's still annoyed.*

"They're meeting us there."

"Well done, bro. See, doesn't it feel good to push through and conquer?"

Burton didn't answer, but he felt something he couldn't put his finger on. Was it personal pride? He shuffled his sore shoulders against the seat to get comfortable. His eyelids were heavy.

Burton woke to the sound of ringing. As he rubbed his eyes and squinted, the words *Unknown Caller* came into focus on the blue touchscreen of the dashboard. Patrick answered and switched the call to speaker as he drove.

"Hello?"

"Patrick Burton," a voice said. It was deep and distorted.

The caller was using some sort of tech to alter their voice. "This is Muhktar."

"How can I help you, Muhktar?" Patrick replied, keeping cool.

"Stop your experiments. The road you're on will result in death and despair."

"For who?"

"Everyone you love."

"Are you mad? It has the potential to—"

"Think about the bigger picture, Patrick." The call ended.

"That was creepy as fuck. How do they have your number?" Burton asked.

"God knows. We're here, though. C'mon, wake up."

"But… the call…"

"There's security all over the place. Stop worrying."

Guards checked Patrick's identification before allowing him to continue.

"Great work, lads, keep it up," Patrick said. "You can never be too careful."

Patrick glanced in his mirror.

"Let them through. They're with me," Patrick ordered before turning to Burton. "O'Fagan and Eliza are right behind us." After everyone parked up, they met up at the front entrance.

"Our adversaries would incinerate this so-called security in seconds," O'Fagan said with certainty as they walked toward the lift. He was hobbling almost as much as Burton. It seemed the restorative qualities of the Elixir weren't permanent when you reached old age. The question however, was just how old was he?

"At least we'll know they're coming," Patrick replied.

"Don't be so sure about that."

"Muhktar called us," Burton blurted out.

"Did they now…" O'Fagan said thoughtfully. "Interesting. It's unlike them to become involved so directly. Muhktar has always preferred to utilise Nicoli as a blunt tool. They are on the verge of playing their hand. We also have great cause for concern. I will explain in a moment."

The group reached the immunology lab. Eliza hadn't said a word, it was unlike her. Burton sat on one of the plastic chairs to take the weight off his battered ankles. O'Fagan let out a deep sigh and addressed everyone.

"Nefertari has disappeared. I haven't seen or heard from her since she left."

The group all started talking at once.

"What?"

"Where can she be?"

"How do you know?"

"I hope she's ok."

"How do we find her?"

"We both carry a tracking device so we know where the other is. The signal has disappeared. I thought it might be because of interference while travelling, but alas—"

Patrick interrupted him. "Aren't you a technophobe?"

"I struggle with the device, but we all have our limitations," O'Fagan replied. He pulled from his pocket a screen slightly larger than a standard mobile phone and held it up. It displayed a GPS map of Bamburgh. "There should be a green dot showing exactly where she is. If she had moved away from Bamburgh, it would update and show us somewhere else. There was a brief blip near the sand dunes, but that was the last thing it showed."

Patrick looked at the device, probably unconvinced that it wasn't just a user error causing the dot to disappear. Without a word, he handed it back.

"Can we go find her?" Eliza asked. "It's my fault – I sent her there."

"The group is fractured. Look at Jonathan. His brave mission tonight has taken a toll. Eliza, you are drained from worrying about your mother. Patrick is—"

Patrick completed the statement before O'Fagan could highlight a weakness. "Wondering why you need your walking stick again."

"Exactly. We are in no state to take on the cult. This might be a trap and there is no time to recharge naturally. We need a boost. There are around six drops of Elixir left. Will a couple be enough for your studies, Patrick?"

"I've also got one of Egan's Violators from the party," Eliza said, placing it on the desk.

"How was the party, Jonathan?" O'Fagan asked with a smirk.

"Awful," Burton replied. Eliza glanced at him but didn't comment. "I took these. Check the photo album." Burton threw his phone to his brother.

"Who are the long-haired guys?" Patrick asked as he scrolled through the images.

"There was a band practicing in the same place that Egan was using as a hideout."

"They need to grow up," Patrick stated.

"Hey, there's nothing wrong with doing something that you love, no matter how old you are," Burton said, defending his fellow dreamers. "Anyway, they saved me from a python. It was the only reptile Egan could get his hands on."

O'Fagan tutted. "Pointless."

"Two huge points, actually." Burton showed the bite on his arm. Patrick bounded over and started checking his brother's eyes, presumably for violet. He placed his palm against Burton's forehead to check his temperature.

"How do you feel?" Patrick asked.

"Horrendous," Burton replied.

"Good," Patrick responded as he continued the examination.

Eliza had walked closer in his peripheral vision.

"The Aesculapian is the only snake that can be used.

There's nothing to worry about. Anyway, I think he'd know about it by now," O'Fagan added.

"Christ, that gave me a fright." Patrick said. He started reviewing the photos that had been taken in the pound-shop lab.

"He's cute," Eliza said, glancing at the band pictures over Patrick's shoulder. Immediately, Burton stood and reached out for the phone, but his brother threw it to him instead.

"Good catch, Jonathan. You're a man of many talents," O'Fagan announced. He always turned his compliments up when he was about to request something.

Burton pinged all the photos to his brother, and one to the band as promised.

"It might be enough," Patrick said, holding the vial up to eye level.

"It will have to be." O'Fagan approached the snake at the back of the lab and rolled up his sleeve.

"Wait – you're using that?" Burton asked.

"It's the only way to administer such a small quantity. Don't be scared."

"Count me out. I need a clear head." Patrick was adamant.

"Should we not keep some for Eliza's mam?" Burton said, leaning forward in his chair. He realised how selfish they'd all been. Eliza looked over at him as if she'd been desperate for someone to suggest it. Their eyes met.

"What's wrong with her?" Patrick asked.

"Cancer. Don't ask for specifics, please. I can't bear to talk about it." Eliza walked behind Burton and began massaging his neck and shoulders. His upper right side was still sore after charging through the crate and then knocking Egan to the ground.

Oh my God, it's heaven. Burton closed his eyes and savoured their contact as her fingertips went under his collar and brushed the top of his chest.

"No, the needs of the many outweigh the few. You're a

good man, Jonathan – it's why I like you. However, as Socrates once said, 'An honest man is always a child'."

"What do you mean by that?" Burton asked.

Patrick glared at O'Fagan. "He means you're naïve, Jonny, and he's right. But you're also the one who risked his neck to get this stuff back."

"Exactly," Eliza said.

"Fine. Let's call it all off and heal one person in the Freeman Hospital," O'Fagan said with heavy sarcasm.

Patrick stood by his brother. "Don't start acting petulant. If Eliza doesn't get a drop, I'm not doing anything else."

"One drop." O'Fagan looked into the vial, then pointed it at Eliza as if it were a loaded weapon. "One drop only. Remember, it's not your first attempt to get this. You only have both your hands thanks to Nefertari."

"Huh? What happened?" Burton asked.

"I was desperate," Eliza said.

"One night, she tried to steal a full vial and run. After a pleasant evening spent planning, I was awoken by a commotion and whipped open the curtains to see Nefertari dragging Eliza by her hair through a downpour."

"She's so damn strong," Eliza murmured.

"She's magnificent," O'Fagan snapped back. "Was I betrayed? Yes. Was I hurt? Possibly. I was ready to take your hand until Nefertari asked a simple question: 'Why?' To lose your parents is one of the hardest things we face in life. To see your guardians grow weaker until your strength surpasses theirs only makes you feel more vulnerable in this world. Nefertari comes from the opposite of a loving home, yet she asked me to stop and think. I am no longer a Column, and I am not bound to their rules any more. Their code is not mine, and that's why we are here." O'Fagan picked up the same bronze locket that had been shared initially with Patrick. He administered a droplet into the container and handed it to Eliza.

"You're not a slave here, Eliza. Are you happy to continue?" Patrick asked.

"Yes. I'll give the droplet to my mother tomorrow. It should ease her pain, but a full cure would need more. David has supported us, and Mam's in her own private room because of him. I'm sorry if I made it sound otherwise."

"It's fine, dear. I understand how hard it is," O'Fagan replied. He stared at the floor in thought, making Burton wonder whether he'd lost someone close to him in similar circumstances.

"I'm trying my best, Eliza," Patrick added. "You have all given me a lot to work with: the vial, the pod, Egan's formulas. I think I'm getting closer."

"Speaking of which…" O'Fagan walked to the tank at the rear of the lab. "There is so little left that this is the only way. We must all take the Elixir."

"Wait – I need to use the bathroom." Burton hurried to the nearest toilet. He dropped his trousers and the contents of his bowels came forth instantly, splattering brown liquid. He was all churned up, and the appearance of a second snake was the final straw. *Jesus Christ. At least I was near a toilet. Could be worse; it could've happened under the HMS Bacon Saver.*

It was a relief more than anything. He washed his hands and stared at himself in the mirror. He repeated, "I can do this," and returned to the group.

Burton and Eliza stood by O'Fagan and held out their bare arms.

"Now remember," O'Fagan began, "from around 300 BCE, the pilgrims who flocked to Asklepion temples would have experiences and visions. Their visions and dreams were recorded, and a priest would prescribe an appropriate therapy based on his interpretation. This is potent stuff. Try to stay in control."

He lifted the snake from the container and poured the allocated Elixir into the serpent's gaping jaws. He pushed the head towards Burton and its teeth clamped around his fore-arm. His second bite of the night.

"You bastard. Get it off."

The pain was short-lived, but then it took only seconds before the effects hit. Burton felt as though he had the oppo-site of a virus, as if his blood had been super-charged and vibrant cells were now multiplying in his system. The pain in his Achilles tendon disappeared and the cuts on his arms and face healed rapidly. He looked around him, but everything and everyone was gone. He was now standing in a field. As he moved forward, the motion was strange, as though he were walking on four legs without arms or hands. He heard a rumble. Enormous trees smashed up from the ground on either side of him and their branches arched above to form a covering over a long path. Burton clopped forward to see a crystal lake waiting. *I'm thirsty. Can I drink from it?*

Burton caught his reflection as he lowered his long neck down to drink. He had transformed into a white stallion.

What's going on? What is this? Oh my God, the power surging through me… it's incredible. It's impossible to describe.

There was another rumble, and a grey cobbled bridge rose from the deep. It was pristine, with no moss or rot. Excess water cascaded in miniature waterfalls from small, square holes along the edges.

There was a figure far away on the other side. They whis-pered a single word that carried on the air.

"Come."

He reared up on his hind legs and galloped across the bridge, the sound of his hooves echoing from the cobbles. As he advanced, the motionless figure became clearer. It was his fantasy. Eliza appeared like a spectre, wearing a long white dress that blew to one side despite the absence of wind. She was flickering in and out of view, like a TV image with poor reception. Burton tried to go faster, fearful she would disap-pear and not return. The apparition smiled and raised her arms high. There was another rumble. *She's been guiding me toward her. She's making everything easy.*

An enormous prism made of thick glass rose slowly from underground. Burton came to a stop beside her, and they watched it rise together. A solid-looking wooden ladder stretched all the way down from the top.

"I will tie you to my ladder," Eliza said.

She threw a rope over his neck and led him towards the transparent shape. Sunbeams bathed his back with warmth. Suddenly, Burton's face was soaking wet.

"Snap out of it!" Patrick shouted.

Burton touched his hair, nose and cheeks before licking water on his top lip. He looked at his hands before pressing his damp black t-shirt on his chest. Patrick had thrown a glass of water in his face to wake him from an idyllic dream.

Through his haze, he could see the real Eliza's irises were glowing green. She was awake and looking right at him. *I wonder what her vision was like.*

"Good trip?" she asked. "How d'you feel out of ten? Because I'm about one million. Hey, you look… healthier."

"I feel incredible, like I could take on the cult all by myself." Burton looked at his palms shaking, as if they could move any mountain that stood in his way.

"Yeah, let's get 'em." Eliza kicked high above her head with the flexibility of a teen gymnast.

O'Fagan straightened his back and threw away his cane. "Do not get ahead of yourselves. The Elixir does not make you a superhero. What you have is the vigour of youth, the energy we ignore and then forget." It was clear that O'Fagan spoke from experience. "Remember, this is a cure for all illnesses, and any real strength you gain must be earned.

Bruises and breaks will heal quickly, but they will hurt you every single time."

"Why do you need to keep taking it?" Burton asked.

"The Elixir makes you comfortable in old age, Jonathan. It has sustained and extended my life but cannot do so indefinitely. I've reached a point where a top-up is required before my final bow. Can you sense it in you? The surge of endless potential, Jonathan?"

"Is this the moment we get sent away to train? I feel a montage coming on." Eliza was in perpetual motion, jogging and jumping on the spot like a child who had eaten too much sugar.

"For ten years, Nefertari's father beat her every day with a wooden stick. He said the child of a yakuza boss needed to be strong. Her intrinsic understanding of pain comes from a place I hope you never know," O'Fagan said.

"What you're trying to say is that our group is low on experience, and we need to be careful," Patrick said, simplifying the point.

"Exactly. You might be quicker and see more clearly, but you can't do anything well unless you put in your ten thousand hours. Nothing comes free in this world," O'Fagan explained.

Patrick played O'Fagan at his own game, reading a quote from his tablet. "Apparently, Socrates said, 'No man has the right to be an amateur in the matter of physical training. It is a shame for a man to grow old without seeing the beauty and strength of which his body is capable.'"

O'Fagan responded with his booming laugh. "You've beaten me to it! He also said, 'Employ your time in improving yourself by other men's writings, so that you shall come easily by what others have laboured hard for.' I fear there isn't enough time for you to read the things I have written, my friend."

"Fuck off," Patrick said with a smirk.

Burton and Eliza looked on, clueless. They were star jumping on the spot like a couple of aerobics enthusiasts.

"If Nefertari returns, she could show us some basics?" Eliza said.

"*When* Nefertari returns, she will," O'Fagan corrected her. "I won't hold my breath that you could ever best a Caballion warrior, but let's put that on hold. Time is of the essence. We must leave tonight."

"If I don't get back home, the wife is going to ask questions. I always work late, but this is getting into 'Is he having an affair?' territory," Patrick said.

"Just tell her you're on the verge of a big breakthrough," Eliza suggested. "I'm sure she'll understand."

"I think I'd rather face Nefertari than Dom when she loses her temper," Patrick said with a laugh.

"She's very fiery," Burton added.

Burton wanted to test out just how much his strength and stamina had naturally improved. He jumped up and grabbed a railing above him, copying Eliza. They both performed pull-ups, but the railing detached and they banged heads as they fell to the ground. The electric light it had hung next to started to flicker. *Christ, it does still hurt.*

"For fuck's sake. Be more careful, Jonny. All of you, be more careful." Patrick was mainly looking at his brother as he spoke. He put his hand on Burton's shoulder. "You've got this. But keep your head screwed on."

Despite the blood dripping onto the floor, their wounds healed. Patrick mopped the excess crimson from his brother's head, which was as good as new within seconds. "Remarkable."

Burton, Eliza, and O'Fagan walked out of Biovax and past the security guards to the car park.

"Shotgun!" Eliza shouted as soon as the car was in view.

Burton ducked for cover behind Patrick's car.

"Not a real one, dummy – the game to get the front seat."

"How old are you?" Burton replied.

"See if you can guess while you're sitting in the back."

O'Fagan had a beautiful, dark blue classic sports car that suited the older gentleman. As Burton took his seat and looked out into the night, he saw his luminous green eyes reflected in the window.

CHAPTER 12
BAMBURGH BONES

The engine roared. O'Fagan had his foot down and the classic car was eating up the road. Burton prayed the old philosopher could see ahead as the windscreen wipers battled against the blizzard. The electricity in the vehicle was palpable as Burton accustomed himself to the power of potential.

"I've never been to Bamburgh, even though it's near to home," Eliza said, lording it up in the front passenger seat. "Can you hear me back there?"

"It's really nice" Burton said. "I've been twice with the family. Last time, Dominique dressed Matty up as a little knight. He looked hilarious."

Eliza turned to look at Burton, and smiled as he showed her a picture of 'Sir Matts-a-lot' on his phone. "Aw, he's so cute."

"Bamburgh Castle has sat on a rocky plateau for nearly one and a half thousand years," O'Fagan said. "It has suffered multiple attacks over the centuries and been rebuilt more than once."

"I know the feeling," Burton joked.

"It's a bit like a broom that's had the handle replaced a

hundred times. Is it still the same broom? The castle can't be that resilient," Eliza asked.

O'Fagan kept his eyes locked on the obscured road. "Although the fortified walls have housed a succession of kings in the past, a family now owns it. They welcome tourists and rent it out for weddings."

"Do you think Nefertari will be there?" Eliza asked. "We can't just walk around Bamburgh shouting her name in the middle of the night."

"The blip near the sand dunes is our only clue." O'Fagan handed the tracking device over. "Here, you take this, Eliza – I struggle to make head nor tail of it."

"I can't even see a dot. It's not bleeping," Eliza said. She shook and tapped the device. "Maybe it's this shitty weather."

"Years ago, I was travelling in Thailand, just after the worst monsoon on record. Now that was horrific. I was trying to help the locals and noticed a young Nefertari rebuilding a house. That night, I saw her resting in soggy filth on the road-side. The poor thing was shivering like a stray dog. All I offered was shelter, and I gained the most loyal friend I ever had."

"I hope she's okay," Eliza replied

"The cult has been quiet. I'm nervous about this," Burton said. He was energised, but edgy. He jumped and hit the top of his head off the roof as his phone vibrated. A text had buzzed in his pocket. It was from Patrick.

> *I'm heading back to the lab. I've had an idea. Will report back.*

He's such a doer. He never waits for things to fall into his lap. Inspired, Burton searched online for facts about the area that could be linked to the Elixir and help.

"It says here that the Bowl Hole bodies were researched at Durham University. They were then laid to rest in the Crypt of St Aiden's," he said. "Could Nefertari be there?"

"We should start there. Maybe this device isn't capturing

the signal because she's..." Eliza gulped and paused. "Underground?"

∼

O'Fagan pulled the car over and stepped out. His nostrils flared as if he were trying to catch the scent of those he hunted. He led the way, trying to remain swift and discreet.

Before long, Burton could see St Aiden's. It was a modest-sized stone church surrounded by gravestones that protruded through the grass like decaying teeth.

"There's nowhere to hide or take cover," Burton whispered to the group.

"Nice observation. Like that isn't obvious at all," Eliza replied.

"Sh!" O'Fagan glared back at them as they crept closer. He veered off to one side and down a narrow set of stone steps. "It looks like they might be expecting us."

O'Fagan eased open a door at the bottom of the steps. "No lock. They've either been here, or they are still here," he whispered.

Burton couldn't prevent himself from worrying, "It feels like a trap."

An aura surrounded the silent, dimly lit tomb. Artificial orange light maintained an authentic medieval tone; it was as if wax candles were still flickering on the dark stone. Wet footprints on the ground showed that heavy soles had undoubtedly passed through. The tracker was bleeping, the high pitch intervals shortening as they moved.

"Nefertari must be in here – it's going crazy." Eliza thrust the tracker towards Burton. "Look."

A green dot flashed in the centre of the device and stated that the subject was *Approx 10 metres* away.

"Sh!" O'Fagan said again. He was looking at something

after climbing to the top of a metal grid staircase. They followed him up.

O'Fagan walked straight past a piece of broken metal lying on the ground and towards a forced opening in the stone. Burton picked up the object and held it like a weapon. The curving Anglo-Saxon design had been part of the display and pulled from the wall. It resembled a cross with a circle around it. The rust was rough against his hand.

"Blood," O'Fagan noted. There were small drips leading inside. He crouched and entered the hole in the wall. Burton squeezed in behind him and looked over O'Fagan's shoulder to see dozens of metal coffins stacked on top of each other. They were all marked with a crucifix, bar one that had been dragged from its resting place and stood up lengthways. There was writing in blood across the cover.

"What does it say?" asked Eliza.

"'APOSTATIS', which is 'Defector' in Greek," O'Fagan explained.

Burton closed his eyes and tightened his grip on the curving metal. The coffin creaked open, but there were no cries or screams. He raised his left hand to his face and peeked through the gaps in his fingers.

A human skeleton faced them. It had a small computer chip jammed into its forehead. Fresh red blood, that was yet to fully dry, highlighted the eye sockets and teeth.

"Nefertari's tracking chip," O'Fagan announced as he dislodged it from the skull. He handed the microchip to Burton, who then handed it to Eliza. She placed the tracking chip and the device in the pocket of her jeans.

Burton's phone rang. *Huh?* Burton didn't receive calls from anyone anymore. He walked back down the stairs and answered with his left hand, which wasn't holding the metal.

"You're ambidextrous?" Eliza observed. "Nice."

"Have you found her?" Patrick asked.

"No, just her tracking chip in a crypt. I'll put you on

speaker." Burton pressed a button so everyone could hear as O'Fagan clambered out of the narrow hole.

"Why have they lead you there?" Patrick asked, trying to analyse the situation. "What's the significance?"

"There must be a connection. Is it a warning?" Eliza asked.

"We are not the first to challenge the cult," O'Fagan said. "These people must have had a good reason to meet. My guess is that this group of souls fought to cure their people in a time when the Elixir was reserved for a king. This pagan, presumably a Viking settler, was one of them. Maybe he was their leader." He projected his voice like a stage actor from the railing at the top of the staircase.

"He looks like he came off second best," Eliza commented.

"So, it's a warning that they might bury us all alive if we persist?" Patrick asked.

"To be blunt, yes. People must ask themselves how they want to be remembered before they sink into the sands of time. The pagan in the coffin met his maker knowing he had at least tried to fight. There is no greater failure than doing nothing," O'Fagan said with certainty. "Unfortunately, the tallest poppy tends to get cut down first. Bravery is therefore a necessity."

"Well, failure isn't a word I acknowledge," Patrick said. "I might not have a horny hat or an axe, but…" He paused. "I think I've done it. I think I've found out how to recreate a stable version of the Elixir."

"How?" O'Fagan gasped in disbelief that bordered on anguish.

"When Eliza and Jonny bumped heads in the lab, their blood mixed on the floor. I analysed it. The combined plasma of both female and male origin subjects allowed me to see a code, a pattern that had remained hidden until now. It was incredible. It was like their DNA was dancing."

"What now?" Eliza asked. She looked over at Burton with wide, hope-filled eyes.

"I need to continue the testing. It could take months. We all know what happened with Egan's formula. I can't risk anything going wrong."

"Bravo, Patrick, bravo. It's not every day someone can match a god." O'Fagan walked down the steps and back outside in deep thought, ignoring the others.

"Wow, incredible, bro." Burton said. He had so much pride to be related to someone so clever, so special.

"Well, thank you both for being so excitable and clumsy," Patrick joked.

"My mother is first, right?" Eliza asked.

"As soon as it's safe. Concentrate on finding Nefertari."

"I'll let you know as soon as we do," Burton said. "Well done, bro."

Burton looked at Eliza. She rubbed a tear away and hugged him with her cheek pressed against his chest. Every step closer to victory was to be celebrated, but every embrace was to be truly cherished.

They headed outside. O'Fagan was standing in the graveyard and looking towards Bamburgh Castle. Flickers of light were visible from the very top. He started speaking without turning around.

"I don't know what to feel. When science matches godliness, can the divine remain remarkable?"

"What now?" Burton asked.

"We go to Bamburgh Castle and meet the person who doesn't want us to cure cancer." O'Fagan walked back towards the car.

"Whoever they are," Eliza said.

"What makes you think they'll be over there?" Burton asked.

"Look at the shape of the light," O'Fagan replied. "They're waiting for us."

The distant fire curved multiple times, creating an S-shape. *Snakes again. Great.*

The castle sat on a vantage point at the top of a hill, overlooking the sea. The group passed old, dormant cannons as they ascended a gravel path. Burton pulled his beanie hat down over his ears and raised the collar of his peacoat to cover his chin.

"How is this place open at this time of night?" Eliza asked.

"You can hire it for weddings and things; it's how they keep it running." Burton replied.

"Sh! Follow in total silence," O'Fagan ordered.

Why is there nobody around? This isn't right.

They entered the castle and continued walking unopposed. As they tiptoed past rows of armour, Burton half expected one of them to swing for him. The interior of the building was like a museum, with all manner of medieval trinkets displayed alongside descriptions of their origins. Old coins and arrowheads had been placed in glass cases alongside fractured skulls.

Eliza touched a mounted crossbow on the wall. "Do you think it works?"

"No, they wouldn't have something so dangerous on display, surely?" Burton replied.

"It's behind a tiny rope, and that stops anyone advancing, right?"

"Maybe they should've just put a red rope around the entire castle to stop all the invaders over the years," Burton replied.

Eliza responded with nervous laughter.

O'Fagan reached into the inside pocket of his coat and drew a gun.

"Shit." Burton gasped. It was a German Luger from World War Two. He had seen them in a video game he played with his friends. The old man's shaking hand suggested his aim might not be the greatest.

"Have you even fired that thing before? You're not filling me with confidence," Eliza asked.

"It's time to be serious. I'll do what I must. I can't fight like I used to, but this might even the odds. The cult doesn't believe in guns – they deem them too loud and impersonal. Loud bangs tend to be bad for keeping secrets."

They advanced up the spiralling castle steps, creeping closer to the top.

Eliza halted and closed her eyes for a moment, as if she was drawing on inner strength.

A gravelly male voice came from the summit.

"What has taken you so long, traitor?" the person said in a contemptuous tone.

O'Fagan sped up and onto the roof with his gun held out in front of him. Eliza and Burton followed until they stood in the middle of a tooth-shaped parapet. The S-shaped fire on the opposite side to the entrance was generating considerable heat and had melted most of the surrounding snow. Nefertari had been chained to the base by her arms and neck, and the fire was burning her back. The constant scorching heat must've been torture, but she wasn't making a sound. Two hunters stood close to her; their crimson robes were fluttering in the wind enough to reveal a glimpse of their moulded body armour underneath. Their vacant green eyes were glowing above their masks to fire a deathly stare. A man who appeared to be wearing a vest of skeletal hands stood calmly with his arms behind his back. He looked over at the group. *What kind of psychopaths dress like this?*

"Shoot him!" Eliza shouted without hesitation.

As O'Fagan took aim, another foot soldier appeared from the group's blind spot and dislocated the philosopher's arm at the elbow, propelling the gun over the castle wall. They followed up with a right hook that O'Fagan blocked with an open palm. He nullified a kick to his front by pushing his attacker's heel straight upward and away. He then returned with a kick of his own into the hunter's standing leg which almost made them buckle. O'Fagan was breathing heavily. Burton had the impression that this was a mere sample of what he'd been capable of a long time ago. After the hunter took a second to recover, their following jab broke through the old man's one-armed guard. The next left hook connected, and the next, and the next. O'Fagan slumped to the floor with blood dripping from his mouth and nose.

Burton moved in front of Eliza and swung the Saxon piece of metal that he'd carried from the church, the weight propelling him forward. His target side-stepped and cracked him across the back of the head with a counterpunch. Everything blurred and Burton tumbled face first onto the ground. He looked back at Eliza to see her legs booted from under her with one kick of a black-soled boot. In desperation, he prayed. *Please God, protect us from this evil.*

Nefertari had reacted to the distraction and used it to her advantage. She flipped her chains around the neck of the closest hunter and created tension by leaning back and pushing the flat of her feet against their chest, suspending her lengthways in the air. As they grasped at the links coiled around their throat and pulled down their mask, the others beat Nefertari in the head, legs and ribs. She did not relent. The guard's neck snapped, and their tongue dangled from an open mouth. Despite these actions, her movement was limited and she was still unable to break free.

The leader ignored all this and smirked. "David, why has it come to this? We used to honour Asklepios daily. We gave the Elixir to those who deserved it most. Yet somehow, I've ended up on a castle roof with this crazed mongrel."

"Nicoli, I presume?" O'Fagan asked.

"Yes. Where are my manners? Nicoli Polydamas. The only remaining Greek blood on the Four Columns. You have ideas above your station, David – tell me, why? What was so wrong with giving honest people a second chance? The numbers were small, but we were always in control."

Nicoli was dressed in black boots, jeans, a beanie hat and bomber jacket over his bone vest. A thick black beard hung under his bulbous nose. There was an arrogant smile coming through all the hair, and Burton caught the glimmer of a green tooth.

"You know why I left," O'Fagan replied. "I wanted to make amends. The second pandemic was the final straw. We must try to help all those in pain, it is our duty."

Burton had been allowed by the guard standing over him to get to his knees.

"Did Asklepios cure the world as cities burned to the ground and children went hungry in Ancient Greece?" Nicoli paced back and forth before them like a defence lawyer in court. Although calm, his words suggested a pent-up aggression that could surface at any moment.

"He wasn't in a position to do so," O'Fagan replied. He spat blood at Nicoli's feet.

"A god could not act?" Nicoli asked with a laugh. "Pain is a necessary part of life, and therefore Asklepios limited the Elixir. It is sacred and should not be bastardised."

Burton sensed a turning of the tide in Nicoli, his speech pattern was quickening, as was his walking from side to side.

"What if a god didn't make it? What if Asklepios was just a man?" Burton shouted out.

"You blaspheming *malakas*. How dare you. I know what your brother is doing." He waved a patronising finger at Burton.

"What his brother *has done*, Poly-dumbass!" Eliza shouted. She threw an icy snowball off Nicoli's face before his guards could react.

"What?" Nicoli replied. He wiped bits of white out of his beard and shot a murderous glare in Eliza's direction. He walked over to Nefertari.

"Eliza, no. Be silent," O'Fagan pleaded.

"I'm tired of this." Nicoli pulled a curved scimitar from a scabbard on his belt and hacked off both of Nefertari's hands. She passed out without so much as a yelp, and her handless arms flopped from their shackles.

"No, you monster!" O'Fagan yelled and lunged forward. The guard extended a spear within a split second and tripped him.

"Not such a good bodyguard now, is she? Everyone put your hands together for Nefertari." Nicoli picked up her severed palms and mimicked clapping in front of Eliza's face, before chucking them aside into a pile of snow. "What did you think was going to happen here?" He squatted level with O'Fagan on the ground. "You've made a mockery of our ways for long enough. Everything you've done has risked the Elixir becoming common knowledge. How could you let it be defiled and abused by those unfit to even look at it?" A hunter pointed a phone at the old philosopher and Nicoli offered a greeting to the device, "Good evening, Muhktar."

A distorted "Do it" came from the phone.

"Do you want to quote Socrates one last time before I slit your throat?" Nicoli asked O'Fagan.

"'The end of life is to be like God, and the soul following God will be like Him.'" O'Fagan glared at his executioner and then into the phone lens. "I am Asklepios."

Burton and Eliza looked at each other and back toward O'Fagan. *Could it actually be him? Is this why the Elixir wore off on him so quickly? Was O'Fagan the mythical healer? Was he two thousand years old? A god?*

Nicoli stood up, snarled, and slashed repeatedly at O'Fagan's throat with his scimitar. Blood droplets sprayed Burton and Eliza's faces where they knelt. O'Fagan's body slumped fully onto the ground and his head was sent rolling across the roof by the wind.

Muhktar's voice continued to demand, "Their eyes look green. They've taken it. Cut her. Now."

As Nicoli sauntered over, his guards held their metal spears across Burton and Eliza's throats from behind. The crushing force was choking Burton and preventing him from making a sound. *This is it. Before I've achieved anything. I've wasted my life.* He prayed Nefertari could somehow spring to life again and save them, but she was motionless. From the corner of his eye, he saw tears trickling down Eliza's cheek.

Nicoli ran the tip of his scimitar down the left side of Eliza's face, and her muted scream forced up past the metal held against her throat.

"Open your eyes, girl," Muhktar demanded. "Open them!"

There was a brief silence.

"They've been blessed," Nicoli announced.

"She'll become a threat," Muhktar said in a deep, muffled voice.

"Then their blessing will be brief." Nicoli stood and adopted his slashing stance.

"Wait," Muhktar said.

Nicoli growled through gritted teeth with his green incisor on display.

"They are children of the Elixir now. Let the boy take one final warning to his brother." As Muhktar spoke, Nicoli walked over to his phone and put it back in his pocket. He stomped back over to Burton and Eliza.

"You are uneducated children." Nicoli used O'Fagan's red scarf to wipe his scimitar clean. "Tell your brother to stop his experiments before things get any worse. Tell him what you've seen here today. Tell him about the mercy of Muhktar. Understand?" He squatted again and tapped his wet hand against Burton's cheek twice. "I thought so."

He turned to Eliza and tied O'Fagan's blood-soaked scarf around her neck before pulling the knot tight. "Blood cannot stain that which is already crimson. Remember, we are maintaining something that has helped people from the shadows for years. The Elixir attracts many unwanted suitors who would use it for their atrocious means. You have no idea what I would've done to your pretty face…"

Nicoli walked to the parapet edge. Nefertari's bronze spear handle was clipped to his back. He turned and waved, before rappelling off the side of the castle with his two remaining hunters. Their whole ambush had been planned. *Why did O'Fagan walk right into this? He must have known what awaited us?*

Burton and Eliza knelt frozen to the spot, they were breathing in unison. Burton was first to brake their staring contest of horror and turned his attention to Nefertari. Eliza shot up and ran to her.

"Cauterise," Nefertari said, just loud enough to be heard.

"Hold her," Eliza ordered Burton and stood by the flaming S-shape.

Burton sat with the warrior lying back between his legs. He held her bleeding stumps up to the serpent flame. They felt like chicken that was fresh out of the fridge. He shut his eyes tight and turned away. The heat against his cheek increased and then came the sound of searing, like meat hitting the pan. The vile burning smell almost made Burton vomit onto his shoulder.

"We need to call an ambulance or she'll die," he said.

"Even with the Elixir?" Eliza asked.

"We can't afford to wait and see."

"How the fuck do we explain this?" Eliza asked.

"Tell the truth. This has gone too far."

"Then our work was for nothing."

"They're going to find O'Fagan's body, Eliza. We have to. You'd better take off that scarf."

She untied the knot with difficulty and placed the blood-soaked fabric into her coat pocket. "Do it. Tell them about everything, apart from the Elixir. We were running odd jobs for O'Fagan, and Nefertari was his friend, okay?" Eliza asked.

"Okay."

"Promise me."

"Okay."

Burton pulled out his phone and rang 999.

"Hello, I'm on top of Bamburgh Castle. I've been attacked, my boss is dead, and another is badly injured. Please hurry."

Burton and Eliza sat huddled with Nefertari between them, trying to keep her warm.

"Please hurry," Eliza whispered.

CHAPTER 13
INTERROGATION

Burton sat patiently in a windowless, pastel blue interrogation room at Newcastle Central Police Station. His chair was bolted to the ground. Affixed to the grey table in front of him was a black metal bar, presumably to attach handcuffs. Burton rubbed his wrists. Another grey chair sat opposite him. His left knee was knocking against the top of the table.

I'll tell the truth. One lie just leads to another.

The door opened and Detective Glover walked in carrying two cups and with a towel draped over his shoulder. His top button was open, and his tie was hanging loose. His eyes were focused, as if processing every aspect of Burton before either of them even spoke.

"Coffee?" Glover asked.

"Yes, please. I'm so cold."

"Yes, you've had quite a night. Here, dry yourself and get warm." Glover handed him the hot towel. It was rough to the touch, but clean enough.

Burton dried his face and hair. Then he took a sip of coffee. The warm steam rising from the cup was heaven as it filled his frozen sinuses.

"Are my friends okay?" Burton asked.

"We're waiting for news from the hospital. Miss Contra is here, in a different room. I'm hoping you can help me tonight, Mr Burton."

"Yes, anything."

"The top of Bamburgh Castle is a bloodbath. Could you tell me how this happened the night before Christmas Eve?"

"Mr O'Fagan's friend Nefertari went missing, and we had evidence to suggest she might be in Bamburgh."

"You had evidence? Son, we're the police."

"I know. Sorry. Somebody had lit a fire at the top of the castle and we thought they might be signalling to us. When we reached the top, there was a man dressed all in black with a big bushy beard. He introduced himself as Nicoli. He and his three associates beat us to the floor."

"Were these associates dressed in black?" Glover asked.

"No, crimson. More like monks in tabards, with Spartan armour underneath. One of them was killed as well."

"Spartan monks? This sounds a little far-fetched, Mr Burton."

"I know it does, but I swear to God it's the truth. Nicoli—"

"The man in black?"

"Yes. He chopped off Nefertari's hands and killed Mr O'Fagan in front of us."

"That must have been terrifying. How did you know the deceased?"

"He was my boss, of sorts. I was unemployed, and he paid me to run odd jobs for him."

"And Miss Contra did the same?"

"Yes. We're a team and do most things together."

"What errands need two people?"

"I had just started. Eliza was showing me the ropes. We collected things and accompanied O'Fagan."

"Were you and the deceased on good terms?"

"Yes. I was so grateful for the job. I just wanted to buy my nephew a Christmas present."

"Did he pay you well?"

"Just a basic salary."

"What was your reason for going to Bamburgh tonight?"

"I thought I'd said? He asked me to... he said he needed some help to find his friend. I'd always assumed she was his bodyguard."

"Why is that?"

"She's tough and always around him, checking the area, that kind of thing."

"So nothing you were doing was illegal, but your mysterious boss needed a bodyguard?

Burton took a deep breath and rubbed his eyes. *I must seem so guilty.*

"Are you tough, Mr Burton?"

"Me? No, I wouldn't hurt a fly."

"What did the deceased do for a living?"

"He was an employment lawyer at Maslow Fairchild Solicitors, I think."

"Can you expand on a piece of evidence?" Glover held up a clear bag that contained O'Fagan's Luger.

"He took it out on the stairs leading to the top of the castle. Someone knocked it out of his hand before he even fired a shot. Honestly, I didn't know he had it until we were nearly on the roof."

"Then he was expecting trouble. Can you tell me why an employment lawyer needs a bodyguard and an illegal German firearm?"

"No sir, I can't."

"Can't or won't?"

"I can't – I don't know." Burton was sweating. "I just did what he told me. I was desperate for money."

"Desperation can make people do idiotic things, Mr Burton. Do you know why Nicoli would want to harm your boss and his bodyguard?"

"No, sir. They seemed to have a history together. There was animosity between them."

"There certainly was, judging by the amount of blood splattered across your clothes. Do you know where Nicoli is?"

"No, that's the first time I've ever seen him, I don't know. You could check the CCTV?"

"You want my job now? Tell me, son, do you think CCTV picks up much in a blizzard?"

"I'm sorry... I wasn't... I don't know."

"And just one more thing. Do you have any photo ID on you?"

"Sorry, I've lost my wallet."

Glover held up another clear plastic bag containing Burton's wallet, which he had dropped while tracking Egan to the Warerooms. "Is this your wallet, Mr Burton?"

"Yes, that looks like mine. Where did you find it? Can I have it back?" Burton reached out to take it, but Glover moved it away without breaking his stare.

"What were you doing on the night of the sixteenth?"

"What has this got to do with catching Nicoli?"

"Just answer the question," Glover replied swiftly.

"I think I went for a walk through the Ouseburn, but I could be wrong. The days are all blending into one this month." Burton gave a nervous smile, which garnered no reaction from Glover.

"Did you wander to the Warerooms?"

"I heard a bang and saw the sirens. I hope nobody was hurt. What happened?"

Glover moved closer so he was inches away from Burton's face. "Now listen here, Mr Burton. You were there during the attack on the Biovax building, you were near the explosion at the Warerooms, you were at the scene of a murder investigation tonight. Hell, the excavation site that was raided recently is right on your doorstep. We even have two recorded 999 calls that confirm your voice pattern. This has all happened in the space of a month. What's going on? D'you think I'm an old fool?"

"No, sir."

"Say it. You think I'm a dumb pig looking for truffles in his own shit." Glover slammed his palm on the desk. The noise made Burton jump in his seat.

"No, sir, I don't."

Glover had started to raise his voice and his bloodshot glare was becoming more threatening. Both good and bad cop were sitting in front of Burton as one entity.

"You're way out of your depth here, son. What is connecting these things together? What do you know about the explosion? If you're afraid, we can protect you."

"I don't know, sir. Please let me go. I've done nothing wrong." Burton's knee kept knocking the underside of the table and water was filling his eyes. The dishonesty was draining him; he wasn't used to it.

Glover drained his coffee cup.

Maybe if I tell him, he'll help. Maybe they can protect us and find Nicoli.

Burton was getting close to blurting out everything, but he thought back to his promise to Eliza.

"I've no doubt that you'll be involved in the next big thing that happens in this city," Glover said. "The more you involve yourself, the more evidence I'll compile. Believe me, I'm recently divorced and I've got all the time in the world to work on this case. I've seen lads like you get in over their head before, and d'you know what always happens? We find them washed up somewhere or suffocated in an empty room with a carrier bag tied over their head. You need guile to survive with rats in the underworld, son."

He crushed the cup and threw it down on the desk. "The force has become a non-entity in recent years. Most of the time, we just observe. We're defunded, disrespected and then hauled over hot coals for not doing our job even though our hands are tied behind our backs. It's a joke. New coppers have gone soft, but I'm from an older generation, and I'm on to you."

Glover stood up and banged on the door. A police officer was waiting to escort Burton back to reception.

As Burton sat and waited for Eliza with his head in his hands, a police officer started telling a story to his colleague behind reception.

"So, I'm sitting in a house in the West End when a huge Alsatian comes in and leaves a steaming pile of turd on the carpet. The man doesn't flinch or apologise, and we continue to discuss a noise complaint. I finish my questioning before adding, 'May I just say, that's one of the most disgusting things I've ever seen in this job.' He replies, 'What are you talking about? It's not even my dog. I thought he was yours?' It wasn't even his dog – it had wandered in off the street! That's Newcastle West End for you."

Their laughter was interrupted as leggy female twins were frog-marched into the station by struggling officers. One girl was swearing, and the other was spitting. Their eyes were vivid violet; they'd clearly each taken a Violator. They were acting like scalded cats in a bag. One of the officers' faces had been clawed. It was revolting and highlighted how important stopping Egan had been.

"Another couple of Violators, nasty ones," a sweating officer announced to his colleagues as he entered the station. *They must be calling anyone who has taken the drug a Violator.*

Ten minutes later, Burton heard a disturbance from the corridor. Eliza was making more noise than both twins put together.

"You've got no business keeping me here and you've got no business questioning me. My boss was just killed! Where is your compassion? Women are out in the snow getting attacked by lunatics with violet eyes and you're treating me like a criminal? Heartless robots, every one of you."

"Calm down, Miss Contra!" shouted Glover. "I said you were free to go, but that could change quickly, especially with your record."

"You should thank me for shining a light on the incompetence of this station," Eliza said with real venom.

"Goodbye. Until the next time."

Eliza entered the reception. She grabbed Burton by the arm, yanked him out of his seat, and slammed out of the police station door. "We need to see Nefertari. Text your brother and tell him what's going on."

Burton looked at his phone. He had sixteen missed calls. The last text message read *'WHERE ARE YOU, ARE YOU OK!?'*

As Eliza rang for a taxi to the hospital, Burton texted back.

> *I'll be at your house in a couple of hours. So much has happened. I don't know where to start.*

The flustered pair took a taxi to the Freeman Hospital and introduced themselves to the receptionist as Nefertari's friends. They were told she was in surgery and to wait for an update. Eliza bought two cups of coffee and they took a seat. An elderly man struggled along a nearby corridor, doubled up over a Zimmer frame and dragging a mobile drip. A young beaming couple breezed past him with their smiles turned up to eleven; they were holding a newborn.

"Circle of life," Eliza muttered. She was looking in the same direction.

"Do you think you'll ever have a family?" Burton asked.

"I'm not sure if I'd want to bring a child into this fucked-up world, to be honest." Eliza returned a forced smile as the proud and elated parents passed. "Do you think you'll ever grow up?" she asked.

"I think I'll probably always have the mind of a child," Burton replied. Eliza had just taken a mouthful of coffee and spat it all over the floor as she struggled to control her laughter. It was a rare glimmer of humour since the harrowing sights they had endured.

"Yeah, you probably will."

As they glanced at each other, everything that had happened evaporated with the steam from their cups. After they had chatted and waited a while longer, a doctor appeared holding a clipboard and signalled them into a private room. He was clearly rushed off his feet. Sweat dripped from his brow and shone below his peppered hair.

"Hi, I'm Doctor Jorge. Your friend is okay, but she's had a hell of a night. We've barely got a word out of her, but she did nod when we mentioned your names as visitors. The good news is that the ice preserved one hand enough to allow for replantation. As it was cleanly severed, it may also regain better function than if it had been pulled off or crushed."

"That sounds promising?"

The doctor nodded. "Her recovery has been remarkable, but the use of the replanted hand depends partially on the regrowth of two types of nerves: sensory nerves that let you feel, and motor nerves that instruct the muscles to move. Nerves grow about an inch per month."

"Will she be able to use it again?" Burton asked.

"The replanted part never regains one hundred percent of its original use. I'd consider sixty to eighty percent an excellent result. The number of inches from the injury to the tip of a finger gives the minimum number of months before the patient may be able to feel something with her fingertip. Physiotherapy is a must, and this can cause a large degree of emotional distress, depending on the patient."

"She's the toughest girl I've ever met," Eliza said.

"Good. That will help her no end. The hand will not look like it did or function as before. She may feel shock, grief, or anger. These feelings are common. I'll be asking her to talk about these feelings with me, her GP, a counsellor, or someone she trusts to help her come to terms with things."

"Can we see her?" Eliza asked.

"She's sleeping now. She lost a lot of blood, and it's taken a lot out of her, literally. I'd say come back tomorrow at 2pm for the usual visiting hours, and we can see how she's doing. Her rate of recovery in this short time has been remarkable."

"Thank you, doctor. Look after her, please," Burton asked.

"That's what I'm here for." Even though the doctor replied to Burton, he was smiling at Eliza. He rushed back to his work.

"He seemed nice," Burton commented.

"Really nice," Eliza responded.

"It sounds like Nef's going to be okay. What now?"

"This." Eliza tapped her chest, where the locket rested under her coat. "I'm going to call in and see my mam before I go."

"Of course. I'm so sorry. I forgot she was here. Would you like me to come in with you?"

"No, it's okay – I'd like to see her by myself."

"I can wait?"

"No, you need to speak to Patrick. I'll be okay. I come here all the time."

Eliza walked along the same corridor into which Dr Jorge had disappeared. Burton waited and took a seat by the front entrance. Eliza seemed to care about Nefertari. The fact that she had cast the final vote to send her to Bamburgh must have weighed on her mind. Nefertari had also intervened and stopped Eliza losing her own hand on the night she stole a vial. Burton didn't budge, he wanted to offer his support in any way he could.

Eliza reappeared after around an hour. She was talking to

Dr Jorge. *That's it. They'll fall in love and get married forever. I've missed my chance again.*

She seen Burton waiting patiently and smiled. Her eyes were red like she'd been rubbing away tears. Dr Jorge was mid-sentence when she walked away from him and planted a soft kiss on Burton's cheek. Eliza grabbed his hand and led him outside.

"How is she?" Burton asked.

"She woke up for around 45 minutes after I dropped the Elixir in her mouth. I spoke to her. It's the most familiar thing in the world to chat, but also the hardest. I keep wondering if it'll be the last moment we ever share. She's quite far gone. I need to get her more, and fast."

"What did you chat about? If you don't mind me asking."

"Me, as always. How I was doing and the people I'd met. I mentioned you."

"Wow, I'm honoured."

"Mam doesn't like me being on my own. She wants me to be a bit more trusting and have a bit more stability in my life. Christ, sorry, I wouldn't normally say this much to anyone. I guess you caught me off guard. Can we change the subject, please?"

"Of course, but you can talk to me any time that you feel the strain. I'm here for you. You know that, right?"

"Thanks, Jon." Eliza linked her arm with Burton's as they walked.

"So, what now? Can Project Panacea continue without O'Fagan or Nefertari?" Burton asked.

"I don't have all the answers, y'know. I'm not a superhero. Next time you think of a question, see if you can answer it by yourself. I know as much as you do." Eliza sniffed and rubbed her eyes with the cuff of her coat.

"I don't have a clue. Maybe Patrick will?"

Eliza shook her head.

CHAPTER 14
BROTHERS

"This is awful. It's out of control." Patrick stood in his sitting room and sighed. For someone who never lost his cool, the news had rattled him. Eliza and Burton sat on the edge of his settee, giving a blow-by-blow account of the horrors they had witnessed in Bamburgh. "This is why I didn't want to get involved. Tino, no! Get in your bed!" Patrick yelled at the excited dog that was trying to coax Burton into wrestling with his rope toy. The fluffy black mutt continued undeterred. "I can't have her knowing about this, do you understand?" Patrick pointed to the ceiling. Dominique was reading Matty a bedtime story upstairs.

"So, what do we do now?" Burton asked.

"We have a nice Christmas," Patrick replied.

"What? But—"

"No buts. Mam and Dad are coming tomorrow, and we are going to make damn sure they enjoy themselves. Do you understand?"

"What about the Elixir? You said you'd made a breakthrough?" Eliza chipped in.

"We must rigorously test every stage, and that will take months. Think about how long it took to produce a vaccine during the last pandemic. I need to decide if I even want to progress."

"You must. Please. Jon, tell him," Eliza pleaded.

"I'm sorry, Eliza," Patrick said, "but I love my family as well. I'm putting them in danger. Jonny, you could've been killed tonight."

Both their voices were getting louder as things got more heated.

"But we owe it to the world." Burton had never been surer about anything in his life.

"Nobody mention a word about this over the next few days," Patrick said. "I'm serious. I work all year to enjoy this one day. Let me have it."

"Nobody mention what?" Dominique asked as she walked into the room draped in expensive-looking red silk pyjamas. Her clothing matched the colour of the wine that filled her glass to the brim.

"Nothing, just a Christmas surprise," Patrick replied and smiled at his wife.

"Jonathan – your clothes… is that blood?" Dominique asked.

"They've been in a car accident, but they're okay," Patrick replied.

"Thank goodness. I won't even ask, I'm just happy you're safe. Are you going to introduce me, Jonathan?"

"Oh yes, sorry. This is my friend Eliza."

"Wow, such a pretty friend. I love your parka – it looks warm as toast. You haven't even taken their coats, Patrick. Come on, I trained you better than that. Tino, stop that." As soon as Dominique spoke, the dog relented and ran to his bed. Patrick also followed his orders.

"Would you like a glass of wine, Eliza? I bet you're ready for one," Dominique asked.

"Oh no, it's okay, I'm going, so—"

Before she had finished her sentence, Dominique had

placed a glass in her hand.

Patrick didn't need to ask his brother. He fetched two beers from the fridge, popped the tops off with a bottle opener and handed one over. "I think you'll be ready for this as well."

He fetched a black T-shirt and jeans for Burton, and Dominique gave Eliza an orange sweater with *Natural Selection* written across the front, plus jeans that were a bit too big. She put on some Christmas music and, before long, the group relaxed. They chatted and laughed as Patrick told funny stories about when he was younger.

"Where will you be spending Christmas, Eliza?" Dominique asked.

"Oh, I don't know. My mam's not very well – she's in hospital. I'll just watch a few films and have an early night at home."

"On your own?"

"Yeah."

"Nobody should spend Christmas alone. You're more than welcome to stay? Jonny will be here, obviously."

What a brilliant suggestion…

Eliza paused, as though trying to decide. "Okay, that's so kind. I'd love to, thank you so much."

"Great." Dominique gave her a cuddle, even though they'd just met.

Patrick nudged Burton, and they clinked their bottles together.

"Okay, bedtime," Dominique said. "Matthias will be up early again. Eliza, I'll show you to your room. Actually, Jonny, the second guest room has no bedding. I was going to change it in the morning before your parents arrived."

"It's okay, Dom, I'll stay on the settee," Burton announced.

"Do I smell or something?" Eliza asked. "Come on, silly, we'll go head to toe if it bothers you that much." She beckoned him over. Burton caught Patrick shaking his head as he walked past.

"Yeah, I'll wake up with Tino licking my face if I stay in here. I know from experience," Burton joked.

"How do you know I won't do the same?" Eliza flicked her tongue out like a gorgeous toad.

As they walked to their room, Dominique pointed out a painting on the wall.

"What do you think?" she asked in a hushed voice.

"Cool. Is it a weeping willow tree? I like those. It has a unique charm. I bet it was expensive," Eliza replied.

"It was a gift from our talented Jonny. Isn't it wonderful?" Dominique looked at the picture with pride and admiration.

"Shut up!" Eliza's eyebrows raised in surprise as she looked at him. "You painted that?"

"Shh, you'll wake Matty," he replied. "I don't think I got the right shade on the grass, but it came out okay."

"It's beautiful and you're brilliant. Goodnight," Dominique said as she opened a door and showed them to their room. *Dom's always been so supportive of me. I'm lucky to have her in my life, never mind Paddy.*

A freshly made double bed was in the middle of the guest room. It was covered with pillows and the duvet colours were coordinated in a scheme of light grey, white, and dark blue. *I don't want her to be uncomfortable. How do I not come across as a perve?*

"Head to toe, then?" Burton asked, looking away as Eliza undressed in front of him.

"I don't want to kiss your big feet goodnight, do I?" Eliza said, almost to herself, as if she was trying to adjust to Burton's over-chivalrous behaviour.

"We'll never be closer than in the *HMS Bacon Saver*

anyway, will we?" Burton replied as he slid in between the soft, clean sheets.

Eliza had a full sleeve of tattoos up her left arm. Burton had noticed them at Cal's party but was too panicked to examine them properly through his wolf mask. One stood out: a Mexican Day of the Dead skull in which the Tyne Bridge formed its frowning mouth.

"Cool tattoo."

"Thanks. The design is called *Dia de la muerta*. It came out great."

"Have you been to Mexico?"

"No, but I'd love to. This reminds me to seize the day wherever I am. You can't cheat death but you can beat it by living, know what I mean?" Eliza was looking up at the ceiling.

"I think so. We should experience everything we can in the short time we have. I went to a Halloween party once in a glow-in-the-dark skeleton onesie. Does that count?"

Eliza turned to look at Burton. "Tell me more," she said.

"It didn't have any pockets for my wallet and phone, so I had to wear my coat all night. I kept needing to explain to people over loud music that I wasn't leaving." Burton looked for any reaction.

"You're such a dork." She sniggered, but then she frowned and broke eye contact. "D'you think this is going to work out? Today was so awful." Eliza lowered her voice to a whisper. "I feel guilty for goofing around, David helped me so much."

"I have no idea. Let's just get through the next couple of days. It's up to Paddy now," Burton whispered. He lay face to face with perfection. Her vivid green eyes were glowing, and every muscle in his body yearned to wrap around her.

"You have to convince him." Eliza sounded desperate, even when whispering.

"I'll try. I'm so pleased you're staying here, though."

"Really?"

Eliza snuggled herself into Burton and her sweet lips kissed his, albeit briefly. She turned away when he tried to kiss her more passionately.

"Goodnight." Eliza pulled Burton's arm over her and rested his hand on her soft breast. Her heart was beating steadily under his palm. *Did she just reject me or not?* Regardless of the answer, it was a warm end to a harrowing day. *No Elixir vision could match this.*

~

"Morning," Burton said. He'd awoken to see that Eliza was sitting up and looking at her phone. "Happy Christmas Eve."

"You were talking in your sleep... a lot!"

"Well, somebody else was snoring," Burton replied.

"Shh, no I wasn't. It must've been the wine." Eliza whacked Burton on the arm.

"Would you like a cup of tea or coffee?"

"Tea, please."

"Okay, five minutes."

Burton put on his brother's jeans and T-shirt, then made his way downstairs. He heard a loud bang followed by punching sounds mixed with dramatic music in the sitting room. When he popped his head around the corner, he saw his little nephew cross-legged and immersed in a superhero cartoon.

"Hey, Sir Matts-a-lot. Happy Christmas Eve."

"Uncle Jonny – yay!" The little guy ran over to his uncle for a big cuddle. "It's Christmas Eve. I'm so excited. Look, I'm watching Mighty-Man." Matty was well-spoken and lacked the rough northern twang of his dad and uncle.

"I don't think I've seen this one before. Who is he fighting?" Burton asked.

"The Spider Mutants have trapped him in a big web."

"Oh no. I bet he won't be stuck for long. He always finds a way out, doesn't he?"

"Yeah, he's the best." Matty punched and kicked back to the settee to watch the end.

"I thought I was the best?" Burton asked.

"Well, after you he is," Matty giggled.

"Hi, Tino." The dog had been nudging Burton's leg the whole time and got a pat on the head for his trouble. "My friend's staying with us for Christmas, Matty. You can meet her soon. She loves Mighty-Man too. I'm just taking her a drink."

"Okay." Matty zoned out again in front of the TV, which looked even bigger next to him.

Patrick was up as well, sizzling bacon in a kitchen fit for a celebrity chef. "We're going to take the dog out soon," he said while flipping the rashers. He already had teas and coffees lined up on the bench for Burton and Eliza.

"I'll ask Eliza."

"No, me and you." Patrick pointed the spatula at Burton with intent. "Dominique will be up soon. They can talk about girly shit for a bit."

"I don't think Eliza likes girly—"

"Get sorted. We're leaving in half an hour. We'll head into the dene."

"Okay."

Burton took Eliza breakfast in bed. She had the covers pulled halfway up her face when he entered the room and peeped over them in playful anticipation.

"Bacon. Gimme."

Burton placed her tea on the bedside table and sat on the end of the bed. "That's my dad's favourite taste on earth – bacon sarnie followed by hot tea. He claims it can't be topped."

"He's got a point," Eliza replied mid-chew, then took a sip of her drink. "When will your parents get here?"

"They're heading up this afternoon. It feels like ages since I've seen them. I'm looking forward to it. Listen, Patrick wants to go for a walk with the dog soon. I'm going to see if I can convince him to continue his research."

"Without me?"

"Maybe brother to brother would be best?"

"What am I going to do here? "

"Chat to Dom? You seemed to get on last night. You should see her collection of designer shoes. It's ridiculous."

"Yeah, she's cool. Although I'll stick to my battered old trainers – they're multipurpose, for all occasions. They were the last present my mam was able to buy me. I look a bit of an eyesore in heels. Don't take no for an answer."

"There are some clean towels here. Take a shower and I'll be back before you know it."

Burton made his way downstairs and munched his bacon sarnie, throwing a piece to Tino, who jumped and caught it in his mouth. Patrick appeared with a lead in his hand. He was wearing a Christmas-pudding bobble hat and a warm black jacket covered in pockets. It looked new and expensive, as always.

"Are you ready? Stick this on – it's an early present." Patrick threw Burton a matching Christmas-pudding bobble hat. "Ooooh, Christmas twins," he said in a high-pitched voice. It was a line from a comedy show they both enjoyed.

"Are we not supposed to be keeping a low profile?"

"I've upped our security – there are guards everywhere. Don't worry."

"That makes me feel slightly better."

A huge laugh came from the top of the stairs. Dominique was looking down at them. "Look at you two, you're so cute. Let me get a picture."

Patrick put his arm around Burton as Dominique pointed her phone at them. Tino was pulling Burton towards the front door.

"That's amazing," Dominique said. "It's going in a frame."

"Can you send it to me?" Burton asked.

"Yes, of course. Sent."

"Okay, honey, see you soon." Patrick let Burton pass before locking the door behind them. Burton could still hear Dominique laughing when it closed.

The brothers walked into Jesmond Dene, which was covered in undisturbed snow. The trees created a canopy of branches as they ventured alongside a frozen stream. Burton spotted a little red robin sitting on the bridge ahead, but Tino bounded forward to scare it off. His barking broke the silence.

"Early bird catches the worm, but I'm not sure how he'll find any this morning," Burton observed.

"Nature can be cruel, but it sure looks good on a Christmas card." Patrick was looking up to the sky, taking deep breaths and generally revelling in the fresh air. "Listen, I know what you're going to ask me, so I'll tell you." He kept looking ahead at Tino snuffling in the snow.

"Go on." Burton was desperate to hear his decision.

"I'm going to do it."

"That's fantastic." Burton was relieved. It was impossible to change Patrick's mind, even on the smallest thing. "What d'you need me to do? How can I help? What can Eliza do?"

"That's the thing. I mean 'I'm' as in *me. I'm* going to do this. I'll carry the burden that comes with it. I don't want you close to any danger. Mam and Dad are getting older now. When this gets out, it will consume my life. You need to be there for them. Everything they need or want, it's all on you. I'm going to be too busy."

"But… but…"

"No buts. This is too important to walk away from, but I need to approach it carefully. Remember, I tried to do the right thing once before and ended up in prison."

"But I've helped so much."

"These people don't mess around. You can't stop them."

"And you can?"

"We've paid for the best private security in the country and they're transforming Biovax into a fortress as we speak."

"How can Biovax afford it?"

"Sometimes favours are worth more than any contract. Maslow Fairchild's been involved, he's amazing at that kind of thing." Patrick handed Burton a gold envelope. "Here, I was going to surprise you tomorrow, but now seems like a good time."

Burton's hands grew colder as he removed them from his pockets and opened the envelope. There was a Christmas card inside with a nativity scene on the front in landscape format. Burton was careful with it, as a card from his brother usually contained a cheque – but this one just had a message:

Jonny

I've pulled some strings and got you an analyst job at Tall Oak Bank. You start on the 4th of January and will earn a wage of 24 grand a year!! You're a top lad and a top brother. Make sure you knuckle down.

Looking forward to a fantastic Christmas with you.
Love Patrick, Dom, Matty & Tino.

"What?" Burton was in shock. "I don't know what to say."

"Thank you, maybe?" Patrick smiled.

"Of course – thank you so much. But Eliza, the Elixir, the cult?"

"You're out of it now. You've done your bit. Leave it to me. I just want you to be safe. It'll be the best thing that ever happened to you."

"But an analyst role – can I even do that? What's this place like? I've never worked in a bank before. I'm an artist."

"You're a bright lad, Jonny. You'll be able to do it with

your eyes closed. Save up and buy a house. It's about time you joined the real world, don't you think?"

"Thanks. I won't let you down." Burton hugged his brother to show gratitude, but he felt conflicted. "But please, if you need my help, let me know."

"You'll be too busy 'go-getting' to care." Patrick patted him on the back to signal the end of the brief embrace.

Tino squatted and produced a steaming turd on the path. "Lovely, Tino, just lovely," Patrick said.

"Aren't you going to pick it up?" Burton asked.

Patrick looked at him and kicked some snow over the top of the stinking brown mound to hide it. He smiled again. "Pick what up?"

Something startled several birds in the trees. Burton looked toward the grass verge.

"It'll just be a guard," Patrick said confidently. "Let's head back."

∾

Both brothers and the dog shook themselves as they entered the house, then removed their wet coats and shoes. Matty ran over and handed Burton a drawing of the photo Dom had taken earlier. *Mery chrismas* was written above two stickmen wearing pudding hats.

"Wow, this is amazing. Can I keep it?" Jonny asked his nephew.

"Yes. Do you like it?"

"It's brilliant. Look at the detail. Is that Tino as well?" Matty beamed and ran off to play with his Mighty-Man action figures on the sitting-room floor.

Patrick received an alert on his phone. He read it and tapped the screen. "Mam and Dad are almost here."

It must have been a heads up from security.

"Where's Eliza?" Burton asked Dominique. "Is she up yet?"

"I'm sorry, Jonny, but she took a call and left while you were away. She was very apologetic and thanked me for last night." Dominique gave him a pitying look. "She seems lovely. It must just be strange for her in another family's house at Christmas. Think of how you'd feel."

"Ah, it's okay, thanks. I'm just nipping to the loo." Burton moped to the downstairs toilet and splashed water on his face. *I can't believe she's gone. Where did she go?* There was a knock on the front door as he exited the downstairs bathroom.

Burton's parents entered the house, wrapped presents were spilling from the top of the large bags they were carrying.

"Matthias, my little angel, happy Christmas Eve." He got a big hug from his grandma.

Matty was jumping on the spot. "Are those for me?"

"Have you been a good boy this year?" she asked.

"I have, I have!"

"Then there might be something good in there for you."

"Yay!" Matty ran off, even more excited than before.

"Hi, son." His dad hugged Patrick, and Dominique took their coats.

As his mother spotted Burton behind them, she did a little accelerated burst toward him for a hug.

"Hey, watch your bad knee," Burton warned.

"I've missed you. Have you enjoyed yourself? You look much better. I knew it would do you good. Doesn't he look much better?" Mrs Burton pointed out.

"Yes, thanks. It's been great."

"What can I smell?" Burton's dad asked.

"Success?" Patrick joked, and his father gave a proud smile.

"Dominique, the house looks beautiful," his mam said.

"Thank you. We have some lamb in the oven. Not too much, though – we don't want to spoil dinner tomorrow."

"Best meal of the year," his dad announced.

"Can we play the action roll game?" Matty asked his uncle.

"Go on, then," Burton said. They went outside, and he covered his eyes. "Okay... action roll!" he shouted, peeping through his fingers.

His nephew and the dog both dropped and pencil rolled across the snow together. Matty hid behind a trampoline.

"Three, two, one... I'm coming to find you," Burton said, and then pretended he didn't know where his nephew was. "Here's Tino – that's not a very good hiding place. Where is Matty? He must've gone to the shop for some sweets." Burton heard his nephew giggle. "I give up. I don't think I'll ever find him."

"Here I am!" Matty sprung up with his arms in the air. He climbed onto the trampoline and started bouncing.

For the rest of the day, they all caught up and built a snowman each in the stately garden. Burton chatted to his parents as if everything was fine. He tried phoning and messaging Eliza five times but received no response.

Ghosted again. I thought she'd be better than that. Eventually, he put his phone down in order to watch a movie the family was enjoying together.

"Here, another gift." Patrick threw him some Santa-themed pyjamas.

"Your brother's so thoughtful, isn't he?" his mother said. "They're great, they look comfy."

Burton and his parents retired as Dom and Patrick began placing presents across the settee and fake snowy footprints on the wooden floor. As Burton climbed into bed, he wrapped his arm around Eliza's pillow and clutched it to his chest. Her intoxicating, fresh scent was still all over it. *Where did you go?*

Burton opened his eyes. It was Christmas morning.

I made it.

Matty ran into the room wearing reindeer-patterned pyjamas. "Get up, Uncle Jonny, get up. It's Christmas!" He climbed onto the bed and started bouncing on it.

Patrick stuck his head around the door. "He's been wanting to do that since four-thirty this morning."

"Has Santa been?" Burton asked.

"I'm going to see. Come on, come on." Matty tried with all his might to drag his uncle out of bed.

"You're keeping him waiting, Uncle Jonny," came Dominique's voice from the hallway.

They all made their way downstairs together to look upon every child's dream: an enormous pile of presents.

"He's been, he's been!" Matty shouted, pointing at the footprints. "Can I open them?" he asked his mother.

"Of course, my son. They're yours. I want to see what Santa has brought for you." Dom put her arm around Patrick and pulled him closer to her. Burton's mam and dad stood with beaming smiles, as if this memory was the greatest gift they could have received themselves.

Matty blitzed through present after present, hurling wrapping paper here, there and everywhere. He showed off his new Mighty-Man rocket. "Look, it does this. And look, it makes laser noises." Matty pressed the buttons and handed it to his uncle to inspect before moving on.

"It reminds me of one I had when I was your age," Burton said.

Burton glanced up from the toy and noticed someone had knocked the head off a snowman in the garden: it was the biggest one, Patrick's.

He nudged Patrick. "Have you seen tha—"

"It's okay," Patrick replied, stopping him from saying

another word and pushing down his arm.

"Oh, Dominique, these moments are so wonderful. It's such a shame that your own family can't be here," Burton's mother said.

"Thank you, I'm just so happy I have you," Dominique replied.

There was a loud knock on the front door.

"Who could this be? That's a rent-man's knock," Burton's dad asked. Tino started barking.

"I'm not sure. Are you expecting someone, Patrick?" Dominique asked.

"Is it Eliza?" Patrick looked at his phone. "Security hasn't sent me any update. What am I paying them for?"

"Who is Eliza? And what security?" their mother asked.

"Just a neighbourhood watch scheme on the estate. The footballer next door had a break-in. I'll see who it is." Patrick walked to the front door, picking up their dad's wooden cane en route.

"He wants broken into for missing that golden chance to score last week," his dad added, but nobody acknowledged him.

Burton looked around and discreetly grabbed a heavy brass candlestick from the dinner table.

Patrick shouted from the porch before he'd even got to the door, "I don't believe it!"

"You still wear your watch, I see," a man said in a Spanish accent.

"Every day, my friend." Burton heard loud pats on the back from the porch. Patrick walked back inside. "Dom, Mam, Dad, Jonny, Matty. I'd like you to meet our guest of honour. A Christmas miracle. May I introduce to you, the one and only Sergio Gamero."

Dominique dropped her cup of coffee, and it smashed on the floor. The scalding liquid splashed across her feet and shattered fragments cut them open.

CHAPTER 15
VIEJO AMIGO

ergio walked into the sitting room wearing a black leather coat, black jeans and heavy black boots. His nose was flat and crooked; it had clearly been broken a few times. One hand remained in his pocket.

Wait a minute – it's the man from the bus that got me my hat back. That was Sergio?

"Hello. It's been far too long. How I have dreamt of this moment." Sergio took off his coat to reveal bare, muscular arms covered in tattoos. There was no trace of the Asklepion mark, as his left forearm had been inked over in solid black. *He's disowned the cult.* He didn't have a left hand, reminding Burton that it had been taken by the Caballion years ago.

Burton noticed his mother was taken aback as she tried to assess their guest. Young Matthias peeped at the man from behind his uncle's leg.

Dominique's perfect hostess facade dropped. She'd hurt herself and was trying to hold back tears as she wiped blood from her feet with her bare hand.

"I hope I didn't startle you. Are you okay?" Sergio asked.

Dominique shook her head and burst into tears.

"She must've been scalded." Burton's mother hurried to

the sink and filled a bowl with cold water. She crouched down with difficulty and started bathing Dominique's cuts.

"Why is mammy crying? Is she okay?" Matty started getting tearful himself. He pulled at Burton's pyjama bottoms.

"Your mam has just spilled some hot coffee on her feet and hurt herself. She'll be fine soon," Burton explained.

Dominique wiped her eyes and smiled at her son. "I'm sorry, I shouldn't be crying at Christmas. Come and give me a hug, then introduce yourself to our guest."

The little boy approached the towering Sergio cautiously. "I'm Matthias. Nice to meet you." He held out his hand.

The Spaniard shook it and ruffled his hair. "Such a well-mannered kid. I'm impressed. I'm Sergio. Do you look after your mama while your dad is working hard?" Sergio asked.

Matty nodded.

"Good boy. You look strong." Sergio feigned some punches on Matty's shoulder. Then he straightened and shook the hands of Mr and Mrs Burton. "And you must be Patrick's parents. Hello."

"Wow, some handshake you have there, Sergio. What is it you do?" Burton's dad asked.

"Well, it gets a lot of use. I've only got the one. Carpentry accident." Sergio held up his stump.

"Sergio is an old business associate," Patrick interjected.

"Your son is a fantastic man, Mr Burton."

"You don't have to tell me. This is my other son, Jonathan."

Burton nodded at Sergio.

"It's been cold out there. Hope you've had a warm hat to wear," Sergio said, alluding to their earlier meeting.

"Yes, thanks," Burton replied with a smirk.

"Am I missing something? Have you met?" Patrick asked.

"It's like I know everyone already. I heard so much about you, inside."

"Inside where?" his mother asked.

"Inside our old office block," Patrick said hurriedly. He obviously didn't want his parents to know another former prisoner was in their house; they'd judge Sergio unfairly.

"This is quite the introduction. Aren't we forgetting it's Christmas Day? On with the festivities!" Patrick handed out drinks and Matty ran back to his presents. The group chatted.

"I feel so guilty – are you okay?" Sergio asked Dominique, looking down at her bloodied feet.

"Don't worry, you're forgiven," Dominique said.

Burton wandered over to his brother in the kitchen. "Maybe he'll help us?"

Patrick didn't avert his eyes from checking the turkey in the oven. "Jonny, shut up. I'm sick of saying this to you. Not on Christmas Day. How many fucking times?"

"I'm sorry, I didn't mean to—"

"What did I say in the dene? Leave it to me."

"Leave what to you?" his mother asked on her way to fill up her glass.

"He's just asking if he can help with anything," Patrick replied.

"I don't think you've asked me that once in thirty-four years," she joked.

Christmas music played, and the family continued to catch up as the smell of dinner wafted through the mansion. In between his preparations, Patrick held court as always, showering the mother and father with hilarious stories that always ended with him coming out on top.

Burton had no stories of his own, but he laughed along and played with Matty.

"Dinner's ready." Patrick shouted. "I've put it out, so help yourselves."

On the large kitchen island were slices of ham, turkey, sausages, roast potatoes, mashed potatoes, turnip, pigs in blankets, cabbage mixed with bacon and chestnuts, parsnips,

Yorkshire puddings, sprouts and more. Dominique had set the table beautifully.

"This looks amazing, Paddy," Burton said.

"I taught you well, son." Mrs Burton hugged Patrick, claiming part of the praise.

"It's here at last. The greatest meal of the year," his dad said. He appeared more excited than Matty had been before opening his presents.

Tino lay under the table, drooling and waiting for scraps. His head was resting on Burton's thigh.

"Is there anything you can't do, *amigo*?" Sergio said as he filled his plate high, as though he hadn't eaten for ten years.

"You have quite the appetite, Sergio," Burton's dad commented in an impressed tone.

"When you've been in situations like Patrick and I, you learn to stock up when you can," Sergio replied. "Isn't that right?"

"Sure is," Patrick replied.

"So how come you aren't with your own family, Sergio?" Burton's mam asked.

"I've been very tied up, Mrs Burton, and I wasn't sure if I'd be welcome,"

"Even at Christmas?" Matty asked.

"Especially at Christmas. I will never forget the magical times in Merida with my beautiful *familia*. We didn't have all this, but we had each other."

"Why would you not be welcome?" she quizzed their guest as she drank more wine.

"I don't think that's a nice thing to be asking, dear." Burton's dad placed his hand over the top of his wife's glass.

"It's okay, Mr Burton. I heard about some things happening in the area and decided to give my *amigo* a call. I hope I'm not intruding," Sergio replied.

"Work opportunities?" his dad asked.

"Yes, something like tha—"

Burton's dad jumped in before Sergio even finished his sentence. "Jonny's been looking for a job. Maybe you could get him involved?"

"Uncle Jonny can do anything too!" Matty shouted, putting his arms high in the air with pride.

"Is that right?" Sergio asked.

"Yes," Matty replied politely and with certainty.

"Well, Dad, have you seen what Paddy got me for Christmas?" Burton handed him the golden card. His father's eyes widened as he read the message, his proud smile grew even larger.

"That's fantastic. I told you everything would work out, didn't I? Well done, Patrick. You're such a good man." He turned to his wife. "He's got him a job."

"You're lucky to have such a good brother," Burton's mam said. "You'll have to roll your sleeves up and make a decent job of this one. Get in early and make an effort."

"I always do. It just hasn't worked out anywhere," Burton replied, looking down at Tino.

The news raised the mood of his parents higher. Everybody pulled crackers, told jokes and ate until they were stuffed.

"What do you call a penguin in the Sahara?" Burton's dad asked.

"I don't know," several people replied.

"*Lost*."

"Go on, Dom, read yours. You've been quiet," Burton's mother encouraged her daughter-in-law.

"What's orange and sounds like a parrot?" Dominique asked.

"No idea."

"A carrot."

A tremendous groan came from all around the table.

Soon, they escaped to the sitting lounge area.

"Is it time for more presents?" Matty asked politely.

"Why don't I give you mine?" Burton asked. He pulled a big box from the corner of the room. "Now, I couldn't get you much last year, but hopefully this will make up for it."

"What is it?" Matty asked.

"Open it and find out."

The excited child started ripping the wrapping until he revealed the latest computer game console, complete with a Mighty-Man game. His nephew stood shaking as he looked at his second favourite hero on the side of a box that was almost as big as him.

"Now when I'm not here, we can play online and chat," Burton said as his speechless nephew hugged his uncle.

"How did you afford that? That's too much. How much was it?" Burton's mother asked.

Dominique was impressed. "Oh my word. Uncle Jonny, that's incredible. They were all sold out. How did you find one?"

"Thanks, bro," Patrick said, "that's too kind."

"Son, you haven't been working," Burton's dad said. "You need to hang on to your money."

"Wow, those things aren't cheap," Sergio added.

Burton smiled.

As other presents were shared, Burton received some rare Lull vinyl records from his brother, including a signed copy of their most famous hit 'Don't Tell a Soul'. He'd also bought him *Knightsblood* graphic novels and a poster from the third movie signed by the actor who played Burton's favourite character, Morality Knight. *All this and a job. What a haul.*

After all the presents were opened and the members of the family were taking a breather, Burton visited the downstairs toilet. Although it had felt like he needed to go, he seemed to be constipated. The Elixir hadn't seemed to fix his bowels; anything psychological was still a burden. He looked at his phone as he waited. After about five minutes, he heard Sergio and Patrick talking in the hallway.

"I've heard some things, *amigo*," Sergio whispered to his friend.

"What things?"

"The Cult of Asklepios in Newcastle. O'Fagan killed in Newcastle. And you, of all people, getting yourself involved. Be very careful that you don't lose it all like I did. *Me entiendes*? Do you understand?"

"Of course," Patrick answered.

"No good comes from the Elixir. I'm going to destroy it all, and anyone who stands in my way. This magic you have today is worth a thousand vials of that poison. And by the way, your security is shit. They didn't even see me coming."

Burton flushed the toilet only after he was certain they'd gone. When he re-joined the group, Sergio was thanking his hosts and saying goodbye.

"Matthias, stay strong. Patrick, you're going to need a diet after all this rich food. Mr and Mrs Burton, thank you for such wonderful company today. And goodbye, Dominique. It has been a pleasure to spend Christmas day with you all."

"Isn't that lovely," Burton's mother said with a smile as Sergio left. Then, before the front door had even closed, she turned to Burton. "So, are you going to tell me about Eliza now?"

"She's just a friend," Burton replied.

"A beautiful friend," Dominique added, taking a sip of red wine from her large glass. Burton guessed his face was probably the same colour as the wine right now.

"Have you met her, Dominique?" his mam asked.

"Yes, she stayed here last night."

"D'you think it could be something more, Jonny?" his dad asked.

"I'm not sure. She's just a friend," Burton replied hastily, to show he was uncomfortable with the line of questioning.

"Well, don't let her get away. You know what happened with the last girl."

Why do they remind me? Do they think I've forgotten? Burton looked out of the patio doors at the remaining snow of Storm Jessica.

"Come on, Matty, let's set this up and have a game of *Mighty-Man Mania*," Burton said, ending the conversation.

The rest of Christmas Day was cosy and happy.

The day after Boxing Day, Patrick drove to the hospital with Burton to see Nefertari.

"Hello, we're here to check on our friend Nefertari," Burton said at the desk.

"Oh yes, I remember you. Let me look," the receptionist replied.

Dr Jorge was rushing past, his stethoscope bouncing on his chest as he jogged to his next emergency. He held up five fingers to Burton and mouthed the words "Five minutes" as he ran along the corridor. After thirty minutes, he reappeared.

"I take it you're here to see Nefertari."

"Yes, of course," Burton replied. Dr Jorge looked worn out, with dark circles around his eyes.

"What's the update, doctor? I'm another friend of hers," Patrick added.

"Maybe you could tell her she needs to come back for these." The doctor rattled some painkillers in his hand.

"What?" Burton was confused.

"She's gone. She disappeared as soon as she came to full consciousness."

"Why did you let her leave?" Patrick asked.

"We can only help people that want to be helped. She'll be experiencing a lot of pain and discomfort. We're investigating how she left the premises without alerting the staff."

"Well, that's certainly one of her talents. Has our friend with the coloured hair been here?" Burton asked.

"Your friend was here yesterday morning and left Nefertari a letter. Her hair was light blue, actually."

"What did the letter say?" Patrick asked.

"I don't make a habit of reading private notes," Dr Jorge said in an irritable tone.

"No problem. Thanks, doctor, we'll try to find them," Burton replied.

"Good luck." Dr Jorge hurried back up the corridor.

"What a dick," Patrick muttered.

"Give him a break. That was probably the only 'rest' he'll get for hours," Burton said.

It wasn't until midnight on New Year's Eve that Burton messaged Eliza again.

> *Happy New Year, Eliza. I hope everything is okay. Can you let me know? Nefertari checked herself out of the hospital.*

As 'Auld Lang Syne' boomed out of Patrick's enormous soundbar, a reply came through at last. Burton almost dropped his phone with excitement as it vibrated.

> *Hi. My Mam passed away on Christmas Day. I'm a wreck. I've lost my best friend. I couldn't stay and ruin it for your family. I'm sorry, I need time to be alone. Take care, Jon. Xxx*

> *I'm so sorry, Eliza. I'm here for you if you need to talk. Please get in touch.*

Burton was gutted. Mainly for his friend, but also because keeping her mother alive was the only reason Eliza had involved herself with the Elixir. Would he ever see her again? *What a selfish thought; the girl just lost her mam.*

Patrick dropped Burton and his parents at home the next day. Burton went straight to his room and put his new Lull record on the turntable. The jangly guitars of 'Don't Tell a Soul' played as the singer reminisced about losing his virginity:

Then something changed
And he felt strong
As she said
Don't tell a soul
But there's something I need you to know
There's something I need you to know
Don't tell a soul
But there's something I want you to feel
There's something I think you should feel

Burton lay on his bed, thinking about Eliza and wondering what to expect from his new job. He was going to be rusty in the real world.

CHAPTER 16
SIXTEEN MONTHS LATER

T he balding bus driver turned in his seat to address the passengers. "Sorry, everyone, the engine's conked out. You'll have to wait on the path for the replacement service. Don't worry, it's already on the way."

Great, I'm going to be late. I'd better text the witch. At least the sun has come out. Spring at last. Getting up in the dark has been a nightmare.

Burton exited the Newcastle-bound bus and stood on the pavement in his navy-blue suit, crisp white shirt and pink tie. He looked down the adjacent streets and over both shoulders. A black car had followed him almost everywhere after the Bamburgh incident – he presumed it was Glover looking for a hot lead on a cold trail. The car was nowhere to be seen.

Burton took out his phone and texted his boss.

> *Hi, Martha. Sorry, the bus has broken down. I'll be about twenty minutes late.*

❧

Tall Oak Bank was divided into departments dedicated to savings, mortgages, insurance and more. There were excellent facilities for staff, including a canteen, gym and games room. However, using them was frowned upon as the time could be used for working.

Burton walked into the open-plan office twenty-six minutes late. It was a bustling atmosphere with colleagues typing, holding team meetings and generally trying to get ahead. Every navy-blue pillar displayed the logo of the company: thin pink rings that looked like the cross-section of a tree. All the male workers were dressed identically to him. *Here we go, another day pretending that I know what's going on. Only eight hours left.*

"What time do you call this?" his colleague Chris said, spinning on his chair and laughing, drawing as much attention to Burton as possible. "Did you have an accident on the bus? Did you kiss a girl and faint? Did you bend over to pick up a pound coin and split your pants?" Chris was six feet eight, with spiky bleached-blond hair, and he looked massive even sitting down. His pink tie blurred with his white shirt as he rotated, he was a spinning top and jack-in-the-box all in one.

"Yes, you're right. I kissed a girl and then filled my pants. Luckily, it was after they'd split, so it all just fell out onto the street. I've put it on your car bonnet for safekeeping," Burton fired back. It wasn't his best comeback ever, but Chris would just get more and more distracting if ignored. In defence of his colleague, the wacky humour made the job bearable most of the time, and his heart was in the right place.

"Can't wait to sniff that. Roll on five-thirty, buddy." Chris offered a fist bump and mimicked an explosion by opening out his fingers slowly after they connected. He never seemed to do any work, but his boss was based in Scotland and rarely visited to check up on him.

Burton's own line manager, Martha, sat scowling through the top of her black-rimmed glasses. She had gaunt features, stunk of cigarette smoke, and her thinning black hair left a trail everywhere she went. There were some straggling hairs on Burton's desk which he brushed away as he sat down. She must have been checking the work he'd printed before leaving last night.

"This isn't good enough, Jonathan."

"I'm sorry. The bus br—"

"I've booked a meeting room. Send me the overdue report, then take a seat in Room F. Thanks."

"But I haven't—"

"Just send what you've done. Meeting room F. I'll be there in a moment."

Burton switched on his computer and stared at the spreadsheet he'd completed in a hurry. The small numbers combined into a magic-eye image as he tried to adopt a business frame of mind. He emailed the analysis, then walked to meeting room F. A smaller room mustn't have been available at short notice, as he knew from experience that this one could sit around twenty people. A large metal table filled the room, surrounded by unpadded office chairs. Three tripod microphones were placed on the table for conference calls; Burton thought they looked like little spaceships, and the language coming out of them often sounded alien. He rarely understood a word of it.

Burton walked to the opposite side of the meeting room and looked through the large window. He could see birds flying around and landing on the edges of the nine-tiered company car park. *They look so free.*

"Take a seat, please." Martha had entered without him noticing. Although the luminous green in his eyes had faded, he noticed traces of the colour in his reflection before he turned around.

"Okay, about this morning. I—"

"Your time-keeping is atrocious, Jonathan."

"But the bus broke down. That's what I've been trying to tell you. Did you get my text?"

"That's no excuse. You should allow enough time to get to work in the morning. It's not the first time this has happened."

"The other time was months ago. I went to the doctors on my dinner break. You know about my mental health issues. Even then, I was only five minutes late. I've not been late since. In fact, I haven't even had a dinner break since."

"We all have problems, Jonathan. And what about this?" Martha let a print-out of his analysis drop from her spindly fingers. She had circled three mistakes on the tiny figures calculated within the table.

"It wasn't finished, I told you."

"I asked you for it two days ago."

"As well as six other things, all apparently urgent. I didn't have the time to do it all. I told you yesterday."

"You left at five-forty-two last night."

"I'm only supposed to work until five-thirty. I had to stay late four times last week."

"You left at five-twenty-seven on Friday."

"I was the only one here! Everyone else had gone home."

"You should've texted me and told me you were leaving early."

"You were on holiday." Burton looked up at the grey panelled ceiling and took a deep breath.

"You still should have told me."

"Do you need to know what time I go to bed? Don't think I haven't seen you timing my trips to the toilet as well. This is getting ridiculous. I'm not standing for it."

"I beg your pardon? Who do you think you're speaking to?"

"Another human being? This is a disgrace. You've got a bee in your bonnet about me and I don't know why. I've done my best and worked hard ever since I arrived here." Burton didn't raise his voice, but he was getting more and more annoyed. Maybe that's what she wanted but he didn't care anymore. He met Martha's glare for the first time and saw the green rings of his irises reflect in the witch's glasses.

"I've never been spoken to like this in all my years of management."

"Well, maybe it's about time someone did. You make the workplace unbearable. You act like you're an emperor – it's pathetic. You're a line manager, and a bad one at that."

"I knew this would happen when I heard you hadn't interviewed for the role. I feel threatened. You're being aggressive, and I need to leave the room."

"What? We're having a discussion."

Martha left the room and five minutes later she returned with her fat friend from reception, whose make-up was an inch thick.

"I'm not being funny, but why is she here?" Burton asked.

"Because I felt threatened. You were shouting at me and being aggressive."

"Give over. This is getting embarrassing. You can't just lie. There's a difference between being angry and aggressive. I didn't even raise my voice."

"Have some respect," the orange bogtroll lookalike replied. "She clearly felt threatened if she left the room."

"I'm not listening to this anymore. I'm done. The bus broke down, and if you won't treat me like an adult, I'm gone. Tell me how you wish to proceed. I'm leaving."

Burton left the meeting room by kicking the door to open it. He stormed back to his desk and typed a quick letter of notice.

"What would you rather be or a wasp?" Chris asked. It was the type of intentionally garbled question he'd often ask to lift Burton's mood.

"Sorry, mate. I've had enough of that witch. I'm leaving."

An auburn-haired girl called Rachel turned around in her desk chair. "What happened?" she asked in concern.

"I can't be bothered to explain it. I'm done. Sorry, Rachel, we've had our last coffee trip."

"Don't let the bastards get you down, buddy. You'll be okay. We can go for a pint soon," Chris said.

"Yeah, and me too," Rachel added, forcing a smile.

Burton picked up his bag and marched out, handing his security pass to the other receptionist at the entrance. He didn't want to give the bogtroll the satisfaction. *I can't believe this is happening again. What will Paddy say? I've made such a mess of everything. Still, felt fucking good putting that evil witch in her place. I wouldn't have done that before I met Eliza. But what am I going to tell my dad? It was unbearable, an eternal dead end. I would've ended up... back the way I was.*

The flowers at the front of his home were blooming. His parents had always nurtured the garden with such care, and from spring onwards it was a real haven. *Everything they've planted and grown has been a success. Everything apart from me.* Burton walked through the door.

"Are you okay? Why are you back so early?" his mam asked.

Burton slumped into his seat in front of the TV. His mother picked up the controller and turned down the booming football commentary.

"I had to leave. She was awful. The bus broke down and she was rollicking me for being late. She said I threatened her, but I didn't even raise my voice. I can't put up with lies like that." Burton didn't look up once.

"She's a nasty piece of work. I knew it the first day you described her. It didn't suit you putting little numbers into little boxes – it's not for you. You're an artist. You'll get something better." His mam was supportive as ever, but his dad stood up and left the room. His mam added, "Are you sure you weren't being too sensitive again?"

"I tried my best. It just didn't work out," Burton replied, still looking down.

"I know you did." His mother put an arm around him.

Burton's dad stomped back in from the kitchen. "It's work. That's what work is. You aren't there to make friends." His dad was rarely angry, but when Burton glanced up he could see a look of shame. "I had some shocking bosses on the building sites. You just have to take it."

"I don't want to fucking take it. What do you know about it, anyway? You've never passed an exam in your life," Burton snarled.

His father held his chest as if experiencing sharp discomfort. He marched upstairs. He was from a stronger generation and had always hidden any pain from his wife and children.

"We don't use language like that in this house," Burton's mam said, pointing to the stairs. "You apologise immediately and let that be the end of it."

"What am I going to tell Paddy?"

"Don't message him – he's going to be on the news at one o'clock to make a big announcement. He wouldn't say what it was but he's sending a car for us soon. Go and apologise now," his mother demanded.

Big announcement? Did he do it? Burton walked upstairs and peeked around the door of his parents' bedroom. His dad was lying on the double bed with his polo shirt rolled up; he was holding his chest. His wrinkles, white hair and overall frailty stood out to Burton like never before.

"Dad, I'm sorry for speaking to you like that. I'm just so frustrated. Nothing ever works out for me. I have no luck. Ever."

His dad didn't even open his eyes; his hand remained pressed on his heart. "I'm trying to help you, son. There's no such thing as luck. It's all about preparation leading to opportunity. You have to be stronger. You need to be more resilient. Be like your brother. You'll get more chances, but you need to be ready to take them. It's not a nice world out there. You can't always be painting pictures. Try to be a man. You need to be a man."

"I will, I'm sorry. Are you okay? Do you need a drink of water or a cup of tea?"

"I'm coming down in twenty minutes to watch the interview."

"Okay."

Burton trundled back to his own room. He had been on the end of many defeats but being a loser in the eyes of his father was the worst. He looked around his bedroom at his gaming console, records, paintbrushes, comics, and *Knightsblood* display models. *I've been in a state of regression for fifteen years. I'm useless.* He lay on his single bed and picked up a book in the hope it would calm him down.

Since the events at Bamburgh, Burton had been reading about Greek philosophy. O'Fagan's comments had inspired him to try and understand some of the concepts. This was his way of honouring his memory. A discussion between Socrates and his student Plato caught his attention. He noticed the statement *Love is a serious mental disease*. The philosophers described love as a 'divine madness', a glimpse of how God viewed the world. It could give you inspiration and enthusiasm to propel you forward, but would just as likely rot you to your very core if left unfulfilled.

Plato also described a Republic in which children were separated from their parents and reared to respect only a Guardian class. He believed it would promote unity and assist in the removal of desire from human nature. As horrific as it sounded, maybe humanity would be better off without so much 'want'.

A lot of what Plato said resonated with Burton – for example, *The first and greatest victory is to conquer yourself.* Burton wondered if he'd ever win that battle. He imagined being bludgeoned into the mud and holding up his broken sword against repeated blows. He needed to rise and become something more.

Burton's mam interrupted his thoughts by shouting up the stairs, "Come on you two! Patrick's on in a minute."

Father and son made their way downstairs into the sitting room.

"I wonder what it is?" Burton's mother asked. "My son on the TV again, I can't believe it. He's done so well."

As the title music and graphics ended, the smile, blonde hair and blue eyes of respected anchor Kim Knowles appeared.

"Good afternoon. Biovax Director Patrick Burton will begin a live press conference in just a moment. He is set to make, in the company's words, 'a huge announcement that will change life as we know it.' Professor Smith from Northumbria University is with us today to help unpack whatever we're about to hear. Hello, Professor. What can we expect from this announcement?"

The bald professor wore a brown tweed jacket complete with beige elbow patches. He had round frameless glasses and a thick grey moustache that he kept stroking, perhaps due to nervousness.

"Thank you, Kim," the professor said in a posh, educated accent. "Let's start with the facts. During the last two pandemics, Biovax couldn't produce any results. Oxford University was, of course, pivotal in producing a vaccination. As was HEAL, the American pharmaceutical giant. In comparison to HEAL, Biovax look like they are selling their wares from a car boot sale in terms of size and quality."

"I don't like him," Burton's mother commented.

"Shh!" his father said.

"Isn't that a little harsh, Professor?" Kim asked. "Biovax is a huge provider of jobs in the North East, and they have a near perfect employee rating. They must do something right?"

"That's because my boy's the boss," Burton's mam interjected.

"Shh!" His dad turned up the TV even louder.

"The staff may be happy, but do they ever get the job done? Biovax is a glorified producer of paracetamol, and Patrick Burton must take a sizeable chunk of the blame."

"Wasn't Patrick a student of yours, Professor?"

"Yes, and I'd say he wasn't even in the top half of his class."

"How do you account for him becoming the head of the company, then?" Kim asked.

Burton's mam glanced at his dad before breaking the law of silence again. "Go on, Kim, you tell him. I've always liked her," she said. It was like she was supporting her favourite team and their roles were reversed. Burton's dad just looked as if he had accepted defeat.

"I'll give him this: although he was arrogant, he always worked effectively when needed. Patrick achieved whatever he set out to do because he had so much self-belief. People also seemed drawn to his personality. When he talked, they listened." Smith had to force the compliment out; it was apparent he wasn't used to giving them.

"So, what are your predictions for this announcement?" Kim asked.

"Maybe they'll be taking on more staff, maybe they'll be closing the plant down altogether. Patrick Burton is slowly becoming a bit of a laughingstock amongst his peers. God knows what he'll say this time. Maybe he's resigning." He pushed his glasses up on his nose, stroked his moustache and sat back in his seat with a smarmy, elitist grin.

"Then let's find out, shall we? We can now cross to Mr Burton, who is live outside the Biovax building. Good afternoon, Mr Burton."

The screen split in two, showing both the studio and Patrick, standing before the front doors of the Biovax building. He put his finger to his ear to hear the anchor.

"Hi, Kim, how are you? It's an important day and I'm pleased to say the sun is shining for this announcement. It will shine all the brighter for many more when I'm finished." He beamed.

"He looks so handsome," his mam said.

"Are you ready to share your announcement? I'm sitting with an old teacher of yours, Professor Smith, who has speculated potential closure for Biovax. This seems unlikely, given your tone. Others have predicted an influx of jobs, which might be closer to the truth?"

"Kim, I'll just get straight to it. We've found a cure for everything, from cancer and AIDS to simple aches and pains. Biovax have created an Elixir that will act on any trauma the body is experiencing." Patrick paused and smiled. *"This is the beginning of the end for physical pain."*

Kim sat speechless with her mouth open. Professor Smith fell off his chair and tried to climb back on and compose himself.

"Did I hear that right?" Burton's dad asked in utter bewilderment.

His mam started crying. "My boy…"

The house phone rang, and more than one mobile phone buzzed. Nobody moved.

"Did you know about this, Jonathan?" his mam asked.

"I knew he was working towards something special that would help the world," Burton said as his mam hugged him.

"Mr Burton, I've been reporting for eight years, and I've never been speechless on air. I don't know what to say. Professor?" Kim looked over at her embarrassed guest.

"Patrick, this is irresponsible and dangerous," Professor Smith said. *"It's impossible."*

"Professor, I understand your concerns, but we are deep into testing and results are showing a 99.9 percent success rate on all known viruses. It's unprecedented. The World Health Organisation has already cleared the Elixir for use."

"Poppycock! Nothing has ever had such accuracy. How have you done this?"

"Hard work, as always. You know me, Professor."

"But how is it made?"

"Magic," Patrick replied, smirking.

"This is a publicity stunt." The senior scientist shook his head and threw his arms out to show the underside of his palms in disbelief. He acted as though he was being pranked and his career was at risk. *"We deserve a better answer than that."*

"I don't want to bore the public, so I'll explain in layperson's terms. The immune system is our own personal army. Once a virus enters the body, it takes time to plan how to stop it. During this time, the virus replicates and grows stronger, and this is how you become sick. Once your immune system fights off a virus, however, it remembers and understands how to defeat it again. Incredible. So this cure, this Elixir, acts as a blueprint in your DNA, a battle plan for your immune system to use during the first wave of any attack."

"Even if it were true, it must have limits!" The professor seemed to be trying to find something to knock Patrick back.

"The Elixir will not regrow severed limbs and early data suggests brain injuries are also complicated. It doesn't make you immortal, only more comfortable in old age, potentially extending your life. Imagine maintaining the strength and energy of your youth while building your knowledge and experience. The Elixir could speed up progress in every profession, from bricklaying to quantum physics."

"You can't grow back an arm? That's terrible for amputees across the world," Smith said, clutching at straws.

"We can't grow you a personality either, but we're working on it." Patrick retorted, stopping the professor in his tracks. Despite the sun, rain droplets were now spitting onto the shoulders of the Biovax CEO.

Kim interjected. *"There are going to be many people clam-*

ouring for this. How do you plan to distribute it? How much will it cost? Can you prove it's safe?"

"Like he'd charge for it," Burton said, dismissing the question. Patrick was his hero.

"We held prior discussions with the British government," Patrick replied, *"but to be honest, I wouldn't trust the current Prime Minister to cut my grass. Anyway, I doubt they could afford it."*

Burton rose from his seat. "What?"

"I've had some fantastic discussions with Maslow and the Biovax board of directors. We will offer the Elixir as a blue-chip cure, two hundred thousand pounds per dose." Patrick stood firm with his arms crossed as the rain got heavier in the Biovax carpark.

Frederick Wortham entered the frame, a large black umbrella held over his head.

He must have hired Wortham after Egan left. But why?

"Who has that kind of money, Mr Burton?" Kim asked. *"You said you were going to end pain."*

"We are a business. Biovax has shareholders. Why should we give the greatest advancement in human history away for free?"

"What about the internet? That was gifted to the world."

"And we all know how that worked out. I'd hardly say the internet has progressed humanity. It needed to have restrictions and be properly policed. It's utilised by child traffickers, arms dealers, and remains out of control to this day."

"How can you stop that from happening to your own creation? I noticed you have amassed a small army around the building," Kim said.

"Biovax will retain exclusive control of the patented formula. You will have to visit our headquarters to have a dose administered. I've also opted for the best security in the country, the British Assault and Reconnaissance Regime for Information and Enforced Regulation."

"That's a mouthful," Kim interjected.

"We call them BARRIER for short. I'm not taking any chances."

"You liar!" Burton shouted at the TV.

"Don't worry, I'm sure he'll get us one, Jonathan," his dad said.

"What about everyone else? He was supposed to give it to the world. This is going to create a huge divide."

"Maybe it's expensive to make?" his mam suggested. "It sounds complicated."

Burton stood in front of the telly with his hands pressing at either side of his head. "He's worse than them. He only got me that job because he needed me out of the way. He sounds like a tyrant."

"Worse than who?" his dad asked.

"Stop it – he's your brother," his mam ordered.

"You don't understand." Burton's entire body tensed up from the top of his neck to the bottom of his feet. He clenched his fists.

Kim continued her questioning: *"I notice you're wearing a 'Vote Fairchild' badge on your suit."*

"Correct Kim. Maslow is renowned for riding big waves and he's a very well-connected man. For me, it was a no-brainer to involve him in the decision-making process. I've got great respect for everything he has achieved. I can see him in Number 10 one day."

"We're almost out of time, Mr Burton. Could you answer one last question?

"Yes, of course."

"How is the Elixir administered, and is it safe?"

"Well, Kim, we've created a patented Biovax container that stores the Elixir and keeps it cool." Patrick held up a gleaming glass pyramid in the palm of his hand. The camera zoomed in to reveal a new Biovax logo; the 'B' was turned on its side to rest on top of a 'V', suggesting a woman, the giver of life. *"And as for your second question..."* Patrick removed the tip of

the pyramid and held it above his head, before pouring the green liquid into his mouth.

"Thank you, Mr Burton. I'm sure we'll speak soon. And thank you to our other guest, Professor Smith. This has been a historic broadcast. We'll be bringing you more at 6pm. I've been Kim Knowles. Start saving your pennies."

"No, Paddy, how could you?" Burton said out loud to the TV screen.

"What's happening to his eyes?" his mother asked.

Patrick's eyes were glowing green for the first time. He stood staring into the camera in the now torrential rain.

CHAPTER 17
FLOWERS IN THE FALLOUT

Outside Biovax, Burton was met with a horde of desperate locals that stretched across the paths, parking areas and grass verges in front of the building. The scene was developing into a music-festival-sized crowd by the minute, with the Biovax building in place of Glastonbury's Pyramid Stage. A parking attendant was writing ticket after ticket and slapping fines on windscreens with glee. *There must be a thousand people here.* As Burton eased his way forward, a fat man in a hoodie with an eyebrow piercing shoved him back.

"I've got a sick two-year-old daughter. D'you think I'm going to let you push in front of me, mate?"

"Sorry, I need to speak to my..." Burton stopped mid-sentence and backed off. *I better not say who I am; they'll lynch me.*

"Yeah, you jog on." The fat man gave a vicious look that said he'd do anything for his baby girl. Arguments and fights were breaking out all around Burton. These people were desperate and had come seeking charity.

A solitary police car sat on a grass verge watching on as

hired BARRIER guards administered their heavy-handed order.

People in the crowd were holding up makeshift cardboard signs displaying painted messages: *CURE MY CANCER, SICK AND BROKE, I'LL DO ANYTHING!* News teams were setting up on the edges and trying to capture the atmosphere, as were opportunist vloggers and selfie-takers looking for 'likes' on their social media channels.

I'm not going to get close. Even if I rang Paddy, I wouldn't get through.

Burton's phone had been buzzing in his pocket over the last couple of hours. He looked at it for the first time since the news broke. There were multiple missed calls and messages, most from people he hadn't spoken to in over ten years. As he scrolled down, however, he saw multiple messages from a name he'd been forcing himself to forget. Eliza.

> *I can't believe him. Why has he done this?*

> *Did you know about this? I trusted you.*

> *Ring me. Why are you ignoring me?*

> *We need to talk about this, it isn't right. He's as bad as they are.*

> *We need to meet now. I'm worried about your family.*

Wow, she doesn't respond to me for months at a time and I'm getting scolded for leaving a message unanswered for two hours?

Burton typed a reply:

> *I had no idea, honestly. I've come to speak to him at Biovax but the place is locked down. Where are you? I'm raging.*

Within seconds, his phone buzzed again.

> *I'm here. Meet me at the nearest bus stop. I'll pick you up if I can get through.*

Burton put his phone back in his pocket and glanced around at the crowd. He caught the eye of an absolute dick from his high school. This guy had once tried to make him kiss a dead rat in the playground before a teacher pulled him away. He was called Pete, and it was clear he'd come to love steroids since leaving education prematurely.

"Hey, Jonny? Jonny Burton?" the bully shouted. "It's me, Pete, from school, your old mate. Is that you? Hey you, Jonny? It's me, Pete Weyland!"

Burton shook his head and tried to act like he didn't know him, but the people surrounding him had taken note.

"Burton? Are you a relation?" the fat man asked.

"Hey, that's Patrick's brother," Pete shouted again, pointing. "He'll know what's going on!"

Someone shoved Burton from behind and his head snapped back as he stumbled forward.

"How do you expect me to pay for the cure, you cruel bastard?" the shover asked.

"Yeah, your brother's supposed to be working class. Shame on you." An old woman and her husband prodded Burton with their walking sticks. A group of boys pelted a pasty at him, followed by a full can of Coke.

"Our dad's ill. Give us the Elixir." Another man pushed Burton to the ground.

Pete booted him in the stomach and laughed, he hadn't changed one bit. Burton curled into a ball and tried to cover his head to protect himself as the crowd kicked him and spat on him. Someone even poured a bag of chips over him; the smell of salt and vinegar made him long to be on Tynemouth beach.

We're finished. Paddy has dragged our family name into the dirt.

Through the ringing in his ears, Burton heard the quick stab of a siren followed by a hissing of gas. He looked from in between his elbows, his hands protecting the back of his head. The lynch mob around him started coughing and holding their eyes but Burton himself was unaffected. Every one of their cheap shots had hurt, but the Elixir seemed to mitigate any serious damage. BARRIER were trying to send a message in front of the news cameras by firing teargas.

A strong, green-clad leg thundered into the back of an aggressor and it sent him crumpling to the ground. Burton heard another crack, and a second person dropped beside him holding their jaw. The fat man was next; the attacker ripped his piercing straight from his eyebrow making him yell in agony while clutching his face. The big eyes above the purple facemask were unmistakable; Eliza stood over Burton and offered her hand.

"For fuck's sake, Frosty – it's me." She pulled the mouth covering down and ruffled her white hair as proof. She was wearing a skin-tight emerald-green jumpsuit, and she'd also added a short black leather jacket over the top to add an element of punk style. A holster was pressed against her right thigh and attached to a leather belt around her slim waste.

"Eliza, how did you… behind you!" Burton pointed and yelled as a raw-eyed Pete Weyland ran at her. As he swung his steroid-filled arm, Eliza ducked under it and cracked him in the ribs with her left fist. Her right followed with an open-palmed strike up into his nose. Burton winced as the bully collapsed, winded and bloodied.

"How did you—"

"Come on, slowcoach." Eliza hoisted Burton up and they ran, barging the horde out of the way.

"This way," she said.

"Wait, isn't that O'Fagan's car?"

"Get in."

Burton clambered into the front seat as Eliza turned the key in the ignition.

"How did you do that? How have you got this car?"

"No time for questions, Frosty. We have to get to your parents' house."

"My parents? Are they in danger?"

"I just hope we can get there in time. Your brother has just declared war on the Cult of Asklepios, and they'll retaliate by killing everyone he loves. That includes your mam and dad." She sped off, zigzagging past abandoned vehicles.

The classic car was being pushed to its limits. Burton gripped the grab handle above his head as the engine roared once again. They sped along the coast road toward a cloud of billowing, black smoke in the distance.

Burton tried calling his mother, then Dominique and Patrick, but all went straight to answerphone. As the car hurtled onward, a military-sized helicopter with dual propellers flew low overhead, back in the direction from which they had come.

"We're nearly there." Burton sat ready to spring the door open.

"Oh no – are we too late?" Eliza asked as she screeched to a halt outside.

Hellish flames were burning his home to black. His mam's beautiful garden resembled a patch of no-mans-land and all the flowers were gone. The word *VLASFIMIA* had been sprayed in red across the front stone wall of the house. It must have been Nicoli's doing, and was presumably Greek for blasphemer. Burton had no time to process any of it. *I have to do something.*

"Eliza... My parents... I need to get inside." Burton held a deep breath and charged toward his front door.

"No, Jon, wait, there might be a—"

At the same moment, Eliza grabbed his arm. An explosion from within the house shattered the double-glazed windows. The backdraft blew the pair back to the front gate and an intense heat burned across Burton's face. He got back to his feet and stood before the impenetrable wall of flame. His yell turned his vocal cords raw.

"What have you done, Paddy?" Burton shouted. He shuffled and edged his way forward, getting close enough to see the partially melted number seven of his front door drop to the ground. *I can't get closer; the pain is too much. I'm burning.*

Eliza yanked him backwards again.

"We don't know that they were inside. Ring Patrick again," Eliza said, trying to calm him down. He was hyperventilating and shaking. Every inch of his exposed skin was blistering.

Two fire engines arrived and stopped behind O'Fagan's car, which was still in the middle of the road. The emergency workers ushered Burton and Eliza back further before spraying their hoses with maximum force.

Burton tried to call Patrick. No answer. He spoke into the answer machine. "Our house has been attacked, it's on fire and I can't get in. Are Mam and Dad with you? Are Dominique and Matty with you?"

A text came through in response.

> *They're with me. I had them collected. Don't worry. Get away from there and call me. We need to talk. They hit my house as well.*

> *You lied to us. This is your fault.*

"Thank god – they're okay." Burton looked up at the sky as if speaking to a higher power. His neighbours stood farther up the street and looked on in concern from a safe distance.

Burton watched his childhood home burn in front of him; the only place in the world where he had felt truly safe. He wiped his cuff on the red paint to smudge the letters on the wall, though he didn't know for sure what they meant.

"We need to go. Come on." Eliza got back into the car.

Burton took one last look at the incinerated building. Everything had been erased.

"Where are we going?" he asked.

"To see an old friend."

The crowd parted to let them through, and Burton noticed his rotund neighbour looking on with tears streaming down his face.

They drove so far into the countryside that Burton hadn't the slightest idea where he was. As Eliza parked up, all he could see apart from hills and sheep was an old boarded-up pub. The battered sign hanging over the door read *The Laughing Heart*.

"Why have we stopped?" Burton asked.

"May I present to you, the Contra family pub."

"It looks… nice," Burton said.

"No need to be polite, Frosty, I know it's a shithole. We had to close during the last pandemic – we weren't making enough money to stay open. It hit a lot of places hard. Then Mam got sick, and, well, the rest is history. David gave me some money, but I hate taking charity. I just accepted enough to get by."

She pushed the door open.

"You don't lock it?" Burton asked.

"You don't need to when you have the toughest woman alive sitting inside."

"Nefertari is here?"

"How did you guess?"

Burton followed Eliza into the lounge area. The place looked as though it had once been a cosy retreat for hikers, but now the air was thick with dust and damp. The maroon carpet squelched and a drip from the ceiling splashed on Burton's shoulder. A bar with rusting gold pumps was in the corner of the room.

"We used to sell four delicious ales. Now the pumps don't work," Eliza said.

"And neither do I." Nefertaris' deep voice came from beside a fruit machine. She wore a black hood over her head, presumably to keep warm. On the table in front of her was a packet of crisps that had been split open.

"Hi, Nefertari, it's been a while. How have you been?" Burton asked.

Nefertari didn't reply. She reached for the crisps, but the dexterity in her fingers didn't allow her to take one. She pushed some off the table using her stump to make the snacks fall onto her right hand. It was painful to watch.

"We thought we'd found the right man. We thought the time was right." She rose and approached Burton, standing so close that he could smell the pickled onion on her breath. "Did you know?" she asked. Her English had improved.

"No, I'm appalled."

Nefertari was still intimidating despite her malfunctioning fist.

"I believe him, Nef – this boy is incapable of lying," Eliza said. "He's terrible at it."

"It's like having a disability. I don't know how people do it and still sleep at night." Burton realised his poor choice of words. "I'm sorry, Nefertari – I didn't mean to make light of your situation. I'm an idiot."

Nefertari backed away, maintaining her gaze, and sat down.

"If you hadn't realised, I'm training to be a badass now." Eliza looked up to the left and put an index finger on her chin. "Or is it badarse? Is that what a British badass is called? A badarse? Or are they still a badass?"

"Have you been drinking from those manky pumps? You sound crazy," Burton replied. *God, I've missed her.*

Eliza unzipped her jumpsuit and pulled the top half down around her waist. She was as toned as an Olympic gymnast. Burton wondered if she'd noticed his jaw hitting the floor.

"Nef has been training me like a dog every day. See, no chocolate cake." Eliza showed off her midriff and ran her fingers from the centre of her black sports bra down to her flat abs. "I'm getting good." She picked up a pink T-shirt from a barstool and put it on. *APOKOLIPSTIK* was emblazoned across the front in a punky black font. *Her favourite band.*

"It was a good idea to leave some clothes here," Burton commented.

"All my stuff is here – we live here," Eliza replied.

"Here?"

"Yep. The hills have come in handy for getting fit."

"You have some catching up to do," Nefertari said. "We're going to need your help to pull this off."

"Pull what off?"

"I need you to prove how serious you are first."

"How?"

"6am tomorrow morning. Cardio." Eliza took a crisp from the packet. "Now ring your bro and see what the hell is going on."

Nefertari leant forward and took the last crisp, using only her mouth to suck it up. She crunched down on it without breaking her judging gaze on Burton.

Burton walked into the gents' bathroom to make his call. Little black bugs were crawling all over the white tiles by the sink. *Yuk, this place is filthy.* He thought about backing out again, but he needed the privacy.

His thumb hovered over Patrick's name on his phone screen. It was as if the damp air wasn't filling his lungs and they weren't expanding like they were meant to. He took one last gulp of air and pressed down on Patrick's name. The phone rang twice before he answered.

"Where are you?" Patrick asked.

"How could you do it?"

"Jonny, you're so naïve. It's your best and worst quality. You're innocent, like a little kid. You've got no guile or understanding of how the world works."

"Ordinary people won't be able to buy the Elixir without selling their soul. It's an absolute fortune."

"I've worked all my life while you've been sitting on the dole. You just don't get it."

"I've tried hard everywhere. It just never worked out."

"One year here, six months there, 'I'm getting bullied', 'I'm not enjoying it'. Grow up. You're just fucking lazy, and I should've told you a long time ago. Why d'you think I didn't want you involved? You have bad luck because you do things badly. I could've got you a job at Biovax, but I knew you'd only mess it up, embarrass me, and then get depressed even more."

Burton started hyperventilating again. *He's right, I'm nothing. I'm worthless.*

His panic attack rendered him speechless as his hero spoke, "I'm selling the Elixir because I'm the CEO of Biovax. We have shareholders and competitors. The company was close to downsizing considerably, I would've lost my job along with most of the staff. I've done what's right for Biovax and for our family."

"Best for our family? Nicoli just blew our fucking houses up!" Burton managed to force out the words through his heaving.

"You'll thank me one day. I'll buy Mam and Dad a bigger house. All this will die down. I tried to help someone once before without thinking it through, remember, and look where it got me. You're just like I was. I'll arrange for you to be picked up and kept safe. Where are you?"

"No."

"No what?"

"I don't want to be picked up. I don't want to be associated with you." Burton hung up and ran to the sink to wretch into it. Bugs crawled over his right hand as he gripped the filthy basin.

CHAPTER 18
COLLARBONE KISSES

I t was sunrise. Burton and Eliza had hiked up one of the jade hills overlooking the pub. Eliza was wearing a white vest and green shorts, while Burton had cut his jeans at the knees and took a light blue Laughing Heart T-shirt from behind the bar. They were each carrying a grey hiking bag full of rocks on their shoulders.

Two rabbits hopped across the path in front of them.

"Looks kind of nice," Eliza said.

"Is that Hadrian's Wall?" Burton asked. The sun was illuminating a long stretch of stacked cobbles.

"Yeah, hikers used to always leave pamphlets about it in the pub. The Romans built it to keep out raiders. Think I remember them saying it was about eighty miles long with a castle every mile. I used to stand here and pretend I was a centurion when I was a little girl."

"That's so cute."

"Whatever happened to that happy little girl?" Eliza kicked a loose stone and watched it tumble down the bank.

"I dreamt about you last night. It was mad," Burton said as they watched the beams of light playing upon the fields below them.

"What was I doing?" Eliza asked.

"We were supposed to meet at a party. You turned up late in a sweatshirt and tracksuit bottoms. A queue of people in black eye masks formed, and they all took turns to kiss your collarbone. I was disgusted and dragged you away. Next thing I knew, we were walking down a street flanked either side by decrepit buildings with smashed windows."

"You're having me on." Eliza whacked Burton's shoulder, and the weight of the bag almost toppled him. "I'm never late."

"Was I right to rescue you?"

"Like I'd ever need rescuing by you. Sounds like you've still not got over Kinky Cal's party, if you ask me." Eliza looked at Burton with humoured disapproval and placed her hands on her hips, lit from behind by the sunrise.

"I've been meaning to ask, what did you see when you took the Elixir? I'm curious."

"Well. I was in an empty cinema and wearing my sweats, funnily enough. Big red curtains pulled back to show an enormous screen. My mam was on it; she was wearing a bright yellow dress and riding a bike with a wicker basket. As I leant forward in my seat, I noticed a muscular arm on the armrest to my left. Our fingers inter-locked, and the harder I squeezed, the closer my mother pedalled towards me on the screen. Then I looked down and suddenly, I was wearing her dress. That's when I woke up."

"What d'you think it means?"

"I think it means I want to be like her, but I need to trust people a bit more. She loved everyone with so much warmth, but my scumbag dad left her to bring me up alone. Mam said I was crying a lot one night and he just packed a bag, claiming it wasn't the life he wanted. Fucking coward."

"What a dick. There are good people out there, though. Don't lose faith altogether."

Eliza scrunched her face, as if she wasn't sure she believed Burton's statement.

"Don't tell anyone about that. Okay, eight miles up and down. And by the way, maybe I enjoy getting my collarbone kissed."

She started sprinting, and Burton followed. They leapt over any obstacle in their path. Burton felt strong. His thigh muscles powered up and down, propelling him forward like an old steam train. The Elixir had certainly improved his engine, he didn't even tire until the final mile. He caught his breath as they came to a halt.

"Okay, warm-up is done."

"Warm-up?" Burton repeated.

"Yep. Now sprint back down to Nefertari. Last one there's a dirty rotter."

She sped up again. Burton tried to follow, but his momentum threw him forward, towards the foot of the hill. He lost his balance and fell face first at Nefertari's feet. Despite some scrapes, the thing that was hurt the most was his pride.

"Slow. Stand," Nefertari said.

She signalled to Eliza, who threw Burton a long, thin branch. He caught it, despite awkwardly resting on one knee. Eliza closed the space between them in a second and cracked him across the shoulder, knocking him fully to the ground.

"Hey, what are you doing?" Burton said, unhappy at the cheap shot. "We just got back."

"Nicoli would not wait," Nefertari shouted, watching on.

Whenever Burton tried to get up, he was taken down. Eliza swept his legs from under him. She pulled and pushed him. She punched and kicked him until he was bloodied.

Burton lay on his back. "Have you brought me here just to be your punch bag?" he asked, rubbing the scratches on his cheeks made by the branch. The sharp splintering pain in his ribs passed, thankfully, within a minute.

"You're here to learn how to do the same," Nefertari said. "Good, Eliza. We will have our breakfast and begin."

"Begin? I'm half dead," Burton moaned.

"Nothing is worth having unless it's hard to get," Eliza said.

She offered Burton her hand, pulled him up, and they went inside the pub.

Burton hobbled to the bar area, pressing his palm against his wounds as they healed.

"What do you even eat here? Just crisps?" he asked. Through the hatch in the kitchen behind the bar, he heard Eliza opening and shutting the microwave door multiple times.

After about five minutes, her face reappeared with an announcement, "Breakfast is served."

She rested three bowls of hot porridge on the bar. "Hope you like it, because you don't have much of a choice. Luckily, we've got sack loads of the stuff. It was a favourite with hikers, and it doesn't go off. It's ideal."

"Do you need any help with yours, Nefertari?" Burton asked.

"No," she replied, with an edge to her voice.

She picked up the spoon, resting the handle in her palm and gripping loosely with her thumb.

"This is quite nice, Eliza, thanks," Burton said, displaying good manners, as always.

"Did you expect anything else from the master chef? What did Patrick say?"

"He wants me to join him in his evil Biovax fortress."

"Are you going to?" Nefertari asked.

"No chance. I won't be part of it."

"Maybe it's something we could use to our advantage," the injured warrior suggested.

"What could I do in there? It's heavily guarded."

"I will teach you to be ghost and then flame," Nefertari replied.

"As soon as we do anything, we'll trigger alarms and alert the guards," Eliza said, leaning through the hatch.

"Neither ghost nor flame cast shadow. They'll never know," the warrior explained.

"You make it sound so easy," Eliza said.

"Anything is easy if you apply yourself." Nefertari took a big mouthful of porridge.

The lessons continued. Burton and Eliza stood ten metres apart beside a shallow stream trickling on a riverbed of pebbles and mossy rocks. They were holding the same wooden staffs that they had wielded earlier. The air was fresh, with only the odd butterfly or bee to disturb them.

"A gentleman never raises his hands to a lady," Burton stated.

"You couldn't hit me anyway, mate," Eliza said in a serious tone.

'Mate'? Am I in the friend zone already?

She spun the staff from side to side in a figure-of-eight motion. Nefertari stood next to Burton and leant in as he looked on in awe.

"See how she move like flowing water?" Nefertari traced a wave motion with her stump. "First, stand sideways. Put your right hand in the middle of the staff and your left on your chest." As Nefertari spoke, Eliza performed a simplified slow and rhythmic version of the spinning technique. "The dory spear was the chief weapon of Hoplites, citizen-soldiers of Ancient Greece. I shortened length to improve my stealth and speed."

"This seems so complicated." Burton tried to spin the stick but kept hitting it against his legs and head. "Is this necessary? We don't have time for this."

"All we have is time. Think of it like drawing a figure of eight, and don't grip tight. Lead with thumb. The more you sweat in peace, the less you'll bleed in battle," Nefertari explained.

Burton dropped the stick. "Sorry."

"This is only the beginning. It won't be long before you're spinning, blocking and cross striking like Eliza."

Eliza exploded into 'flame', spinning the staff like an inferno and unleashing a flurry of varying attacks that stopped just short of Burton's nose.

"Not bad for a lady, huh?" Eliza blew a strand of purple hair out of her face, then turned and walked back ten metres.

"Again," Nefertari demanded as Burton's pitiful spinning continued.

Over the next few hours, 'Again' was a word Burton became tired of hearing. He couldn't seem to pick up the technique. They practised all day, and he lost track of time.

"There's a question I've been meaning to ask, Nef," Burton said, desperate for a rest and using his question to blag one. "Where do the Caballion come from?

"They are lost souls, people with no direction."

"Why's that?" Eliza asked.

"When someone in that mental state is offered purpose, they are malleable."

"Don't I know it," Burton commented under his breath.

"We make them loyal and driven. Many people just want to belong to something. We can teach the rest."

"Beats joining a choir," Eliza said.

"At the beginning of our civil war, there were eight. Now two left to kill. In Bamburgh, I was ambushed. The walls of the crypt were too narrow to swing my spear." Nefertari seemed to be seething at herself.

"What chance do we have if they bested you?" Burton asked.

"I was not beaten. I am still breathing. While chained, I killed one. The flesh can go on if the mind is willing. Pain can help us move forward."

"Amen to that," Eliza said. "What happened to your partner? The other hunter David trained?"

"Dead," Nefertari replied.

"These people really don't want change, do they?" Eliza asked, but Nefertari didn't respond.

"I suppose it's easy to get stuck in your ways. If this is a cult, are there followers or subjects?" Burton asked.

"The Elixir has saved many lives. Those blessed will always offer help if they see this." Nefertari showed the damaged tattoo on the underside of her wrist. "They are rarely dangerous, because we vet our targets. Saving someone's life is often enough to convince them to keep our secret."

"I bet," Eliza said.

"If they don't keep secret..." Nefertari glanced at Burton and stopped her sentence. The awkward silence suggested only death.

"How did O'Fagan find you, Eliza?" Burton asked. He had just about caught his breath and the sweat was cooling on his back.

"The hospital. He'd overheard me talking to my mam."

"David made a mistake with his last hunter and chose strength over soul. I had to kill him. David learned the lesson that we build muscle easier than spirit. It's why I wanted the both of you. It wasn't all about your brother, Jonathan."

"You chose us?" Eliza asked.

"David didn't have long left. I was to become the new Column and you were to be my Caballion," Nefertari explained.

"I've never been chosen for anything before," Burton said.

"Enough of this. I think it's time we touched on 'Ghost'."

Nefertari said. The sun was setting behind the hills. "Today has run away from us."

Burton propped himself up with his branch. "Run away? It's been never-ending."

"How do we become Ghost?" Nefertari asked as they started walking back to the pub.

"Intelligence," Eliza answered, like a star pupil.

"And how do we gain intelligence?"

"Planning," Eliza answered again.

"Good. Buildings, surroundings, people, weather. Do you think it was accident that I wore white the first night you saw me, Jonathan?"

"I guess not," he replied.

"If you don't look ahead, you'll always find trouble at the door," Nefertari instructed as they approached the Laughing Heart. "Use your phone to monitor Patrick's interviews in the coming days."

They entered. Burton started scrolling on his phone and plonked himself down on a barstool.

"He's been interviewed on every news channel. There are headlines like 'Costly Cure' and 'The Bitterest Pill'. Very negative stuff. There are thousands outside Biovax now. Does the TV work?"

Nefertari used the butt of her new silver spear to hit the power switch of an old TV in the corner of the bar. Patrick's face appeared.

"I know you're desperate, but please go home. We can't offer charity. Our distribution is limited, hence the high price. There are certain behaviours and characteristics of the Elixir that require slow production until we complete further research. Vessel creation and storage, for example, are paramount. Now if you excuse me, I must get back to work."

Patrick didn't look his calm and collected self as he headed through the Biovax double doors to a cacophony of booing and abuse.

Following his departure, news anchor Kim Knowles spoke to a full panel of smartly dressed and well-groomed experts.

"Greg, is what we are seeing here just marketing 101?"

"Kim, I think we might be seeing the most high-profile example of early adopter marketing ever. We see it in the tech world every day. The latest and coolest gadget comes in at a premium price. After some time perfecting the product and ironing out the bugs, it slowly becomes available and affordable to a mass market," Greg explained.

"That's fine, but what about those with sick relatives? What do they do right now? This might be a good question for economics expert Sarah Barkley."

"You raise a very worrying point, Kim. To secure a place on the Biovax waiting list, we may see a huge fire sale of assets. Entire families selling their homes and anything of value in order to purchase one vial to save someone they love. The value of everything will be driven down."

"Then this could see a rise in homelessness, crime and prostitu-tion," Kim added.

"Exactly. The economy could crash like we've never seen before, even worse than during Wave 2 or the last energy crisis. Of course, there will always be those looking to take advantage. It could get very nasty, and quickly."

"So if you were going to sell your home, you'd suggest doing it while the prices are high?" Kim asked.

"Mine is already up for sale. 22 Starlingdale, five bedrooms, huge south-facing garden – please contact me. My number is—" Sarah said before being cut off.

"I've been Kim Knowles, and this has been the North East News."

"Everything is fucked. This could start a war." Nefertari switched off the TV using her spear once again. "There were interesting things, did you hear?"

"Blah blah blah, that's what I heard," Eliza replied as she completed press-up after press-up.

"He said there was a crowd there," Burton added.

"Yes, and?" Nefertari urged.

Burton tried to recall the whole interview. "He said that production was slow because of... what did he call it, vessel creation?"

"Exactly. Biovax is big, but not big enough to store all materials. They may require regular delivery," Nefertari said.

"What does that mean?" Eliza asked.

"A potential route into the building and also a potential target for Mukhtar and Nicoli to hurt him." Nefertari held the knuckle of her index finger to her mouth. She was planning.

"How did Nicoli and Mukhtar become Columns, if they're so crazy?" Eliza asked.

"Nicoli had his position handed down to him from his respected father, who lived to be 152. He was a legendary and wise leader. Nicoli got the position easily, even though he didn't deserve it."

Burton swallowed, thinking of the parallel to his job at Tall Oak Bank.

"David would never tell me about Muhktar, even after they butchered Gorgone. Maybe we will learn more in the coming days and months."

"Who's up for porridge?" Eliza asked. She sounded as though she needed a break from the heavy conversation filled with death and betrayal.

"Again?" Burton asked.

"You better get used to it. We're up early again tomorrow." Eliza looked at Burton with a certain drive in her narrowed eyes.

"About that. Do you seriously expect me to become a Spartan warrior? I'm not like you. I couldn't beat up a room full of people in a million years. It's just not the way I'm made. I'm an artist and a creator, not a destroyer." Burton's tone was open, honest and matter of fact.

"I agree," Nefertari responded.

"Then why have I been hitting myself in the face with a branch all day?"

"You were not made that way, but you are no longer how you were made."

"What do you mean?"

"Elixir is a gift from God. You will never be like me, but you can become the best version of yourself: harder, stronger and faster. Maybe you will even stand up for yourself one day. Wallowing is waste. Take action, take control."

"Well said, Nef," Eliza said from the hatch. "What is it David used to say? You will be greeted at the gates of Hell by the person you could have been. That's freaked me out ever since I heard it."

"Thanks for sharing," Burton said, as a shiver ran up his back.

"Until I conquer my injuries, you two are my hands," Nefertari said. "I will do what I can to make you strong. The three of us are in this together. Get some rest. We have an early start."

Day after day, the pattern continued. Burton ran, fought, jumped, quipped, laughed, shot, spun, sighed, balanced, and watched the news. Seeing Eliza standing in the sun was a joy, even from the friend zone. She made him want to be braver, and her positive spirit motivated him. Burton also noticed muscles developing on his shoulders and arms for the first time in his entire life. He even flexed once or twice in the bathroom mirror when nobody was around bar the bugs.

One morning, they were balanced on top of Hadrian's Wall. Nefertari looked on, analysing their every movement as always. Eliza lunged at Burton with her staff, knocking him off for the tenth time in as many minutes. In his frustration, Burton stood and crashed the wooden staff down on his thigh, splitting it in half. Holding one piece in his right hand, he advanced, feeling more balanced and unhindered. As Eliza jabbed out with the butt of her practice weapon again, Burton dodged it for the first time and whacked the shortened piece of wood off her hip.

"Ow. Is that the first time you've hit me? Hurts more than I realised."

Eliza hopped down and advanced, but Burton side-stepped her swing and spanked her backside twice with the stick. He bounced on his toes and cheered for an invisible crowd.

"Hey, get that chuffed look off your face," Eliza said, rubbing her left buttock. She kicked Burton's wrist and sent the stick flying out of his hand and into the nearby stream. Then she smashed her staff up between his legs. Burton collapsed onto the grass, holding his balls. She had been holding back.

"And still the champion of the world!" Eliza put her foot on Burton's back and rolled him into the water.

"Come on, that's a bit much, isn't it?" Burton lay on his side and coughed as the stream trickled against his cheek. "Why are you even still involved in all this – revenge?" he blurted out. As soon as the words left his mouth, he realised how harsh he sounded.

Eliza's smile straightened. "D'you think I'm that selfish? You're not the only one trying to be a better person. My mam's gone, but I'm not," she replied.

"Very good, Jonathan. It looks like it might suit you to try something more… Roman." Nefertari broke the tension, ignoring the squabble between her students. Burton and Eliza stood in silence whilst Nefertari walked down to the pub. She returned after ten minutes holding a new weapon. "This belonged to David."

She handed a short sword to Burton. It was the one from David's office. The handle looked like bone, with worn finger grooves that formed a smooth and comfortable grip. The round bronze pommel at the hilt matched the inlays of the rosewood scabbard. Burton drew the blade three-quarters of the way from its case and watched the light bounce off the hilt. There was an inscription in Latin running up it: *Vivamus, Moriendum Est.*

"David told me it meant 'Let us live, since we must die'. Roman foot soldiers adopted the gladius from the Greeks. It is sharp on both sides, a thrusting and cutting weapon that will suit your natural fighting style. In Livy's account of the Macedonian wars, the Macedonian soldiers were horrified by the dismembered bodies this weapon left in its wake."

"Dismembered bodies? That's not me. I've tried to tell you a thousand times." Burton was reluctant to even remove the weapon fully from its sheath.

"See if that's the case when your life in danger, or when someone you love is begging for help. You need to defend yourself and others around you."

"What would you rather have, gladioli?" Eliza chimed in with another perfect put-down.

"It is better to be a warrior in a garden than a gardener in a war," Nefertari said. "A real man is not passive and meek. You should be dangerous, and others should be aware of that."

In his anger, Burton pulled the blade free and slashed into the air. The gladius felt balanced and already an extension of his own arm. He found it much easier to wield than the staff.

"Check you out! You're looking the part for once," Eliza said.

Burton put the sword back into the sheath and handed it to Nefertari. "I don't want to use this on anyone."

"We can't win this war with a paintbrush," Eliza said.

"Am I not supposed to pull my sacred weapon from a mythical stone or something, anyway?" Burton asked, with more than a hint of sarcasm.

Eliza grabbed the gladius, unsheathed it, and rammed the blade hard into a tree trunk. "There you go. It's yours to pull out whenever you want to stop being such a wuss."

Weeks passed and the Biovax media circus grew with still no dose being administered. The only noteworthy thing Patrick had mentioned was that he'd signed a deal with both NASA and Newcastle Utd Football Club, which would make them the flagship sports team using the Elixir once it was available. Other teams had challenged this, but Patrick had likened it to taking a vitamin supplement or eating a healthy diet. Fans were excited at the prospect of an injury-free season. Some of the world's top older players were linked with transfers to the team. Burton thought about how excited his dad would be. Missing his parents, he rang his mother, but there was no answer. A text came through two hours later.

> *Son, where are you? I've been worried. We are being treated well in the Biovax building, it's lovely to get meals made for me. It's like a five-star hotel. Get yourself here.*

> *Mam, look, I know he's way more successful than me and he's got loads of money, but like you've always said, money isn't everything. I don't believe what he's doing is right.*

Burton's phone rang in his hand. It was Patrick. When Burton answered it, there was silence at the other end.

"Paddy?" Burton spoke first, but there was still silence. "Paddy? Are you there?"

"Come to the back of Biovax at 11pm. I'll tell the guards to guide you in. The crowd is a little quieter there. I'll explain myself this one and only time."

"I just don't underst—"

Before Burton finished speaking, the phone went dead.

"This is a fantastic opportunity. The set-up and security of Biovax will have changed, how you say, dramatically." Nefertari sat in her favourite spot by the fruit machine, talking to Burton and Eliza after he had shared the news. "I need you to be alert. I'll break it down for you."

Burton looked up from his press-up regime. "Okay, the simpler the better."

Eliza chipped in each time she completed a sit-up at the other side of the lounge. "Yeah – this one's – got the – memory of a – fish, and a forgetful – one at that."

"When have I ever forgotten something you've said?" Burton asked.

"Okay, how far apart – were the castles – on Hadrian's Wall?" Eliza sat up and paused.

"One mile," Burton answered, lightning fast.

"Okay, lucky guess. What's my favourite band?" Eliza wrapped her arm across her chest where the logo was emblazoned on her sweat-drenched T-shirt.

"Apokolipstik," Burton answered again.

"Okay, well… how many ales are on sale in the bar? Without looking," Eliza asked.

Little did she know, he could see a reflection in the windowpane behind her. He took his time.

"None, but if it was open there would be four," Burton answered.

"Three out of three? No way, you cheated."

Eliza pounced on Burton like a wild cat and pinned him down. He put his hands around her waist as she looked around.

"The reflection's in the bloody window, you cheater."

"Hey, there wasn't a rule that said I couldn't use a reflection."

"Reflect this." Eliza went to give Burton a playful slap, but he caught her wrist in his left hand while lying on his back.

"Children. Please." Their sensei sounded like a fed-up schoolteacher.

"Progress at last, huh?" Eliza stood up from the floor. "Sorry, Nef, what will he need to look for?" Eliza was still looking at Burton as she spoke.

"One. You need to keep an awareness of how you access the building. Patrick will request that you use an entrance away from the crowd. Two. Note how many guards you pass. Three. Try to identify any security cameras on the route you take."

"Will you have a high-tech spy gadget to disarm them all?" Burton asked.

"No. Four. Analyse your brother's words. Look for openings, like we have done each night during his interviews. Five. Find out where Patrick is creating and storing the Elixir."

"Easy," Eliza said, rubbing the sweat off her face with a towel.

"Easy? I don't know about that."

"You need to be confident. Your emotions are always written on your face. Silence them, or Patrick will know something is going on," Nefertari said.

"Frosty's an open book," Eliza said, looking straight at him.

"Am I a good read?" Burton asked.

"Sometimes. Don't know if I'd call you a page turner."

"We'd better get a move on; it'll take a couple of hours to get there."

"Repeat the steps," Nefertari demanded.

"One. Access. Two. Guards. Three. Cameras. Four. Patrick analysis. Five. Elixir location."

"Good. Take deep breaths. Speak balanced and don't joke or fidget. Pretend he's still the brother you loved."

"He is. That's never going to change. I'd love him if he dropped a nuclear bomb on an orphanage."

CHAPTER 19
SNAKE PIT

"**G**ood luck. I'll try to stay as close as I can." Eliza dropped Burton off a couple of miles away from Biovax. It was one of those indecisive days that he had always hated, with intermittent cloudbursts and bright sunshine in between. Luckily, he'd opted to put on a dark blue cagoule. Upon arrival at the building, he estimated there were around two hundred people at the back entrance. Many were edging forward, but it was easier to navigate unnoticed than at the front of the building. A huge yellow crane towered over the horde, presumably erected to move materials and make alterations to the building. Burton heard hammering and sawing from behind three large, corrugated shutters. *They must be strengthening every aspect of their HQ.*

"Please, my boy is dying!" a young woman cried from behind a *NO ENTRY* sign. Two BARRIER guards stood silent on either side of silver double doors. Their uniforms resembled police riot gear, only they were dark grey with a luminous yellow trim around their helmet and cuffs. Yellow ID numbers were emblazoned across the front of their bullet and stab proof vests: #82 and #90. The woman ran towards them screaming, "Please, I must speak with Mr Burton!"

Without warning, #90 stepped forward and slammed an electric baton into her stomach. She collapsed on all fours. #82 moved in and smashed her across the back. The poor woman's face was flattened into the tarmac. The guard took a couple of steps back and looked like he was going to kick her.

"Stop!" Burton shouted.

He sprinted towards them. As #82 swung his leg at the woman, Burton kicked into the guard's ankle, making him miss and spin. #90 swung his baton, but Burton ducked and cracked him in the ribs with his left fist. He felt a surge on his back as another swing connected, the violent vibration travelled down into his legs. He staggered into a metal fence and pushed his fingers through the mesh to steady himself. On his left, the frantic woman was dizzied and getting to her feet.

"Go!" Burton shouted, but she continued towards the door. Another baton strike surged against the base of Burton's spine and made him yelp.

#82 reached for his holster. *How much force are they allowed to use?* The guard removed a taser gun and shot at the woman. She collapsed to the ground again, convulsing.

"Your turn, ginger," #90 said and drew his own yellow taser.

Burton put his hands in the air. "Wait, I'm Jonathan Burton. I'm here to speak with my brother Patrick, your boss."

The guard's finger remained on the trigger. #82 stepped over to Burton and patted him down from behind.

"He has no ID but matches the description."

"Slap a restraint on him and take him through," #90 said.

"Put your hands behind your back," #82 instructed. He applied a sharp, plastic restraint around Burton's wrists and led him through the entrance, roughing him up all the way with shoves in the back. Burton noticed a playing card stuck to #82's helmet: the king of clubs. They walked down a long, narrow corridor, which acted as a funnel into the building and presumably stopped any crowds entering en masse. The glass panels were lit every ten metres by tiny blue lights on the floor of the walkway.

"I really hope you're not who you say you are. You better pray you're telling the truth," the limping guard threatened, pushing Burton on the shoulder to usher him along.

"That woman was lying on the floor. She was defence-less," Burton said.

"Well, it wasn't her floor," the guard replied. "I was just doing my job."

"You used unnecessary force."

"Don't break the law and you don't get my force. She was trespassing."

"She was desperate – all of those people are." Burton noticed a black sphere with a blinking red light on the ceiling. *The first security camera.*

"Turn around," #82 ordered.

Before the lift doors opened, the guard took a picture of Burton using a phone protected in a thick casing. He held a key card against a panel and pressed a series of buttons: up, up, down, down, up. Within moments, the lift doors made a pinging sound. Burton repeated the sequence over and over in his head.

"Get in." The guard pushed him through the doors as soon as they opened. "I'm supposed to clock off at half ten. I should be on my way home," he grumbled as he hit floor five and nine in quick succession. The lift closed and the code flashed green. *Up, up, down, down, up, 5, 9.*

"When we get out of this lift, I'll receive confirmation from the gaffer. If you ain't Jonathan Burton, I'm gonna take you into a quiet room and fill it with your noise. You understand?"

Burton received a shove in the back again as soon as the lift doors opened. He could hear the guard dragging his dead leg behind him.

"Wait there," #82 ordered again.

Floor five opened into a holding room with another camera above. It was a small arsenal. Helmets, armour, batons and rifles lined the walls, waiting for the slightest reason to be used.

The guard checked his phone.

"Nothing." He pressed a button on the left ear area of his helmet. "Troublemaker claiming to be the gaffer's brother. Threatening and violent, but I have everything under control, no back-up needed. No confirmation from boss yet."

Comms in the helmets.

The pair waited.

"Okay, looks like it's the little room for you, mate." The guard swiped his security pass again and pushed Burton through. They were inside Biovax.

"I'm Jonathan Burton – let me go. I haven't been threatening or violent."

"Threatening and violent? That doesn't sound like my baby brother. Let him go." Patrick came walking confidently down the corridor towards them.

The guard's demeanour changed. He lowered his head to submit to the alpha and didn't make eye contact. "I'm sorry, Mr Burton. He's the fourth person who's said it this week. I was just making sure."

"You were just doing your job, a fine one as well. Think nothing of it. Great work," Patrick assured the guard as he hurried to remove Burton's wrist ties before limping away.

"Are you okay, Jonny?" Patrick asked.

"That guard just nearly killed a poor woman outside."

Patrick reached for his pocket and pulled out his phone.

"Commander, guard #82 has broken dress code. Please get your men in check. He has a playing card taped to his head, and he looks ridiculous. To make matters worse, he's just been over-physical with a member of my family. Remove him from your roster."

"He's fired?" Burton asked.

"Gone. Follow me."

The two walked to Patrick's office and the older brother sat at the desk behind his laptop computer. Burton admired the family photos on the wall, especially one of them in their matching Christmas pudding hats. Patrick signalled for Burton to sit opposite him. Blueprints of Biovax were spread across his desk.

"What was that?" Patrick asked.

"What?"

"My update said you attacked the guards? I've never seen you throw a punch in your life. *You* made a BARRIER soldier limp? You're usually the definition of a pacifist."

"I've been taking self-defence classes since the events at Bamburgh. Just in case Nicoli comes back."

"That's pretty smart, bro. I didn't think you had it in you. Has there been any sign of him?"

"Not a thing. Have you seen anything?"

"There is something, yes." Patrick walked around Burton and blocked the only door. "The vial deliveries aren't making it here from Gateshead. They're being hijacked. I've got four delivery drivers with no hands kicking off lawsuits. Our first twenty clients have been waiting two months for a product I can't provide. This is my once-in-a-lifetime opportunity, and it's being lost. What do you know about it?"

"Nothing," Burton replied.

"Don't lie," Patrick snarled, and pulled Burton toward him by the collar of his cagoule. The sudden scuffle knocked the family pictures from the wall.

"How could I have known? I haven't even spoken to you."

Burton knocked his brother's arms away with ease; it was a surprise to both of them. Patrick turned away and rubbed his left forearm.

"Everyone is against me."

Burton stood up straight. "The Elixir should be shared. I thought you agreed. I've never seen you like this."

"The world isn't that simple – I told you on the phone. Every opportunity is blood in the water. First, the big sharks arrive and have their fill, then the smaller fish get the leftovers until there's nothing left."

"So, are you the big shark?"

"Animals don't get ideas above their station. That's how evolution works. I've learned a lot listening to my wife's seminars all these years, Maslow as well. What O'Fagan suggested is the equivalent of swimming up to a shark and slapping your dick in its face. My genius needs to go through the appropriate channels."

"Genius? You could start another world war."

"Perhaps – or I could become the most revered scientist of all time. I've been to prison. I've got a northern accent. The establishment doesn't want people like me to succeed. They like their champions to be from Oxford or Cambridge and speak like the King. I was sure our pandemic vaccine was right, 100 percent, in fact. There was definitely foul play. Did you see the way my old professor spoke to me on the news?"

"I did, actually."

"Well, that's an example of the type of person I need to dominate. I need to silence these people as I advance. Take the casing, for example. I've discovered that the Elixir needs to be stored in a special thermal casing that keeps it at minus ten degrees. Even the shape of the container is important. Triangles play a big role in how materials gain their internal strength. In common metal atomic lattices, there are three basic arrangements: face-centre cubic, body-centre cubic and hexagonal close-packed. They have three-dimensional arrangements and base atomic layers of—"

"Triangles are strong, I get you. I think." Burton said, cutting his brother off. It was the first time he'd ever done it, and Patrick shot him a foul look before letting out a deep breath.

"The blood in the water is attracting bigger mouths, and in this business you need to satisfy the food chain. We are trying to expand a wing of the building to bring production in-house, but the crowd is slowing any growth. The shareholders are getting edgy."

"Look, it's not about business or personal pride, it's about what's right. You shouldn't give a damn about shareholders," Burton replied.

"That's why you're thirty-six and living with your parents. Haven't you realised that doing the right thing gets you nowhere? The moral high ground is a very lonely place."

"Fuck you and fuck your stupid company," Burton spat.

Patrick walked to a window and looked out over the horde. Many booed at the sight of his silhouette. As Burton looked over Patrick's shoulder, he saw some people in the crowd sinking to their knees to beg, bow, or perhaps even worship the Biovax CEO. Patrick shut the blinds.

"So why do they deserve an Elixir? What great value would these people bring to the world?" Patrick asked.

"Every person has value, Paddy. Think about what Mam always said. Everyone knows something you don't and is better at something than you are. You should treat them with respect. Listen to them, learn from them."

"They have value if they can pay. Most of them probably can't even make a cup of instant coffee."

"Have you heard yourself? Who are you turning into? Mam and Dad must be ashamed."

"It's not a question of personal wealth. The money is being reinvested to find more answers."

"But what will Matty say when he's older?"

"I hope he won't be a loser like you, a little fish. Mam knows how hard my decision has been. I speak to her every evening. You've never seen me like this because I don't whine about every minor problem like you do. I get on with it. I'm a man, and I'm changing the world."

Burton's tone remained sarcastic even as the conversation reached boiling point. "Well, you won't get far without your trucks and their 'precious cargo'. What a shame. If they're all getting stopped, then maybe someone in your team isn't as trustworthy as you think they are. Egan wasn't loyal either, maybe these people have realised something I couldn't."

"I'm responsible for everyone in this company. I need to lead. Look, I'm giving you the option now: drop all this and stay, or leave and don't come back. You're my brother, and I don't want you to get hurt. You've never had an issue sharing the spoils of my success in the past. Why start now?" Patrick held out his hand to Burton, perhaps expecting the same submissive response the guard gave him earlier.

Burton looked Patrick right in the eye. "No."

"Follow me." Patrick stood up and walked to the corner of his office, where there was a large cityscape photo of Newcastle, featuring the quayside. Underneath there was a small golden plaque that read *Newcastle at Night*. Patrick pressed the plaque. Burton heard a click and Patrick pushed the wall. It was a concealed door.

"You really are turning into a supervillain," Burton said in disbelief.

"This just saves me a ten-minute walk to the immunology lab whenever I need to examine the tanks." Patrick's feet clanked along a metal walkway.

"Tanks?" Burton asked as he followed. The dark and narrow passageway seemed to curve down for an age. He attempted to loosen the front of his collar from habit, but Patrick had ripped it away already.

"Come in." Patrick said.

Inside was a nightmarish pet shop that contained glass compartment upon glass compartment.

"Aesculapian snakes are scattered all around the forests of

Greece. Only one in a hundred can harbour the Elixir and then transmit it via venom. You might see a few snakeskin belts and boots around the building."

"That's not fucking funny." Burton took a few steps back. Slow-moving reptiles were all around him. Each case contained a white synthetic arm that the snakes were biting down on at intervals. Green liquid flowed through corrugated tubes into the ceiling and walls. Burton took a deep breath as he experienced a familiar tightening pain in his chest.

A screen on the back wall displayed a map. Before it stood Dr Frederick Wortham, who was looking at a silver tablet with one eyebrow raised. The screen zoomed in on an ancient aqueduct. Wortham plugged a data drive into the side of his tablet, the type usually used to save a project.

"I approached Frederick to help us find any remaining buried temples in the world," Patrick explained. "We can't have our competitors finding anything, can we? Why wait for a trickle of water when you can find the lake?"

"That sounds like something O'Fagan would've said," Burton replied.

"He was a fossil of a man. Our methods are way more advanced. Isn't that right, Mr Wortham?"

"Yes, Mr Burton. Eighty percent of the ocean is still uncharted, for example. All you need is patience and endeavour to find real treasure." Wortham was like Egan 2.0, only he excelled in a different area. Patrick seemed to be drawn to the overly studious type. He liked to have a book-worm by his side to balance out his own academic short-comings.

"Would you mind giving my brother and I a moment, Frederick?"

"There is breaking news that you need to see first." Frederick picked up his tablet again and pressed a few buttons. Now the wall screen showed a broadcast from the Prime Minister, who was stood behind a lectern outside of 10

Downing Street. The unlikeable Eton alumnus had dark shadows under his eyes and his blue suit was creased all over. He had a face like a Boxer dog that hadn't been given a treat in weeks.

"People of the United Kingdom. Our combined efforts across two pandemics were incredible, something each one of you should be proud of. We followed the guidance of science and pummelled the infection rate into the dust until normal life could resume. Concerts, pubs, packed football stadiums, and holidays abroad all returned as local businesses recovered. However, it is with great regret that I stand here today to bring you terrible news. We have identified a new virus capable of disrupting our way of life again, but this time, it is only infecting our young ones. Wave 3 has broken out in Newcastle at the Freeman Hospital, specifically the children's ward. I urge you to keep your little ones indoors until we establish what has triggered this and how we can combat it. I'm sure many of you will look to Biovax for answers, but based on our conversations I doubt that they will do the right thing. For now, I urge you to remember this slogan: 'No play for a brighter day'. I will update further as and when I can. Thank you." The Prime Minister picked up his notes and walked back into Number 10.

Burton stormed over to his brother so there was barely an inch between their faces. "Patrick, give them the formula. Kids are going to die."

Wortham looked for an answer from his boss. "How do you wish to proceed?"

"Please. Give my brother and I a moment, Dr Wortham," Patrick asked again.

"As you wish," he replied, and exited the snake pit.

Patrick walked to a red metal door at the rear of the lab. It had *CAUTION* written across it in large white stencilled lettering. The door was also bordered by thick yellow and black diagonal lines. Patrick picked up a tablet and hovered his index finger above the screen as if he were about to press something.

"Here's the deal, Jonny. That was not breaking news. Maslow Fairchild warned me that the government was going to try to force my hand."

"What d'you mean? They planned this?" Burton's head flinched back. Patrick held up a silver data drive that glimmered under the flickering light.

"Watch this."

The sagging jowls of the Prime Minister reappeared on the screen. A camera had captured a conversation inside Downing Street. He was talking to a random associate Burton had never seen. The figure was carrying an umber-coloured suitcase.

"Make sure it's contained. Make sure it's controlled. Make sure it's believable. The last thing I need is another scandal. This is bleak, but we could be looking at war if we don't give them something soon. Let's face it, most of the little northern buggers are going to die anyway."

The Prime Minister tutted and shook his head. His minor response was not worthy of his grave order. The clip ended.

"Maslow has informed me that the PM is getting pressure from America, Russia, China and others for the formula," Patrick explained.

"That video needs to be released now. Why isn't it already on the news?"

"It's leverage, and the timing isn't right."

"Timing?" Burton asked.

"Why d'you think it's so rare to see an honourable Prime Minister or president? It's a horrific business filled with back-stabbing and deception. Maslow wants to hold on to this information for now, and I'm going to respect his request. He's a powerful ally. Plus, the poor kids are already infected."

"But it makes you look so much worse. How do you know Maslow's not planning the same fate for you?"

"I feel for those families, I really do. But this is business. The

Biovax board has been clear – there will be no charity. People want what they can't have, it's human nature. We'll save more lives in the long run, trust me. I need to keep them onside for now until I complete my research. It's a difficult balancing act."

"Fuck you." Burton threw an arm up and turned away.

"You don't agree with what I'm doing? That's fine. You can remain ignorant and I won't give it a second thought. But should you and your friends disrupt what I'm doing... well, I will have no choice but to retaliate. Don't let the door hit your arse on the way out." Patrick moved away from the red door and started examining each snake tank.

Burton made a fist.

"But the kids? What if your own son was one of them?" he said again, only to be ignored. "What did you see when you took the Elixir? What was your vision? A dictatorship? A mountain of money with you at the top?"

"None of your fucking business," Patrick replied without looking at his brother. "You don't understand. I'm being stronger than you realise, for all of us."

A BARRIER guard entered the lab and escorted Burton out of the building. There was no rough treatment, and the guard even apologised for not holding the door open.

As soon as he was outside, Burton bustled through the crowd. He repeated the code for the lift over and over in his head.

Each time someone from the horde moved towards him, he put his head down and changed direction. As soon as he was free of the crowd, he typed the memorised information into his phone before he forgot.

Is that right? Damn, I'm not sure. It's making my head hurt.

Eliza appeared in the corner of his eye and matched his stride, walking with him as he exited the area. "You miss me? A few people on the edge recognised you, so they had to go sleepy-byes." She tapped the tranq gun holstered on her hip.

"Nobody noticed. Sick people are dropping like flies every second."

"On the edge is ok, there's no risk of them being trampled. Good luck to any ambulances trying to get near the front, though," Burton replied.

"Have you seen the Prime Minister's update? Eliza asked.

"Yep, and Paddy's not doing a thing about it. We need to act fast."

"You're joking. Why not? Actually, save the explanation for Nef. How about some Apokolipstik in the car?" Eliza wound down the car windows and blasted her favourite band's title track. Burton was preoccupied with his brother's megalomania to say much on the journey home.

She puts on her Apokolipstik
To go and break a few hearts
That girl makes medicine sick
You should've known from the start
A femme fatality
You'll wish you'd never been born
Ain't nothing new to me
I've seen her do it before

~

"My aim is getting better, Nef," Eliza said as she took off her belt and holster.

"Sit down and tell me everything," Nefertari said as Burton walked through the door of the Laughing Heart.

He begun to relay everything he could remember, every step, every word.

"First things first. The code for the lift is up, up, down, down, up, five, nine." Burton looked up from his phone to see Eliza had taken out a tattoo needle.

"What's that for?" Burton asked.

"A tattoo artist used to be a regular when I was younger. Customers let me practise on them when they'd had a few but I was shit. Here, write it on the underside of my right arm."

"It'll scar your body for life. Wouldn't a biro do?"

"I thought you liked art? Doesn't bother me. It's like a level select cheat in a retro game: up, up, down, down, up, five, nine."

"She's right. Your phone could get broken, or paper could get wet." Nefertari added.

"I wasn't even thinking like that. I just didn't have a pen. I've done it before." Eliza plonked her leg up on a bar stool and rolled up the leg on her tactical suit to reveal the words *Dentist on Tuesday @ 2.30* written on her calf.

Burton shook his head. "How does it even work?" He took the needle and tried to accustom himself to the weight and shape.

"Just put your foot on the pedal and draw," Eliza said.

He sat by her and tapped his right foot against the small, round pedal. The needle started to buzz. He drew arrows just below the inside of her elbow to represent the code, followed by a 5 and a 9. It was crude, but there was something sensual about piercing her skin. A deeper connection was being made between them.

"You're a natural! Thanks," Eliza said. Her arm healed without the need to even wipe it.

"You should get it as well, Jonathan," Nefertari suggested.

"Me? No way. I'll just remember it."

"Here, hold your arm out, Frosty. Don't be a baby."

Reluctantly, Burton held out his right arm, underside upwards. He closed his eyes as the needle scratched into him. The idea of being permanently marked was way worse than the pain itself. It was over within seconds. He looked. It was red and puffy, but the code was clear. Eliza had even added a tiny smiley face.

"Now we're tatt-twins."

Burton shook his head, and for once he didn't return her smile. "I hope it's worth it."

He finished relaying everything to Nefertari.

"It sounds like Nicoli is getting to the trucks. How?" Nefertari asked.

"Someone inside must be passing on the information," Burton replied.

"Maybe Mukhtar has a hold on someone he works with?" Eliza added.

"Or maybe someone he trusts is working against him. Who does your brother trust, Jonathan?" Nefertari asked.

"Not me, anymore. Frederick Wortham was there, the archaeologist. Paddy's also enamoured with Maslow Fairchild."

"Christ, we'll be screwed if it's Maslow. Seems like he's got everyone in his pocket," Eliza said.

"Well, get this. Maslow shared evidence with him that the Prime Minister ordered Wave 3 to be started on purpose. I've seen it."

"Fucking hell!" Eliza replied.

"Why?" Nefertari asked. She picked up a kitchen knife and tapped the blade against the table.

"The formula. They want it. They're trying to guilt Patrick into handing his research over. That's why they targeted children specifically."

"This is huge," Eliza said.

"It is," Nefertari agreed, "but we can't tackle a government now. As David used to say, a mountain is only conquered with small steps."

"We need to get enough Elixir to save those kids," Burton said.

"The vials are being manufactured somewhere off-site. He must've mentioned something?" Nefertari stabbed the knife into the table three times as she processed the information.

"Actually, yes, he did. They need a special thermal casing to keep them cool. He can't manufacture them in his building, so he outsources to a Gateshead-based company," Burton said.

"Bingo." Eliza had been leaning against the bar, but now she stood up and started swiping on her phone.

Burton got to his feet again too. "We could follow a truck?"

"You're getting the hang of this," Nefertari said. She scraped the knife across the surface of the bar.

"Here we go," Eliza said, clearly chuffed with herself for finding the information in a flash. "Vanderling Group is a manufacturing business specialising in thermal devices in Gateshead, right on the doorstep. Guess who's a majority shareholder? Maslow. That's where we're going next."

Burton wasn't sold. He stood in thought, scratching his hairy chin. He hadn't been able to shave for a while. "That seems too easy, doesn't it?"

"Patrick probably wasn't banking on the empty containers being a target," Eliza replied.

"That's not my brother. Paddy thinks everything through. He was a chess champion when he was younger and he's always ten steps ahead."

"Eliza, I have placed my tracker on your spear for emergencies," Nef said.

"Does it not have to be put, y'know, in me?" Eliza asked.

"I wouldn't want someone trying to remove it from you like they did me. They are small enough to attach to most things. It will still work."

"That must've been so painful," Eliza said.

Nefertari didn't even flinch. "Jonathan, take the gladius. Any of the above situations you listed could be very dangerous. Nicoli is a violent man." She threw a knife up in the air and it hurtled down towards her only hand.

"Nef!" Eliza shouted as the knife dropped.

The point landed in between Nefertari's spread fingers and stabbed into the wood.

"What are you doing?" Eliza asked in horror.

"You haven't been the only one working on your weakness every day."

Burton looked over Eliza's shoulder to see that the kitchen knife stuck out from the centre of a triangle Nefertari had carved into the bar.

Burton walked outside and looked at the gladius sticking into the tree trunk. It was wedged up to the hilt. He gripped the bone handle and pulled. It was jammed tight. He took a deep breath, then pressed his foot against the bark for purchase and yanked again. Every muscle strained under immense pressure until he finally flew backwards onto the grass with the sword in his hand. He stood and pointed the sap-covered gladius into the air, imagining himself on a promotional poster for a Hollywood blockbuster. *Well, I guess I might be worthy after all…*

CHAPTER 20
DEAD AHEAD

Burton and Eliza waited until morning before heading to Gateshead, a large town on the other side of the River Tyne. Heat waves made the road ahead appear to ripple, and it wasn't even midday. They drove past the Angel of the North, a huge copper-coloured sculpture of a figure with rectangular wings. The corrugated titan overlooked the surrounding area.

Eliza glanced up. "How tall d'you think that is? A hundred feet?"

"Maybe less? I'd love to have a massive statue made of me," Burton replied, daydreaming as he looked at it through the window of the passenger seat.

"Are you a wannabe dictator as well? Do all Burtons just want everyone to bow down to them?" Eliza asked.

"I mean for doing something worthy of remembrance. Although, I can't deny it would be nice if someone listened to me now and again."

"I listen," Eliza said as she changed gear.

"Would you listen to my orders?"

"I doubt it – only if I was still waitressing. How would you like your steak, sir?" Eliza said, mimicking a high-pitched southern American accent. "Actually, let me guess – well done?"

"Correct," Burton replied.

"Anyway, it's just a massive angel. It's not of anyone in particular."

"I know that. But you see footballers by the stadium, or military leaders dotted around."

"Look at the statues pulled down in the London riots. Some were of slave traders. Get them in the bottom of a river and leave them there."

"But on the flipside, you could get one if you scored 206 goals for Newcastle Utd."

"Well, if you want to be immortalised, you better get busy. I don't think you're going to break into professional football at your age, even with the Elixir and a new pair of boots. Look, we're getting close. I'll park up at the Angel and we can walk from there."

Burton laid the gladius in the footwell and exited the car without it. He didn't want to draw any unwanted attention and also hoped their summer apparel would help them blend in. He was still wearing the Laughing Heart T-shirt with cut-off jeans, whilst Eliza wore her Apokolipstik T-shirt and black leggings.

"We're hardly dressed appropriately for a battle are we?" Burton asked.

"You're joking, aren't you? I'm sweating like a pig in a butchers. I couldn't cope in a tactical suit today."

"What if there's trouble?"

Eliza shook her head. "Do you always expect the worst? It can get a little draining. Let's just see what happens, yeah? Go with the flow. We're safer undercover."

"Sorry, I just like to be prepared. I'll stop moaning."

Burton rolled his shoulders and neck to loosen some of the tension as they walked toward the unknown. He glanced at Eliza again. She was looking cool in her new orange-framed sunglasses. *Man, we should've just gone to the beach and had a pint.*

～

The Vanderling building was situated in a winding business park. The weathered sign at the front entrance named over a dozen businesses: Garry's Garage, NOS Electronics, and Tools Worldwide, to name but a few. Burton felt less manly just reading it. As they walked further into the industrial park, they came across a forklift truck reversing and beeping. Men wearing hard hats and high-vis jackets were standing next to it. One of the workers shouted directions in a broad northern accent that even Burton found difficult to decipher.

A single BARRIER guard protected the front door of the Vanderling building in the distance.

"Not many women around, are there?" Eliza pointed out.

"They'd get wolf whistled to death," Burton replied.

"I wonder if there's a word for that."

"Me and my mate Adam used to say it was 'cocker block' if a pub had no girls inside," Burton reminisced.

Eliza laughed. "As in chocker block and full of cocks?"

"Exactly."

Eliza surveyed the front of the building, "Where is this pub? I like the sound of it. They'd get a smack in the chops if they whistled, though."

"There's no space to load anything here," Burton said. "Let's check out the back."

The pair fell silent as they approached the rear of the single-storey building.

"Fuck me. Look," Eliza whispered. A large black freight lorry was parked at the back of the building. It had a golden Biovax logo emblazoned across the side. A sweaty topless man in cargo shorts was using a pallet truck to pull a large crate onto a tail lift at the rear of the vehicle. His biceps were like footballs and his skinhead reflected the sun's rays. One BARRIER guard, #24, stood by the truck as the man worked.

"He's loading something on," Burton said. "It might be the vials?"

"One way to find out."

Eliza put her purple hair into pigtails and jogged forward, away from Burton.

"Wait." Burton hissed.

The guard held out his taser as he edged towards her. "Stay there, Miss. Not one step closer." He pressed the side of his helmet. "Random girl at the back entrance. Looks ditzy. No back-up required. I'll move her on."

Eliza started talking to the labourer like a stereotypical dumb blonde. "Hey mister, I've been trying to put my bed together and it won't fasten. D'you know where I could get some good screws?"

The labourer looked at Eliza and whistled. "Alright, darlin', if you want a good screw, I'm your man." He had a cockney accent and started smiling like he couldn't believe his luck. He walked over and patted the metal shoulder pad of the guard as if to say, *'It's okay, I've got this covered'*.

"You've got enormous arms," Eliza said flirtatiously, touching his bicep.

"I just have to finish this one job, petal."

"No, I need the screws now. Just take me. Show me where the shop is, and I might let you test the bed out later?"

She can make guys do whatever she wants. It's like hypnosis.

"You have a job to do – get on with it." #24 ordered as he lowered the taser.

"Come on, pal. I'm just helping this damsel in distress. I'll be a few minutes." The labourer winked at the guard. "Come on, man, it's bro code."

"Five minutes, or you'll be reported and removed from your position."

"It'll have to be a quicky. Come with me." The labourer

beckoned Eliza toward an entrance covered by thin PVC drapes. She turned and mimicked the cockney's dim wink to Burton as he led her away through the translucent flaps.

What do I do now? I've only got five minutes. I need to take out the guard. How, though? Look at that armour. Burton looked around for inspiration. *If I attack him, he'll alert his mate. He'd kick my arse anyway.*

The guard strolled around the truck and casually checked his environment. A rustling came from the branches of a nearby tree, and the guard blasted his taser up with lightning-fast reaction. Two thin yellow cables zipped out of his weapon, and a small creature exploded. Blood splattered across the green leaves. The guard pressed a button on the handle, and the cords wound back into the barrel to charge.

"Four squirrels terminated. I'm two ahead now," the guard boasted with his hand to his ear; he was mimicking the Austrian accent of an iconic action movie star.

The sound attracted him. Maybe I could lure him away. I'm running out of time.

Burton picked up a broken piece of concrete and looked around to see three rusty yellow skips, twenty metres away. Two looked full, but one was empty, with *leaker* sprayed in white paint along the front.

Here we go. Let's see if empty vessels really do make the most noise.

Burton threw the concrete. It skimmed off a wet piece of wood and into the leaker with a clang.

The guard aimed fast and edged towards the skip before remembering his weapon hadn't charged. He holstered it and moved closer. Burton used the huge black truck to provide cover between them. He crouched down and hurried toward the crate that was just about to be loaded via the tail lift. The metal hinges of the crate creaked as he peeped underneath the lid. *Jackpot.*

The box contained empty pyramid vials stacked neatly.

Burton took one from inside, but then heard armour clunking closer beside the lorry. He eased the lid back down, but the creak of its hinges made the guard's footsteps halt. Burton slid to the side and placed his back against one of the enormous rear wheels. *I can't budge or I'll be seen.*

"Thank you so much, Marco. Call me later when you've finished," Eliza said with a raised voice from behind the PVC flaps. The guard was examining the crate mere metres away, but now his footsteps moved toward Eliza's voice.

"You've been four minutes and fifty-six seconds. You almost lost your job, Marco."

"Be cool, twenty-four, we're back already."

Burton remained crouched and rushed back to the gate. He let out a sigh of relief as he pressed his back up against the outer wall, then peered over his shoulder.

"Never abandon your task again, even if another trollop passes by. Keep your head down while I move the slag on. Do you understand?"

Eliza waved her index finger at #24. "Hey, tin man, shut your fucking face. You shouldn't talk about women like that."

"What's a little flat-chested tart like you going to do about it? Go away and grow yourself some tits."

Eliza handed her packet of screws to Marco. "What am *I* going to do about it?"

"Oh, scary," #24 mocked.

No, no, no. Don't do it. Burton shook his head, hoping Eliza would see. He flashed the vial in her direction.

Eliza used her left foot to hoof the guard on the side of his knee – a part of the body that wasn't armoured or padded. After he was knocked off balance, she cracked his nose with a straight right. The taser in his holster pinged; it had charged.

The guard staggered back, holding his face. Burton ran at him from behind and grabbed his left arm before he could press the communicator. #24 drew his recharged taser, but Eliza pushed his wrist up into the air as he let the shot go. She kneed the guard in the stomach repeatedly, and he wheezed as all the air left his body. As Burton pushed off the helmet from behind, Eliza cracked #24 with a right hook and his teeth scattered across the tarmac like dice. He was knocked out cold on the hottest day of the year.

"I'm a 36C, you piece of shit," Eliza said as she leant over the unconscious guard, who had fallen backward onto Burton.

Her temper was something else. Burton crawled out from underneath the guard.

Marco stood clutching the packet of screws. "I think your boobs look lovely," he said, besotted. He held out the packet for Eliza.

"It's okay. I think I might just have a few loose, but I'm fine with that. You keep 'em." Eliza smiled and walked off.

Sorry, mate, it's straws you're clutching at. Bit like myself.

A muffled voice came from inside the empty helmet. Burton placed it on his head and heard a voice saying, "Are you deaf? I asked you if that was squirrel number five."

Impressions weren't his strong point, but Burton went for it. "Five terminated." He threw down the helmet and jogged after Eliza.

"I'll call you!" Marco shouted from the distance. Eliza ignored him.

She bossed Burton out of the gate. "Come on, you dummy. Let's get into position."

"*I'm* the dummy? You just put them on high alert. What now?"

"We wait and follow the van. Nicoli is sure to show."

"Isn't it weird that there were only two guards?" Burton asked.

"Well, it's just the containers. There's nothing valuable inside," Eliza replied.

"Paddy said they were important. I've told you; he was a chess champion. It doesn't feel right."

"I don't know. Let's not look a gift horse in the mouth, yeah?"

At the mention of 'horse', Burton was stirred by the memory of Cal's party and his Elixir dream state. *Christ, so much has happened since I first seen her sitting on the wall.*

There was only one entrance into the business park. They returned to the car and drove closer to the Vanderling building now they had the lie of the land.

"We could wait all day," Burton moaned.

"It's a stakeout. They could move at any time, might be two minutes."

"It could be hours." Burton let out a sigh.

"Then I guess we'll have to wait. Lucky for you, I've got the glove box of your dreams."

"Excuse me?"

Eliza reached with her left hand to open the glove box compartment, revealing an Aladdin's cave of snacks. "There's some salt & vinegar nuts, cheese & onion crisps, a bottle of Coke and a bar of chocolate. Help yourself."

"I love Nolbertos' Nuts. You're well stocked up." Burton grabbed the packet.

"That's not all – dig a little deeper," Eliza teased.

Burton touched a smooth, cold plastic shape with rubbery buttons. "No. Way. Is this what I think it is?" he asked.

"Yes. Way," Eliza replied, mimicking him perfectly.

Burton pulled out a handheld gaming system with an LCD screen and a bright pink custom border.

"It's not the newest one, I couldn't afford it. Three games, though: *Tiger Alliance*, *Velocity Raptors* and *Shogunner 8*."

"This is outstanding. All my favourite things in one car. We can take turns. You've played a blinder here."

Eliza turned away, trying to hide her smile. "One of us still needs to keep watch."

Hours passed. They spent it jumping, shooting, climbing, racing, solving puzzles and scoffing. The catchy, repetitive music and power-up sound effects of *Velocity Raptors* filled the car.

"Do you think we can follow the truck without being seen?" Eliza asked. "The roads will be empty later. By the way, I'm so beating your time on the Wicked Ravine level."

"It's rush hour now. We've got a few hours at least. Wait, hang on – look." To Burton's surprise, the huge black truck edged out of the junction and came to a halt at the traffic lights.

"They're moving at the busiest time? That doesn't make any sense." Eliza threw the game device into Burton's lap and put the key into the ignition. "At least it'll be relatively easy to stay hidden." She moved within a few cars of the truck as it crawled towards the green light. The pursuit was on.

"Maybe broad daylight gives protection for the transport?" Burton wondered aloud as they followed.

"This is going to be the slowest car chase ever," Eliza replied, looking dead ahead. "Wait, there are road signs on the bridge. There weren't any earlier. They're saying the Tyne Bridge is closed. They never close it apart from during the Great North Run."

Burton scratched his stubbly cheek. "I doubt maintenance would start during rush hour. Something's up."

The Biovax truck drove straight past the signs blocking the road and onto the empty bridge. Surrounding cars honked their horns in disbelief.

"Looks like they've made themselves a shortcut. Here we go." Eliza gripped the wheel and gave it a sharp tug to follow the truck.

Suddenly, there was a gigantic explosion at the far end of the Tyne Bridge; fire and smoke billowed up. Eliza smashed the brakes to perform an emergency stop, making the hand-held game fall off Burton's lap. As he reached down to the floor, he felt the cold bronze pommel of the gladius graze against the backs of his fingers. He picked it up.

"What the fuck was that? Should I reverse?" Eliza was looking back over her shoulder. There was a hissing sound followed by a trail of thin white smoke; Burton turned to see that four cars had exploded behind them. Hopefully the drivers had abandoned their vehicles before the missile hit, it was impossible to tell.

"They're firing fucking rockets. Get to the side of the bridge, now!" Eliza yelled.

"We're trapped." Burton rolled out of the car and crawled on his elbows to the left edge of the bridge. Eliza moved to the right. Burton clipped the gladius scabbard to the belt of his jean shorts. The skin of his elbows and knees was grazed as quickly as it healed. *The cult is ambushing the truck and we're caught in the middle.*

Then he heard Nicoli's gravelly voice from the far end of the bridge. Burton looked up to see him walking towards the Biovax transport. "Get out of the truck now and I may spare you, driver. You have ten seconds."

Metal clicked together as Nicoli reloaded an RPG launcher. *They don't use guns, but they fire rockets?*

Burton lay with his chest and chin on the pavement. A sign had been fastened to the bridge next to him that read *DON'T JUMP, YOU HAVE WORTH*. Flaming carcasses of a fire engine and maintenance vehicle blocked the road ahead. Nicoli stood alone with an RPG launcher resting on his shoulder. He glanced over in Burton's direction. Burton longed for the time when all RPG had meant to him was 'Role Playing Game'.

"Ah, two for the price of one. This was never my style, but Muhktar convinced me to try and be more direct. Some people only listen if you're loud." Nicoli grinned through his thick black beard and patted the top of his launcher like a pet.

"You'll fucking pay for what you did!" Eliza shouted as she stood up. She extended her silver metal spear with the press of a button.

"Make that three for the price of one. Tell me, how is that gender-confused freak? Did he live?" Nicoli snarled and made a spiralling motion with his index finger. Burton looked behind him to see two hunters approaching them.

"Eliza, behind us. Caballion!" Burton shouted.

"Driver, you have five seconds. Four. Three." Nicoli took aim as he continued to count down.

The driver exited the truck and put his hands behind his head. He was tall and lean. Burton struggled to make out his features behind the helmet visor. There was a yellow #1 on his grey armoured chest plate.

"Tell me your name, followed swiftly by the next delivery date on the schedule. If you lie, I will murder your entire family. Speak now, before I put a rocket in between your teeth."

"I am Number One, the commander of BARRIER." The elite guard touched his earpiece. "Now! Take them alive."

"Wrong answer." Nicoli lifted the RPG, but at the same time #1 drew his taser and fired electrified cables into Nicoli's skeletal vest. The Greek didn't flinch; the bone armour had stopped the electricity conducting. The shutter at the rear of the truck opened and multiple BARRIER soldiers emerged.

"Make that about twenty-five for the price of one."

The commander yanked on the taser cords, and the sudden pull made Nicoli stumble forward and drop the launcher. Half of the guards moved in as he drew his scimitar. The Greek maimed the first two mercilessly with wild slashes to their necks. The others slowed their advance as Nicoli begged for them to take him on. Commander #1 threw the

RPG over the side, before locking his gaze on the vicious Column.

Meanwhile, the remaining guards at the rear of the truck pointed their tasers and electrified batons at all targets, including Burton and Eliza.

"Get down on the ground now!" one guard ordered, but the hunters continued to walk nonchalantly toward them.

The Caballion took longer strides to close the remaining space. Their metal weapons clashed against BARRIER armour as they entered close-quarters combat. As Burton had witnessed before, they threw down canisters and fought within black smoke. Leather straps flapped around their waist as they pirouetted between precise strikes and stabs with their spears.

"Heat vision!" a trooper instructed, and they adjusted their helmets accordingly. They had been briefed and prepared.

Glancing behind him, Burton saw that Nicoli had been overpowered at the cost of several more soldiers. They had his arms behind his back and his face pressed into the ground.

"Doesn't look like you expected this one, did you?" the commander yelled into Nicoli's ear.

Eliza cracked the helmet off one guard and shoved the butt of her spear into his throat. He let out a noise that Burton had never heard before, like a pigeon squawking into a wet tomato. She crouched low and swept the legs of another guard who ran in behind her. It was as if she had developed a sixth sense.

Trying to keep his back to the edge of the bridge, Burton ducked under a baton as it swung for his head. There was no choice: he drew the gladius from its sheath and pointed it towards an oncoming aggressor. His arm was shaking, and his nerves seemed to transfer all the way to the tip of his quivering blade.

"Careful you don't cut yourself," #84 taunted.

Burton recognised the guard's change in movement in preparation for an incoming attack. He stepped to one side, making the guard miss him by six inches. Solid training had quickened his reactions. The baton clanged across the railing of the bridge as he dodged another attack. The inaccurate strike had presented the easy target of an outstretched arm. In that split second, Burton channelled every rejection he'd ever had and hacked down with a primal scream. #84 dropped to the floor and cried out in agony as his arm was severed, the bone splintering like the snapped stick of an ice lolly. A surge of power almost immobilised Burton, but the gladius became steadier in his hand.

The Caballion lit red flares and moved at speed to nullify the heat vision capability of the guards. They were adapting. At one point, they were back-to-back with Burton as a helicopter thundered above.

"Cease your antisocial behaviour," a pre-recorded voice boomed.

It burned his senses out. All Burton could see were the ripples of electrical batons rising high into the black and red clouds. He heard Eliza shout out in pain, distracting him further. A random strike hit him in the stomach. Another bashed into his chest and sent him stumbling backwards towards the front of the Biovax truck.

"Clever, huh? A trap within a trap," he heard the commander shouting in Nicoli's ear.

"Within a trap. Some people only listen if you're loud," Nicoli repeated. He sounded cocky for someone with his face pressed into the ground.

Another trap? No…

Burton sheathed his weapon, twisted, and pushed off on his right foot in the direction of Eliza's grunts. She resembled a punch-drunk boxer against the ropes and the outnumbering guards were beating her relentlessly. Burton charged through them and used his momentum to carry Eliza over the side. He pulled his bloodied friend into an embrace as they hurtled down. The heat of a third explosion came from above, like someone had opened a huge oven door. Burton closed his eyes seconds before they hit the water. *God loves a trier…*

Every bone in his legs should have shattered on impact and the undercurrent should have dragged them both to a murky grave, but neither happened. Burton had vitality, energy, and strength. He ignored the pain and battled through the water, fighting against the blood of his city. The Tyne had sent a thousand ships to war, but now was waging one of its own on anyone who entered.

She is not yours…

Burton held Eliza tight as he pulled with his free hand and kicked with everything he had. Shrapnel and screws from the broken bridge zipped into the water like deadly metal rain. Each blast of energy got him closer to the edge, but the current was trying to drag their bodies downward. Burton pushed up and up while shielding Eliza from harm. *Not like this. You can't take her away, not again…*

Gradually, he manoeuvred closer to the side of the river. All he could hear was chaos each time he bobbed up for air. A hand was stretching from a ladder on the quayside.

"Over here!" voices yelled, distorted from underneath the water.

Burton pushed Eliza toward the outstretched arm and looked back to see the Tyne Bridge collapse in on itself.

CHAPTER 21
FATBERG IN THE RAVECAVE

Burton opened his eyes. He coughed and spluttered as dirty river water escaped from every hole onto an old mattress. Sitting up, he moved to the edge of the bed and placed his bare feet on the rubbery floor. Everything was blurry. It was hard for him to even see his own fingers.

"Where am I? Where is she?" Burton shouted, wiping at his eyes and face. He stood on jelly legs and waved his arm in different directions. He hadn't felt this vulnerable since his escape from the Warerooms, when every car had seemed like a vicious beast approaching. *Come on! Elixir, do your thing.*

"You've certainly found your voice since the last time we met."

Burton couldn't fail to recognise the colossal outline and voice. Nobody had a stature like Kolo Holloway.

"Kolo?" Burton relaxed but kept rubbing and squinting his eyes.

"Got it in one."

"Where am I? Where's Eliza?"

"Your girl is resting in the room next door. My wife is in there, don't worry. Here." Kolo threw a towel at Burton, but it hit him in the face; he hadn't been able to react. "You're in the

Bigg Market – the Sugarcane Club, to be precise. I used to bounce here back in the day, but now it's another Maslow building."

"Maslow Fairchild? Is there anything he doesn't own?"

"Yeah, the businessman. Most of the pubs have closed, people don't have much disposable income anymore. Maslow has been buying up businesses and offering some of his real estate to the homeless. It's great PR. Some folk say he's going to run for Prime Minister one day. Cal recovered, but he stopped throwing his parties and I was out of a job. I applied to keep the peace here. I've had some unholy scraps of late."

As Kolo became more visible, Burton noticed he had bandages around his knuckles, butterfly stitches above his left eye, and a couple of nasty scars on his forearms.

"How many people live like this?" Burton asked.

"Feels like half of Newcastle, and it's only increased since the news of the third wave broke. I was on my way here to start my shift and saw bodies being pulled from the water; I didn't even realise it was you at first. Then *boom*, the bridge disintegrated." Kolo mimed an explosion.

Burton squelched back into his trainers and looked around. The once-vibrant dancefloor of the Sugarcane Club was now filled with rows of basic bunk beds with thin black frames and white sheet covers. Scattered around each bed was a mix of expensive designer bags, branded sports holdalls and supermarket carrier bags. They all appeared to be full of the essentials to live, such as tinned food and water. Burton glanced out of an arched window and saw more homeless people congregating below them at the entrance of the building. *They must be waiting for a chance to get a roof over their heads.*

Burton looked around for Eliza.

"She's over there. Apologies for separating you, but there are hardly any beds," Kolo said, pointing her out.

Eliza was lying unconscious on a top bunk. A greasy-haired shirtless man wearing baggy orange pants stood below her. His left hand was touching her bare feet, and the right was rummaging around in his crotch.

"Hey, get off her! I'll fucking kill you!" Burton moved forward, but Kolo's tree-trunk arm stopped him.

"What are you doing, Mr Harris? You've been warned about this kind of thing before. For the love of god, the girl isn't even awake." The deep timbre of Kolo's voice filled the room without effort.

The other lodgers were uninterested; this must have been happening regularly. Burton circled the slimeball.

"I've done nothing, you dumb nig—"

"Get your things together and leave," Kolo ordered, without reacting to the beginning of the foulest possible insult.

"I've got nowhere to go. You're such a big man, aren't you?" The fetishist was hard to read. He switched from fear to bravado and back again every five seconds.

Burton noticed a glimmer at the back of Harris's baggy orange pants. He was reaching for it.

"Kolo, knife!" Burton shouted.

The pervert screamed as his flick knife bounced off the floor. Kolo had grabbed the lunging arm and twisted it.

"I tried to give you a chance," Kolo said. He sighed as he frog-marched Harris away.

Eliza appeared peaceful as she lay on the bed with her eyes closed. Despite the fall, she was unscathed and without any cuts or bumps. There was a sound like a heavy suitcase being slung onto a baggage carousel; Burton glanced out of an arched window. Kolo had thrown Harris down the stone steps. The pervert limped away as Kolo allowed a new tenant to enter.

"Tyra, Tyra, where you at?" Kolo asked when he returned.

A small lady wearing a light blue pinafore over a white blouse came in carrying a bucket of water and a cloth.

"I told you to watch her, babe. Where've you been?"

"I thought you said, 'wash her'. I was just getting some clean water to wipe her face, babe. She's filthy."

"Harris was up to his old tricks again, so I asked him to leave."

"I told you to kick the creep out last time."

"He's gone. That's the end of it." Kolo turned. "Jonny, this is my wife, Tyra. Tyra, this is my old school friend, Jonny,"

She gave Burton a warm smile.

"Pleased to meet you. What do you do here?" Burton asked.

"I volunteer. It's good for the soul. Plus, I just feel safer around my man. We're living through dark days."

"You can say that again," Burton said with a nod. "They do say that in times of tragedy that you should look to those trying to help."

"A lot of people are in need, and it's getting worse. It's absolute mayhem outside. What's happened to the bridge?" Tyra looked to Kolo for answers.

"I was hoping Jonny could tell us, considering he was just fished out of the Tyne."

"Maybe the news will shed some light on it. We were just walking across the bridge and before we knew it we were here," Burton replied. He played ignorant, keeping an eye on Eliza at all times.

Residents were watching an old TV in a breakout space. Tyra mopped the dirt from Eliza's face, brow, and neck as they listened. The headline *Terror on the Tyne* flashed up on the screen, then cut to a close-up of the anchor, Kim Knowles.

"Good evening. The Tyne Bridge, a defining symbol of the North East, has been destroyed. Police are calling it a potential terrorist attack and are urging Newcastle residents to stay away from the quayside and city centre until they can confirm the streets are safe.

"Phone footage from a jogger captured the catastrophe. It shows a Biovax transport being halted by a man in black. The following

images are harrowing, and some viewers may wish to look away now."

The video showed the Tyne Bridge from a distance as the Biovax lorry screeched to a halt. Amid the fire and smoke, all that was visible were stick men battling. Two silhouettes dropped from the bridge and explosions ignited all along the underside until it crumbled.

"We can now speak to Patrick Burton, head of Biovax. Patrick, hello."

"Hi, Kim."

"Are you able to shed any light on what has happened this afternoon?"

"I think I can, Kim. First, I need to address all the families of our brave BARRIER guards. Please have hope. We have teams searching the entire area for survivors."

"We echo that. It's a tragedy. Has anyone been found?"

"The BARRIER commander pulled himself from a pile of twisted metal only moments ago. He might make it. We've spoken."

"That's good news. What happened? What was in the truck?"

"The truck was a decoy. Over the last couple of months, we have been trying to transport large numbers of Elixir containers to Biovax HQ. You may have seen me display them in promotional material. A terrorist cell has been intercepting the trucks and destroying them. As you can imagine, it has slowed production."

"There has been a lot of pressure on you from those ready to purchase. Some have suggested it's merely a marketing ploy, but Biovax has over-promised and under-delivered before. Are you worried that you won't meet the demand?" Kim asked.

"It hasn't helped. Everyone must remember this process is revolutionary, and genius takes time."

"Sorry to halt the interview, Mr Burton. For those fond of the bridge, I'm just receiving breaking news in my ear that Maslow Fairchild has promised to fund a full rebuild, and work will begin as soon as the area is safe. An early social media poll suggests that the new bridge will be completely flat, in order to appease the two

percent of voters who were offended by the curve of the previous structure." Kim turned her attention back to Patrick. *"Sorry again, Mr Burton, I'm sure you won't mind hearing of your friend's generosity."*

"Not at all. That's great news."

"Do you have any idea who the terrorists are? We know you've had run-ins with activist groups before, such as Three Blind Mice."

"The Commander shared a report, and it's my understanding that a group known as the Cult of Asklepios are opposing me. We cannot even begin our process until we stabilise production. It breaks my heart to tell you that my brother's girlfriend Eliza Contra is a member of this group. If you see either of them, please contact the police and ask for Detective Glover. She's dangerous. Jonny has been brainwashed."

The faces of Burton and Eliza flashed on the screen. It was the picture Patrick had taken when Eliza was giving him a massage. In a different context, it would have looked comical; the look on his face was one of pure ecstasy.

Everyone in the vicinity stared at Burton, including Kolo. A whispering circle formed. Instinctively, Burton stepped towards Eliza's bunk bed to protect her.

"These people have given everything to save up for a cure," Kolo said. "Their homes, their bodies, their dignity, and God knows what else. Give me one reason why I shouldn't let them rip you apart." He gave Burton a look worse than he'd given Harris.

Burton heard Tyra putting her water bucket down behind him, then soapy water sloshing onto the floor.

Eliza coughed and spluttered in her bed. She was waking up.

"Wait. Eliza, don't move," Burton said as she came to her senses. He turned his attention back to the residents. "I can explain. We weren't trying to stop the truck; we were trying to help it get through. We just got caught in the middle."

"Middle of what?" a stranger asked.

"The cult and BARRIER," Burton replied.

"That's rubbish. He's trying to save his skin," an exhausted-looking woman shouted.

"Do you know what my wife has been through to get anywhere near enough money?" A man put his hairy arm around his significant other with tears in his eyes. Other members of the crowd began sharing their own tales, getting louder as they all struggled to be heard. One angry man stepped forward, only to be blocked by Kolo.

Burton tried to explain. "We think it's inhumane to charge so much. It's unfair to everyone. I've tried to tell Patrick. He's just turning you against us."

"Where are we?" Eliza held her head and rubbed her eyes. "Who are all these people? Kolo? Is that you, Jon?"

She dropped to the floor from the top bunk and stood unsteadily beside Burton. She linked her arm around his to balance herself as she slid her feet into her trainers.

The rabble continued to give their reasons to be added to Patrick's list. Most of it was incoherent.

"They think you blew up the Tyne Bridge," Burton whispered to Eliza. She seemed far more fragile than normal and was shaking from top to bottom.

"Look at their eyes glowing green." A teenage girl with dreadlocks pointed out.

"They've already had it – maybe they have more," someone else suggested. The sweaty circle closed in, looking to Kolo for the all-clear to pounce.

"We wanted to see where these were made." Eliza opened Burton's soggy backpack and held out the empty pyramid vial.

The crowd all yelled over each other, not realising it was just the casing.

"She has it."

"They have an Elixir!"

"Give it to me."

"We deserve it more than anyone."

"It could cure the children."

"Oh my god, it's here."

"Get it off them, Tony."

"How much can we offer them? What do you have?"

"Lad, she'll do anything. She's good, anything you can think of. Just give it to us."

Eliza held the pyramid vial in front of her like a grenade without a pin. "One step closer and I'll smash it onto the floor."

The attention of the crowd was diverted as Detective Glover's voice shouted up the stone stairs from the entrance. "We believe this Maslow building is housing a wanted terrorist – Eliza Contra. Come out with your hands above your head."

"That pervert must have grassed us up," Burton whispered.

"What pervert?" Eliza asked without taking her eyes from the crowd.

"I'll tell you later."

"Make a path behind us toward a window."

Burton edged the crowd out of the way as Eliza mimicked smashing the vial on the floor.

"We'll have to jump," Burton said, attempting to slide it open. "It's jammed."

"Stop right there!" Glover had seen them through the bodies, and now tried to push himself closer.

"You want this? Here you go." Burton grabbed the vial and threw it over to Glover, who caught it before slipping on the wet floor. Around thirty people dived on top of the detective in the biggest 'pile-on' Burton had seen since high school. Several officers tried to assist him but didn't make physical contact for fear of being reprimanded.

"What are you doing? I'm a policeman. Have some respect!" Glover's voice was the only thing that could escape the mound of bodies. The crowd argued on the pile and wrestled each other.

"Give me it."

"Where has it gone?"

"Who has it? I'll kill you."

This was their chance to get away.

"How high are we?" Eliza asked Burton.

"The first floor, I think. Maybe the second."

He inhaled deeply, then took two steps back. He ran at the window and shattered through the thick glass. As his feet hit the pavement, pain shot up through his legs and into his back. He collapsed. A second later, Eliza thudded off the ground beside him and cracked her head off the concrete.

"Eliza!"

As Burton stood, his body felt like it was dealing with severe trauma from the landing. Sharp stabbing pains shot up his legs and spine. He felt damaged, but they needed to keep going. He hoisted Eliza up by the armpits.

"Pretty spontaneous, Frosty – that's more like it," Eliza muttered, forcing a grin. She could barely open her eyes.

Burton wrapped her left arm across his shoulder, and they limped along the cobbled street. Within minutes they reached the end of an alley, where blue lights flashed in either direction.

Burton couldn't bear the thought of them taking her away from him.

"Where can we go? There'll be blockades everywhere. You're a wanted terrorist," Burton said. He looked around frantically for an escape route and something caught his eye. "Remember *Knightsblood 2*, when the Morality Knight used the underground caves to evade the Dragon Lord? Is that too crazy?" He gestured down at a grate on the street.

"We've got no choice. You don't have a peg for my nose though, do you?" Eliza crouched gingerly and heaved up the drain cover. "Here, hold this."

Burton held the edge as she jammed her staff into a small gap to pry it open further.

"Oh my god, it stinks." They both retched and turned their faces away from the drain.

"But the disease, the dirt," Burton said, mortified.

"You can't catch anything from stuff like that anymore, remember? The bright lights up here are hurting my head, anyway."

Eliza climbed down a ladder, and Burton had no choice but to follow. They were like two rats scurrying into a hole.

"Christ, this is the worst thing I've smelt in my entire life." Burton dropped from the grimy ladder and splashed onto the floor. The sewer was narrow, dark, and rectangular.

"D'you think I can't smell it?"

"No, but—"

"Stop bloody whinging about it, then. Oh, thanks for saving my life, though."

"You're welcome. It's mad how we can see down here. Has the Elixir given us night vision? I don't think we'll understand what we can and can't do until we've lived with it for a while."

They came to a grey concrete archway with the graffitied word *RAVECAVE* spray-painted along the top in thick white lettering.

"I remember seeing something about kids partying in a sewer near the Tyne Bridge. Wonder if it was here?" Burton pondered.

"Shitty venue," Eliza said as she sploshed along.

"Literally. Who the hell would want to party down here?" Burton half expected to hear the ghostly laugh of a deceased child.

They ducked under the arch and entered a larger square space. Upon a raised concrete platform were the remains of a lighting rig. An old red generator lay dormant in the corner.

"They must've used that to power the lights and music," Eliza said, walking over to it.

"Hardly looks safe, does it? Kids are so bloody stupid."

"Illegal, underground and rave are three words that will always get teenage tongues a-talkin. They probably had it during lockdown when they weren't allowed to party. Fair play to them."

"Fair play? Someone could've been electrocuted."

Eliza shrugged. "Part of the fun, isn't it?"

"Remind me to never accept a party invite from you in the future," Burton joked.

"Even if I let you kiss my collarbone?"

"Shut up! I can't believe you even remember that."

Eliza squatted down and looked at the generator. "D'you reckon this still works? I wouldn't mind seeing this hovel in all of its glory. It's not plugged in anywhere. Stinks of petrol, though." She pulled a cord to rev it up, but nothing happened.

"Wonder if that has any in?" A red plastic petrol can was floating in the sewage water in the corner. Burton fetched it, shook the can, and trickled what remained into the generator.

"Here we go." Eliza pulled the cord again, and the machine revved into a chunter. "It's alive!" she shouted, and the echo of her voice filled the halls of filth.

Dim lights sparked across the rig and *RAVECAVE* appeared in a variety of neon colours on every spare inch of the wall. Droves of rats looked as if they were having a mini rave of their own around the edges of the square space.

"The kids used a black-light rig," Burton commented. "That's clever."

"Looks pretty cool. The rats seem to like it."

A speaker sizzled as it played a distorted version of the dance classic 'Love Reload' by Watercooler Crew. A fat rat sitting on top seemed to be enjoying the vibration, until the music died after ten seconds.

Eliza pointed. "Look at that big one – he reminds me of my old fiancé."

Burton didn't react. "Listen, Eliza, before we move on, can I speak to you about something?"

"Sure, but make it quick."

"In the Maslow building, I walked in on a guy touching your feet and rubbing himself. We sorted him out."

Eliza scrunched up the corner of her mouth and shook her head. "It's okay. There are creeps everywhere. He's not the first and he won't be the last. I've got used to it now. Thanks for getting rid of the sicko for me."

"That's not all."

"What else?"

"I'm sorry if I've made you feel uncomfortable. You've tried to be my friend, but I couldn't see past how pretty and sexy you are. It's like I've tried to pursue you rather than just getting to know you. I'm not like the other scumbags, and I don't want to be. I want to be better."

"You're sweet. Look, I'm as friendly as I am flirty, and I use it a lot. People see me as a mad pixie girl, but it's just been my way of coping with everything over the last few years. It's been so hard, and I'm not always myself. Anyway, I've never thought about you as anything threatening. Honestly, I think you're quite unique in a good way. I must be rubbing off on you."

"There you go again," Burton said with a smile.

Eliza gave another wicked little grin in return. Their green eyes locked in the neon hollow as they traded future memories.

"Seriously though, you're more than that," Burton said. "You're confident, hilarious, spontaneous and just, well... so damn cool. You've got a spirit that I've never seen in anyone. Speaking with you makes me feel like... like what I imagine Dante Gabriel Rossetti felt painting Beata Beatrix, or—"

"Please stop. Christ, you lay it on thick, don't you? I'm not some heavenly creature. You've not mentioned that I'm thirty and I can't form any kind of friendship or relationship that lasts. Must be a reason for that, right? Or that my eyes are too big for my face and I look like an alien. You know what they called me in high school? Roswell. And if I'm so perfect, why did my fiancé leave me? D'you know that I went to see *Knightsblood 2* by myself? I took a pad and paper so people would think I was a reviewer instead of a loner. Sad, isn't it? The quicker you stop looking for perfection, the quicker you'll get a date."

"True perfection has to be imperfect," Burton mumbled.

"Whatever." She rolled her eyes. "Look, there's a torch over there."

Dismissing Burton's compliments, she splashed over to a collapsible chair that had fallen on its side. She produced a rubber torch and shone it under her chin to make a spooky face.

"Let's go," she said.

They waded for an hour through stinking corridors and brown water that became deeper and deeper. Burton was so embarrassed that he wasn't sure what to say or do. The smell was also getting worse; it reeked of rotting meat.

"What the hell is that?" Burton could see a huge, light pink square blocking the entire route through. It was shiny and bulging, like the bodybuilder's veiny, oiled bicep at Cal's party.

"Christ, it's a fatberg," Eliza answered.

"What the hell is a fatberg?"

"I heard about them on the radio. It's a congealed mass of all the stuff that shouldn't be flushed."

"It's like something out of a horror film." The flesh-coloured mass appeared to rumble as if it were alive.

"I'll be right back..." Eliza said, quoting the popular horror line and mimicked nervous shaking, before extending her staff and jamming it into the blockage.

"Rank," Burton said, watching on.

"Are you going to help or what?"

As Burton got closer, he made out condoms, crisp packets and wet wipes. He drew his gladius and sliced at the mass as if it were a gammon joint. Some bits were softer than others. He had flashbacks to the BARRIER guard's arm and felt sick to his stomach.

"Was there anything on the radio about how thick these things are?" Burton asked.

"Think they're random. One was the size of an elephant."

"Great." Matted sewage dropped into the water as Burton stabbed at it. Although he was sweating, he couldn't bear to wipe his mucky arm across his brow.

Eliza continued to prod and twist. "That was an example of a small one. There was a fatberg in London the size of eleven double-decker buses."

They excavated for hours before creating a slippery gap just big enough to edge through. The fatberg became harder the closer they got to the centre.

"I'm done with being in here – we're getting out at the next ladder." Even Eliza sounded fed up, which wasn't her style.

Burton was a swamp creature, but at least the sewage level lowered to his ankles once they reached the other side.

"Finally, a fucking ladder." Eliza climbed up first and her denim legs dripped more filth all over Burton as he followed.

The fresh air hitting his nostrils was like a natural high; he'd almost got used to the putrid stench of Newcastle's bowels. A brown puddle formed at their feet on the pavement as they tried to get their bearings.

"Where are we? How far did we get?" Eliza asked.

"I think we're at the bottom of Gosforth High Street. The blockades are behind us now," Burton replied. He looked down the long street and shook his head at the economic downgrade of the area. "Most places have their shutters down indefinitely, but there still might be people around. We need to go before we're recognised."

Eliza wasn't listening. "Look over there, a massive gym. Are you thinking what I'm thinking?" She didn't wait for an answer and ran towards it.

"Wait, we'll be spotted. They'll smell us coming. Wait!" Burton ran after her as she sneaked around the back of the building.

"What are you doing?"

"Gyms are only allowed to open now if they're well ventilated. Most of them think that means keeping their fire escape doors slightly open. I never pay to work out. Come on." Eliza dragged him towards the fire escape.

She was right. They slid inside.

The walls were bright yellow and had motivational slogans written across them in a bold black font: *YOU ARE OVERPOWERED* and *BECOME THE META* greeted them as they entered. Chatting friends looked on from an elevated row of treadmills, a strongman squatted under enormous weight, and a lad with twig arms attempted to bench-press a bar with nothing attached. None of them paid much notice, they were only interested in bettering themselves. Burton followed Eliza to the men's changing room, slaloming between two exposed penises. *Put them away, for fuck's sake; it's so unnecessary.*

Eliza ran straight past the shower and to the next doorway. The unmistakable smell of chlorine hit them, and she paused for the first time as they reached the pool.

"Goodbye, stench." She stripped out of her stinking clothes before sprinting past the 'no running in the pool area' sign and cannonballing into the deep end. Her laugh echoed as she plunged under the surface.

Burton dropped his backpack, removed his own dishrag clothing and followed. They both bobbed up together. Eliza appeared angelic against the pattern of water rippling across the ceiling and tiled walls. She was a heavenly creature and nobody, including her, would ever change Burton's mind.

"This is the first time I've been wet today and not hated it," Eliza announced.

"Same. Pleased I don't have to carry you this time."

"You cheeky bastard. Are you saying I've eaten too much porridge?" Eliza laughed and splashed Burton's face.

"Hey!"

Eliza swam closer and spat out water. She was looking directly at him, and was just about to speak when an old man wearing goggles, a blue swim cap and long red and white trunks from the 1950's waddled in.

"We need to go," Burton said. "We can't keep messing around. We need to regroup with Nef."

Her face dropped.

Burton cupped his manhood with his left hand as he climbed out and shuffled in the general direction of his underpants.

"Never mind those, peachy, get over here!" Eliza shouted from a storage cupboard.

Swimming floats and armbands flew out the door as he walked toward it. First she threw a towel at him, followed by an XXL yellow staff T-shirt with *Level Up* written on the front, followed by a pair of navy-blue tracksuit bottoms. Eliza had put on a red *Level Up* sweatshirt and a pair of yellow lycra shorts.

"Comfy, aren't they? Let's get out of here."

As soon as Burton was ready, they exited via the fire escape and headed into a nearby street.

"Stop!" Nefertari called from the other side of the road.

"What are you doing here?" Eliza shouted back.

CHAPTER 22
UNBREAKABLE

Nefertari walked towards Burton and Eliza with the tracker in her hand. She carried a huge holdall across her back.

"The tracker in my staff was for emergencies only," Eliza said. She stomped her right foot slightly and sounded like a huffy teenager claiming their need for independence to a parent.

"That's what this is. We need to get off the street. Follow me." Nefertari looked both ways and crossed the road into a narrow side alley that led into Gosforth Park. The group sat on a wooden picnic bench surrounded by shrubs, trees and an overflowing bin. The parallel lines of trees formed a leafy archway over them. Burton could hear the moans of two Wimbledon wannabes as they volleyed a tennis ball back and forth nearby. It was a pleasant summer's evening, and the air was clear. Birds tweeted above them in the remaining light of day.

"When I saw what had happened at the Tyne Bridge, I feared for you," Nefertari said. "I hitchhiked. Tell me everything."

When Burton and Eliza were in the middle of explaining

recent events, Nefertari threw the tracker to the ground and yelled in frustration.

The tennis players' rally stopped and one of them looked over his shoulder in their direction.

"Shh!" Burton tried to calm his friend down. "What's wrong? I thought you would be pleased?"

"I wanted to do it. I wanted to be the one to kill Nicoli. Shit, *Kuso!*" Nefertari swore in her mother tongue.

"What about your hand?" Eliza asked.

"My hand is fine." Nefertari picked up the tracker and rattled it in front of Eliza. "If I can hold this, I can hold a weapon, and if I can hold a weapon, I can kill any man. We must move fast while Patrick is distracted."

"The heist?" Burton asked.

"Yes, we must save the children."

"Tonight?" Eliza added.

"Yes."

"Look at the state of us. We can't storm an evil headquarters dressed as personal trainers." Burton wasn't even joking as he looked down at his bright yellow *Level Up* T-shirt and Eliza's lycra shorts.

Nefertari patted the huge black holdall on the table. "For you both."

Burton unzipped the bag. It contained tactical clothing, as well as two tranq guns, a pair of Wayfinder binoculars, and two smoke bombs. His clothing looked slightly bulkier than Eliza's, with a ballistic design more suited to defence than speed. Firstly, he applied dark green trousers and black boots. Burton didn't bother to cover himself as he changed; he was past caring about his appearance. Next, he put on a black body armour vest that gave the impression of prominent pectoral muscles. His arms were protected by two pointed metal bracers that almost reached the elbow. Finally, he applied a baltea belt that featured black and white leather straps. Confidence grew, he felt strong and ready to dominate.

They continued the conversation.

"Did Nicoli have my staff?" Nefertari asked.

"No, he didn't, just an RPG and scimitar," Eliza replied.

Nefertari looked pleased her weapon hadn't been lost to the deep. "I knew he wouldn't be skilled enough to wield it."

"Who will have it now?" Burton asked.

"He must've given it to Mukhtar in tribute," Nefertari replied without hesitation. She was also strapping on something, and her arm was now covered in shining silver metal up to her elbow joint. *I'd hate to be on the end of that…*

"He calls you a mongrel, but he's the one fetching sticks," Eliza said.

"Am I right in thinking the cult are defeated? One hunter was arrested at Biovax, you killed another in Bamburgh, and two were on the bridge with Nicoli. Muhktar is all that's left."

"You are correct, but expect anything. Patrick reported that there were survivors," Nefertari replied.

"Actually… Nicoli said something that didn't make sense, Nef." Burton said. "He called you gender confused."

Eliza fired a dagger glance at him.

Nefertari stood up and put her arms behind her back. She looked up to the sky, as if thinking of a far-off land.

"What do you think drove my father to train me so close to my death?" Nefertari asked.

"I thought it was to protect you and make you strong," Burton replied. "Because you were the daughter of a Yakuza boss."

"Partly. Except my father didn't have a daughter. In his eyes, he had a son called Takeo. His son was effeminate and liked chibi dolls and cherry blossom. The taller Takeo grew, the more the father beat and broke him. Each time father put the pieces back together, he prayed they would make a man. One day, the teenage Takeo was trying on his mother's lipstick in secret when both his parents entered the room. Before Takeo could say anything, his mother put her arm around him and claimed he looked as beautiful as the Egyptian Queen Nefertari. Father struck her to the ground and screamed of his humiliation. He scolded her for 'enabling' behaviour.

"As tears flowed, a rival clan burst into the house, but Father was in no position to fight. They mocked his weak genes and laughed at his 'ladyboy' son. They kept asking how he could live with the shame. Takeo overpowered them, bested them, and slaughtered them. Standing ankle deep in their blood, Takeo asked if the brutal skills had honoured Father. He just pointed at the door. The soul of Takeo stayed with his mother forever, but Nefertari walked into the streets of Tokyo that night. I never saw them again. I'm sorry I never told you, Eliza: although they labelled me a boy at birth, I identify as female. I don't want special treatment; this is just who I am." Nefertari showed no sign of emotion despite the harrowing tale.

Eliza embraced her friend. "It's okay, Nef, I know."

"It makes no difference to me – you're here and that's all that matters." Burton also hugged his sensei. "We are three points of a triangle and you're at the top. We're unbreakable."

"For a better world," Eliza said, squeezing tighter.

"We take too long. We must discuss the plan of attack." Nefertari stepped away from their hold. "Mukhtar is attempting to dent your brother's progress and credibility. They'll blow up the whole Biovax building if they can."

"My priority is my family – they'll be in the panic room," Burton said. "Then we get the Elixir and bolt to the Freeman Hospital. It's not essential, but grab Wortham's data drive if the opportunity presents itself. We can do it – I know we can."

He felt energy, motivation, and purpose soaring through him. He started bouncing and stretching on the grass, then picked up his gladius from the park bench and clipped it to his new belt.

"Are you with me?"

"This was not David's plan, but..." Nefertari looked straight past Burton. "But it will be enough to honour him."

"I'm in." Eliza holstered her tranq gun and pushed her arms into her leather jacket. The handle of her staff snapped securely to a magnet on her left shoulder.

"Hey, you were right! It's them!" A sweaty tennis player in a white polo shirt dropped his racket and turned to run.

"Shit! Shit! Run!" his friend replied.

"Sorry, guys, time to visit snooze-town." Burton drew his tranq gun and downed the man on the left. Eliza dropped the other. Multiple tennis balls rolled out of the men's sports bags and down the path. Two ace shots.

"Game, set and match," Eliza said, holstering her weapon.

Burton turned to address the others. "Once we get there, Eliza, you drum up the crowd at the front of the Biovax building. When BARRIER move their resources toward the angry mob, me and Nef will nullify the guards at the rear. We'll take the elevator to Patrick's storeroom and through his office passageway to the lab. Once we grab the Elixirs, we'll escape the way we came in with my family."

"Let's do this. I've never seen you so focused and bossy, Frosty. Did I mention you look like a Viking with that beard and armour? I like it – you look powerful." Eliza pulled the black hood of the tactical suit from underneath the collar of her jacket, then reached both arms into the air with interlocking fingers to perform a stretch. Burton noticed his own clothing had a black-and-white-striped mask to cover his mouth, it reminded him of his old scarf.

"Nice colour choice."

"I had it made especially," Nefertari said. "It is the colour of the Aesculapian snake, remember, not just your football team."

"How could I forget?" Burton joked, thinking back to the time he'd swung a lamp at her the first time they'd met. *That's so thoughtful. I didn't think she was capable of that.*

"You will both need to wear them so the crowd doesn't recognise you," Nefertari instructed.

Eliza pulled her purple mask up over her nose and looked straight at Burton. "How do I look?"

"Like you bought a 'Sexy Ninja' costume from the fancy dress shop."

"How can I help you find your fun today?" Eliza replied, mimicking the creepy tone of Flowerpeckers' greeting. They both sniggered.

"If you need to do anything, now is the time. There is no going back," Nefertari said.

Her words brought them back down to earth.

"It feels like we need to save our progress," Eliza said to Burton apprehensively.

～

"Okay. What the fuck are they?" Eliza whispered.

The sun was setting behind the Biovax building as the group lay on one of the grassy vantage points that overlooked the horde. The sky was a mixture of pastel pink and orange; it gave a punch-tinted wash across everything in front of them. Eliza handed the pair of Wayfinder binoculars to Burton. He looked into the twilight to see two newly constructed watchtowers.

Jesus Christ... At the top of each tower, far above the crowd on forty-foot-high grey metal supports, stood two BARRIER guards within a pyramid shell. They were evaluating the area by shining neon blue searchlights that resembled eyes. The platform rotated slowly on an axle from left to right. A loud solitary *clunk* could be heard each time they switched direction.

"The inverted metal legs and big eyes make them look like fucking dinosaurs," Eliza said.

"Shame they don't stomp around. We could've called them T-Mechs," Burton suggested with a smirk.

"Shut up, Jon," Eliza replied, and whacked him with her elbow.

A fracas broke out in the crowd, and the blue beams shone in that direction. A deafening siren began. It sounded like an orphaned elephant trumpeting through a distorting microphone.

"Cease your antisocial behaviour," a voice boomed. Around five guards ran towards the fracas and the trouble-makers stopped in their tracks.

Eliza rubbed her right hand across her ribs and hips, as if remembering the pain from her beating on the Tyne Bridge.

"They're so intimidating," she said. For once, she seemed to have no intention of rushing in. "What am I supposed to do? Maybe I could shoot the guards on the tower? Or maybe we can take them down together?"

Burton handed the Wayfinders to Nefertari.

"Regardless of how intimidating they appear, the towers are stationary, and the guards will only add to your distrac-tion," Nefertari said as she analysed their obstacles coolly.

Below them, people pulled elderly relatives and sick chil-dren away from the neon beams as BARRIER dealt out their rough justice. *How can the police allow this? Why don't they step in? A flashing blue light is supposed to represent help, not brutality.* Burton looked toward the other grass bank where the officers had been sitting since the start of it all. Glover was smoking a cigarette and marching along the front of a growing number of squad cars. *What will it take for you to act?*

"The art of war is to win without fighting. Our plan is the same. Keep them busy. Survival belongs to those who can adapt."

"Yeah, but I'll be absolute toast if they gang up on me again."

"Adapt. Your army is in front of you. Drag their attention

around the horde. Cause chaos. Give BARRIER one thousand fires to extinguish."

"You could've said mech-stinguish, if—"

"For fuck's sake, Jon, not now. I've already told you it's not funny." Eliza said in a raised voice. She wasn't in a playful mood. It was as if their personalities had flipped at the last hurdle. Her eyes welled up, like Burton had seen when she had talked about her mother. She was afraid. "I don't want anyone else to get hurt because of me. These people have been through enough."

"Remember, this is not a dance," Nefertari warned. "Do whatever you can to gain an advantage over your opponent. Be aggressive. Be instinctive. Be like an animal. Hesitation will cause your death."

"Wait, what's going on?" Burton said. "Look."

Patches of the crowd were becoming frantic and violent without encouragement. Multiple bright violet dots appeared across the horde. It resembled 'Starry Night over the Rhône' by Vincent Van Gogh.

"Looks like someone might be down there handing out Violator pods," he said. "This has reached a tipping point."

"Egan?" Eliza asked.

"He must be convincing people to try his formula. The police have been useless. How did they let him get away? It must've been when the explosion happened at the Ware-rooms. The Violators are going to tear everyone apart."

"Eliza, go now," Nefertari ordered. "We'll never have a better chance. It appears that every opposing faction is attacking Biovax tonight."

"Okay, I'm on it. See you shortly... I hope." Eliza set off towards the far end of the crowd.

"Follow me." Nefertari edged around the outskirts in the opposite direction.

"Will she be okay?" Burton's voice cracked and the words didn't quite come out properly.

"She has blossomed like the trees in Takeo's garden. Eliza is remarkable. Follow me and stay low."

Threats, insults and incoherent rambling started growing louder from the horde. The beams snapped on one location after another. The T-Mechs were going cross-eyed.

"Predictable," Nefertari said.

Burton let out a deep breath and raised his eyebrows to relieve the tension in his forehead. The growing number of Violators weren't like zombies from any movie or game – they were worse. They were acting on impulse, but displayed self-awareness that the undead in fiction always seemed to lack. Some had even started working together.

BARRIER formed a well-drilled line across the front of the building and the unruly sea of violet turned its attention to the grey wall. Patrick's army were carrying body-length riot shields and clashed their batons against the front of them in unison. Their display of power was perfectly in sync.

The words "Cease your antisocial behaviour" repeated on a loop. The unrest became a roar, and the roar became a riot. Things were thrown and fires were lit. Fights were erupting every few metres. Burton's plan had combined with whatever Egan had concocted, and the result was pure carnage.

Tear gas launched from the watchtowers as the defensive line took two steps forward. A group of guards planted their shields and mounted rifles on top of them to increase the steadiness of their aim. They opened fire.

"Go," Nefertari instructed.

"But they're shooting everyone," Burton replied. His breathing shortened as he looked at the dystopian horror in front of him. Newcastle – his city – had become a war zone. *This is all my fault.*

"My ribs, I think they're broken. Help. I've been shot." A reporter was crawling towards the edge of the crowd and shouting at his cameraman. Influencers circled the team and vlogged the incident, their phones outstretched to record themselves. They offered no help to the reporter but yelled "Like and subscribe" as he tried to catch his breath.

Nefertari took a deep sniff and crouched down to pick something up. "No blood. Rubber bullets. Crowd control only."

They continued to work around the edge of the horde.

"Shit, there's three?" Burton said. A third watchtower had been partially erected by the back entrance. A guard was climbing up to the platform.

"Your intel has been poor," Nefertari said, frowning as she calculated a new plan. "Look, one thick cable comes from the right support clamp and attaches to the piece above."

"Almost like an Achilles tendon," Burton said.

"Yes, it must provide power to the searchlights. I will cut it."

"You'll get electrocuted."

"Battery power only. I can take it."

She stalked towards her target like a tiger in the wild. Burton also moved in, trying to locate an undetected angle. A hiss accompanied a thin trail of smoke and the platform exploded into pieces. The backdraft blew the guards, Nefertari and Burton off their feet like ragdolls.

Burton opened his eyes to see the bright yellow paint of the unmanned crane. It provided welcome cover as he pulled himself up and rested against it. The legs of the watchtower had fallen outwards and pinned maniac Violators underneath.

The explosion had caused ringing in Burton's ears, adding an additional layer to his disorientation. The Biovax punch bowl had been spiked and then stirred. *This is too much.* Another missile whistled into the side of the building and shattered several windows. The still-conscious BARRIER guards charged into the surrounding woodland in search of the shooter.

One of them, #22, noticed Burton and broke away from his

squad. As he raised his rifle, three Violators leapt onto him from different angles and dragged him to the ground, scratching and biting him. It was a horrifying sight to behold as chunks of flesh were torn by talon shaped fingers.

There was no sign of Eliza. *I hope she can protect at least some of these innocent people.*

Burton checked on Nefertari and held up his arm to signal he was okay. She nodded in return. To his amazement, a char-grilled Nicoli walked from the grass verge behind her. His bushy beard and eyebrows had been burnt away, and his face was yet to heal. His skeletal vest was the only identifier that remained. It was soaked in fresh blood that had presumably belonged to members of the recent search party. His eyes locked on Nefertari.

"Mongrel! Are you not going to give me a wave?" Nicoli taunted.

Nefertari raised her head, standing unchallenged amongst the mayhem. Even those not in their right mind were keeping their distance. Nicoli pointed the tip of his scimitar towards her.

"Do not interfere and stay exactly where you are," she shouted to Burton as she extended her baton.

"You don't always have to fight alone," he replied. "I can help."

Nefertari charged at the man who had taken her hand.

Their weapons clashed together. Nicoli took a step forward and made three wild slashes. Nefertari took several quick steps backwards to create space between them; her foot-work was impeccable. Burton growled, he wanted to run closer, but remained beside the crane as instructed.

"All I wanted was for things to stay the same," Nicoli said. "How does that make me a villain? We helped so many people. You know O'Fagan was only trying to save his ancient skin, right? He didn't care about anyone. The blas-phemer just needed a constant stream of Elixir to see another year." He waved the tip of his scimitar to gesture at the horde. "Look at the turmoil his plan has caused. This is why we follow the word of Asklepios to the letter. Re-join us and I promise I'll forgive your *trans*-gressions." Nicoli gave another toothless smile as he circled around her.

"You are nothing."

"Wrong. I am your phantom pain," Nicoli replied and lunged forward for a head strike. Nefertari pushed it aside with a grimace and aimed a stab at his body that made Nicoli skip back.

Nefertari glanced at her arm stump before raising her baton. "I have prayed for this day."

As he advanced again, Nefertari smashed her weapon down against her metal arm, aiming sparks into Nicoli's face. He held his elbow up to protect his pockmarked nose.

"You fucking dirty mongrel," Nicoli said. He advanced and slashed wildly, three times. The last swipe connected only slightly, but it knocked her hand at an awkward angle. Nefertari's fingers sprung open, and her baton dropped to the ground.

"Time to meet your master, bitch." Nicoli sneered.

Wait, has she been leading him into this position?

"You finally get it," Nefertari replied, "I am a bitch." Another three predictable slashes followed from Nicoli. *The tiger is guiding the tamer.*

"Come on, hot stuff, give me a kiss." Nicoli taunted and pouted as he moved beneath the arm of the yellow crane. He glanced up.

"Now!" Nefertari shouted.

Burton had no time to doubt himself. He pulled a lever marked 'release' on the crane's controls, unleashing a ton of metal girders and poles over the Greek's head.

Somehow, Nicoli remained standing after the debris fell. Blood was trickling from his ears, and he was rocking from side to side. Nefertari marched towards him and powered her metal stump through his chest armour. His bone trophies shattered into fragments. She picked up a metal pole and skewered it through his heart.

"Hell hath no fury like me," Nefertari said as she stood over the corpse.

Burton ran over and nudged Nicoli's body with his foot to check he was dead.

"How does it feel to work as a team?" he asked.

Nefertari ignored the question. "Let's go," she said, and ran for the back entrance.

Burton grabbed a key card from the belt of a downed guard and moved into the narrow walkway. The explosion had damaged the controls, and the security doors wouldn't close behind them. The walkway lights were also damaged, creating a flashing blue strobe effect within the corridor. Purple-eyed lunatics followed them into the narrow passage. One Violator ignored them entirely and ripped the security camera off the ceiling as the others advanced. Burton swiped the card, glanced at the tattoo on his forearm, and entered the code as Nefertari pushed an aggressor away to buy some time. *Up, up, down, down, up.*

The lift pinged, and they continued to oppose the Violators as they stepped backwards into it. Burton hit number five and then nine as arms reached for them. Although the code lit up in green across the panel, the Violators prevented the doors from closing. Burton kicked and pushed the bodies away, but he was reluctant to use any fatal techniques. These people were desperate, just like he had been. All those nights struggling to sleep and lying awake consumed by jealousy, longing, aggression and fear; they were horrific. The Violators deserved another chance, like he had right now.

A stocky man grabbed Burton's left hand and bent his fingers back. He responded by kicking him in the beer belly with the flat of his foot. It knocked the brute away, and the man's wide frame carried the other Violators backwards with him. The doors closed and Nefertari gave a slow nod of approval.

Burton's reconnaissance mission had been worthwhile. *Maybe luck is just preparation leading to opportunity after all, thanks Dad.* He watched as the cuts and scratches healed on his arms in a moment of respite.

"You've come a long way, Jon," Nefertari said. "Just remember that any kind of pain is a lesson. Own it. Bruises, breaks and blood are nothing; embrace them and you'll be capable of anything. Believe in your ability to move forward and you *will* move forward."

Burton nodded in agreement. The lift pinged. He set himself to fight again.

The room was empty; it seemed that BARRIER had deployed fully. A single remaining helmet sat on the wooden changing bench. Burton lowered it onto his head to hear concerned voices communicating via the earpiece.

"Watchtower C is down, Commander. A missile came out of nowhere. Over."

"Watchtower B has also been… dismantled. Over."

"The crowd continues to cause havoc despite Watchtower A applying tear-gas canisters. A green blur just sliced the power cable and survived the shock. Visibility is low. Over."

"Sir, the security camera is down at the back entrance. Over."

"They'll storm the building within the hour. Over."

"If they get within ten metres of the building, use live rounds. Boss's orders." Burton recognised the voice of the commander from the bridge.

"We need to hurry. They're going to fire on the crowd for real." Burton swiped the key card on the panel, but the door didn't open. He tried it again. "Huh? Why won't it work?" He swiped again.

Nefertari knocked him away with her blunt arm. "Don't try anything else."

"Perhaps the room locks down after full deployment?" Burton replied.

"Perhaps your memory isn't as good as you think it is." She looked up at an air vent. "Could you fit in there?"

"There's nothing wrong with my memory. Here, give me a boost." Burton stepped onto Nefertari's hand and she hoisted his entire weight up with one arm. He removed the air vent with a dull *clunk* and climbed inside.

The vent was thick with dust that blackened the underside of his arms as he pulled himself along. *This isn't so bad, I was wading through a lot worse earlier*. A door pinged below, but the vent was too narrow to turn back. It must have been the guard returning for his helmet. He was muttering to himself.

"As if I needed a shit just before deployment. The lads will never let me hear the end of it."

Burton heard another sharp crack, like the sound of a boiled egg being sliced open. He moved his elbows at a quicker pace to drag himself forward and dropped through a second vent at the first opportunity. Nefertari was standing at the other side of the corridor wiping red yolk from her metal arm. She had entered the corridor by force as the guard had gone through the door.

Burton beckoned as they crept through the deserted hallways. "This way."

"Nobody here. It seems strange," Nefertari was almost robotic as she surveyed every door and corner.

"This is Patrick's director's floor. Staff were told to work from home this week due to growing hostility outside the building. Patrick deemed it unsafe."

"No guards either? I don't like this."

"Well, apart from... that guy." Burton pointed to Nefertari's arm, which she held in an attempt to stop red droplets leaving a trail.

Burton entered Patrick's empty office and approached the

Newcastle cityscape. He pushed the bronze plaque and pulled the picture down at the bottom right corner.

"The Elixirs should be through here. We'll find my family, grab some vials and get the fuck out," Burton said.

They edged through the passage into Patrick's laboratory.

"I told you never to come back," Patrick said. He was working diligently in his flowing white lab coat. BARRIER guards lined the edges of the room, and all of them aimed rifles at the intruders.

They were trapped inside the snake pit.

CHAPTER 23
FAMILY FIRST

"Your weapons – place them on the ground," Patrick ordered.

Burton knelt in order to lay down his gladius and tranq gun. "What are you doing here? I thought you'd be in the panic room. Are Mam and Dad safe? Are Dom and Matty okay? It's crazy out there."

"They're going to be fine," Patrick said. His gaze shifted to Nefertari. "I won't ask again."

"No," Nefertari said simply.

The guards re-stressed their aim by prodding their rifles forward.

"Nef, we're surrounded. What are you doing?" Burton asked.

"I don't believe he'll let guards open fire in this room. The reptiles are worth billions. If they're killed or escape, he's finished. I will defeat all guards in a fair fight." Nefertari looked at Patrick. "One step closer and the tanks shatter," she threatened, holding out her metal-coated arm.

"Fine, go ahead. How about the one right next to you?" Patrick suggested.

Nefertari jabbed, and the snake inside slithered back. She

struck the tank again, but her metal stump only thudded against it.

"Bulletproof, fireproof and shatterproof," Patrick said.

A guard blasted a blank round into Nefertari's kneecap. She dropped momentarily before standing up again. The other guards exchanged quick glances with each other. *Not even a gunshot can hurt her? She wasn't joking in the lift.*

Burton stepped closer to his brother. Patrick held out his hand to stop the agitated guards from doing anything rash.

"I've tried to protect you, Jonny. I know how fragile you are. Let's face it, the only thing that can shatter around here is your mental health. I didn't want that. I didn't want your paper-thin confidence to be ripped apart again. You were doing so well."

"What are you talking about? I've never felt better."

"Really? Mam and Dad gave you every opportunity to succeed in life, only to be rewarded with pulling you from your lonely doldrums every day. What kind of payback is this for them, brother? What kind of payback is it for me? You look ridiculous."

Patrick was standing in front of the Alpha tank and the huge black-and-white reptile had risen on full display behind him. Its forked tongue kept stabbing out as Patrick looked at his younger brother from underneath his lowered brow.

"Why are you saying this?" Nefertari asked.

Patrick input a code into his tablet: 11-92-12. Burton could see the reflection in the tank, the same trick he'd used on Eliza in the Laughing Heart. The red reinforced door marked *CAUTION* clicked and opened automatically beside his older brother

Patrick entered the room and the guards ushered Burton and Nefertari in behind him. The temperature plummeted and everyone's breath became visible. A layer of smoke licked against their ankles; it was as if they were on top of a black cloud. Two seven-foot-tall cast-iron cylinders stood in the centre of the room, each with clear corrugated tubes entering them at the top. It looked as though Elixir from the snake pit was being pumped directly inside. Circular gauges on the side of each chamber vibrated violently, the pins inside were making an aggressive buzzing sound.

"The evolution of the Abaton," Patrick announced, referencing the chambers of healing that O'Fagan had once spoken about.

"What are they?" Burton asked.

"Our home was burned to the ground. Mam would've been baking cakes, Dad was probably watching the sports news. The Caballion had barricaded the doors from the outside."

The contents of Burton's stomach pushed up into his throat. "You said you got them out... you said they were with you... I've spoken to them."

Patrick took an old mobile phone from the pocket of his lab coat and started typing. The phone's casing was charred, with traces of pink underneath.

"Who are you texting?" Burton asked.

"You."

"My phone was lost in the Tyne Bridge explosion."

"Oh well. The message was, 'Love you son'."

"What? They were from you?"

"I thought one of Mam's orders would be more likely to get you here to safety. I didn't expect the sarcastic mouthful you gave me instead. You've been spending too much time with that girl."

Patrick put the phone in his pocket and hit a red button on the side of each Abaton. They opened slowly to reveal thick glass chambers filled with Elixir. The murky green liquid was disturbed and rippling.

"There's something in there," Nefertari said, limping forward to one of the Abatons. The BARRIER guards took a couple of steps back.

"I'm trying to save them, Jonny. They were burned and injured, but I kept them alive. I'm pumping ninety percent of the Elixir we generate into these Abatons, and I need the funds raised from the rest to complete my research. Biovax wouldn't have dared sanction this if I'd told them. They lack the vision, even Maslow."

A blackened figure slammed scorched hands against the inside of the glass. Pieces of their fingers were breaking off and regenerating with each contact. Skin and body parts attempted to regrow around the carbonised skeletal construct. The liquid filled with bubbles from the mouth area, muffling their scream.

"The face. It's… Mam? No, it can't be. She's in pain. Mam, can you hear me? They didn't escape? What's happening? Where's Dad?"

"I can save her. Do you understand? Her smile, her words of encouragement, I can bring it all back." Patrick's tone remained assured and confident despite the horrific image in front of him.

"This is a torture chamber," Nefertari said. "We must stop this. She is prisoner in her own body."

"Do you know what happens to resurrected folk in Greek mythology?" Patrick asked Burton. "Divinity. Immortality. Don't you want their love forever? I certainly do."

Burton froze as he watched his own mother break apart and reassemble over and over. He could only assume his father was hidden amongst the liquid of the other Abaton. Time crawled around him. He looked at the guards, Patrick and his… 'parents'. *How did it come to this? How did we end up here?* He struggled to catch his breath as an invisible force tried to rip his heart from his chest. He was turning catatonic. The nerves of his spine ignited, his hands shook, his shoulders locked, his lips became numb.

Nefertari seemed to speak from the ether. "If you won't

help her, then I will." She limped towards the console and raised her arm to smash it down.

"No!" Burton yelled. Time returned to full speed, and he leapt after her. He caught Nefertari's arm, then dragged her away. He attempted a sleeper hold around her neck, something Nefertari herself had taught him in the emerald hills.

"Don't," he pleaded. "I need them."

"They are not your parents. This is barbaric."

Nefertari ducked out of the hold, spun and kicked. She connected into his stomach with the ferocity of an iron mule, despite the bullet wound in her kneecap. Burton flew backwards, clunking off the second chamber. For a moment, his father's one-eyed face appeared silently in the tank before disappearing into the liquid. He was still prepared to hide the agonising pain from his son. *Dad?*

Nefertari scissor-kicked a guard out of the way and bludgeoned another with her metal arm. She raised it above the console again. Burton drew his gladius and threw it into his friend's back without hesitation. The blade wedged into her, and the upward pointing limb froze in position.

Patrick gave a nod. He'd been waiting. The guards all flicked a switch on their rifles and fired. Nefertari dropped to her knees, and blood patches spread across her white tactical suit like a watercolour painting.

"For a better world," she whispered before falling face first onto the laboratory floor.

"We must study her," Patrick ordered. "Nefertari has had Elixir running through her body for many years. We could learn something from her organs and push our research forward. Take her to Wortham on the helipad and wait for me. Jonny, that must've been hard, but I'm proud of you. Family first, always."

A guard pulled out the gladius from Nefertari's back and handed it to Burton before dragging her away.

They think I'm on their side? What have I done? Burton knelt, sobbing, in front of the Abaton chambers. "I'm so sorry for everything. Please don't leave me. Please stay with me." His nerves were on fire and his hands were shaking.

"Can you see why I didn't show you? I hate it when you're like this. I'm so close to bringing them back." Patrick pressed buttons to close the chambers before dropping to his knees too. Burton's older brother looked directly into his eyes and held his head in place to stop it dipping. "I promise you, I can do it. I can do anything. I've always been able to do it all. Right?"

An automated female voice came over the speaker system. *"New order completed – ten million pounds."*

"More money for our cause. Do you understand now? These chambers cost a fortune to run. Biovax is haemorrhaging money and the board will notice before long. I'm writing it off as research and development while they're blinded by greed. I'll mass-produce the Elixir. I'll make Biovax the biggest company in the world. I'll save a billion sick kids. Right now, though, I'm focused on them." Patrick gestured at the Abaton chambers. "Can you forgive me? More importantly, will you help me?"

Patrick stood up and held out his right hand. This time, Burton accepted. *He's been doing it all for Mam and Dad, for me, for us…*

"Family first," Burton muttered through his sniffling.

Commander #1 entered the lab, still applying his damaged grey armour.

"What are you doing, Commander?" Patrick asked. "You should be resting."

"I know, boss – but someone has your wife. They're in the main reception with a gun to her head."

Patrick hurried out the lab with his white coat flapping behind him. The Commander and Burton followed.

"But the panic room was secure?" Patrick asked.

"Not one guard is responding, sir."

"My son?"

"We are searching."

"Fuck!" Patrick yelled and pulled at his hair with both hands. He turned and looked back at Burton. "Where is your friend, Jonny, the pretty one?" he asked.

Burton was silent.

"Where is she? Your family is in danger." Patrick shook him by the shoulders and slapped him across the face. Patrick was dismayed but still calculating his next move by identifying all potential threats.

Burton became limp as his brother shook him. It hadn't been part of the plan, but Eliza was erratic. *Surely she wouldn't do anything to hurt Dom or Matty?*

"We had come here to steal a box of Elixirs and get the family to safety. Eliza was in the crowd, causing a distraction and protecting the sick. It won't be her," he replied.

As he followed at Patrick's heel, he turned to look back. He tried to contemplate the pain his parents were experiencing with every passing second.

Burton had betrayed his ally and broken the triangle. *Nefertari, I'm so sorry. My friend. My sensei. I'm so sorry.*

CHAPTER 24
DIVINE MADNESS

T he brothers stood with Commander #1 at the top of the grand staircase in Biovax reception. In the centre of the marble floor below, a hunter was pressing a pistol into Dominique's silken hair. The full width of the entrance behind them was made entirely of reinforced glass, providing a widescreen display of the ongoing war outside. Glancing left and right, Burton saw that BARRIER guards had lined the balconies above, pointing rifles down at the assailant.

"What do you want? Name it – anything!" Patrick shouted.

"To get your attention," Dominique said, and stepped forward without resistance.

"Dom, what's going on?" Patrick shouted.

Her 'captor' pressed a small square detonator on their belt and set off a chain of explosions under the parallel balconies. The soldiers dropped twenty feet under a heavy layer of rubble. The entire reception now had a border that resembled a charcoal sketch as the plants and sofas burned into nothing. *They've planned it all.*

Sergio pulled down his mask and hood. "Don't look so

shocked, *amigo*. If we can blow up your bridge, we can certainly deal with a few poorly trained soldiers."

"Dom?" Patrick asked.

He began to walk down the stairs, but Commander #1 stepped in front of him. "I don't recommend that, sir."

Patrick brushed past him and continued to descend.

Sergio looked at his old cellmate with pity. "I told you in confidence about the Cult of Asklepios. You knew what happened to my *familia*. The day I left for England I gave my sister the tracker in case anything went wrong. I gave you that watch in the hope that she would find you instead of me. I wanted her to be happy."

Sister?

Patrick removed the watch and threw it at his wife's feet.

"Is this true?" he asked.

"I am Dominique, the dutiful housewife. I am Sofia, the flower girl. I am Muhktar, the vengeful Column. But I am also… so sorry, Patrick," his wife said, forcing her words out.

"No, she can't be," Patrick muttered to himself.

"O'Fagan was in charge when the killers came for my family," she said with a heavy sigh. "He left me broken but alive, unable to finish what he started. His Caballion butchered my brother and parents on the other side of a sun-baked wall."

"Why did he spare you?" Patrick asked.

"The atrocities he committed weighed heavy on him. I guess it was the beginning of his new ideology – Project Panacea, I believe he called it. In the years that followed, I travelled the world and chased whispers. I was a poor flower girl, but I was pretty. I'll leave it to your imagination how I raised enough money to travel. The degradation made me numb, but scraps of information were my fuel. I tracked him down before realising it wouldn't be satisfying enough to kill him quickly."

"What did you do?" Patrick asked.

"I begged to be trained. I told him I was lost and without purpose."

"Didn't he recognise you?" Patrick asked.

"Deep down he knew, but we never spoke of it. After years of serving Asklepios, I completed every Caballion trial and O'Fagan cast the final vote to make me a Column. He was haunted by the memory of Merida, and I think he looked upon my Asklepion conversion as some kind of twisted penance."

Outside, a woman foaming at the mouth slammed face first against the glass as a wounded guard blasted her with rifle fire at close quarters. The doors were cracking under immense pressure from the horde.

Somehow, the war outside didn't distract Patrick and Dominique from their conversation.

"When I attempted to share my plan with Sergio, the tracker led me to you," Dominique continued. "Despite all my calculations, I never planned on falling in love. You were like a warm fire in the bleakest winter. Patrick, you managed the impossible and distracted me for years. However, even as I held our new-born son, my heart was trapped inside a vacuum and didn't feel full. I couldn't rest. I had to make our world a better place for Matthias. It was a maternal instinct, a calling from Mother Nature herself."

Sergio circled his sister, shooting any guards who regained consciousness. Commander #1 maintained his aim on the Spaniard.

"Sir, please," Commander #1 begged.

"So, you brought down the cult from within?" Patrick asked as he reached the bottom of the steps. He was almost within reach of his wife and the time for questioning was nearing an end.

"Yes, but O'Fagan watched me closely. He wanted to swell our global population by mass-producing Elixir, whereas I wanted to get rid of every last drop. Gorgone was merely a slave to tradition, caught in the middle. Nicoli just wanted O'Fagan dead. His ambitions aligned with mine, which made him easy to manipulate. The cult was dismantled, and I was well on my way to eradicating the poison – until O'Fagan played his ultimate card."

"By approaching me?" Patrick asked.

"Sadly, yes." Dominique ran her fingers through her perfect hair and rubbed the back of her neck. Despite everything, Patrick still seemed enamoured by her beauty, his eyes were entranced on her.

"He thought I would support you and focus on our family. Instead, I explored your weaknesses under the guise of the Three Blind Mice activist group. Nothing got to you like the vaccine we tampered with. All those nights you spent locked away in your study were just as hard for me. I know it sounds cruel, but I thought O'Fagan would move on if Biovax went out of business. I was trying to save you from all of this. I underestimated your resolve. It only made you more determined."

"You ungrateful… Your eyes aren't even green." Patrick shot an outstretched palm toward Dominique's face to highlight his point and took another couple of steps forward. He still couldn't bring himself to insult her.

"A full blood transfusion. I didn't want a drop of that poison in my veins a minute longer than it had to be, and neither should anyone else." Dominique glanced at her brother.

Sergio returned to his sister's side. It seemed strange to see him draped in crimson armour instead of black.

"But the Elixir isn't poison. We could've helped so many people." Burton spoke quietly for the first time, unsure if anyone had heard him. Every sentence from Dominique produced tears, which evaporated, as if the green circles in his eyes were burning them away.

"There are seven billion people on this planet, Jonny.

Remember, if there were no insects or worms, we would cease to exist within ten years. If humans didn't exist, the planet would thrive. The oceans are filling with plastic and the air with pollution. We kill, destroy, burn and drain. Natural selection might not be enough. We should be thinning our numbers down."

"Is that how you justified attacking my parents?" Patrick asked, vitriol now creeping into his tone.

"I had no choice. Nicoli wanted to send a message, and I needed to maintain a position of strength. I tried to warn you multiple times, and even let Jonny go free in Bamburgh. If nothing else, I hope it helps you to understand my pain. I've had that same feeling in the pit of my stomach since I was thirteen," Dominique said.

Another body crashed against the glass panel, and then another. The horde had overpowered the BARRIER guards, and the entrance was under immense pressure.

Sergio looked over his shoulder before stepping in front of his sister. "And look at the level of destruction it has caused," he said. "Look at what is happening outside. Imagine this chaos on a global scale – there will be a nuclear war before another Christmas. We must destroy these vials of acid rain. Look at us – we were good people once. I warned you, *amigo*, the Elixir brings death, not life."

Patrick ushered Commander #1 forward but at the same moment the Spaniard opened fire. The bullets ripped through the gaps in the damaged armour. BARRIER's champion was dead quicker than you could pierce the film on a microwavable meal.

"I love you, husband, but your knowledge is far too dangerous. I promise that Matthias will always remember the best of you."

Patrick yelled and charged at Sergio, only to be knocked down by his friend with ease. He'd never trained for this. The sight of her husband collapsing made Dominique raise her hand to her face.

Sergio put his arm on his sister's shoulder to comfort her. "It's okay, Sofia." He rubbed her back as tears dripped onto her index finger that was resting like a bridge under her eyes. "Do you want me to finish him? I can do this for you. I will do anything for you."

Sensing a distraction, Burton closed the distance between him and Sergio, and sliced down with his gladius to protect Patrick. Sergio stepped sideways, dodging the attack, then threw his gun a short distance to his sister before extending a pointed baton.

"One bullet left, *hermana*. Protect yourself."

Burton stood side-on to his opponent, as he'd been taught. He held the gladius behind him and waited for an opportunity; he didn't want to overextend, like the guard on the Tyne Bridge.

Sergio's eyes flashed green as he flailed his weapon. Burton evaded by bouncing away. He feinted a sword swing, then stepped in with a straight jab of his left fist. The Spaniard's teeth crunched against his bare knuckles. All those months of sparring with Eliza were paying off. *I'm doing it, I'm fighting back.*

"I didn't think you had it in you." Sergio wiped blood from his lips and spat to the side. "I might be rusty, but what can a boy do against a man?

The Spanish bull charged in, unafraid, and smashed his baton down against Burton's blocking gladius. Burton's wrist gave way under the ferocious attack and the sword clanged off the marble floor. Then a straight kick to his stomach knocked him onto his back like a stranded turtle.

Stamping feet crushed Burton's chest like dropping anvils. It was like every panic attack he'd ever experienced, combined into one. *All my suffering has prepared me for this moment – I can take it.*

He rolled away and clambered up again, raising his arms in a fighting stance. Then came dizziness. Multiple versions of Sergio approached and lunged at Burton; his vision went from blurry to white. It was as if a bomb had gone off in his face.

I can take it. He started swinging wildly, but the strikes were coming too fast for the Elixir to heal him. He suffered a smash to his nose, a boot to his ankles, and a crack to the ribs. The taste of copper flooded into his mouth. *Detach from the pain, I must detach from the pain.*

Only a voice gave Burton faith that he might not be seconds from death. His big brother had risen to save him and was threatening Sergio.

"Get away from him."

"*Amigo*, why did you get involved?"

It sounded as though a couple of Patrick's punches connected before something more final: a gunshot.

Burton lay still. His vision cleared enough for him to make out Dominique, who was cradling Patrick's head and kissing him.

"Paddy!" Burton yelled. He stretched out his arm towards his fallen brother. He couldn't move or even crawl. He just lay on his stomach with his chin against the cold ground.

"I'm sorry, my love," Dominique said softly. "I felt the pull of a stronger emotion."

"What can be stronger than divine madness?" Burton asked, then laughed. He replied in place of his brother who lay lifeless. "Real love is never defeated."

Project Panacea had underlined the importance of being virtuous above wealth and power. It had also torn the Burton family apart and pitted an entire city against them. O'Fagan had orchestrated an echo of Plato's teachings in his *Republic*. The old man couldn't lose, even in death. *Maybe he was Asklepios after all…*

Burton rolled onto his back and looked at new stars

through the high glass ceiling. Tears welled in his eyes, but he only laughed harder. His mouth wouldn't straighten or even curve into a frown. He couldn't stop smiling. The guilt of feeling depressed had left him, even though he was at his lowest.

Dominique pointed the gun at him. "I hope Eliza was worth dying for, Jonny."

She squeezed the trigger and the hammer clicked. The clip was empty. In her grief, she'd forgotten.

"We've had an absolute blast!" a voice shouted from the top of the staircase. Not too late to the party, I hope?"

Eliza leapt from halfway down and landed beside Burton. She slammed her silver metal staff on the ground, then spun her weapon around her body and above her head.

Burton tried again to stand but couldn't. His wrist and ankle were broken. All he could do was mutter "Muhktar" and point to Dominique. *I must detach myself from the pain. I have to get up and help.*

"No way – really? You're Muhktar?" Eliza asked. She was covered in soot and her leather jacket was all scuffed. "I was certain it was Maslow."

"Yes." Dominique replied. Her voice now lacked any emotion.

She kicked off her heels and ripped her red dress at the waist to give her greater mobility. The final Column had muscular thighs and arms that only stood out to Burton now she was a potential threat. Dominique pulled the bronze staff of Asklepios from her shoulder and extended it. She mimicked Eliza's routine.

"Sergio, kill the archaeologist before he leaves and find his data bank," she said. "I'll meet you where we planned. Tell Matthias that his mother won't be long."

Sergio took one last look at his downed cellmate before running up the steps and into the main building.

Eliza and Dominique circled each other, their footwork almost identical.

"The cult is finished," Dominique stated. "I've cut the head off the snake –metaphorically speaking, of course. After all these years of sacrifice, I've almost done it."

Rubble and the bodies of BARRIER soldiers surrounded them; Violators pressed up against the reinforced entrance, and some of their arms had broken through the glass.

Eliza was the first to attack. Each of her combination strikes were parried effortlessly.

"Predictable. You can't bat your lashes at me," Dominique taunted. She coiled low, before springing backward and simultaneously cracking Eliza across the head.

"My mam would be here if it wasn't for you," Eliza replied. "All the people outside would now be healthy if it wasn't for you."

She tried again, but Dominique put all her weight on her back leg and raised her right knee. Holding her spear like a brush, she swept away each attempt by Eliza to land a low blow. The Column countered again and pushed forward into a powerful kick. Her bare heel cracked into the centre of Eliza's chest and sent her reeling backwards into the grabbing, scratching and groping wall of Violator arms. Nothing could have prepared her for this beating.

It's my fault. I wasn't a good enough sparring partner. Burton tried to push himself from the floor again, but excruciating pain shot up into his arm. *I can take it. I have to be a man.*

"You're a bad advert for the Elixir. Maybe I should let you live," Dominique said.

Eliza wrestled free from the grasping arms. Her eye was purple and swollen. Dominique walked over to Burton and slammed the ornate spear tip into his shoulder. The muscles around the injury burned. All he could do was scream. He was impaled.

"Trust me, you do not want to live without your family.

This is an act of mercy, Jonny. You are such a sweet boy, but I cannot let the curse of the Elixir continue. This is the end."

Eliza stood straight, took three strides back, and sent her own weapon whistling like a javelin into the ceiling. Broken shards rained down, covering the floor in a deluge of tiny razors. Burton covered his face with his left forearm. After the patter of sharp glass rain subsided, he looked at Dominique.

His sister-in-law could no longer move freely. Each step was shredding her feet, and her bloody footprints had already left a trail of abstract expressionism on the shiny white marble floor. She looked around, planning her next move.

"You've left yourself defenceless, Eliza," Dominique said through gritted teeth.

"You should've chosen better footwear for the occasion," Eliza replied, seeming confident that she had regained control. She wiped blood away from her nose with her wrist.

Then she picked up one of Dominique's red designer shoes and crunched across the broken glass toward her opponent at pace. She skidded away from a desperate jab before slamming the heel into her opponent's left eye socket. Dominique dropped to the ground.

The bronze staff of Asklepios rolled towards Eliza and nudged her toe. She picked it up and blew a hanging strand of purple hair away from her face. She had adapted, and she had won.

Dominique lay motionless, but somehow managed to speak. "Your family is gone, Jonny. It's your fault... all of this. And for what? To impress a girl?" She looked up at Eliza with her remaining eye, her hand covering the wound as blood pooled around the back of her head.

Eliza raised the staff above her head. "This is for my mam."

No...

Burton dragged himself across the floor on his belly and grabbed the bottom of the weapon before it swung.

"She's already beaten," he said.

"Muhktar will never be beaten," Eliza replied. "We aren't heroes, Jon, we're just two broken souls."

Her resistance didn't subside. She kicked out at his wrist.

Burton knew what was coming. He closed his eyes as Eliza bludgeoned her opponent into a paste, cursing as she rained down blow after blow. Each swing was accompanied by a sound like a spindly crate of rotten fruit being crushed.

Burton let out a sigh of relief as the horrific noise subsided.

Eliza helped him up. "Here, use this," she said, offering the wet bloodied spear as a walking stick.

"I'll be okay," Burton replied, trying to hide the pain even though his body and mind felt beyond repair. He didn't know what to say. Eliza was acting as though nothing had happened.

Burton limped over to his brother.

"Don't give that piece of shit the time of day," Eliza said.

"He had his reasons." Burton experienced flashbacks of the good times he'd spent with Patrick: penalty kicks in the back garden, his brother buying him his first beer, and every Christmas day. A few tears dropped over Patrick's chest and bullet wound.

He crouched and placed his hand on Patrick's heart, then noticed sharp pieces of plastic inside the top pocket of his brother's lab coat. The bullet had shattered the data bank containing the evidence against the Prime Minister. But that was a problem for another day.

"I can carry him," Burton said with certainty.

"You can't, and there's no time. He's gone – leave him."

Then Eliza stormed over and turned Burton to look at her. "Jonny, where's Nef? We need to get out of here. The horde is about to break in, and I don't want to be around when they do. I barely escaped them before."

"I'm sorry. They got her too."

"What do you mean?"

"BARRIER took her away. Eliza, I think she might be dead." Burton left out the important part of the story, terrified of her reaction. Her aggression scared him more than anything else that they had faced tonight.

"Follow me."

Burton stepped backward, looking at Patrick. "He's my hero. I won't leave him."

His gladius scraped against the marble as he struggled to pick it up from the floor. His wrist cracked and crunched as he tightened his grip on the handle and clipped it to his belt. Savage pain shot up his ankle as he lifted Patrick from the floor and rested his brother's full weight across his bloodied shoulders. He shut his watery eyes tight and gritted his teeth, reaching to the banister with his left hand to steady himself. He whimpered as he ascended.

He looked back to see Eliza standing dejected as the wall of arms continued to reach and grab for her from behind. The Violators were about to break into the building.

CHAPTER 25
THE GUARDIAN CLASS

Burton exited the narrow walkway behind Patrick's office and struggled between the reptile tanks. He laid Patrick's motionless body by the alpha snake tank and glanced into the foliage. The demonic head snapped against the side and scraped its fangs against the glass. Burton didn't flinch; he glared right back into the serpent's hate-filled eyes before concentrating on the task at hand.

He turned his attention to the control panel. The display of the tablet screen was state-of-the art and appeared way more advanced than anything Burton was used to. An automated female voice asked the user to place their hand on the outline provided. Burton held Patrick's hand against it.

Patrick Burton print match detected. Authorisation confirmed.

"What are you doing?" Eliza asked.

"I need to find Matty."

He pressed a tab marked *Entry*, and was presented with multiple options:

- *Office*
- *Alpha Tank*
- *Support Tanks (Press for subgroup)*

- *Chamber Entry*
- *Abaton 1 (Press for subgroup)*
- *Abaton 2 (Press for subgroup)*
- *Panic room (Open)*
- *Lockdown (Compromised)*
- *Cellar Door Elevator*
- *Helipad Access*
- *Security View*

Burton pressed *Security View*, and multiple surveillance images appeared. Some had been destroyed and displayed only static, but others painted a vivid picture.

"The horde's broken through," Burton announced. It occurred to him that Dominique's remains would have been mauled.

"We need to be faster," Eliza replied.

To Burton's surprise, he saw that Glover had led the police inside the canteen. They were restraining as many Violators as possible. *I wonder if that was their order, to wait until the horde crossed the threshold into the building? If only they'd helped from the beginning.*

Swiping between camera feeds, he spotted Sergio fighting through a tunnel with Matty hanging on his back.

"He's with Sergio. He's protected. Thank God. We have time."

"No, we don't!" Eliza replied.

Burton pressed *Chamber Entry*. The instruction *Please enter passcode* displayed. Burton remembered the sequence: 11-92-12. It was from Patrick's favourite film, in a scene where the big brother confuses his siblings as they try to do multiplication.

The red reinforced door marked *CAUTION* opened and they walked through.

"What is this place?" Eliza asked from behind him. She looked around the Abaton Chambers, then examined the crates. "Look." She held up an empty vial to show Burton.

"My parents were killed in the fire. Paddy was trying to… resurrect them. Their bodies are inside these cylinders."

"I'm so sorry, Jon. It's my fault. I got you into this. I used you." Her bottom lip trembled slightly.

"Eliza, stop. I need to tell you something. Nef tried to destroy this place straight away, but I literally stabbed her in the back. I was in shock. Then the guards shot her as she stood defenceless." Burton shook his head, disgusted at himself. He didn't know if his conscience would ever be clear.

Eliza changed her stance. She extended the bronze spear in front of her and raised her chin slightly indicating her disapproval. *Is she going to attack me?*

"You did *what*?"

"Mam and Dad are all I've got. I was taken by surprise. Please, forgive me."

"I had to watch my mother disappear, remember? But Nef was on our side. She was our friend. We were a triangle."

Eliza sidestepped, tracing a semicircle around Burton.

"I'm on your side. Please. It was a mistake. Like the one you made when Nef spared you – it's the same."

"I didn't hurt anyone directly. Don't turn this back on me," Eliza replied. She thrust the point of her weapon toward him.

"But it would've completely derailed everything."

"I trusted you."

"You used me! You literally just admitted it." Burton raised his palms and didn't reach for his gladius, knowing it would only escalate the situation. The point of the dory spear was millimetres from his Adam's apple. "Please forgive me."

Eliza lowered her weapon, but her look hurt Burton more than any attack could. He had walked through the friend zone, entered a red mist, and ended up sitting on a pile of her indifference.

"Look," she said after what seemed an eternity, "we can fill these empty vials. But *you* need to let your parents go."

"How can I go on without them?" Burton asked.

"You'll see them again," Eliza said with certainty.

In that moment, Burton realised that despite being surrounded by religious zealots for so long, they'd never shared their own thoughts on the great beyond. *Eliza believes in the afterlife?*

A low rumble snapped him back into reality.

"What was that?" he asked.

"What?"

"That noise." He heard another rumbling.

The helipad access doors opened and Wortham appeared. There wasn't a speck of dirt or blood on his clothing. Two BARRIER guards stood either side of him in the narrow service elevator. The only weapon raised was Eliza's spear; she appeared ready to skewer all three.

"There's still a chance to save Patrick. Get him in the lift. Now!" Wortham ordered. It seemed he'd been watching everything from his own tablet. The guards made to advance, but Burton and Eliza instinctively blocked their path.

"Why should we let you have him?" Eliza asked.

"He's dead and buried if you don't. Here, take this. Call it a trade." Wortham pulled a data drive from his tablet and threw it across to Eliza, who caught it. She glanced at Burton and they both nodded. The soldiers dragged his brother into the service elevator as Eliza closed the *CAUTION* door behind them.

"We'll take him to the helicopter," Wortham announced as the guards tore Patrick's shirt off and embalmed his chest in the full contents of a vial. It seemed they'd been drilled on what to do in these circumstances.

"But he's been shot in the chest," Burton said.

"We can't lose him. We'll take him to the best of the best. Maslow has already told the surgeons that we're on our way."

"Where's Nef?" Eliza asked, aloof to Patrick's fate.

"We're taking her as well, Elixir subjects are essential to our research. We want her alive. Follow us up. There's not enough room for six. Trust me."

"I don't. We'll find you, but we've got another job to do first," Burton said.

Eliza lowered her spear as the lift doors closed. She paused and looked at the lift with her head tilted, as if she also wasn't convinced.

Within a minute, the words *Helipad Access* flashed red on the tablet. Eliza pressed the button to call the lift, but each press resulted in the grinding sound of cogs and cables malfunctioning.

"Out of order?" Burton asked.

"You're damn right he is. That weasel's fucking dead when I catch him. He's swindled us."

"We'll get to him, don't worry. If he manages to keep Paddy and Nef alive somehow, then I don't care. It was obvious he was up to something."

Burton swiped through the security streams on the tablet to see the police unwittingly funnelling Violators toward their location. Egan was with them, high on his own supply. He was hunched over, and his tongue was licking all around his mouth as he ran. The scientist hadn't had a haircut in a long time, and the bedraggled bush of brown straw was almost down to his shoulders. His faded shirt was ripped open under his soiled lab coat to reveal his bare chest. The dweeb appeared more threatening now that he was running with a pack. He was yelling Patrick's name.

"What's happening?" Eliza shouted.

"The police and the Violators are close."

"We need to fill these vials now," Eliza ordered.

Burton looked at the options displayed on the screen. "I've got an idea, but I need to time it right."

"No – help me now. Hurry."

"I need to try."

He watched what looked like fifty Violators running toward the lab doors and opened them using the tablet controls. As they rampaged inside, he pressed *Lock* to stop the police following. His next move was to open the snake tanks. A chorus of hisses could be heard from the next room. Burton paused, looking at the Alpha tank on the screen. He gulped and pressed 'release'. The threatened snakes bit down into the Violators and hung from all parts of their bodies. The alpha rose above the scrawny Egan and clamped its jaws onto his neck. He stood in a dream state. *It's working. Paddy's formula is cancelling out Egan's. Thank God.*

As Glover looked through the glass wall of the lab, he seemed to recognise what was happening as the violet faded from Egan's eyes and his wild threat was nullified. The detective barked orders and signalled to his officers what was happening. Burton held a button and announced the passcode into the corridor for Glover to hear so he could arrest the cured Violators and have the snakes contained: "11-92-12."

Glover looked up at the security camera. "I recognise that voice," he said, his eyes narrowing. "Thanks."

Burton turned back to the Abatons and placed his forehead against the cold metal of his father's chamber.

"Goodbye, Dad. I'll try to become half the man you wanted me to be."

Burton turned taps that lined the circumference of each Abaton and placed a pyramid vial under each. He heard the clunking of pipes followed by flowing liquid that sounded like water draining from a full bath. Elixir spilled from them. Eliza stacked the vials into crates as soon as each one filled. It was crazy to think that the precious commodity they'd battled for was now splashing onto the floor and being wasted.

"Hurry! You need to help," she said.

Burton pressed his cheek against his mother's Abaton.

"Mam, your constant positivity should've made me invincible. I wish I could've paid back your support somehow. I wish I could've made you proud. Thank you for everything."

"We... will... watch... over... you."

Burton fell backwards as the ghostly whisper came from his mother's chamber. *Did I imagine that?* He slammed the button on the side, and it eased open.

"Is she still in there?" Burton asked himself.

Eliza grabbed two large crates and pushed up from a squat. Her arms were straining. "Help me."

"Wait." Burton pressed the button on the side on the chamber again several times, hoping to make it speed up. "C'mon, c'mon, c'mon!" As the glass became visible, he looked through the two-inch gap. The drained chamber was empty.

"They're too heavy." Eliza was wobbling, trying to keep her back straight.

Burton hit *Cellar Door Elevator* on the tablet and grabbed the top crate. His shoulder and wrist were in agony, but they could still function; it was a pain he would have to ignore and hide, just like his dad would've done. A large square mechanised platform started to lower toward the back of the room, it had no walls, only yellow safety railings around the sides.

"Quick." Eliza skipped onto the platform. The vials clinked in their crate like bottles of wine as she moved.

Burton hopped on and they sank into a delivery tunnel. *This must've been how Patrick intended to receive the vials from Gateshead.* The tunnel was well lit and void of any violence or explosions. *This is the first bit of peace in what seems like forever.*

"Home free?" Eliza asked. She blew hair from her face. "It feels like I'm spending half my life underground with you."

"We're not out yet," Burton replied.

After the initial vertical drop, the lift carried them horizontally to an entrance alongside a stretch of road intended for the Biovax delivery trucks.

"Where do you think this will lead?" Burton asked.

"Somewhere quiet where nothing is on fire... I hope." Eliza replied.

They approached huge grey metal doors where the trucks would have entered. *I'll find you Matty. Hang on.* A smaller side door opened with the press of a button marked *Exit.*

They were greeted by wild lilac flowers either side of the road. They looked mostly grey under the full moon.

"Have we escaped?" Burton asked.

He put down the crate to give his arms a rest, and Eliza did the same. They held each other without saying a word. He was embracing a beautiful girl with a sense of achievement. Wasn't this what he'd prayed to the sky for on each trip to the Wallsend Job Centre? It was as if he'd made a deal with the devil. Burton struggled to comprehend the amount of loss he'd experienced to reach this moment.

"Your brother kept a lot of blueprints on his desk, Jonathan." A Spanish voice said.

Sergio looked exhausted and wounded from battling through the Biovax corridors. He hobbled from the long grass with his only hand gripping Matty's shoulder. Tino the dog ran over and jumped up at Eliza for a pet.

"Uncle Jonny, I'm scared." Matty said, his bottom lip was trembling.

"Don't be scared," Burton said. "We're just playing a game. Knights again, like Bamburgh Castle when you were Sir Matts-a-lot. Remember?"

"Wortham has gone," Sergio said. "Tell me where. I made our nephew a priority. You owe it to me."

"Let him go," Burton replied, ignoring the demand.

"Young Matthias will be coming with Sofia and I."

"Sofia?" Eliza whispered.

"He means Dominique," Burton whispered.

"As in Muhktar?

"Yep."

Eliza stepped forward. "Good luck with that. She was looking a bit pasty last time I saw her."

Sergio growled at Eliza.

"I know what family means to you, but this life is not for Matty," Burton said.

"He will be raised to be strong. But there are a few loose ends to deal with first. Yourselves included." Sergio stood firm, despite sweating, bleeding and breathing heavily. He put his hand around the back of his nephew's neck as if to claim him.

"He's just a child. He shouldn't see this," Eliza said. She extended the staff of Asklepios, but Burton held out an arm to stop her advancing.

"Wait," he ordered. Then he addressed Sergio. "You saved him. I know you have a heart. You want to make amends for what happened in Merida – I get it. Even after what you've done to us, I understand. You're not a killer. Please, I'm begging you. Leave. Don't make me do this."

"I made a promise to make my sister happy," Sergio replied.

Burton drew the gladius from its sheath. This man had already beaten him within an inch of his life tonight, but losing again was not an option. *Let us live, since we must die.*

"Action roll!" Burton yelled, and immediately his nephew and canine began playing their favourite game. Matty wrestled free from Sergio and pencil rolled into the long grass, giggling alongside his faithful dog. As Sergio looked down and reached out, Burton rushed in and sliced off his remaining hand before driving his gladius into the Spaniard's stomach. The pressure was like a knife in a steak pie as the sword pushed all the way through and crunched against his backbone. The instinctive strike was swift and silent. As Burton looked directly into Sergio's eyes, the vivid green faded.

"He's going nowhere." Burton pulled out the gladius and

shoved Sergio into the long grass with a single movement. His quick death had been successfully hidden from the eyes of his nephew. "Family first, always."

"We definitely aren't heroes," Eliza muttered to herself.

"Matty, come out," Burton shouted, wiping his weapon quickly. "We need to go. I can't find you. You win."

"Where did Daddy's friend go?" Matty asked as he toddled out from his hiding place.

"He had to go back to Spain, but he said he'll send you a present," Burton replied.

"Yay!" Matty did his little present dance, shaking his bottom.

Tino ran over to Eliza and lay at her feet. She stood with the bronze staff of Asklepios held in her left hand, resembling the statue O'Fagan had showed them at the beginning of their journey. The pose was fit for a goddess.

Matty and Tino played together in front as they walked away.

"How will we ever find peace after all this?" Burton asked.

"That's too hard for me, Frosty," Eliza replied.

"I used to lie in bed praying for love and excitement. This is the result. I've lost everything to find it. I'm cursed."

"But you found it?"

"The night you left your note, I was planning on doing something irreversible."

"The note telling you to meet me on the Pit Heap?"

"Yeah. I've learned a lot since then. You can't cheat death, but you can beat it by living to your full potential. You taught me that, Eliza, and I never want to be without you. I promise I'll be strong. I promise I'll never leave you. Just make it easy for me, for once? I'm begging you. Please."

"Christ, you pick your moments. Desperation isn't sexy, y'know. That's Eliza's tip of the day." She leant against a picket fence and looked across the field of moonlit lilac. "Last time we were in a sewer, now we're standing beside a

Spaniard on a permanent siesta. I don't know, okay? I've told you what I think about all that stuff. We're not on the same page. Plus, what you did to Nef... it's... unforgivable. Can we just get to the hospital, please?" She picked up the crates and straightened. "You don't give up easy do you, Frosty?"

"That's one good thing that comes from living with a mental illness, Eliza –you become resilient. I'll never give up on you. No matter what stage you think we're at, I'm here and I'm yours whenever you want me. I'm desperate, because you mean everything to me. You saved my life."

The vials continued to clink as they reached a worn track in the grass. Eliza had fallen silent, and she couldn't even look in Burton's direction. *Have I come all this way just to lose her?*

CHAPTER 26
THE FIRST OF MANY?

B urton and Eliza walked into the reception of the children's ward at the Freeman Hospital. They were drenched in the blood, sweat, and tears of everyone who had stood in their way. Matty sat down wearing a protective facemask, swinging his legs as he watched Tino through the automatic door; Burton had told his nephew it was his mission.

Eliza approached the receptionist and began speaking quickly before they were recognised through the dirt on their faces. "Before you raise the alarm, you might be interested in what we have in these crates."

The receptionist looked panicked. She took a deep inhale before responding, "Is it a bomb? Please god, no. There are sick children here. We've got no money."

Burton looked at the waiting area. A man was reading a newspaper; the front page had his and Eliza's faces plastered across it with the headline *Terror on the Tyne* written above.

"We're here to help." Burton opened a crate and handed over a vial of Elixir. A woman who looked as though she hadn't slept for a month entered the building, sobbing. As she approached them, she saw the distinctive vial being handed over.

"Is that what I think it is? Who does it belong to? Is it lost? I lost one... earlier... I put it down and walked away. Please, my daughter has Wave 3. She hasn't got long. The doctors have tried everything. Please. How much?"

"We haven't verified anything, miss. If you'd just like to wait a moment," the receptionist replied, trying to signal her colleague.

Eliza took a vial from the crate and handed it to the woman. "It's real, and it's free."

The mother held the vial, staring at it.

"Are you an angel?" The woman kissed Eliza and got soot all over her pale face. She ran off into the ward.

"Wait, miss. We don't know what that is!" the receptionist shouted.

"Oh my god, that felt so good. Try it." Eliza handed Burton a vial.

More parents gathered as word went around the ward.

"What's going on here?" an exhausted-looking doctor asked the receptionist. She pointed her biro at the vial-filled crate. "Is that what I think it is?" he said, dumbfounded.

Within ten minutes, the troubled woman burst out of the double doors looking euphoric. "My baby is awake! My baby is talking! She told me she loved me! It's real!"

The caution of the crowd evaporated, and the remaining Elixirs were distributed within seconds. After a few minutes more, fathers and mothers approached Burton and Eliza in floods of joyous tears offering unbreakable bear hugs.

"I think you need to see this," a nurse said, beckoning to Burton and Eliza. Burton ushered Matty over, and they followed her.

As they walked through the double doors into the children's ward, the sound of laughter and jubilance overwhelmed the beeping of healthy heart rates. Kids sat up in their hospital beds with bright green eyes and smiles. They were free of pain and ready to play.

Eliza walked from bed to bed and high-fived each of the little ones. She turned to look at Burton, who was smiling and holding his nephew's hand. Burton looked up and thought of his parents and brother. *This is the moment I wanted. This is for you.*

A little boy with a plastic tube up his nose tugged Burton's trouser leg. "Can I ask you something?"

"Sure, buddy, go ahead." Burton crouched so that he was on the boy's level.

"My dad said you're a better hero than Mighty-Man. Can you fly?"

Burton looked over to the dad, who nodded and wiped tears from his eyes.

"Uncle Jonny can do anything," Matty answered with certainty.

"You know what?" Burton said.

"What?" both boys asked in unison.

"All I do is try really hard, and sometimes that's enough to do great things."

"Why only sometimes?" the child asked.

"Things don't always work out the way you want them to, but you've always got a chance if you never give up. That's what Mighty-Man does, and he's amazing."

"Yeah, he is!" Both boys bounced on the spot and giggled together.

"What's your name?" The father asked as he walked over.

"Jon. Nice to meet you." They shook hands. For the first time, Burton felt that he had an identity. He'd been called Jonny, Jonathan, Jon, Frosty, ginger pubes and worse; now he believed in himself.

"How can we ever repay you?" the father asked.

Burton looked at all the hopeful families packed into the

ward. They were free of pain, at least for today. "This is enough."

"I'll think of something, mate. I've got a few contacts." The elated father was already planning.

Eliza addressed the room. "Okay, kids, we need to get going. Y'all be good."

They left the ward to rapturous applause and cheers. Eliza held Burton's right hand and Matty held the other as they went to collect Tino.

~

They walked past an abandoned pub with a blackboard outside, it had *Antibodies, live and in your face tonight!! Bring your own booze!!!* scribbled on it. Despite everything, art had also endured. Burton chuckled to himself as Tino scampered in front of Eliza to sniff a lamppost.

"Our lives have changed forever," Eliza said. "This feels more like the beginning than the end."

"How?" Burton asked.

"Because I've got this." Eliza unzipped the top of her ripped tactical suit and reached into her black sports bra. She pulled out Wortham's data drive. The word *Copy* was written on its side.

"We have all the known locations of the Elixir."

"We do. But I'm going to find Nef before anything else. You also have something more important to deal with." Eliza glanced in Matty's direction as he toddled along beside them.

"You're right. He comes first now, and he'll need some stability for a while. How will I tell him?"

"Tell me what?" Matty had been absorbing their conversation like a sponge, without letting on.

"That we're going to Tynemouth beach tomorrow and we're going to get the biggest ice cream you've ever seen."

"Yay! Will Mammy and Daddy be there? I want to see them," Matty asked.

Burton gulped and squeezed his nephew's hand. "You bet."

"Hey, Sir Matts-a-lot, would you mind walking Tino for a bit?" Eliza asked and handed him the lead.

"Sure, but I'm getting really tired. My little legs are sore."

"Well, your uncle might buy you some sweets for energy. How about that?"

"Yay!"

As Matty started his sweetie dance, the adults stopped and spoke in hushed voices.

"I need to charter a plane for Butrint," Eliza said.

"Now? Why?"

"I can't waste any time. Nef wouldn't wait. Even if they save her, she could end up worse off."

"Worse than being dead? How?"

"She won't be free."

Eliza's response triggered a memory of the birds flying above the Tall Oak multi-storey car park.

"How will you pay?"

"It's okay. O'Fagan accumulated a lot of money over the years. He created accounts for Nef and me. He wanted to make sure we continued Project Panacea if anything happened to him. I guess I can say money's no object, for the first time in my life. I didn't want to tell you, after seeing how your brother changed. I needed to know you were still in it for the right reasons."

"Once this little guy is sorted, I'll pay Maslow Fairchild a visit. There might also be a few Violators in the city that need to be taken care of," Burton replied.

"You're a lot more sure of yourself these days. And did I mention that beard suits you? You look a bit more rugged."

"You did. I'll find you again, Eliza," Burton said without

hesitation. He snapped the tracker onto her belt without breaking eye contact.

"I know you will."

Burton held Eliza by the waist, the tips of his fingers brushing her skin through the rips in her tactical suit. Their lips met for only a second before she pulled away, as always.

He'd crawled from an abyss to grab her hand and be dragged into the light. He was ready to restart, reset and reconnect. He was alive. He loved the Samurai Dye smell of her hair, her sarcastic tone, her quirky humour, her laugh, her rashness, her directness, her bravery, her friendship, her body, her tattoos, those big green circle eyes. Their DNA was dancing, and he prayed it wouldn't be for the final time. Eliza was the Elixir he'd searched for all his life.

"Yuk," Matty said.

"Well, Frosty. Guess I'll be seeing you," Eliza said, then briefly licked her top lip. All Burton could do was look at her. "In the event of an emergency, passengers are expected to get on with it. There are no exits on your left or right. This is a one-way flight. Buckle up for Butrint."

He didn't want to let go. Eliza pulled her arm away, blew Matty a kiss, and ran without looking back.

"Bye," Matty shouted, waving.

For now, Jon Burton was a guardian. He had a purpose. As he walked with Matty and Tino, colours radiated from the surrounding buildings and every breath seemed rejuvenating. The sadness of losing his parents was deep, but it hadn't manifested in a conventional way. How he'd feel one hour, one day, one month or one year from now was anyone's guess. Burton promised himself he'd never let Matty see any sadness or pain. He would be strong like his own father and do everything in his power to make this boy happy until Patrick returned.

The dual bladed Biovax helicopter flew overhead.

"Wow, cool," Matty said, looking up. Jon squeezed his

nephew's hand again and gazed up, wondering what the future might hold.

I have value and worth. I'm sensitive, gentle and have respect for people. I'm also kind, honest and loving. Although society might say differently, these things make me more of a man, not less. I confused being harmless with being virtuous, but now I've grown some teeth. I will never give up, and that makes me dangerous. To be this way is to be strong, and no storm over my city will ever keep me down again.

EPILOGUE

"**A**nd finally. A mysterious bronze statue of two faceless figures has been left outside of the Children's Ward of Newcastle Freeman Hospital. The female figure is holding a long staff, while the male is carrying an open crate. Children can be seen looking up at them. An inscription reads, 'Knights of the North.'

"In a statement released today, hospital officials claim they did not commission the statue, but all colleagues are unanimously opposed to it being removed.

"It's nice for the kids," a smiling nurse said. "It shows there are selfless people out there ready to fight for what's right."

From the studio, Kim Knowles commented, "We have beaten Wave 3, and this is a great symbol of how there will always be someone to help you get through tough times."

"Well, you got your statue, Frosty." Eliza smiled to herself and turned off the stream of the North East News. She threw her tablet onto the white sheets of the hotel bed and wedged open a window frame. To feel any breeze in the dry heat of Butrint would be welcome. According to Albanian tour guides, the temperature was due to Sirocco, a Mediterranean wind that blew in from the Sahara.

Eliza used her Wayfinders to examine a collection of sturdy white tents in the distance. She'd been watching the site for a week. Local mercenaries were guarding the base of an aqueduct, and she had wondered whether Wortham could be inside. For a second, a tent flapped open, and Eliza thought she saw the glimmering metal handle of a wheelchair and the tip of a boxer's braid. *Nef!?*

Eliza looked into a body-length mirror to examine her new sand-coloured tactical suit. She flipped the handle of her dory spear and clipped it to her back. She was prepared to do anything to rescue her friend. The feeling of personal pride she'd experienced in the hospital was also playing on her mind. She wanted it, again and again. Eliza felt closer to her mother with every act of kindness.

"For a better world," she whispered, then squeezed her right hand into a fist and headed for the door.

A NOTE FROM THE AUTHOR

First of all, thank you. I am eternally grateful that you have given my words your time and hope they resonated with you in a meaningful way. As this is my debut novel, I need to ask one further favour…

Please go to Amazon and leave a review.

By sharing your star rating, you will add validation to the quality within these pages and help others discover my story.

I hope to share more adventures from Jon & Eliza in the future. For a better world!

ABOUT THE AUTHOR

D.G. Mooney was born a stone's throw away from St James' Park in Newcastle, 1984. He chased the dream of becoming a world famous guitarist, before focusing on the more attainable career of world famous author. He's a passionate Newcastle Utd supporter, and can be found shouting at referees on most Saturday afternoons. Howay the lads!

For updates on future projects, please sign up to the author's Elixir Club and social media channels:

🐦 twitter.com/themoonwolf
📷 instagram.com/themoonwolf
▶️ youtube.com/themoonwolf
🅖 goodreads.com/dgmooney

ACKNOWLEDGMENTS

It's impossible to put into words what these people mean to me. I'll keep it brief:

Mam and Dad: You always approach each day with humour, heart and determination. Your example is inspiring and the reason I'll never give up.

My Brothers: Having you in my corner makes me feel like I can take on any challenge.

My nieces and nephews: You're hilarious and unstoppable. Thank you for your energy and enthusiasm.

My best mate: Watch my best man speech again, I meant every word and still do.

Special mention for A.W: You've encouraged me to keep writing from the inception of these characters. I'll never forget your support.

Printed in Poland
by Amazon Fulfillment
Poland Sp. z o.o., Wrocław

26478867R00197